the Last martian sunset

JON VASSA

Black Rose Writing | Texas

ISBN: 978-1-68433-293-9
PUBLISHED BY BLACK ROSE WRITING
www.blackrosewriting.com

Printed in the United States of America
Suggested Retail Price (SRP) $20.95

The Last Martian Sunset is printed in font

To Kaye,

The one who dragged me out of my head and sat me behind a typewriter.

the Last
Martian sunset

CHAPTER 1

The young man froze as he stood amongst the giant crowd. Blinding lights winked from every corner, begging for his attention. He took a deep breath, focused on his feet, and shuffled tighter into the crowd.

Visit every booth, his father had told him. *The last fair is the most important. Don't screw it up.*

The young man closed his eyes. *This is your chance*, he thought. *Never budge, never let go.* He reopened his eyes to the bright signs and the brimming crowd.

A man walked to the front of the mass of people, standing as a barrier between the students and the vibrant auditorium. He was flanked by four officers gazing intently into the crowd, their Maglaz rifles clearly in view on their shoulders.

"Group forty-six, you will have thirty minutes to explore the job fair behind me. If you see a red flash on your Vlex, then please skip those booths."

The man glanced at his watch. "Anyone reported to be seeking unsolicited interviews at a booth will be escorted out by security. You have thirty minutes, starting now."

The young man raced within the stampede. He rushed to one of the most popular booths that everyone else was headed to. *Earth's One Bank.* As he approached it, his transparent piece of glass flashed a stark red rejection in his hand. "Damn it," he said.

Xan bowed out and continued jogging through the maze of presentations. "I don't want to work for a bank anyway," he whispered to himself. "That's not my goal."

As he passed the different booths, he received more red flashes than green or yellow ones. He continued his aimless drift amongst the crowd, hypnotised by its rhythm and his red blinking device. Pain throbbed in his chest and fear crept into his mind.

He saw his grandfather patting him on the shoulder as a young child. The old man smiling at him with pride.

He grimaced at the memory and pushed with determination towards the *Food Science* stalls. He clenched his fists and marched straight for the cheese booth, only to receive a red flash from his Vlex. It didn't stop him. He pushed on past the other rejected students, and right by a security officer.

"Don't budge. Don't slip. Keep moving," he muttered under his breath.

A blinking red light flashed on his Vlex. "Ignore it," he growled. Then an alarm beeped. He grit his teeth and elbowed right up to the booth when a tight grip snatched him under the arm.

A security officer held onto him. The heavyset man dragged Xan away, pushing him into a less crowded area. Xan thought about going back, then stopped as he made eye contact with the guard who held up his rifle.

Xan's fists loosened. He gazed around him and saw a sign that said *The New Colony*. He laughed to himself.

"You idiot. You could have gotten yourself killed."

There were fewer booths in this area and an even thinner crowd. Xan bit his upper lip as he scanned the visual presentations. *Get the hell out of here before you get roped into something you'll later regret.*

He turned his gaze and caught eyes with a pilot standing nearby. The man raised a thick eyebrow at him, and Xan glanced at the three-dimensional presentation behind the man. *Sioux Air, Your Own Place Amongst the Stars!* A holographic cargo ship landed in a busy spaceport where massive vehicles rolled up next to it. The ship doors opened, and the vehicles dragged its contents out and onto the runway.

Xan backed away from the booth. His glass device flashed green. He paused a moment to contemplate the offer. *First one of the day.*

The pilot squinted his eyes at Xan and grinned a sharp white smile. "There's more than most will ever see up there."

Averting his eyes, Xan nodded and hurried off. He picked up his pace and stopped when another green flash blipped across his device. As he lifted his eyes, he saw a stern woman watching him.

GH1 Recruitment Company.

Xan slipped his Vlex into his pocket and rubbed his wet palms together. She never took her gaze from him. He studied her presentation.

"Hello," she said, "and welcome to the future."

Xan faked a smile and squinted his eyes. *You can't be serious lady.*

"Interested in Mars?"

Xan scratched the side of his arm while he watched the holographic presentation behind her. A happy group of employees boarded a giant ship, their arms around one another and waving bye to their families.

"I've never thought about it."

"Now's a good time."

"It's so far away though."

She refocused on him. "Mars is going through a tremendous growth spurt right now. It'd be a shame to miss out on it."

Xan chewed the corner of his lip.

She inhaled deeply and continued speaking. "They predict that the economies of both Martian cities will eclipse the economies of Earth's five biggest cities within the next two decades," she said.

"Yeah right. Be serious."

"I am. And so should you. Let me send you some charts. You have your Vlex?"

The young man lifted the rectangular piece of glass from his pocket. "Sure, right here."

"Look for yourself then."

Three-dimensional graphs rose out of his screen. He noticed they were the same graphs as those on her presentation.

"The biggest companies are investing in the new frontier," she said. "You realise the smartest people in life don't go where the money is, but where it'll be."

Xan coughed. "Yeah, I've always thought that. It's the reason I came here." *That, and everywhere else flat out rejected me.*

She tapped her Vlex, and a bright red Mars appeared behind her. The planet twirled in a slow axis, reflecting in his eyes. He opened his mouth to say something then closed it.

A holograph of a grey city replaced the red planet. It was filled with smog, hovercrafts, and people walking the ground like ants. He knew this city. It was the only one he'd ever known.

"Let's take a realistic view at your options here on Earth," she said. "The average person like you will be up against nearly eighty-million new graduates like yourself. Now, that's not even considering the forty-million from last quarter's batch, who, keep in mind, are still hunting for precious jobs. Even factories are cut-throat these days."

His existence was reduced to nothing more than a number on a screen. His Vlex showed him the newest model of androids with upgraded capabilities and the predicted number of jobs they'd swipe.

He closed his eyes for a second. *He saw the red planet surrounded by stars.*

The lady cleared her throat. Xan opened his eyes and nodded his head.

"The interest rates on business loans are atrocious," she continued. "It binds an average small business owner to their loans for over seventy-nine years these days. Who'll ever pay off that debt? You? Your children?"

The young man opened his mouth then closed it.

She watched him closely as uncertainty washed over his face. "I know what you're going to say. What if you create a big business like Mr. Vlex? No point even toying with such ideas, they'll leave you bone dry in an underground shack. The man himself attested his success to nothing more than luck."

A picture of VlexCo's founder flashed across his screen with a quote: *My success? I'd say it was being in the right place at the right time. So let's call it luck.*

The young man read the quote twice.

"There used to be a choice for people like you," she continued. "You could choose if you wanted to be successful. But the world doesn't work that way anymore. There's not enough room anymore to cater to individual personalities and preferences."

She paused for a minute.

The young man eyed her, waiting for more. "That's it?" he whispered.

A bright red planet appeared on his Vlex, the same as the one on the presentation. His pupils widened. The red glint burned straight into his mind.

She watched with a sly grin. "Then," she added, "there are those few who make their own way in life. The smart ones I told you about earlier. Someone who takes the risk to go where the money will be rather than to place their hopes on useless daydreams."

Xan drifted his attention back to the red planet. Every time he looked, a mist of hope wafted through his heart up into his head. *Am I the type who makes my destiny?* he thought. *I couldn't even get the marks I needed in school to be a –*

"Even companies like VlexCo are looking to expand their markets up there," she said. "Mars is the newest frontier. Let's face it, Earth is overcrowded, and those that hold the wealth aren't distributing it any time soon. If you want to break free from all the old systems and give yourself a chance, then go somewhere fresh."

It can't be that easy. She has no clue how bad I've done.

"Have you ever seen either of the Martian cities?"

The young man shook his head. "I didn't know there were cities up there. I thought it was full of atmospheric stations."

She rolled her eyes. "That's a common misconception." She tapped her Vlex fast. The presentation showed him images of red hills with small white domes planted along them. The picture expanded upwards to show a city full of circular skyscrapers, each of them rounded to withstand the Martian winds. The streets lay open, and tiny sand rovers sifted through the city with ease. Then the screen went blank.

She stared at the screen for a moment and sighed. "There's more up there than most people realise. What a shame. To fight your whole life for basic survival among the rest."

The young man bit his upper lip. His thoughts were racing around the red planet.

She glanced at her Vlex, then back at him. "You're in the School of Business?"

"Yes," he said, "but I wanted to be a food scientist."

She shook her head. "It's too late for that. You're either born a scientist or not. And food is tough to enter even for the rich."

Xan chewed his inner cheeks to keep himself from speaking.

She arched her eyebrows. "Mars is a serious place," she said. "It's no longer stuck in the frontier days. There's no better time to go than now."

He breathed a single laugh.

"I'll leave you with my details if you find you're interested."

The young man saw her contact appear on his Vlex. A tiny red planet hung in the corner near her name. He touched the little globe and watched it spin a little in the corner.

"Take your time and think it over," she said.

"I will. Thanks."

She gave him a faint smile, and he returned it.

Xan moved back into the crowd. All the bodies seemed distant somehow. They didn't feel permanent anymore. He could escape them for the first time. He knew a place where they didn't go.

His Vlex alerted him of more rejections as he walked through the auditorium. They stung less and reminded him more of the red planet.

When his time ran out, he exited the building, and it felt like he was back on Earth. His thoughts shackled him down to his family, comforts, and career. The grey haze nipped at his eyes and burned in his chest.

It's a nice thought. If only.

CHAPTER 2

An older man with grey hair stood upon a VlexCo podium before a giant auditorium of students, reading a speech off his Vlex. His eyes were blank, and his voice was emotionless as he read each word. "For those of you graduating next week," he said, "please fill out your surveys before our next class. Otherwise we won't be able to process your certificates."

The man looked at the silent audience. He touched his podium and the auditorium lit up with green flashing Vlexes. The students rose to their feet and dashed out into the crowded hall.

Xan seeped into the crowd. Blue lights illuminated the large hallways with advertisements. *VlexCo – Quality Made in Quantity!* Each time he glanced at an ad up on the wall, it would find its way onto his Vlex.

He was then shown a submerged city with two beautiful people sitting under water in a round submersible.

EXTREME TOURS! Are you an EXTREME TOURIST? I bet so! Right now Extreme Tours is offering a special deal on submerged city tours. Book your trip to Old Manhattan today!

Xan swiped the advertisement away.

A faint buzz sounded in the halls and cut off all of the students' Vlexes. Everything turned dark, and silence lingered in the air. All at once, every single screen turned on to broadcast a video of a high-ranking military officer. "This is an emergency broadcast," he said. "Several bombings have taken place at 3:12 P.M. GMT in the following locations: New King's London, Port-Frisco, East Delhi, and Kuala-Lumpur-Singapura."

The man paused and seemed to look at every student in the eye. "The source and motivation behind these attacks are still being investigated," he said. "If you see any suspicious-looking persons or articles, please inform the authorities immediately. One call could save thousands of lives. Thank you."

The young man saw an information packet appear on his Vlex. *Red Alert Status. Continue with normal operations. Be on the alert for any suspicious-looking persons in or around the university area. All underground passages should be avoided. Contact the authorities immediately if you have any concerns.*

"Thanks," he muttered, discarding the post.

The crowd resumed its pace, and Xan followed along all the way to his next classroom. As he entered the auditorium, a number popped up on his Vlex: *2193*. Xan looked at the numbers beside each row of seats as he walked past them. He found the row *2100-2199* and sat in his designated chair.

The auditorium soon filled to capacity. The room was dim until an older woman walked across the stage, and a podium rose from the ground. The woman stood behind the podium. "Good afternoon," she said. "Let's get started."

She spoke as if she were speaking only to herself – her tone stayed flat, and her eyes remained glued to the podium. "Last class, we left off in the middle of the first underground revolution," she said with a sigh. "Okay. After the government military forces had broken through their primary stronghold, the Arkanal group surrendered. The battle lasted seventy-five days, during which they subdued the remaining terrorists.

"Their leader Abrams Kiegal Simoranaf was not present at the time of the capture. In fact, they didn't manage to locate him or his most loyal followers. The government suspected that the group created a fake leader figure to conceal the true identities of their leaders. In fact, the government only managed to collect oral accounts of Abrams. He was described as an aloof leader, often under the influence of illegal substances. The only document found that was claimed to be written by Abrams himself was a poem titled *The Prophet of Arkanal.*

"In the poem, the prophet consumes a drug that is said to be a gift from heaven. The drug grants the consumer with the eyes of God forever. The prophet corrects the perceived imbalances of the world by recruiting a military regime to overthrow the Earth's governments. After the coup, the world enters into a state of utopia, where all concepts of money and possessions vanish. In the end, the prophet is raised up to heaven to become one of the gods ruling the Earthly realm. Many speculate that the leader wrote the poem in an autobiographical delusion."

The professor stopped for a moment to cough. She pulled out a piece of cloth from her jacket and wiped her mouth. She took her time putting the cloth back, letting her eyes linger upon the dark audience, and then back down on the podium.

"They sentenced the majority of those captured to labor camps or execution centres," she continued. "Soon after the battle, Earth's government created a law prohibiting religious gatherings from taking place. The prohibition lasted for thirty years before they overturned it. During those years, bombings were limited in size and number, but never completely ceased."

Xan found it difficult to follow the lecture. Students on Earth had listened to the same message over and over from their earliest days at school. They all watched government funded cartoons and sang nursery rhymes on how to be good citizens.

His mind drifted to his pending graduation. The safety raft that was keeping him afloat until now had already sunk. He could see a few rafts floating in the sea, and the millions of eyes watching them, just like him. Who would nab the coveted jobs first?

"The Great Divide War brought about a worldwide recession," the professor said. "During those times, the government found it difficult to enforce its laws, which allowed illegal activities to flourish with ease."

Hovercraft sales might give me the right connection I need, he thought. *General sales would be working through the ranks but manageable. Factory work... maybe. It depends on the product.*

"...the first appearance of the Neo-Arkanal group," his professor continued. "They were already controlling several factions around the world by the time they'd announced their existence. The government couldn't trace the location of their headquarters as that information was hidden from even their top-ranking followers. A large number of government spies were killed under suspicious circumstances, causing some to speculate that the group had ties within the government itself."

Am I chasing a hopeless fantasy? he thought. *No one switches jobs after they've landed one. It's become illegal in most places now, with the latest android legislation.*

"The government passed a law banning all Earth citizens from living underground. However, it was hard to enforce it as there were already far too many people living underground at that time."

It's not fair. I never had a real chance.

"The government reacted swiftly, destroying the ship mid-journey. The ramifications lead many to speculate that..."

We all have to pick something. Worst comes to worst, I'll find myself without a job, dead in the streets by the next week. Shit, I'd take a job at the train station before that.

"...tracing back to the original attack. Since then, the government has stepped up its search efforts to round up those who are suspected to be affiliated with terrorist groups. This is why we now have..."

I might even meet a wife there. What would it matter at that point though? Where the heck could we live?

"As the population grew, those pressures remained heavy on the government. After the second androidic boom, more jobs were rendered obsolete, which in turn widened the socio-economic gap even more. Dissension brewed..."

We might have a chance at the flat lottery if we have a kid. The lottery is fair, no? Everyone gets their chance. We could make it.

"...keeping more jobs in the course of events. The law still stands today even after receiving harsh scrutiny from companies and scientists alike. Advancements to android development are still greatly stifled and linger in menial upgrades."

Or if I go big like Mr. Vlex. The young man laughed aloud. *It's possible.*

"We'll close here today. Next class will be our final meeting until the next quarter, and to those of you graduating, it will be our farewell," the professor concluded.

The professor stopped to look out at the audience and then pressed her VlexCo podium. The auditorium shone green, and the crowd rushed outside and mixed with the masses pouring into the halls.

Xan allowed his thoughts to wander in the ads shining down on him. One, in particular, caught his eye. It was an ad showing a luxurious penthouse inside a well-enclosed dome orbiting the Earth.

The ad appeared on his Vlex and spoke to him. *Searching for an escape from Earth? Sioux Property is launching ten-thousand new satellite units this coming June. Why pay lunar prices for an overcrowded dust bowl when you could float closer to home for a fraction of the price? Sioux Property is the largest developer of private homes in the solar system. We always deliver the right touch, for an even finer price. No need to look any further. We'll be seeing you in June.*

Images of satellite homes appeared on his screen. He looked at the large complexes floating above the Earth. He saw happy families laughing together. Bold red lettering appeared on his Vlex: *Does Not Qualify.*

"I know that," he said.

The grey haze swept his focus back outside, and the polluted air dug deep into his lungs. Advertisements lit up the streets around him.

A woman placed a cream full of nanobots on her wrinkles. The ad entered his Vlex.

'Damn it,' he said.

Our cream not only turns you into a younger woman... the young man quickly swiped the ad away. "I doubt your cream will turn me into a woman."

Another ad showed a man spraying himself with a small tube. *Oxytocin spray*, it said. *Make yourself irresistible to the opposite sex with nature's fragrance. Forget sweet perfumes, let biology take its course. We only harvest the most potent strands of synthetic oxytocin to give you men that cutting edge. Never worry about finding a wife again. Also available, our new Vasopressin spray. Now that you've got her, you've got to keep her.*

He found himself being squeezed into a mass of bodies as he moved through the narrow station entrance. Inside the train station, he gazed at the flickering ads above. A small red orb stopped him in his place. The red planet hung over him. *Come to Mars. Every day is an adventure. Book your trip today. But be warned, you might not ever want to leave.*

He saw sand rovers full of beautiful people laughing as they rode up the sanded hills. *Every day is an adventure. Come to Mars. Every day is an adventure. Come to Mars.* Repeated in his head.

"Adventure," he said.

Find your breath of fresh air in our spacious cities, the ad continued.

The crowd pushed him through the station, breaking his line of sight. He kept with the swarm and wedged himself onto the packed train.

The glint of red pricked his mind, and a drop of desire bled its way down to that dark crevice of untouched dreams. *It's too far*, he thought. *I couldn't afford the transport. I don't even know what type of job I could get. I have to focus on my interviews. Then focus on getting a wife.*

A glided stop placed him at his exit. He left the hovertrain and floated along with the rest of the crowd. Glittering ads sparkled in his eye with persuasive buys and unrealistic dreams he'd never touch.

Putting his sights to the floor, he watched the marching feet surround him. He placed his foot in the small space behind the person in front of him, inching his way through the congested mass, micro step by micro-step.

Xan stepped into his housing complex. He shuffled into the lift and rose to his floor. He weaved through the maze of identical doors until he reached his home. He waved his Vlex over the door and slid it out of the way after it beeped its approval.

Inside, a small concrete floor held a tiny table in place and a couch with conspicuous frays in its corners. Xan went to a cabinet and took out a container full of water. He poured himself a small glass and placed it back in the cabinet.

"You have used six water credits," the cabinet said. "You have twelve-thousand and sixteen credits remaining. Thank you."

The door behind him opened. A man with dark bags under his eyes walked through and put down his black work bag on the floor. He glanced at his son for a moment before throwing off his shoes. "Pour me a glass too," he said. The large man fell down into a seat near the table.

Xan poured another glass. "You have used six water credits. You have twelve-thousand and ten credits remaining. Thank you."

His father pointed to the seat across from him. "Sit," he said. He pulled out his Vlex and tapped on it as the young man sat down. "Why did you go to so few booths this time?" his father asked. "I told you the more you go to, the better your chances are at getting a job."

His father kept scrolling through his Vlex, sighing intermittently. The plump man shook his head with a disgusted sigh. "Hovertrain station?" He squinted at his kid. "Son, really?"

"I didn't visit it though," said Xan.

"Why didn't you go to the Bank? That's a good company. Why are you missing all the good ones? God. I've told you about this."

"I wanted to but – "

His father shifted fast in his seat. "Mars?" The man let out a sardonic laugh.

Xan shook his head.

His father sighed. "Did you go visit that section?"

"You said to check out every booth."

"Not the shitty ones."

Xan crossed his arms. "How do you know Mars is shitty? You've never been. Smart people don't go where the money is but where it'll be."

His father looked at him with grey eyes. "Where did you hear that, from some promoter? Don't be so naïve. Of course, they made up a wonderful speech about how great the place is. There's a reason they have to promote it. Because it's probably a shit hole."

The young man felt the red orb sink lower in that darkened crevice. His shoulders rounded and his back hunched.

"It's a scam," his father said. "The only people making money up there are the big guys. Unless you find the money to start a mining business, you shouldn't bother."

Xan felt a hot coal burn in his chest. Mars wasn't a scam. Living on Earth was the scam.

His father let out a small laugh. "You didn't even visit Tox Hovercrafts?"

"I didn't have time to go there again," said Xan. "I've spoken to them at the last five fairs anyway."

"You should've talked with them six. This is one of the Earth's largest companies. It doesn't look good to the business when you do the bare minimum. Damn. We'll let's consider that one gone. Good going."

The young man put his eyes down and waited for the session to end.

His father sat at the table in silence, drinking his glass of water, letting the moment linger for his son. "Do you even care?" he asked.

"Yes."

His father watched him, his eyes cold. He put his glass down and shook his head. "Just leave," he said. "So what if you want to ruin your life. I'm done helping your ass. Thank god I had a second child."

The young man stood from the table and put his glass back into the cabinet. He then walked past his father and into his small room. A tiny bed took up most of the room with barely enough space for a tiny desk crammed in the corner beside it. The young man sat at his chair and placed his Vlex in a groove in his desk. A screen lit up above his desk, filled with pictures of an assortment of cheeses, while a virtual keyboard was projected near his hands.

He typed: *Mars is a Scam*. His screen flooded with various articles.

The government looks favourably upon those wishing to emigrate to Mars. Visa approvals are faster than those for satellite homes and lunar dwellings.

Another article read: *There are great companies to work for on Mars. Don't be scammed by Earth's jobs. Mars is ready for the future's best. Come to Mars! Every day is an adventure!*

A picture of the red orb peeked out from behind all the files. The young man clicked on it. It hung bright on his wall. He watched it spin in the surrounding darkness.

Current temperature in Meridien City: Twenty-five degrees Celsius. Current temperature in Mons City: Twenty-seven degrees Celsius.

CHAPTER 3

He felt piercing malice behind every eye contact he made with other fresh graduates. They wanted him dead. To clear an opening for themselves. *How many of these people will commit suicide after today?* he thought. *When those few precious jobs are filled.*

"Well," his father said. "We'll see how this turns out. Try to get something to afford you a living."

Xan ignored his father as he rubbed his damp palms together.

His father laughed. "Damn," he said. "Our odds were never this high. How many students do you think are here? I knew the population was growing, but when you see it for yourself."

His mother exhaled. "Our parents said the same about our generation," she said.

The young man's perception changed to accommodate his father's fear. The room seemed to grow with more people than he knew. Each person he saw represented a taken job. Each person represented another flat taken. Another spouse taken. Another life lived.

"Do you think you'll get the hovercraft position?" his sister asked.

Xan stared into the sea of people. The auditorium engulfed his senses. "I don't know."

His father leaned into their conversation. "If you get in with them you're set for life. Sales are the future. I'm sure you'll be able to find a wife there. Give it a few years, and you'll be moving into your own flat. That is when you decide to have kids. Stick to two; otherwise the government will put you in a different tax bracket."

"Okay. Thanks," said Xan.

"Speaking of, we'd better get to your first interview. They'll want to see that you're punctual. What's the first one?" his father asked.

Xan glanced at his Vlex, even though he'd already memorised the schedule. "Tox Hovercrafts."

His father raised his thin dark eyebrows. "Really? They still want to interview you? After you avoided their booth at the last fair?"

"They didn't take away my prior reservation," said Xan.

His father smirked. "Fine. Let's go then. Get this over with."

They left the auditorium and joined the crowded streets. Xan had his entire day packed with interviews. The companies wasted no time in filling up the positions.

His father ambled behind them, spouting off his mouth. "It's always been competitive, but I believe this generation has it the worst," he said. "To be honest, this is the best position someone like you could ever land. You're not smart enough to go into the sciences, and you don't have the attention to detail for finance. Those kids have a knack for it. Not the way you've performed though. You're in with the majority of grads now. Keep your fingers crossed. Hope for the best."

They reached the first building. His family piled against the wall, staying out of the pedestrians' way. His father continued rambling on to no one in particular.

His mother moved to stand beside him. She was a beautiful woman with a natural smile and a pleasant gaze. His sister took after her and had the same black hair and clear eyes.

Xan looked into the crowd, at the buildings, and then the hovercrafts zooming above them.

His mother held his shoulders gently, grabbing his attention. "Remember," she said. "The more people there are, the more the need there is for more salesmen."

"Sure," he whispered.

"You have enough anxiety, but son, you have to land a job today. Your odds will never be this good." She turned back to stand with the rest of his family and gave him a pleasant nod.

He tried to smile, but it was fake. The young man stepped through the doors into a large white lobby where he saw a glass pyramid sitting on a crystalline pedestal. He moved towards it and touched his Vlex to its side and watched them both light up. His Vlex received instructions to proceed through the building.

He took a huge elevator lift and arrived at the interviewing hall. Xan paused for a moment in front of the four wide double doors to compose himself and then stepped into the giant room. He came face to face with a roomful of other prospective hires.

There was a large table at the front of the room with three disinterested persons behind, all tapping away at their Vlexes and ignoring the crowd gathering around them.

Xan looked around the room but avoided making eye contact with anyone else.

One interviewer stood up. He cleared his throat and studied the crowd. He brought his Vlex below his nose and read from a script.

"Hello everyone," he said. "You are all here today for the first round of interviews with Tox Hovercrafts. We can only take in twelve of you this quarter, so most you will be leaving us today."

Xan looked around the giant room filled with over four hundred people. *Twelve?* He thought. *How the hell can they only take in twelve?*

"Now, let's not waste any time here." The man tapped on his Vlex and then several red flashes erupted in the audience.

Everyone with red screens looked around the room in confusion. The interviewer glanced up from his Vlex and eyed the room for a moment. "For those of you who've just received the red screen, we ask that you, please exit the room quietly. Based on a computer-generated analysis, we've concluded that you're not the candidates we're looking for. Thanks."

More than half of the crowd sifted out of the room. The young man watched them leave. Some were crying, some had their eyes set on the door as they headed purposefully for their next interviews.

The remaining group moved closer to the interviewer's table.

"Okay," the interviewer said. "Next, we'll ask the rest of you to begin a presentation to sell our newest brand of hovercrafts. We can assess your performance from your Vlexes. Please begin."

The room exploded in humming voices. Everyone spoke into their Vlexes as they read the scripts given to them. The young man talked with as much enthusiasm as he could. He tried to keep his voice clear and his words concise.

"Okay, thank you." The interviewer tapped on his Vlex, and the room lighted up with more red screens. "If you've received a red screen, please leave quietly. Thank you."

While the others were leaving the room, the interviewer spoke. "Next, we need each one of you to pair off with the person beside you. Your partner will have the same number as you."

Xan looked down at the number fifty-six and paired up with the person to his right. It was a girl his age with straight black hair.

The interviewer pointed at his Vlex in the air. "We'll be sending you a dialogue between a sales rep and a customer. You will practice these with your partner. You may begin."

Xan saw that he had been assigned the role of the customer. The girl he'd partnered with began her sales pitch. "Hello sir, welcome to Tox Hovercrafts. I'm here to help you with all of your hovercraft needs. I see from your recent searches you are interested in the Tox-2000 model - " The instance she paused, her screen flashed red.

"Fuck," she said. "Fuck!"

He avoided looking at her. She remained where she was, glaring at him. Other pairs were breaking apart with failed applicants. Eventually, she turned away and went out the back.

"Okay. For the rest of you, we're going to do the same exercise."

The number twenty-three showed on his Vlex. He paired with a young man his age standing to the left of him. This time, Xan was the sales representative.

"Hi sir, welcome to Tox Hovercrafts," he said. "I'm here to help you with all of your hovercraft needs. I see from your recent searches you're interested in buying a full-sized hovercraft, specifically the Tox-FS-800?"

"Yes," his partner said. "That's the one. I'm looking for a hovercraft that can transport my entire family to our new satellite home. We've added another grandchild to the family, so the old model will no longer do."

"I see," said Xan. "Here, let me show you the specifications of the Tox-FS-800. When you purchase the full-sized Tox-FS-800, you'll be flying in the Earth's finest hovercraft to date. As you'll notice here in the file, the Tox-FS-800 model is fully equipped with eight comfortable seats and extra storage space in the boot. I believe this will suit you and your family well."

The customer began his dialogue again. The two racketed back and forth without missing a beat. At the end of the conversation, they both stood still waiting for their results. The computers analysed their speeches and took the better of them.

Xan saw his partner's Vlex turn red. His partner stood there with his mouth open. "You've got to be kidding me. You've got to be kidding me."

Xan kept his head down. His partner growled under his breath and clenched his fists. "Screw you. Screw this whole damn company. How the hell do they give this retard my place?"

Xan ignored him and kept his focus on the ground. The interviewer stood again and eyed Xan's partner. "We ask once more that all failed applicants leave quietly."

Xan's partner glanced up at the table. He shot a glare at the Xan, the interviewer, and then left the room.

The interviewer sighed out of boredom as he watched the last person leave the room.

"Okay," he said. "We'll be giving each one of you a topic for the next task. You're to stand in front of the room and give a speech based on your given topic. Please refer to the number on your Vlex for your speaking order."

The number seven appeared across Xan's screen, and he went to stand in line with the rest. The first speaker went up to the front. Her topic was on the societal implications behind the religious prohibition.

Xan wiped away the sweat that was forming on his forehead. The next person went up. She produced a wonderful speech. Xan felt even more uncomfortable. The next candidate spoke well. Xan picked at the grit under his fingernails. Next, it was another boy's turn for his speech.

Xan panicked when his turn came. He stood before everyone and saw his topic appear: *The Extinction of the Nova Scotian Cod and Its Global Impact on Canadian Trading Routes.*

"Seriously?"

Xan stood before the group. His Vlex shook in his nervous hands. He tried to clear his throat. He started his speech then found himself cut off mid-way through. The interviewers rolled their eyes in annoyance. Xan looked down at his Vlex blinking red.

The interviewer cleared his throat. Xan saw the next person waiting to take his place. Xan put his head down and walked past the rest. Some sneered at him as he passed by. This was their livelihood too.

Xan left the building with his head low. He didn't want to walk out of the lobby. He could hear his father talking outside, over the rushing crowds.

"Suicide rates are so high," his father said. "There's always a spike this time of year. Too many people on this planet. That's how nature works though. Somebody has to go." His father spat a dry laugh.

His mother sighed. "Would you drop it?" she said. "What are you even talking about?"

The young man stepped outside. He saw his mother turn to him, and his father stop talking. They both looked him in the eye. His mother opened her mouth to say something but then stopped.

His father shook his head. His eyes were filled with disappointment. "You blew it?" he said.

Xan kept his mouth shut and walked off to the next interview. His sister caught up with him and walked alongside him, not saying a word. He appreciated her presence.

He entered the next interview and reached the same level as before – the point when he had to speak on a topic. He cleared his throat and spoke with vigour. But his speech on twenty-first-century oil production didn't get him the position.

"God, you're pissing away all the good ones," his father said. "What are you doing in there? I landed the first interview I had thirty-six years ago. Do you need me to walk you through the steps or something?"

Xan left for the next building, not listening to his father's speech.

His father shook his head and followed behind him. "What's the next one? Sioux Freight?"

Xan looked at his Vlex. "No, Sioux Manufacturing."

His father rubbed his chin. "At least the pay is good. You'll be lucky to snag this one."

Xan walked in.

His father let out a grunt. "You aren't serious are you?"

Xan ignored him.

His father stepped up behind him through the door. "You're a dead giveaway. They'll see right through you if you walk in looking depressed. At least pretend to be something. Go in with some confidence."

Xan pressed onward. He went through the building and into the interview. It was the worst yet. He didn't make it past the second round. He stayed inside the lobby for some time, listening to his father blab to everyone out the door.

"Between the three of us," his father said, "we knew he wouldn't make it. The kid never had it in him. Turned out to be a bit of a dud."

"Why would you say that?" his sister said.

"Let's stop talking about this," his mother said.

Xan stepped outside, and his father quickly stopped talking. His father knew from Xan's expression that he did not make the cut.

"Bottom of the pile," Xan's father whispered under his breath.

"One left," said Xan.

His mother moved towards him. "Where is it?"

"Train station."

His father took in a deep breath and let it out slowly through his nose.

Xan lined up for the interview. *Bottom of the pile? Seriously, bottom of the pile is an underground shack or a bottle full of sleeping pills in your gut.* He looked around at the other defeated faces.

Over half left with rejections. At the final part of the interview, Xan made his speech and found himself accepted for the job. A huge wave of relief flooded over him. He felt tears in his eyes but kept them dry as he walked outside with a new title: *Hovertrain Conductor.*

His mother congratulated him along with his sister. Xan tried to smile, but it felt too painful.

"You did well," said his mother. "Thank you son."

Wiping his eyes with the back of his hand, he cleared his vision and saw a giant gate in the distance. Barbed wire circled the top while armed guards patrolled below. All food plants looked the same.

"They still let those androids run the trains?" said his father.

Xan nodded his head.

"How many years until they let them run it completely?"

"Doesn't matter."

"Sure. You know how everything works in this world. Congratulations son and welcome to the rest of your life."

Xan opened his mouth.

"You're stuck now." His father turned away from the family, pulled his jacket's collar up, and disappeared from sight.

CHAPTER 4

His grandfather smiled at him, patting him on the back, his face filled with pride.

Xan looked down at his feet like a child. "I couldn't do it," he said. "I didn't make it happen."

His grandfather smiled. He held the young man by the shoulders, saying nothing.

A loud buzz awoke him from his dream. He reached over and turned off his alarm. The midnight train waited for him to carry its passengers from stop to stop.

He slid out of bed, threw on his conductor's jacket and went to the kitchen. Xan glanced at his Vlex as he snatched a thin package from the cabinet and ripped it open with his teeth. He poured a glob of mush out of the packet into a bowl, set his Vlex down, and turned on the cooker.

After a few seconds, his meal was done. He opened the cooker and looked at his constructed meal inside. Mock eggs with fake bacon laying neatly atop them.

When he finished his breakfast, he ran out the door and down the hall. He slipped into the crowded lift and descended to the ground floor with everyone else. The lift doors opened, and the crowd rushed out, merging with the masses outside.

Advertisements covered the streets, glistening in every inch of each building's face. Passing by a large food plant, Xan lowered his eyes and nearly bumped into a scientist on his way.

The woman glared at him, then went through the first gate and out of sight. Xan tried to ignore her glare as he marched across the street into the nearest hovertrain station.

He headed to the train manager's booth where a decrepit old man sat inside a tall round booth, his eyes glazed over, and his mouth agape. Xan glanced up at him, then tapped his Vlex on a glass pyramid outside the man's booth.

Both devices flashed yellow. A message confirmed that he had clocked in on time and a list of daily instructions appeared: *Normal Hovertrain Operations Today Unless Otherwise Specified*.

Xan sighed and slumped towards the hovertrain pulling into the station. A thrush of wind swirled around him as the hovertrain stopped. The conductor's door slid open, and Xan hopped inside.

The other conductor didn't acknowledge him. She carried on flipping the safety switches and tidied up the area before she left. Xan closed the door behind her and went over to the conductor's seat right next to the deactivated android, who was waiting for the manager to give the green light to go.

The young man watched the station manager's booth for his clearance. A small green light flashed, and he pressed the left button, activating the android beside him. The android sprang to life and sped the train off.

Xan watched the blue track beneath them while they glided along the dark tunnels. Tiny lights on the wall meshed into a blur as they zoomed by. The train approached the next station, and Xan waited for the manager's clearance to enter.

A green light flashed, and Xan proceeded. The android brought the train to a stop. He deactivated the android and waited for the next green light. The light came. Xan activated the bot. The train moved round its circular loop, activating the robot and deactivating his own mind. He welcomed any break in this pattern. Anything to keep his mind from melding into the collective null.

The train's window blinked. It was outlined in red light with a warning message that the train read out to him: "Track obstruction. Track obstruction. Please verify."

He looked out the window and saw a few large rats scampering around the tracks. He pressed the clearance button, allowing the train to proceed.

"Just wait for the day when they allow you to take care of these things," he said to the android. "I assume that'll be it for me."

The android focused on his mission with blind intention. It didn't respond to human noise.

The train stopped. A crowd of people left, and a new crowd came on board. A green light flashed, and Xan pressed the button. The android woke and died again. Coloured lights controlled their lives.

The days went by in the same loop, and the months flew under the radar without a blip.

One day, a man tried to climb over the glass walls to throw himself onto the tracks in front of the moving train. Xan pressed the emergency button. The train came to a halt, and a group of station officials pulled the man down.

That was the most excitement he had experienced in his job. That moment only lasted a few minutes, and then the green lights put him back into a trance. Blinking beside him, the robot glided the train above the tracks. Xan talked to this clicking machine more than any mortal man.

He didn't see the months slide by him, nor did he feel his life swirling into an open drain. The only interaction he had with another human was before his break. The stop came, and the conductor's door slid open.

"Good morning," said the old man, entering the train.

"Good morning," said Xan with a smile.

The older man readied his things. He then broke the normal routine. "How you doing kid?"

Xan felt unsure how to answer.

The older man held out his hand. "Good to see you."

Slowly, Xan reached out and grasped his hand into a shake.

"You ever need any help, come tell me. No one else is watching out for us."

"Oh."

"See you tomorrow."

Xan grinned to himself as he stepped out of the train, feeling light for once. "What a nice guy," he said. "No one ever talks to me down here. Never. And he even shook my hand."

Xan let out a laugh. The crowds paid no attention to him as he stood watching the train speed off to another station. He took in a deep breath and turned over his shoulder, looking at the farthest wall across the station where the food stalls lay burrowed in the walls like narrow cubes.

Xan put his hands in his pockets and walked towards them. It didn't matter that much to him what he ate. All foods were the same. *Fish and Chips* was nothing more than reconstructed vegetables. *Ancient Indian Cuisine* was no different. They made everything in rounded cookers and from the same few plants remaining on Earth.

The young man looked at his options. He went to a traditional Japanese stall and ordered a mock *Katsu-Don.*

Xan found a lone bench protruding from the grey wall and sat watching the crowd go about its way.

EMERGENCY ALERT. MULTIPLE BOMBINGS HAVE TAKEN PLACE IN THE FOLLOWING AREAS: NEW KING'S LONDON, NEO HO CHI MINH, RUSSIO-KIEV...

The list went on. He ignored the terrorist nuisance. All the ads in the station were replaced with the announcement. The rounded ceiling projected a giant feed for everyone to see.

"Dear citizens of Earth," said the lady on the screen. "We come before you today with saddened hearts as another terrorist attack has taken place.

"We, your government are working tirelessly to rid this planet of such evils. We only ask that you, as citizens of Earth, stay alert and report any suspicious persons or articles. If you are ever concerned, we ask that you notify the authorities immediately."

The woman paused. "Each one of you will receive information packets with further instructions on how this will affect your day. Thank you."

The lady vanished, and the ads resumed their noise again. Xan's Vlex alerted him of a new message: *Continue with normal operations.*

The crowd moved along without any change in pace. The ads continued selling, and the young man continued eating. He finished his break and returned to the train. He entered his designated train and switched places with the middle-aged man inside.

The green light came, the button pressed, the android clicked, and the train went down the track. The morning rose, and the young man ended his shift. He left the station and walked with the busy crowd back towards his house.

Before he realised it, he had reached his building. Xan stopped himself before entering. He pulled away from the crowd and piled into the crowded lift.

Xan entered the empty house. Silence ticked inside his mind. Everyone was gone. They had just started their own daily grind. He wouldn't see any of them for a couple of years. At least not until his shift changed.

Xan drifted to the cabinet and poured himself a glass of water. He finished his water and went into his room. He sat at his desk and turned on the news. A screen appeared on the wall above him.

A happy family gathered around a beautiful table, eating a large mock chicken. Every one of them was laughing and smiling.

"Braxton's premium family dinners. For the special nights with the special people in your life. Our packages have been reconstructed with such precision that you won't be able to tell they've been processed. Take some home for your family today."

The ad changed. *An older woman was being led into a tunnel of white light. A lone chair sat in the middle of the giant white room. A scientist held her hand as he sat her in the chair. She smiled up at him.* "Looking for a way out? Is legal euthanasia still a few years off? We can help."

He changed the station.

"Next, we'll be talking with Earth's Head of Security about the recent bombings and how they plan to thwart these terrorist threats. Stay tuned to see what our government plans to do and how you can play a vital part."

Another commercial began. *A red wind blew fine dust around a sleek machine.* "Come to Mars. Every day is an Adventure." *The screen focused on a man driving his new sandrover. A beautiful woman sat beside him, and their children giggled in the back.* "Ever thought about Mars?" *the man said.* "Neither had I."

His wife smiled at the camera and the children waved.

"Then again not everyone is ready for paradise."

"Dad," *said his daughter.* "Can we keep going?"

He turned around, pat her hand, and winked at the camera. "We're having fun. Why aren't you?"

The man turned his sandrover on and zipped out of sight.

Xan turned off his Vlex and climbed into his bed. He allowed the red sands to billow in his mind. Soft touches placed their warmth upon a creviced dream.

I'm already working for the station, he thought. *They'll want the fresh graduates up there. There's no point in trying.*

Xan turned inside his bed and closed his eyes.

He rode in his sandrover, racing down the Martian hills. He turned the wheel back and forth, weaving the machine like a pit viper in the sand. Dust flew around him like a gentle cloud.

The skies glimmered above him. There was no smog to be found.

A sad drone of repetition knocked on his heart. The air stilled. The dust froze in place.

Xan opened his eyes. He touched his Vlex and brought it up to see the time. His arms fell back into his bed. Xan sighed. *What if I never show back up?* He knew his time was limited. The station needed him. But it felt like he'd just fallen asleep. Almost every night felt the same.

***

Government officials crawled within the station. They were standing at the walls, following random individuals, or patrolling in tight groups with dogs at their legs and rifles at their shoulders. Xan slowed his pace as he spied the people around him, and meandered towards the manager's booth.

He looked over his shoulder as he tapped his Vlex on the glass pyramid, then turned back to see a red light flash between them. A message appeared: *Please remain where you are.*

"The hell is this?"

He pushed his back against the manager's booth, standing near the pyramid, eyeing the area for any clues. His eyes locked in on a government official clad in a long dark jacket and a pair of black sunglasses, who was weaving steadily through the crowd.

Xan swallowed hard. He tried not to stare at the man, thinking that he could be going anywhere else. The man halted in front of Xan and cleared his throat. Xan glanced up and tried to smile.

The man extended his large hand. "Vlex," he said.

Xan hesitated.

The man snatched it out of his hand and placed it upon a larger glass device in his hands. The tall man studied it for a moment. "You're to come with me," he said.

"I'm sorry?"

The man paused, raising his eyebrows. "I said, you're to come with me. Unless you prefer to be detained, which can easily be arranged."

Xan shook his head. "Sorry. Right. I-I didn't - "

The man sighed loudly and deliberately. "Follow me," he said, cocking his head towards a blank wall.

Xan glanced at a group of people standing behind the tall man. They were dressed similarly, with long coats and dark glasses, except for one man, who wore a strange pair of eyewear he'd never seen before.

The tall man ushered Xan to the side of the wall, and the group trailed behind them. Xan walked along with his head down and kept his hands in his pockets. The tall man took out his Vlex and waved it in front of the vacant wall. It slid to the side, opening up to a narrow passageway with dim lights spaced perfectly apart throughout.

The tall man pushed Xan inside and pointed down the hall for him to keep walking. Xan complied. He looked nervously at his surroundings, noticing tiny silver triangles lining the black walls.

The tall man gripped Xan's shoulder, making him stop beside one triangle, and swiped his Vlex in front of it. It opened to a small, dark room. 'Get in,' he said.

Xan stepped into the room and stood motionless. The tall man entered behind him, with three other men following and standing guard up against the wall.

The tall man pointed to a dark chair. "Sit," he said.

Xan took a seat, folding his hands in his lap.

The tall man tapped on his Vlex across the table. "How long have you worked with Ra?"

Xan looked up and around the room. "Who is that?"

Placing his Vlex on the table, the tall man rubbed his forehead and sighed. "Do you not switch positions with him every morning at six-forty-five?"

Xan left his mouth open. "I - I didn't know his name was Ra."

The man tapped his finger upon his knee. It was a loud thump that sounded like water dripping from a tap. "Please answer the original question."

Xan shook his head, unsure of how to answer. He couldn't think. There was so little noise and light that it made him feel anxious like he'd never known how stressed his body was until this precise moment.

The man tapped a little faster. "How long have you worked with Ra?"

Xan barked out an answer quick, "Almost a year. Since I worked here."

The man looked down at his Vlex and then back at Xan. "In that time did you ever talk with him?"

Xan shifted in his seat. "I said hello or good morning."

The man tapped his finger faster and with more strength. "I need a simple yes or no."

"Yes."

The man examined him. "In your conversations, did the two of you ever talk about his living arrangements?"

Xan looked around the room. "Living arrangements? No. We only said hello or good morning."

The man looked back at one of the figures standing against the wall. It was the lady wearing a strange pair of glasses around her face. She gave the interrogator a faint nod.

The man turned back around. "Have you ever been to the city's underground?"

Xan felt a rush of hot blood surging through his face. "No! Of course not. I don't even know how to get there."

The lady in the back gave another small nod.

The man kept his eyes down on his Vlex. "A simple yes or no will suffice." He reached down near his feet and pulled up a sleek metal case that he dropped loudly upon the table.

"Have you ever taken any illegal drugs?" he asked.

"No."

He snapped the latches back and opened the case. He took out two round cylinders and set the cylinders down between the two of them. He interlaced fingers into his lap and watched Xan for some time, allowing the unbearable silence to linger.

Then he stood up, took hold of the two cylinders, and walked over to Xan. "Then you'd be willing to take a drug scan?"

Xan furled his brow. "Okay. Fine."

The interrogator moved towards Xan and opened one of the small cylinders. It was full of a shiny blue liquid. "Please place your index finger here," said the man.

Xan dipped his index finger into the blue liquid. A cooling sensation prickled through it. "Ouch," he said, shaking his finger.

The pain refused to subside. Xan kept shaking his hand, trying to swish it away. The blue crept up his arm, sweeping over his hand. "Oww," he said. "Ouch!"

Needles stabbed into his skin, refusing to stop in its incessant climb. Xan stood from his seat and shook his arm, feeling his bicep being overtaken by the sharp pain. The man stood back behind his seat and watched.

Xan felt his face go black. He fell to the floor and curled his body into the fetal position, trying to get some relief. He couldn't stop coughing as the spikes pricked under his nails. He shook uncontrollably on the floor and tried his best to ask for help.

Only gurgles emerged from his mouth. His vision faded into a blur as he saw a dark figure towering over him. "Lift your hand," he heard.

Xan couldn't uncurl his arm, nor his tiny forefinger. Eventually, the man reached down and took his hand with force, and shoved his finger into the second cylinder.

A pink liquid rippled through his body, flushing out the shiny blue one. The needles released their pricks from his skin. The snake around his lungs uncoiled, allowing him to breathe normally again. The man let go of his hand and screwed the tops back onto the containers.

Xan lay on the floor, still feeling cold, with the driest sensation in his mouth he'd ever felt. Nervous shivers convulsed through his body, while his mind could only think of water. "I need something drink," he whispered.

The man ignored him.

"Can I please have some water?"

The man placed the containers back into the metal case. "You can get some when you leave."

"Please?"

The man continued closing his case. "You'll get it when you leave," he said, snapping the locks on the case and holding it to his side.

Xan struggled to his feet using the chair to brace himself.

"That's all," said the man.

The door slid open, and the man held out his palm, asking him to leave.

Xan wobbled through the door, holding onto the walls for balance, nearly tripping into the narrow hallway. One of the dark figures walked behind him, holding his elbow. He guided Xan to the exit, then opened the wall and shoved him outside into the crowded station.

Xan fell with a daze and struggled to push himself up. All he could think of was water. The door slid shut behind him. Xan reached out for the walls, stumbling over his feet, the same command repeating in his head: *Just get to the food stalls. Just get to the food stalls.*

He bumped into others as he tried to navigate the station and fell to the ground, losing focus of the food stalls. He tried to crawl towards the wall. A commuter kneed him in the face. He fell again and coughed endlessly.

Xan couldn't pull himself up through the rushing crowd. Strong bumps knocked him further into the mass of people. A sharp heel stepped on his hand. The young man screamed. Another person bumped into his temple and then another. Swiping his weak fists at the people, he tried to find a chance to stand. People died in peak rush hour all the time. Trampled to death under feet racing to work.

He felt someone grab him under his arm, inching him up off the ground. A bald man in a white uniform lifted him up. Rough shoulders knocked the man to the ground. A group of teenagers kicked the man's mechanical crutch further away.

Xan tried to claw his way onto his hands and knees. Between the fast walking legs, he saw the blurry man steady himself on his mechanical crutch, and soon Xan felt a hand on the back of his collar.

They reached the brightly lit food stalls, and Xan felt himself shoved inside one and sat down on a small metal stool in the back.

"People die on the floors every day," said the man in the white uniform.

"Use your head kid. Fall near the walls or somewhere safer."

Xan forced himself to say the only thing he could think of. "Water?"

"Hold on," said the man. "Just hold on."

The man slapped a warm cup of water in his hand. Xan tipped it back and spewed the water out, coughing from the immediate sensation.

The man looked back at him. "Drink it slowly," he said.

Xan wiped his mouth and tried again. His vision returned and his bones lessened their ache. "Thank you," he said between breaths. "Thank you."

The bald man shook his head and mumbled under his breath. Xan finished the glass and looked up at the man. His crutch lay propped beside him as he leaned against the stall's counter. "Drug scan?" said the man, not turning to face Xan.

"How'd you know?"

"They're swarming today," he said. "To protect and serve." The cook shivered. "Be thankful they let you go."

Xan eyed his empty glass.

"One of your coworkers?" said the cook.

"Excuse me?"

"They asked you about one of them?"

Xan nodded. "I didn't even know his name."

The bald man let out a faint snort and then scratched the few remaining threads on the back of his head. "None of us do. But that doesn't stop 'em either way."

Xan rubbed his chest, feeling the recent pain like a bad memory more than a physical ailment now.

"It's standard procedure," said the cook. "If you've worked in this world long enough, you'll get yourself one at some point. Especially down here. They don't care how loose the tie is."

Xan shuffled in his seat and looked around the stall. There were a few round cookers, just like his own, up against the back counter, and boxes of mush packets on the floor and hanging up above the ceiling.

The man supported himself up on the counter. "You've got be careful who you talk to here. Do what you have to and be on your way." He flicked his hand out through the station.

"I do," said Xan. "Believe me."

The station continued to hum. The mass of bodies flowed in various directions.

"You think my coworker was a terrorist?" said Xan.

The bald man drew in a deep breath before he spoke. "Hard to say. Did he just go missing?"

"I saw him yesterday."

The man shook his head. "God knows then. All you can do is wait. He might show up one day later and then again he might not."

Xan placed his cup on the counter and looked through the side door and then back to the cook. He wondered if he should get up and go, as the man still hadn't faced him. *Maybe this is a polite way of telling me to leave?*

The man wiped his counter with an old rag and then pointed towards one of the other stalls. "There's a lady in the seventh-floor cube, three columns over that had a nasty scan a few years back," he said. "Gone for over a month. No word. Then one day she's back. Like nothings happened."

The cook laughed with a dry bitter tone. "She never told us what happened - but then again, she doesn't really talk to anyone anymore." He laughed with pity. "Poor girl, never been the same. All twitchy now. Barely able to take an order. But that's what we get for being poor and working down here in the station."

Xan felt a speckle of blood from his lower lip. He was unaware he had a nervous habit of biting it.

"Read a history book. We used to make a living," said the cook. "People took pride in their work. To wear a uniform like yours, you'd have to be properly trained. More than pushing a stupid button."

"A month?"

"Or more," said the cook. "Found out she was living underground. Then they probably found out they were the ones that forced her down there."

Xan's nerves jumbled inside his gut. "She lives down there, and they let her work up here?"

The cook hissed as he rubbed his leg. "Tons of people live downstairs and work up here. Don't be surprised if you find yourself hunting flats there yourself one day."

The young man picked the dead skin off his chapped lips.

The cook turned to him. "They didn't teach you about this stuff in school?"

Xan squinted at the man, with half a smile stuck on his face.

The man frowned. "It's a shame they can't be honest. What do you kids think happens with the rest of us, without nice jobs or spouses to share the load?"

Xan cleared his throat. "Family house?"

"And if your parents are dead? No flat gets passed down any more kid."

Xan smashed his eyebrows into a furl. "There are plenty of schemes in place. Sibling flats."

The cook shook his head. "What do you care? Is that your dream in life, to survive?"

Xan paused.

The cook had a serious look. "What I'm saying is most of this is for show."

"You're messing with my head."

"Everyone learns it at some point. It's no secret either."

Xan didn't enjoy being in the stall anymore. He pulled out his Vlex and saw a message on it from the station: *Please return to the station manager's booth for further instructions.* He leaned out the stall. "Thanks for the water," he said.

The cook faced him. "Sure."

Xan went out by the side.

"Hey?" called the cook.

Xan turned to the front counter.

The cook held up his hand with the dirty rag still in it. "I'm not trying to mess with you, all right? I assumed you already knew."

Xan nodded. "Sure," he said, as he disappeared into the crowd.

CHAPTER 5

Xan took his break and perused the food stalls that were jammed into the wall in every available space. Ever since the drug scan, he had done his best to avoid the cook who had helped him by avoiding an entire section of vendors, just to keep safe.

Instead, he approached another stall, where an older lady stood behind the counter. She looked haggard with a pathetic hairnet that did little to contain her wiry hair. Xan smiled and placed his order. The lady pulled out a packet of mush, dumped it into the round cooker while doing her best to manage a strong twitch that jerked her head to the side.

Xan didn't bring attention to it. She already knew, and there was no need to be rude about it.

Soon a dish full of fake chicken made its way to his hands. He tapped his Vlex on the counter's pyramid and went to eat at one of the abandoned benches.

Photos of huge flats adorned the ad space on the wall before him. *Earth's Prime Minister approves. With more government flats being built every day. Have you considered a government flat today?*

The young man laughed.

Government warning. Be careful of terrorists posing as religious practitioners. The right choice is always to report. Remember that one call could save millions of lives.

The young man took his eyes from the ads and noticed a familiar face emerging from the crowd. "What are you doing here?" he said.

His sister Ima sat at the bench with him and drooped her shoulders. "I signed up for a graduation prep course today," she said. "It's supposed to help."

"You still have two years left," said Xan.

She glanced at him. "It was dad's idea. He said he didn't want another..."

Xan kept his eyes on the crowd and then drew in a deep breath.

Ima looked down for a moment. "They only had the early morning classes left, so I took them."

"Right," he said. "Are they helpful?"

She drew her lips into the corner of her mouth. "I haven't started yet," she said. "What do you think, did they help you?"

He pointed to the embroidered conductor tag on his jacket. "Draw your own conclusions."

Her face went red. "Better than nothing."

He put his hand in the air. "I almost nabbed a spot with Vox. So, maybe if I'd started my prep earlier."

She looked down at his food, trying to avoid eye contact with him.

Xan licked the back of his teeth, leaving his mouth open.

"Are you mad that I came?"

"Nah, I'm hungry."

She pursed her lips.

He tapped his fork on his meal. Then he spotted a ring on her finger. He pointed his fork at her hand. "I've seen that somewhere before."

Ima placed her other hand on top of the ring.

Xan picked up his meal. "You trying to impress someone?"

"No. I think it looks nice."

"Does mom know you're wearing it?"

Ima's crossed her legs and pivoted to the other side. "It's fake anyway."

"Dad still tried to pawn it off when Aunt Hana died you know?"

"How's your breakfast?"

He spoke with his mouth full. "This is dinner."

"Either way, how is it?"

"Fine. Tastes the same as every other dish." He stabbed at the mock chicken and took a few more bites. "You wanna try?"

"No thanks."

He pointed to the food stalls around them. "What are your plans Ima? You have two years left. What's the focus of your studies?"

She searched for a moment. "Hospitality."

"You'd better study hard."

"You sound like dad."

The young man looked at his Vlex and saw his break had ended. He rubbed his eyes. "What do you want to do?" he said. "Not what you think you should do."

"I just want a job."

Xan moved to stand but stopped midway. "That's it?"

She grimaced at him.

Xan picked up his plate and threw it in the nearest recycling bin and walked back to the bench.

"You'll be fine," he said. "Practice your interviews as much as possible, and you'll ace it."

She wrinkled a faint smile.

He let out a heavy exhale. "It's not what you think, the outside world." He nudged her with his elbow. "I want to tell you more, but I'm still learning myself."

"Never mind."

His Vlex vibrated. He glanced at the time.

"I wish there was another way for us."

He saw the time again and let go of her. "Forget what I've said. Yeah?"

She bobbed her head a little.

"I have to go. If you see mom, tell her I said hello."

"Sure."

Xan ran back to the train, mumbling to himself. The android sat deactivated at his side. Xan waited for the green light. The green light shone. He woke the android up and the train glided through the blue tunnel haze. "Shut your damn mouth," he said, thinking of his dad. "Who are you to complain?"

The room shouted to him: "Track obstruction. Track obstruction. Please verify."

He looked out the red blinking glass and saw another family of rats. He cleared the train and continued down the track.

"See, he's getting along with his rodent kids," said Xan. "I bet you don't have to worry about flats, dreams, and career choices. It's eat, sleep, and shit for you."

The train stopped at its final station. He left the conductor's seat and merged with the streaming crowd. Numerous ads begged for his attention. One, in particular, caused his heart to beat faster. It was of two beautiful faces walking hand in hand in an opulent city. The woman turned from her partner, winking at the audience. *Every day is an adventure on Mars. Why don't you make your trip here today?*

"I doubt she'd message me back now," he said. "I'm sure Mars has a one job track policy too."

Xan took hold of his Vlex and searched for the Mars recruiter's contact. He stood by the wall, away from the rushing crowd. He found the contact he'd made at the job fair over a year ago, just waiting beneath his thumb, ready to connect. One little tap of his thumb. It took so little to alter his life. One little tap.

The young man stood watching his thumb, waiting for it to move. "What harm would it do at this point?" he mused. "Everyone else ignores you, so what if she rejects you as well?"

The thought of his mother and sister held him back. He let out a sigh and placed his Vlex back in his pocket. He stood against the wall outside the station, watching the human wave drift by him. "We're all trapped here?" he said.

"In a sense."

He turned in shock, wondering who had heard him. The bald cook leaned against the wall beside him, his crutch holding up the weight of his bad leg.

Xan moved away from him a little. "What are you doing?"

The cook smiled. "You're not the only one who enjoys watching the sea of people."

The young man measured him up and down.

"There's no one answer for anyone," said the cook.

Xan held his thought a second. "Who's asking any questions?" he said. "Especially of you and I?"

The man cocked his head to the side and laughed through his teeth. "Hindsight," he said. "A curse to know what you should've done without ever being able to change the outcome."

Xan didn't move. His eyes went across the street to the armed gate in the distance.

"We're so god damned intelligent, yet we can't stop fighting each other, or learn how to share what we've got with one another."

"Was it always this claustrophobic?"

The man shifted his posture against the wall, fixing his shoulder into a more comfortable position. "Who knows?"

Another ad shone in the distance with a red orb hanging in space. *Every day is an adventure.*

Xan bobbed his head. "Why do they treat us this way? I have wants and desires like anybody else."

"They'll never take the time to understand our plight. That'd be too much of an inconvenience on their way of life."

"They wouldn't hesitate to drug test me again?"

"Not for a second."

"I took three years of human right courses and never heard a mention of these drug tests. What a lie."

"That's why they teach us. Who do you think curates these materials? Educating the masses is one thing, but what about the minority controlling most of the wealth? They make their own institutions far away from us to learn whatever they want."

Silence resumed in the empty space.

Xan glanced at his Vlex. He saw the contact sitting beneath his thumb. A green button to connect. On the train, he pressed the button for everyone else, but could he press this one for himself?

The young man turned to the cook beside him. "I want to escape this life."

"Try some perspective underground," said the cook. "I find it's healthy."

Xan laughed. "It's illegal. We'll get shot if we step foot there."

"No, it's not, and no one's going to shoot you for going."

The young man watched him. He studied his eyes for a while. "We turn to terrorism? Guys like us?"

"Be a little more sensitive, kid. There are plenty of good people down there. Hard working men and women getting by just fine."

"What do you mean by that?"

The man pointed his finger towards the ads. "Look at what you're sold for a moment," he said. "What do you see? Houses. Flats. Government programs. The government doing its best to care for us. The government looking out for our best interests. What do you think when you see it?"

The young man watched an ad across the street. Two siblings were moving into a flat together. The room was filled with nice furniture he'd never known existed. The view was nice. The people were beautiful.

"Looks nice," he said.

"It looks nice, but it's a complete lie. These programs and schemes they talk about are nothing more than a diversion from the truth. No one's pinching any more credits from the big dogs to make us more houses."

A sputtering hovercraft caught his attention overhead for a second.

The cook cracked his neck and shifted against the wall. "Let's say you're in my shoes one day. You've never married, or you both work in the station. What do you think your life'll be like then? Where are you going to go from there?"

The young man kept his eyes on the sputtering hovercraft. "I'll be a station manager living with my parents?"

"And when they go?"

Xan shook his head. "Live with my sister if she's single. Or apply for the single flat lottery?"

The cook laughed. "They don't exist. That's what I'm saying."

Xan squinted his eyes.

The man laughed at himself. "Wait until they send you the letter."

"What letter?"

"When they find out you're single and still living in your parents' flat at my age. You'll get it. It's a nice list of places you can go once they die. And I can tell you from personal experience, the ones you mentioned aren't in it."

The young man lifted himself off the wall.

"I don't know why they keep this information from us," said the cook. "I wish they would've told me early on. Could've saved me a lot of time and grief trying to live above ground."

Xan looked down below his feet. "Would it have changed anything for you?"

"Without a doubt."

"Is it safe underground?"

"Safe enough."

Xan looked at the ground. He nodded his head. "Show me," he said. "Let me see it for myself."

"If that's what you want."

CHAPTER 6

The sun rose high in the air while the two men walked through the city. They stopped at a large entrance from which people were trickling in and out. The man cocked his head towards the dark staircase.

"Here it is," he said. "Still want to check it out?"

Xan saw a stream of people exiting and entering. They were people he thought of as good upstanding citizens. He even caught sight of a few conductors leaving the area. "Yeah," he said.

The cook proceeded down the dim uneven steps with care. With hesitation, the young man followed. Sounds of the city muddled into a dull hum while both their feet echoed up and down the dim passageway.

Tripping over an awkward step, Xan grabbed the wall, almost knocking down the cook.

"You want my crutch?"

Xan drew his hand off the wall, feeling a sticky grime on his palm. The cook continued on, turning out of sight into a smaller passage. Xan hurried behind him.

The man put his body flat against the wall, letting another person squeeze by. Xan followed suit and let the woman pass. They slid the rest of the way through, out into another larger tunnel with a faint light glowing at its base.

This is it, Xan thought. *I can't believe I'm doing this.*

The air felt damp, chilled by a few degrees, and smelled of musk and water rot. Xan paused at the last step to place his hand over his nose. The man turned back to face him.

"Most of these places were bunkers built after the twenty days of fire."

"That's right."

"Other than that, I've only ever heard of how dangerous they are."

The cook dug his knuckles into his leg muscles. "Either you figure out this life for yourself or let others tell you what to do for the rest of your days." He growled as he dug deeper into his leg.

Xan kept in place.

"Sorry kid, I have to keep moving," said the cook. "You can find your way back up?"

Xan nodded.

"Good luck." The cook moved on, relying on his crutch.

Xan watched him go. Then inched down the final few steps. "Wait!"

The cook kept moving. "I can't stop. You're either in or out."

Leaping down the last step, Xan jogged through the entranced and emerged into the dim city. He stood in shock, gazing at the slanted flats built on top of one another with no regard for symmetry. There were a few tall buildings that stood almost upright, but Xan was sure it was an illusion because the floors were uneven beneath his feet.

The cook hobbled into a building near them. Xan blinked a few times, broke his gaze, and legged it into the shop. *Herm's Antiques.*

Xan took out his Vlex and tried to find the right place to swipe it in front of the door. He waved it around three more times until the cook twisted the knob open. A small bell dinged above the frame.

"Best you don't come down here alone."

Xan crossed his arms and stepped inside.

The shop lay filled with clutter. Heaps of open shelves brimmed with old discarded items. Wires burst from their ledges down onto the rusted floors, while an older shopkeeper stood at the front counter, dissecting an antique with his tools.

The shopkeeper paid no attention to his new customers. He tapped the side of his spectacles, and a pair of thicker lens fell over the ones already in place, magnifying the antique in his workstation. He carefully adjusted a thin pointed tool inside the contraption, and zapped blue sparks as he welded the innards of the device.

Glancing around the shop, Xan noticed another man and woman speaking to one another. He looked back at the shopkeeper who was pursing his lips in concentration while he tinkered with the antique on his desk. After some time, the shopkeeper shot up his head, somehow knowing he was being watched and eyed Xan with his thick glasses.

Xan ducked beneath the lopsided shelf and saw a pile of outdated Vlexes, almost every model since the original.

Drifting further, Xan stood face to face with the old shopkeeper and let out a gasp. The older man greased his hair down with his hand.

"Looking for something?" he said.

"Oh, uh, no."

The shopkeeper raised his eyebrows at him and smirked. He snatched the item from Xan's hand and examined it a few times.

"Conductor, are you?" The older man pulled at a few of the pins sticking out of the orb-like device.

"That's right."

The shopkeeper twisted the orb with a rough snap, and the contraption clicked inside. "We have underground trains that require more than knowledge than a simple push of two separate buttons."

The door rang behind them as the other two customers left the shop. The shopkeeper tossed the object back on the rack.

"You have any real skill? They don't breed you kids for it anymore do they?"

Xan swallowed hard.

The shopkeeper picked up another antique. He twisted it two different directions, and a red glow erupted from it.

"It's a pity. Men and women used to do more."

Xan nodded.

The shopkeeper put the object back and picked up another one. The new device hovered over his hand, bouncing up and down before it landed in his palm.

They were distracted by the sound of clutter falling to the ground behind them. The cook was ambling towards them, his crutch snagged in loose wires.

The shopkeeper turned around to eye the cook. "You two looking for something in particular?" he said.

The cook pat his crutch. "A simple tune-up if you mind."

The shopkeeper held his hand open and beckoned towards himself. "Bring it here."

The cook reached the shopkeeper, grabbed hold of a metal shelf, and let the shopkeeper take the crutch. The shopkeeper turned it in his hands a few times and handed it back. "Twenty-nine credits."

"How long will it take?"

"Thirty minutes. Take a spare from the rack over there and come back."

The shopkeeper strode to the counter, set the crutch on it and readied his tool kit beside.

The cook stretched his arms between the shelves and lumbered off to the rack of spare crutches. He dragged out an old metal one and put it down to the floor.

Xan picked up an old pair of leather goggles from a bin. He turned them over and saw a faded symbol engraved in the leather. It was a circle with wings around it.

The cook nudged him. "You ready?"

He placed the goggles back. "Yeah, let's go."

They waved to the shopkeeper and left the store. The cook walked further into the city and Xan followed.

"Is it possible there's cheese down here?"

"That's a tough one."

"Can we search some out?"

"I've got one more thing to take care of though."

"Oh, okay."

They walked in silence through the dim city. The paths shifted from narrow to large in confusing directions. There was no grid layout, every street jutted out as randomly as the buildings stacked about them.

Going further, Xan caught wind of a noxious smell. He looked inside the buildings to see where it came from.

They continued down a narrow path, in between houses where people sat crammed into giant rooms. Xan noticed they had tiny blankets under them. There were a few older folks inside, staring off to nowhere or mumbling to themselves with their toothless grins.

The paths weaved in awkward directions, turning from dirt to cement and back to dirt again. The horrid smell grew more pungent along specific areas, but Xan could never locate it. They squeezed down a narrow passageway and stopped by a small shop door. *Advanced Gears and Parts.*

"In here," said the cook, stepping in.

Hovercraft parts teemed inside. The layout felt organised compared to anywhere else underground, and the giant hanging tubes were held neatly together by rusty binds.

An older woman with long white hair came from the corner of the room to meet them. She held the hem of her white jacket as she approached.

"Good morning gentlemen," she said. "Anything I can help you with?"

Her eyes scrutinised them, yet at the same time, she was careful not to seem too invasive. She stood tall and thin, appearing healthier than most.

"I'm a returning customer," said the cook. "Wanted to check out the filtration devices you have."

Xan looked at him with shock. "You have a hovercraft? How'd you afford it?"

The woman creased a wry smile and then waved for them to follow. They stopped at a metal rack full of old engines. The lady touched a bolt on the bottom engine and stepped back. The floor moved back on its own, revealing a hidden stairwell.

"Watch your heads," she said.

They tiptoed down into a room full of radiant green tanks. Xan looked inside the transparent tanks full of green liquid. He saw meaty objects floating inside, with tiny bubbles rising from the bottom to keep them afloat.

"Are these hearts?" Xan said.

The cook tapped the glass. "Yes."

Xan spied the other tanks in the room. He noticed kidneys, eyes, lungs, and other vital organs, all floating in green bubbles.

"I hope you haven't experienced any problems with our products?" said the woman. "We maintain the highest quality within our facility. And I can assure you that you won't find any growers around here better than us."

"No, it's something else this time," said the cook.

They stood next to a tank full of bobbing kidneys.

"Where did you get these?" Xan whispered.

The older lady stared at the bubbles. She turned towards him, a green light reflecting off her spectacles. "We grow these ourselves," she said. "Not a single clone was stolen."

Xan turned back to another tank. A floating eye lolled in the bubbles with an aimless gaze.

The lady turned to speak to the cook, the both of them walking down the path, away from him.

Grey hearts had tangled aortas as they floated amongst the others. *That can't be good for them*, he thought. *I doubt they're even licensed. Look at how messy this is. Does he really believe her? There is no way they got the resources to grow their own organs without stealing from someone.*

After some time, the cook returned. "You ready?"

The young man pulled away from the tank. "Yes."

They left the organ farm and weaved back through the slanted city. Xan thought of the room full of bright tanks along the way and not to mention the distracting smell that arose wherever it pleased.

Neither of them spoke on the way back.

Xan looked at all the homes they passed on the way. It surprised him to see one with bright white tiles and new furniture inside. They picked up his repaired crutch and climbed the steps back above ground.

They both leaned against the walls to watch the pedestrians go about their days for some time. Xan kept his Vlex out, staring at the recruiter's contact, occasionally glancing at the barbed wire gate in the distance. His thumb hovered over the button to connect.

The cook eventually propped himself up and said he was tired. Xan nodded and waved him goodbye, but remained where he stood, looking at the contact. Not that he particularly wanted to stay or leave. He felt in the middle of someplace without any door.

A slight breeze dragged by him and for a second he thought he felt a pelt of red sand in it. *Smart people don't go where the money is but where it'll be.*

Where the cheese will be? he thought.

CHAPTER 7

"Isn't anyone else coming?" he asked.

"No," she said. "Were you expecting someone?"

He glanced around the tiny room. "I guess not."

Xan had never been to a one-on-one interview before. He sat across a sleek desk from the recruiter he'd met at the career fair more than a year ago.

She tapped on her desk, moving holograms here and there. "Right," she said. "We should go over your options first before we discuss logistics."

Xan sat up straight. "I heard about a goat farm on Mars," he said. "Maybe they have some positions available?"

She scrunched her nose. "Don't bother with them. They don't need any train conductors mucking about. These are professional scientists, so unless you've attained an advanced degree in animal husbandry or cheese fermentation, please don't embarrass yourself."

He settled back into his seat.

She paused a moment over her Vlex. "Right. Let's see. Now that we've gotten the fluff out of the way. We have an open position in Mons for a maintenance cleaner."

"What's that?"

She raised an eyebrow. "Someone who maintains the city's appearance..."

He shook his head. "I'm sorry, I don't know what that means."

She rolled her eyes. "If you see rubbish on the ground, you pick it up. If you see a dirty window, you clean it."

"You mean android work?"

"We conserve more energy by using human labour on Mars."

"There are no androids there?"

She took in a deep breath to answer him. "Yes, they have androids up there, just not so many."

"Oh," he said. "I can breathe the outside air?"

"Yes, it's terraformed." Growling, she tapped on her desk. "Fine. Let's look at some other positions then."

After a few moments, she said, "We have an opening for a new cook on a freighter. Do I need to explain to you what a cook does?"

"No. Thanks though."

She pursed her lips a moment and composed herself before speaking again. "So? Is that a yes?"

"I won't be living on Mars though? I'll be on a ship the whole time?"

"Technically yes. But you can spend two weeks on Mars and Earth during transits."

"No," he said.

"Okay... Let's see what else we have." She continued tapping on her desk, opening more holograms. "There are openings in our mines. We always need new hands for extraction." She tried to smile after this.

"Isn't it dangerous?"

Her face remained stoic. "There have been casualties, yes, but the mining companies are putting in new systems to better ensure the safety of their workers."

Xan scratched the back of his head. "Are there any androids there?"

She looked over her Vlex at him with a raised eyebrow. "A few?"

"Doesn't feel right."

She went back to her tapping. "We have a factory looking for some processors. Should we look at something else or should we continue wasting our time?"

He held up his hand. "Wait. No. That sounds interesting."

"Good." The lady opened the details on her Vlex then smirked. "They even have a couple of androids there."

What is she implying? he thought.

"The company is looking for applicants to fill positions and, as a bonus, they'll sponsor your transport up to Mars."

Xan tapped his leg. "Free transport?" he said. "Do you know if the factories are close to the cheese farm?"

She lowered her Vlex to the table. "The farm is there for those who can afford it. Not to mention it's heavily guarded. Same as Earth farms. Can we please leave the farm alone for a minute?"

He looked down at the desk, rubbing his finger on it. "Sure."

"Now, back to the factory. Do you want the position or not?"

***

The young man ignited the android who took the hovertrain to the next station. The train stopped, and he switched places with the other conductor in silence. He pushed through the crowd towards the food stalls and rushed to the counter.

"Katsu-don?" asked the cook.

"No. Give me something new today."

The cook laughed. "Thirty minutes downstairs and your tastebuds have changed?"

"I'm leaving," he said.

The cook eyed him for a moment. "Oh."

Xan squinted his eyes.

"Mars?"

"How'd you know?"

"I saw it on your Vlex the other day. I spoke with a recruiter myself years back, but they don't let old men on their ships."

"Sorry."

The cook inhaled and let out a large breath. "When are you leaving?"

"On the next flight. About three weeks away."

The cook rubbed his face. "Let me throw some mush in the cooker real fast." He turned into the stall and grabbed a packet.

Xan leaned against the counter, tapping it with his finger.

The cook returned. "Damn kid. You really did it. You're actually leaving?"

"Yeah."

"Shit. I wish I'd been like that in my youth."

Xan lowered his head.

The cook reached across the counter and pulled him up out of his slouch. "That's good for you," he said. "Don't feel bad. Honest. I've already made my path."

The cooker dinged in the back. The cook turned to prepare the meal.

Xan pulled out his Vlex. He tapped it on the transparent pyramid sitting on the counter. It flashed green after accepting his payment.

The cook returned with the meal. "Did you tell your parents?"

"Not yet."

"Tell them what you know, kid. It's for the best."

"I sure hope so."

The cook slid the meal towards Xan. Xan looked at it. His thoughts were still. His mouth didn't move.

"You don't have much time," said the cook. "Go eat before you're back in the train."

"I feel strange."

The man wiped the already clean counter with his dirty rag. "If your parents aren't happy with your decision, then remember, you won't be seeing much of them anyhow."

Xan picked up the meal and nodded his head. "There's nothing here for me."

He waved the dirty rag towards the benches in the distance. "Quit thinking and go eat."

Xan drifted away and sat on a lonely bench. He watched the crowds running around him. For the second time in his life, he felt detached. In less than a month's time, he'd be on a ship heading to the fourth planet. Within a year, he'd be tossing red sand in the air.

* * *

Xan stepped into his home. He turned on his Vlex but saw no new notifications. "It's only a matter of time now," he whispered. He knew they'd see his activity. They'd see the job shift in their notifications. It was only a matter of time. He went to his room and shut his eyes. Sleep embraced him.

His door trembled with furious pounds. He heard his father screaming on the other side. He rubbed his eyes and stood up, sliding the door open to his angry father outside.

His father jabbed his thumb over his shoulder. "Get out here," he said. "Get your ass out here right now!"

Xan complied. He walked outside past his father. The old man pinched the back of his son's neck forcefully, pushing him into a seat.

"Sit your ass down."

Dropping into the seat across Xan, his father wrinkled his meaty face into a scowl and bared his teeth at his son. "What is this?" he said.

Xan shrugged his shoulders.

"No. Don't give me that bullshit. You tell me right now what this nonsense is. The heck are you doing, taking another job for?"

Xan laughed. "Thought you might be happy."

His father tapped on his Vlex a few times and pushed it towards his son. "So. You went to an interview. Correct?"

"Yes."

"Three days ago?"

"Yes."

His father glanced at the Vlex again. "An interview for a factory?"

Xan looked down at his water. He didn't answer his father.

"Correct?"

After some time he nodded. "Yes."

His father leaned forward on the table. "A factory where?"

The young man shook his head. He refused to make eye contact.

His father's tone rose. "A factory where?"

"Mars."

"Right. On fucking Mars!" His father slammed his fist onto the table. He pulled them up once more and slammed them down again. His face turned blood red.

Xan used to cower at these episodes. He would squirm until it was over. But now he couldn't feel anything. He only felt the warmth of the Martian sun. The fist pounding the table was a threat with an expiration date on it. *No more talks*, he thought. *No more power plays*.

His father drew his fist back and grew nervous at his son's calm composure. He grabbed his son's Vlex and tapped on it. He made a few grunts and mumbled some curses. He examined his son closely. "You think you're some hot shot? You think you're something smart over there?"

Xan shook his head. "No?"

"Don't play games with me boy! You think I'm dumb? I know what you're playing at!"

Xan opened his hands in the air. "What am I playing at?"

"You're trying to hurt your mother. You think you'll get more attention from it. All because you failed to get a proper job."

"What attention do I need? And the last time I checked, being a train conductor is a proper job, with proper pay. So tell me, what the hell isn't proper in your expert opinion? What makes you, working for the sanitation department any different? You still push a red and green button all day too!"

His father threw his Vlex at him. He punched his knuckles into the table, this time causing a dent. "THE SANITATION DEPARTMENT IS MORE PRESTIGIOUS THAN YOUR LITTLE CONDUCTING NONSENSE! WE PROVIDE THE WORLD WITH CLEAN WATER TO DRINK. WHAT DO YOU DO? YOU PUSH A DAMN BUTTON FROM STATION TO STATION!"

The door slid open. His mother came out, red-eyed, and had her arms crossed.

His father turned to her. "Go ahead. Tell him what you think."

She rubbed underneath her eyes. "People are trying to sleep. Can you both keep it down?"

His father bore his yellow teeth at her.

"Grow up," she said.

His mouth fell open.

Her eyes rolled in her worn face. She blinked a few more times and then looked at her son. "Do you really want to go to Mars?" she asked.

"Yes."

"Are your prospects better there?"

"Yes!" he shouted.

She pinched the bridge of her nose. "Well then, good luck. We wish you the best." Then she gave him a gentle nod and went back into her room.

His father sat at the table and glared at his son. Xan didn't flinch. He kept his quiet composure while his heart raced inside his chest.

His father tapped the table a few more times then threw his chair back and to the ground. He stomped back into his bedroom, leaving his son alone.

The room stayed quiet except for the sound of traffic below. Xan stood to get a new glass of water and sat back down at the table. He opened his Vlex to look at all the items they suggested he get.

Suggested Items for Mars:
Industrial Boots
Water Pouches (three or more litres)
Protective Eyewear (sand goggles)
Ullum Brand Long Coat

He placed his Vlex down and sighed.

CHAPTER 8

Xan sat still, waiting to press the button. His eyes stared blankly out the train window.

"Excuse me?"

He turned his head. He saw the next conductor waiting to take her position.

"Right. Sorry," he said, slipping out of the train. He went through the crowd. It didn't bother him the way it used to. He already felt fond of them for some reason, as if they were just a soft memory from his past. He proceeded to the food stalls and stood at the counter.

"This is it?" said the cook.

Xan nodded.

He studied the young man. "You don't look excited."

Xan rubbed his hands together "Yeah. No. Maybe I'm tired."

The cook watched him another minute. "You want something to eat before you go?"

"Sure."

The cook took down a packet and threw it into the cooker. The young man tapped his Vlex on the pyramid. Both devices lit up green. "Where am I going?"

"Mars."

"Why do I need industrial boots?"

The cook was busy preparing the meal. "They don't have streets up there?"

"They do, but not like here."

The cook dug out the reconstructed dish and threw it into a container. "I wouldn't think about it," he said. "No use anyhow. What'll happen will happen."

He handed over the container. Xan held it with both hands. His eyes were caught in a daze.

The cook wiped his forehead with the dirty rag in his hands. "How long's the trip?"

"Three months."

"I thought it was longer?"

Xan shook his head still caught in a daze. "It depends on the alignment between the two planets," he said blankly.

"That's not too bad," said the cook.

"Yeah?"

"Is there anything you feel particularly excited about?"

Xan nodded. "Sandrovers and the cheese farms."

The cook tried to laugh. "At least you have something to look forward to." He walked out and over to Xan then patted him on the back. "You should get out of here. Nothing's changing anytime soon."

"Thanks," said the young man.

"No worries." The cook reached over the counter, pulling a box from underneath. "Take this with you."

"What is it?"

"It's from Herm's."

Xan panicked a little. "It's not a gun, is it?"

The cook grinned. "You're headed to a new land," he said. "There were plenty of stories from the frontier days."

The young man thrust the box back into the cook's hands. "Shit! No. Don't give me this."

The cook pushed it back towards him with a serious face. "Kid... Calm down, it was only a joke."

Xan rubbed his eyes. "Sorry. I'm sorry."

"Don't worry about it," said the cook. "Go on and get out of here. Seriously. Nothing's changing."

Xan nodded. He took the box back and looked at the cook. "Thanks."

He gave the young man a strong pat on the back. "Have fun on Mars kid," he said. "Go enjoy life."

"I'll try."

The cook pushed him towards the exit. "Don't worry about it so much. Your mind can think you into a hole if you allow it."

Xan walked through the crowd. He turned and gave a small wave, then made his way to the exit.

The glowing ads blurred before him. Every single person meshed into foreign objects he'd soon be leaving far behind.

Come to Mars. Every day is an adventure.

"Three months is nothing," he said to himself.

A beautiful city covered the ad. Circular skyscrapers rose tall in the red Martian lands. *Ready to leave Earth behind? Come to Mars, there's plenty of space.*

Xan reached his home. He sat down at the little table and eyed the gift. He pulled the edges up and peered inside. A pair of goggles with a brown leather strap lay at the bottom. It was the same pair he had looked at in the store. He caressed the emblem carved into the side. There was something regal about those goggles.

"Thanks," he whispered to the vacant room.

The door slid open, and his mother walked through with a box in her hands. "Oh. You're here?" she said.

The young man nodded. "Yeah. What are you doing?"

"I took the day off. I needed to take care of some things, but I finished earlier than expected."

"I see." She pulled out a pair of industrial boots from one of her boxes. "I accidentally bought the wrong pair of boots," she said. "Maybe you want them?"

He smiled. "Sure. I could use them."

She put the boots on the floor next to him and then placed the other boxes on the table. "I thought about visiting the electric park today," she said. "You could join me if you'd like?"

Xan placed his sand goggles back in the box. "That'd be great."

They left the flat and went to the station. His mother didn't ask him anything about Mars. He said nothing about it either. They climbed aboard the hovertrain and transferred lines. They got out at their stop and walked the rest of the way to the park.

A giant quad of buildings stood connected with the electric park that occupied the top floors. Xan craned his head up to see it.

"Your sister wants to join us," his mother said.

"What about school?"

"She got out early."

That's convenient, he thought.

They sat down on a bench outside to wait for her. His mother talked about nothing in particular. Food, politics, the usual. Her voice was strained, but she tried to keep it strong.

After some time, they saw Ima approaching. "Have you been here long?"

she said.

"A few minutes," his mother said.

Xan stood up from the bench to greet her. "Since when do they let college bums out of class?"

"It's not that important."

"Come on," their mother said. "Let's go."

They walked into the large building and went into the lift. He stood beside his sister. "How are your classes going?"

She snorted. "Stupid."

"That bad?"

"Yeah."

"You're lucky to be out of it," she said.

"Don't be so sure," he said.

They turned their attention to the lift doors. It stopped at a few floors before reaching the top. They exited the lift and headed to the park. A large transparent pyramid stood on a pedestal before the door. His mother tapped her Vlex on it. A blue light flashed between them both.

The door spoke to them. "Party of three," it said. "Please wait for the next available park."

"It's easy for you to say," Ima said.

"What is?"

She shook her head. "While you're off riding in the sand, I'll be stuck in a giant auditorium full of competitive assholes. Sounds a lot more fun than that."

"Dear," their mother said.

She glanced at their mother. "It's true."

Their mother rested her hand on Ima's back and let out a controlled sigh.

A door down the hallway lit up with a green outline.

"That's ours," said Xan.

The group moved into the dark room. A tiny outline of words rested in the middle of the wall. A menu of options waited for them to pick whatever they wanted.

"Let's try the Andromeda galaxy," his sister said.

"Why don't you let your brother choose first?"

Xan shook his head. "Andromeda sounds fine."

Ima tapped on her Vlex.

"Deep Space File 0032-091," the room said.

The dark room became immersed in speckles of light as stars lit up all around them. The temperature dropped to mimic the coldness of space. Strong scents wafted through the air and a low sound hummed in the background.

Xan pushed his sister towards the wall. "Go see what that star tastes like," he said.

"Gross. No one licks the walls here."

A burning comet flew by with an icy blue gleam. They watched it rip through the dark sky. It flew by a dying star which had descended into its final blinks of light. Each of their eyes focused on it as the violet rings pulsed from its crimson centre.

"Speed up the time," said Xan.

The comets zoomed by while the changing colours bled faster. All eyes were focused on the dying star. Its core rippled brilliant hues as the family stayed silent to its death.

"Do you think this'll happen to our star?" Ima said.

"Someday," Xan said. "Everything dies."

"I know it's going to die," Ima said. "But I mean while we're still alive?"

Xan shrugged. "Who knows?"

A green ripple emanated from the star, and the violet rings mixed with the gaseous colours. Deep space was peaceful even though they had just witnessed one of its celestial beings die. They watched the star's final streaks of colour fade as stillness took its place.

"What's next?" Ima asked.

Xan looked at the options on his Vlex. From ancient Earth landscapes to journeys on Saturn's rings. "We've never tried this one," he said.

"Ancient Earth Farm File 0028-001," the room spoke.

The dark starry sky transformed into a bright green pasture with white clouds hanging in the air. Their eyes widened to the open space. In the distance, a herd of animals galloped as fast as their awkward bodies could towards a red and white house.

His sister laughed. "What are those?"

Xan squinted. "Cows," he said.

"What are they doing?"

Xan shrugged his shoulders. "Why are you asking me?"

"You picked it."

The large animals rushed into the red house and gathered inside the giant room. A few humans sat below the beasts and pulled at the rubbery pink skin on their undersides. Streams of white liquid jetted through the air into deep metal pails.

"What are they doing?" Ima asked.

"They're collecting milk for cheese," he said.

Ima stuck her tongue out. "Blah. That's disgusting. They get cheese from there?"

"Yeah."

"Why do people pay so much for it?" she said. "Have they seen how it's made?"

Their mother laughed. "You've tried it before. When you were young."

Ima shook her head. "No, I haven't."

Her mother smiled. "Yes, you have. Even though you might not remember."

Xan watched the animals. He saw the farmers changing out the pails for new ones. "I can still remember it," he said.

"Where was I?" his sister said.

"You were too young."

"It's still gross."

He laughed but felt a burn in his eyes. He closed them to stop any tears from falling.

His whole family had gathered together, even grandparents were there. His mother was standing off to the side, keeping stoic and calm. His father was talking loudly enough for everyone to hear about how important his job was, but no one listened.

His grandfather stood at the table, carefully opening a brown package. Everyone watched it unfold. Xan stayed in the periphery. His grandfather grabbed a wired knife and gently cut it into pieces. He handed a piece to Xan's mother first. She smiled at her father warmly.

Soon, everyone but Ima had a taste. His grandfather's radiance shone through the cramped room. He laughed like a proud man. It was now Ima's turn. Everyone gathered around Ima to see her reaction to the cheese. Her little body shook with a wince and puckered lips. The room erupted with laughter.

His grandfather turned his head a few times, searching the room. When his eyes landed on young Xan, he smiled. He took another piece of the cheese and approached the child.

Xan opened his eyes. It was all too much for him to take. He clenched his jaw and shook his head. His mother and sister continued talking amongst themselves.

"I thought he was in cargo maintenance?" said Ima.

"Yes, dear, and cheese was said cargo."

Xan turned his attention back to the farm. He watched the humans squeeze jets of milk from the animals. Their time in the park was nearing an end. "Why don't you choose the last?" he said to his mother.

His mother picked one out.

"Ancient Earth Landscapes File 0007-098," the room said.

"What'd you pick?"

"You'll see."

The farm disappeared, and a new scene took its place. They stood surrounded by a red, yellow, and orange landscape. The altitude was high enough for them to watch the colours sway in the gentle winds that pulled along top the ocean of leaves. Each tree splashed its paint onto the canvas while the sun began its golden descent.

Xan stepped closer to the walls. "Where is this?" he asked.

His mother put her chin up as she gazed at the landscape. "North America," she said.

"What's the title?"

His mother glanced at her Vlex. "Autumn in the Blue Ridge." She almost smiled at the scene.

"It's nice," said Ima.

The sun sank lower behind the waving trees. The day turned to a reddened night until the golden blast exchanged its power for a purple glow. Soon, night took over with speckled stars in a blackened sky.

"That's cool," he said. "You can see the stars."

The bright thumbnail moon kissed its blue light on the foliage below. Then the beautiful scene got interrupted. A set of numbers flashed on the screen abrasively.

10...9...8...7...

"Time's up," he whispered.

His mother stared at the walls, keeping her eyes away from her two children. She said nothing.

3...2...1

The door automatically opened. His mother put her head down for a moment, then sniffed a great breath, and turned towards it.

They slowly left the room.

"That was fun," he said.

"Except for the cheese," his sister added. "I can't believe you guys fed it to me when I was a kid."

Their mother feigned a smile while her mind resided elsewhere.

The Earth grasped them back into its smog. It blurred their eyes with bright advertisements everywhere they walked. The crowded mass of people restrained their pace while towers hovered over them like giants in the land.

Xan felt a bitter peace come over him. It was hard to look at his family right then. He didn't expect to feel this way. Not when he was so excited at the same time.

His sister moved to his side. "Can you see the stars like that on Mars?"

He glanced into the smog-filled air that hung like puffy dresses around the skyscraper's midsections. "I hope so."

She stepped closer to his side. "What about a moon?"

He smiled and then let it go. "I'll let you know when I get there."

They were back in their flat. The young man drifted into his room and gave his small bag a final check. Everything was in order. He went back outside and placed his bag on the little table.

"Well... "

The door opened suddenly, and his father stumbled inside with a package in his hands. Everyone froze to look between him and Xan. His father looked Xan in the eye and then went straight into his bedroom.

Xan glanced at his mother and sister. "I'd better go," he said.

His father returned and sat down at the table with the package in his hands.

"I went to buy a coat today," he said. "And the damn salesman gave me this damn coat I can't even wear!"

It was the exact brand the young man needed on Mars.

His father picked up the coat, letting its tail fall down to the floor. "Some bloody Ullum brand coat." He turned it around, examining it from the back. "God knows what he was thinking. He wasn't thinking, that's what. These stupid salesmen can't get anything right. I asked for a normal coat and what do I get? What an ass."

Xan didn't know what to do. His father lay the coat flat on the table, studying it for some time. Then he threw it at his son.

"You might as well take it," he said. "Better than tossing it out."

Xan hesitated. Everyone watched him. He nervously slipped his hands through the sleeves and fixed it around his shoulders. It fit perfectly.

"Thanks," he said.

His father swished his hand in the air. "Don't thank me. It's that salesman's fault. He's an idiot. I don't know how he got such a position in life anyhow."

Xan stood silently beside the table, leaving one finger around the straps of his bag. No one moved, and no one talked for some time. He didn't know how to break the moment. The imaginary wall of ice that had frozen each of them in place.

What to say. His fingers wrapped tightly around his small bag. "Well…"

His mother nodded, and sister stood next to him.

He picked up his bag with a quick tug. "Okay then." He threw it over his shoulder and waited.

"Best not to be late," his father said.

Xan nodded. "Wouldn't want that."

His father mumbled, "Or they might not let you on."

Xan took a few steps towards the door. He slid it open and waited to take his first step out. He turned back and waved to his family. "See you guys."

He stepped outside and closed the door. A chorus of goodbyes flooded through the door crack as it shut behind him.

The hallways were vacant and silent for once. He touched the walls, wondering if he'd ever see it in person again.

"Bye," he whispered.

CHAPTER 9

Please keep an eye out for any suspicious persons within the spaceport. Do not hesitate to send security a notification. One message could save millions of lives. Thank you.

With more flights leaving each day, we help you fit travels around your busy schedule. Sioux Air. Whether you leave the mesosphere or not, we'll take you there.

The android grabbed the young man's attention. "Thank you for checking in," it said. "Please proceed."

Xan walked through a thin film that scanned him for contraband items. The machine beeped with a green light, which gave him the final clearance to board.

A loud intercom boomed in the spaceport. "We'd like to remind all Martian visitors of the planet's strict anti-drug and anti-gun laws. Passengers found with illegal items will be immediately reported to the authorities. Thank you."

Xan entered the large ship, following the directions from his Vlex. He kept it at eye level to watch it outline the correct doors for him to step through. He weaved along the narrow passages through small metal openings and narrow corridors.

Xan saw a group of people pushing inside one of the crew decks. It had barely enough room to hold everyone. He entered near the back. The room reminded him of his interviews, only the ceilings were closer to his head now.

A lady in an official uniform stood before the group, intent on fixing one of her shoulder pads while the last few passengers squeezed in. She kept straightening her shoulder pads and then her cap every few seconds. A gentle ding sounded through the crew deck, and her focus turned to the room.

"Hello," she said. "I see that everyone is here. Let's begin then."

She slowly eyed each person in the crowd. "While you are aboard this ship," she said, "you will be under my charge. There is a zero-tolerance policy I abide by with every crew I take in. Any form of misconduct will be dealt with appropriately."

She studied the crowd purposefully. Her eyes lingered from person to person. "I hope that is clear because I will only say it once," she said. "GH1 has paid for each of your trips to Mars. You are now formally registered as our employees for the duration of this trip. Uniforms have been prepared in your quarters, and I have already assigned tasks to you."

There were a few murmuring voices in the crowd.

The lady snapped her gaze back to them. "Now isn't a time for opinions." She pursed her lips and scanned the crowd again.

"Your assignments will be sent to you through your Vlexes. You have ten minutes to find your cabins and to unpack before we have our first official meeting."

Xan looked at the others in the room, careful not to let the lady catch him doing so. Everyone stood stiffly. There was a nervous energy running through the air.

The lady cleared her throat. "Get to it," she said.

The room stirred like an angry mob as everyone rushed for the door, putting their Vlexes up to their faces to let it guide them to their cabins.

Xan looked through his Vlex, watching it outline each turn he needed to take. He walked down the narrow metal halls. Each passage looked exactly the same to him — rusted in the corners and covered in peeling green paint.

Xan's Vlex outlined a small door for him, and he paused for a moment. Once he confirmed it was his cabin, Xan pried it open. The door screeched a loud mental twang that reverberated inside the tiny room. His new roommates turned to the door.

"Sorry," he said, but none of them responded.

The room was nothing more than a wall with indented beds stacked five-high. Xan, being the last to arrive, climbed to the top. His bag wouldn't fit, and his body could barely manage to squeeze in. The end of his nose was almost touching the ceiling.

"Good god," he said.

He went back down and opened his tiny locker to place his bag inside. With no time left to spare, his Vlex alerted him to his next task.

All employees are to put on their designated uniforms. No employee is ever to be seen outside their quarters without their uniforms on. If an employee is spotted violating this rule, their managers have the right to punish them in any manner they deem fit.

Xan let out a small laugh after he read it. He saw that none of his other roommates were laughing. They were already slipping into their uniforms without talking or looking at each other.

Xan grabbed the last hanging uniform and did his best to change in the cramped space.

Report to the crew deck at once. Briefing will begin in five minutes. Duties will follow in fifteen.

He tugged on his uniform and made sure everything was in place. The other four roommates had already left for the crew deck. Xan tossed the rest of his clothes into his tiny locker and ran down the halls to make it to the meeting in time. He looked around for his fellow roommates but they weren't to be found.

The same lady stood before them on a tiny platform. She wore black leather boots that clacked slowly from heal to toe. The lady paused for a moment to fix her shoulder pad and then her dark cap on her head.

"Tonight," she said, "will be your first night of duties. Those of you under my command will handle room management."

She paused. "I expect every one of you to follow my instructions without question. I think it's important to remind you all of what it means to be on this ship. Being here grants you nothing. This is not Earth, and this is not Mars. This is a ship floating in the space between the two."

A grin creased along her lips. "I'm one of the best managers on this ship." Her eyes moved slowly. "I achieved managerial bonuses for three years in a row, and I don't intend to let up on that streak. Do you understand?"

No one moved.

"I said, do you understand?"

Everyone nodded quickly.

She smiled. "Good. Because I will do whatever it takes to win. And I'm sure by the end of this trip you will thank me for what I've taught you. Other employees would kill to have me as their boss. Believe me."

Xan wasn't sure about that. The lady reminded him of one of his primary school teachers. Miss Delosia. *God forbid we mixed up our integers or had trouble with our grammar.* Xan had thought it was normal for teachers to smack their students on the head or shove their faces into their books until they screamed sorry loudly enough.

Xan shook his head. *Don't think about that now.*

The lady put her hands behind her back. "Please keep in mind that we aren't obliged to let you off when we land. There is a detainment area on this ship. We are not required by any government to submit a list of our remaining passengers - especially those in confinement."

Her smile faded as her eyes worked around the room. "I will not tolerate any back talking, ineptitude, nor any form of laziness. You are being sponsored by your companies to fly on this ship. You'd better show your upmost appreciation for this gracious offer."

She growled a little. "Now, a few ground rules. You are to clean the cabins without being seen by any of the guests. If the passengers return to their suites before you've finished your duties, you have to complete your current task and contact me immediately.

"Next, you are not to interact with any of the paying guests on the ship. If you see them returning, do not communicate with them unless they talk to you first. Even then, we ask that you do your best to keep out of sight. Most of our guests would prefer to avoid persons such as yourselves.

"Lastly, most of the functions in your Vlexes have now been disabled. You are only allowed to use them to communicate with your superiors. You can also use them as clocks, and nothing else."

She stopped to smash her forefinger onto her Vlex. "That's all. I have sent your first tasks."

Everyone looked down at their Vlexes as the room buzzed with instructions.

Xan rushed out of the opposite door with the rest of the group into a beautiful hallway. He was surprised that such a place existed on the ship. His pace slowed. The hall had carpeting on the floor, and the walls were painted a royal blue. He gazed at his co-workers marching like soldiers heading into battle.

"They're pretty serious up here," he said to another young man. His co-worker ignored him, keeping his head down as he rushed away.

Xan stopped when his Vlex flashed green. He was outside a guest cabin, where a sleek golden light fixture hung at the side of the wall. He flashed his Vlex in front of the door, and it slid open for him. He stepped in. The room was huge and nicely furnished.

His Vlex buzzed. He looked down at it and went to a cabinet, picking out his cleaning supplies. There were several tubes with different descriptions on them.

Carpet Freshener.

Xan looked down at his Vlex for further instructions.

Carpet Freshener: Grasp handle firmly and press the top button twice to activate.

He pressed twice, turning it on.

Next, hold the second button to scan the carpet.

As he did, a red beam expanded into a grid, covering the entire floor. Then a light at the top of the tube blinked.

While holding the second button, press the third button to activate the tracers.

He did as told and watched red spots illuminate within the grid. The tube blinked.

Finally, hold the second and third buttons to activate the freshening cycle and freshen up spotted areas.

Xan held the tube over the spotted areas on the floor and watched them disappear from the carpeting and rug. After some time, he finished cleaning the living area and moved to the rest of the suite. He almost panicked when he saw the bathtub in the bathroom.

"Good lord, how many credits does it take to fill up this thing?"

He didn't waste his time calculating the answer to his question and instead kept on cleaning. He had nearly finished his work when he heard the door slide open.

He stopped what he was doing and tried to slip out of the suite without being seen. A man wearing a crisp suit and white gloves was walking through the room. He scrunched up his nose like he had smelled something noxious. His head was entirely bald and was gleaming under the lights.

Xan tried to avoid eye contact as he approached the door.

"Excuse me?" said the man.

Xan froze at the door.

"I said, excuse me?"

Xan bowed his head. "Yes, sir?"

"What are you doing? Where do you think you're going? Get back here and finish your work."

Xan put his head down even lower. "Yes sir. Sorry."

He went back to the bathroom and sent a message to the manager, alerting her of his situation. Before long, he heard the doorbell ring. The man in the living room answered the door. Xan peeked out to see his manager talking with the bald man.

The man wore a wry grin across his face as he spoke. "No, it's not a problem," said the man. "Explain it to him though. He might need that type of thing."

His manager plastered the smile of a salesman on her face. "I'm sorry again for the inconvenience."

The bald man pursed his lips and moved away from the door. His manager drew in a large breath, gritted her teeth, and approached Xan in the bathroom.

"Sorry, I didn't know what to do."

"You didn't read all or your files, did you?" she asked.

"I thought I did?"

She grabbed his Vlex and pointed to an unopened file. "This one." She jabbed at the file. "This is your specific situation."

He read the file and realised what had happened. "He's the butler?"

She slapped the Vlex into his chest.

"Right," she said. "We're not worried about the butler seeing you."

"I thought he was a VIP."

She laughed, malice dripping as she spoke. "It's your job to read this. Not mine." She tried to keep her tone professional in the butler's presence, but it was steadily rising.

She threw her forefinger up in the air near his face. "That's one," she whispered. "Don't push your limits."

Xan bowed his head in shame. The manager looked around, shaking her head, and muttering to herself.

"Finish your work," she said. "And try to do a better job of it. This place looks terrible."

She left him and apologised to the butler before going. The door closed and Xan went back to his work.

Sink Freshener: Mini Edition. First, hold the second button...

Mumbled words drifted through the suite. "Hate these ships. Hiring classless runts to take care of us. I hope he doesn't have some disease."

Xan listened to the butler droning on in the other room. Soon, he finished his work and went back into the living area. "Sorry sir," he said. "My mistake."

The butler glanced over at Xan with disgust. "See to it that you don't let it happen again," he said.

The butler wasted no time with him and turned away to busy himself elsewhere. Xan drifted back through the beautiful hall and into the crew deck with the rest.

The manager stood at the front of the group, watching everyone arrive, like a butcher watching their prime cuts walking through the abattoir.

"We ran into some problems today," she said. "I'm not happy about that." Her eyes scanned through the workers and paused for a moment on his.

"I sent you the files you needed," she said. "To those of you who read them, thank you.

"Tonight will be the easiest night you'll ever have on board this ship. From now on, your cleaning duties will only get more intensive. Your suites can request cleanings at any time they wish. So don't become accustomed to your sleep patterns.

"Also, tomorrow, each one of you will shoulder additional cleaning duties, on top of the suites you are currently managing." She paused. "Those of you who received the green light are free to go. Everyone else, please stay behind."

The crowd lit in flashing green lights while Xan felt stranded with his blank Vlex. Everyone dispersed except him.

"Come closer," she said.

He inched towards her with his head bowed.

"Closer."

He took a few more steps forward.

"I still can't see you."

Looking up at her, he swallowed and took a larger step. He felt uncomfortable at how close they were.

Her eyes never left his.

"I'm really sorry," he said.

"Oh, I wouldn't want you to feel bad," she said. "It's not like you knew to read every file I sent you. Why would you need to read files marked important on your Vlex?"

Xan's shoulder drooped, and his heart sank.

"Look at me when I'm talking to you."

He turned his head up to look into her eyes. He felt a cold numbness sink over his body.

She stopped to take a breath.

"I'm sorry," he said.

She stared at him with a gaze he didn't quite understand. Something made his pulse rage differently. Her eyes cut through his marrow and wrapped around his veins.

"We often receive workers from the slums," she said. "Heads full of bad wires and undiagnosed illnesses. So, from now on, we can do this one of two ways. I'll let you figure out what they are."

"Yes, ma'am."

"Hurry along now."

He turned away from her and marched out the door. He kept his focus on the floor all the way back to his quarters. The door screeched as he opened it. The room bathed in bright light and howling noise. His roommates shifted in their tiny beds and mumbled at him. Xan crawled up to his sleeping ledge and shut his eyes to rest.

A buzz shook through his bed, beckoning for him. "Mmm?"

He lifted his Vlex: *Room cleaning request.*

"Damn."

His roommates were sound asleep as he approached the screaming door. "Sorry," he whispered, but their grunts were clear about their annoyances.

He slipped through the crew's deck and down the beautiful hall. The butler made no notice of the young man stepping in.

Bathroom Dryer Tube: Grasp the tube firmly and press…

Halfway through cleaning, he heard the door slide open. Xan peered outside and saw that the butler had left. "Thank goodness," he said.

Xan cleaned the rest of the suite in peace. He moved through the room, wondering what it would feel like to live in such luxury. He touched the beautiful rug on the floor and even bent down to smell its fibres. He went into the kitchen and looked at the three rounded cookers on the counter and laughed to himself.

"What do they need three of them for?"

As he finished his chores, he stopped at the fridge, wondering how to clean it. He looked through his Vlex for instructions but found nothing relevant. He opened the fridge a crack and saw a clean storage space. Everything was well organised inside.

At the bottom, he saw a storage box filled with white chunks of food. Xan's eyes widened as he opened the drawer.

"Cheese," he said to himself. "My God."

"It's a self-cleaning fridge," he heard behind him.

He jumped back and slammed the door shut. "I didn't know," he said.

The butler stood in the doorway. "Of course. Typical of your kind."

"I'm sorry."

The butler kept his poise. "It'd be a shame to catch you in there again," he said.

Please don't tell her, he thought. *Give me a chance.*

The butler hesitated before moving to another room.

Xan finished his tasks and quickly left the suite. He ran down the halls and back to his room and woke up his roommates as he opened the door. He climbed up to his bed and shut his eyes for some sleep.

Within a few minutes, his Vlex vibrated again.

CHAPTER 10

Abandoned bags lay unpacked underneath his eyes as he stood in the crew deck for the morning's brief.

"Your ratings are awful," she said. "From now on, I'll be inspecting each one of you as you clean. If your performance continues at such levels, then we'll discover your inner motivation together. The way my prior crew did."

She placed a box on the table and rested her index finger on it. After some time, she opened the box and took out a circular device. She lifted out a large metal brace that looked like it could fit across a person's neck.

She had a small smile across her lips. "Does anyone know what these are?"

No one responded.

"They're banned on Earth," she said.

Xan tried to figure out what it was.

She stroked the ring. "The good old days, I'm sure," she said. "Back when service sectors had more command over its workers."

She brought it close to her chest with a nice squeeze and then returned it to the box. Xan looked around the room for hints of a joke. No one laughed. He rubbed the back of his neck.

The manager drew in a deep breath and let out a loud sigh. "After you've finished cleaning your suites today, you'll be assigned a new task. You are to report to your posts immediately. Don't let me catch you fooling around."

Everyone moved out of the deck and into the hall. Xan followed the crowd, not speaking to anyone on the way.

Ceiling Re-Freshener: Hold the tube and press...

The butler made his passive hum in the stifled air. He moved back and forth with various items in his hands, keeping himself busy. Xan cleaned the master bedroom, keeping his head low. The butler came into the room while he was there and opened one of the cabinet drawers with a gasp.

Xan spied the butler from the corner of his eye. The butler tinkered within the cabinet then kneeled on the floor and opened a large safe at the bottom. He placed a box of jewellery inside and locked it, turning over his shoulder to take a quick look at the young man.

"A bit nosy aren't we?" he said. "That's a very poor quality for a maid."

Xan went back to cleaning. "Sorry, I didn't mean to look."

The butler snorted. "Cliches. You people always speak in them. How many times have I heard this? Almost the same exact phrasing. Yet, after a month or two, I find another similarity. Hands in the fridge or lose gems in their pockets."

Xan swallowed hard.

"To talk with his manager or not? That is the question."

The butler never spoke directly to him but more to himself, looking at the walls or right ahead.

Xan continued his cleaning, and the butler left. As he rounded up his duties, he saw a message from his Vlex: *Guests Returning in Five Minutes. Please finish chores and leave before then.* He took his cleaning supplies and put them back in their containers. There was a loud splashing sound in the living room as he closed the door on his cleaning supplies.

The butler put his hand up to his mouth. "Oh my," he said.

Xan stepped outside and saw the butler standing over a fallen plate, dripping orange goop onto the carpeted floor.

The butler walked away from the scene, shaking his head. "Clumsy, clumsy."

Xan stared in disbelief. "You can't be serious," he said. He ran back to the cabinet and took out his cleaning supplies. He threw the container near the stain and picked up the dish to toss it through the wash. He looked down at the time on his Vlex. There were only a few minutes for him to clean up before they got back.

He rushed to the orange mess and shuffled through the different tubes in his pack. *Bathroom Enhancement Shiner. Secondary Duster. Deep Carpet Cleaner. Wet Vac.* "That's it," he said, grabbing the tube, and vacuuming up the orange slop. Time kept ticking closer to the moment the guests would arrive.

The orange mess didn't want to leave the carpet without a fight.

"Come on," he urged.

"Tick tock," said the butler. "Oh, sir, I understand," he said to the wall. "I don't even like looking at such people. He's been a nuisance from the moment we arrived."

The stain kept an orange residue inside the carpet's fibres. Xan threw the Wet Vac into his container and dug out the Deep Carpet Clearer. "Come on, you piece of shit."

The butler went to the door, bowing as if his master was entering. "Good evening, Sir. Good evening Ma'am."

The carpet's colour slowly returned to their original shade. Xan hugged the cleaning tube. "Thank you, thank you, thank you."

Then with one last freshen the mess vanished. Xan wasted no time in throwing his tubes back into the container and shoving them in the cleaning cabinet. The butler glanced out of the corner of his eye. Xan ran past him and took the dish out of the wash and returned it to its rightful place. The butler followed him with his eyes as Xan walked out the door. He rushed through the hall, keeping his head down. He saw that several guests were returning to their suites, and he slipped back into the crew's deck.

The manager eyed him. "About time," she mumbled. "Now that everyone is here." She lifted her Vlex up and held her thumb over it.

The workers remained motionless. She tapped her thumb on her Vlex and then lowered it to her side. "I'm sending all of you your new assignments now."

Xan looked down at his Vlex. *Flight deck and Captain's quarters.* He glanced at the person next to him: *Mess Hall.*

The crowd moved. He left the room again with the rest. He soon branched away, weaving down new hallways he'd never been before. He followed the directions on his Vlex and arrived at the flight deck.

Unoccupied, flashed his screen. *Cleaning access granted.*

The double doors slid open in unison. The bridge had a dim blue and violet glow inside. Giant windows wrapped around the deck, giving him a panoramic view of the heavens he'd always dreamed of. Xan felt a sacred peace wash over him on his first step inside.

A shiver ran down his back, not of fear but of a reminder that he was still alive. He laughed without meaning to. He slowly walked over towards the few androids that sat near the windows. He presumed they were controlling the ship.

The doors slid open behind him. "What are you doing?" the manager said. "Why aren't you working?"

Xan turned to her. "I can't find the cleaning tubes."

She went to the corner of the room and opened a hidden cabinet. "And you thought the androids might have them?"

He picked the supplies out of the cabinet.

"I have given you a very delicate assignment," she said.

He placed the cleaning tubes on the ground.

His manager stood with her arms behind her back. "Touch none of the controls," she said. "Don't clean the androids, don't even look at them. Don't bump into any of the pedestals and don't ever, ever sit in the captain's chair."

She waited for a response; her eyebrows raised high.

"Yes ma'am," he said.

"Come with me. I'll show you the rest of your tasks."

She opened the doors and walked down the hall. He followed beside her, watching her every step along the way.

"You are to clean the Captain's room along with the rest of the quarters on this hall."

She stopped outside the captain's door and tapped on her Vlex, opening the room. "Go on."

He stepped inside. A lush bed lay in the middle of the room, squared by a mahogany frame and velvet drapes. The thing that caught his eye the most was the oval-shaped window where the stars gathered outside.

His manager slowly drew closer to him. Xan felt his heart rush with a hot burn. He didn't know why suddenly she stood so close.

Her eyes peered into his. "This is the captain's room," she said. "You're expected to clean it every day. Don't rummage through any of his drawers or fiddle with anything he might consider private."

Xan swallowed. "Yes, ma'am."

She moved away from him and floated around the room in a strange trance. He never expected to see her this way. She always bossed everyone around, never pausing, never blanking out.

He did not know what to do, so he casually walked towards the window and gazed at the stars. He saw a red one blinking in the distance.

"Looking at the stars?" she whispered in his ear.

He didn't turn. He stood still like a lamb paralysed in the warm breath of a starving wolf.

She moved behind his ear to speak to him. "I know your type," she said. "Worked down in the trudges for a year, then thought you'd take a stab at Mars. Every day is an adventure? No?"

He felt her draw away from his ear.

"Look at me while I'm talking to you!" she snapped.

He twisted to face her.

"The flight deck is a difficult task to manage. Let me say it again, be careful. I want no more mistakes. Especially from you."

His voice shook as it left his throat. "Yes ma'am."

"The other cabins along this hall need cleaning too. Your Vlex has the rest of your instructions from here on."

He nodded.

She didn't smile at him as she turned out the door.

Xan took out the cleaning supplies and went through the captain's room. He would gaze out the oval window at sea of stars at every chance he got.

His Vlex buzzed with a frantic jitter. The suite needed cleaning. *Did they kill someone in there? Jeez.* He quickly put up his supplies and rushed down the halls to the suite.

The butler was inside mumbling to himself. "I really hope they spray them down before they let them on the ship..."

The young man kept to his work. He tried to ignore the butler's words as best as he could.

Xan was glad to finish in the suite and return to the flight deck. When he arrived, however, he saw a message across his Vlex.

Flight Deck Occupied: Do Not Enter.

"Damn," he said, and turned away.

In time, his day drew to an end, and he went back to his tiny bed up in the wall. When he laid down, he could not move his bones as they were so tired. Sleep took him in an instance and left him as quickly as his roommates entered and exited the room throughout the night.

The door was loud, and the lights were bright in the hall. After three hours of attempted sleep, he woke and got out of his bunk.

He went down the ladder and opened the small door near the lockers that opened to a narrow passage leading to the communal showers. When he stepped inside, he saw a lone cleaner working there with his head down and back slumped.

Xan ignored him and went into the stall at the end. He shut the door and twisted the faucets. A blast of cold salt water hit his skin like acid. The surge brightened his eyes, waking him to his daily grind.

Xan slowly backed into the cold water. There was a scratching noise along the stalls which he ignored. The ship made a lot of funny noises anyway. The engines emitted a jarring hum he still had not gotten used to, and not to mention the clanking doors that open and shut on every floor of the ship.

Then he heard a throat clearing behind him. He turned quickly to see a face peeking through a square opening in the stall.

"What the hell are you doing?" Xan shouted. He grabbed his towel and wrapped it around himself. "You sick fuck!"

"I'm sorry," said the man. "I really am."

"What is wrong with you? What kind of pervert are you?"

The man shook his head fast. "I'm not. I swear. Give me a second to explain, I wanted to have a chat."

"Close that up and leave me alone. I'm not like that."

He felt enraged that such people could exist. He turned off his shower and placed his hand on the door.

"Oh no. No no no. It's not like that," said the man. "Not in the slightest. This is the only way I can talk with other people on this ship. It's creepy, but there's no other way without getting into trouble."

Xan dropped his hand from the door and grit his teeth. "There has to be another way," he said. "You can't go invading another person's privacy so flippantly."

"Trust me, I've been on this ship for two years now. This is the only way."

Xan looked at the man's face and let out a heavy sigh. He could see the man was about a decade older than himself.

"Two years?" he said. "Are you a permanent worker or something?"

The man laughed with a bitter air. "No," he said. "I'm paying my dues back to Earth."

"For what?"

"For wanting to return," said the man.

Xan paused. "I thought Earth sponsored the return trips," he said. "That's what they said."

The man nodded. "They do, but you must put in a few years to step foot there again."

Xan tightened his towel at his waist.

"Turn the shower back on," said the man. "So no one can hear us."

Xan switched it on and turned the showerhead away from himself. "What's with all the secrecy up here?" he asked. "Why doesn't anyone talk to each other?"

"Control, I presume. Have you ever heard of the mutinies in the old days?"

"Vaguely."

"That's what I assume, but nothing would surprise me at this point in life."

Xan looked around the stall again. "You're creepy, you know?"

The man laughed. "Give it a year or two, and you'd be doing the same."

Xan bobbed his head a little. "I'm not sure."

An echo sounded through the bathroom. Someone else had entered.

"Good luck,'" said the man. "Catch you around."

The little, hidden slot closed up, and Xan turned off his shower. He quickly left the stall and returned to his bedroom and readied himself for his day.

CHAPTER 11

Xan went about another day's work. The repetitive cycle sank into a familiar groove of hum drum monotony that turned his mind off and kept his body numb. "Ninety-seven more days," he said to himself.

He left the flight deck and went down the hall to clean the cabins. Someone occupied the Captain's room, so he went to the next one. He opened the door and saw his manager standing inside, hands behind her back. His face contorted.

"What are you doing?" she said. "Move."

He rushed into the room and took out the cleaning supplies.

She stalked him from behind. "What type of behaviour is this? I'm evaluating you, you know?"

He took the cleaning tubes and started his work while the manager circled him, taking notes on her Vlex.

Ninety-seven more days, he thought. *Just ninety-seven more days and you don't have to see her dumb face ever again. What type of behaviour is this? You really have to ask? I'll tell you what kind of behaviour this is. It's of a stupid kid who doesn't know whether he should jump left or right or if he's overlooked small tiny detail that will land him in the ship's prison for the rest of his life.*

She groaned to herself and shook her head. "That's how you clean?"

Looking down at the carpet freshener, checked his grip and held it with both hands. *What more do you want from me?*

She rubbed her forehead with a sigh.

Speeding through the tasks, he continued on with his best effort, ignoring each little comment she made.

"No wonder," she said, as she watched him freshen the ceilings.

He ignored her and continue cleaning. Xan took the bathroom dryer and tried to click it on. Nothing. He tried again. Still nothing.

"Piece of junk," he muttered under his breath. He started hitting it in a bid to get it to start when he realised that his fingers were on the wrong buttons.

His manager rolled her eyes. "I'm sending you another set of instructions on how to use the devices properly," she said. "We have a simpler version for... well, you might be able to understand them better."

He shook his head and bared his teeth. *Come on*, he thought. *Don't give into the bitch. She's trying to egg you on. She wants you to blow up and smash her face in with -*

"Is something wrong?"

"No, ma'am."

He finished up his tasks and stopped to have a final check through. There was nothing else he could think to do. He stood in the middle of the room, looking as if a cloud of dust might crop up from under the door or a giant wad of hair might roll out from under the bed.

She frowned. "Are you done?"

Xan bit his upper lip and then opened his mouth but said nothing.

She sighed. "This is your job. If you think you're done, then fine. Let me tick off a few more things under this evaluation."

She walked through the room, making her disappointment clearly known as she examined the area.

"Well, that's done then. At least you have a chance to pass the final uniform check."

Xan touched his collar reflexively.

She pointed to the middle of the room. "Here."

Dragging his feet, he went to the spot and put his eyes to the floor. She touched the flap on his shoulder and then lightly brushed her hands down his arms. Circling him, she came face to face with him and moved closer to his chest.

Xan's heart started pounding as she touched the collar at his neck. "Nervous?" she whispered.

"No ma'am."

Her face came closer to his, and soon she was slowly rubbing her cheek along his. His chest felt cold as his pulse raced.

"Let's play a little game," she said, unbuttoning his collar. "You look warm."

Her hands glided down his chest to his navel then back to his neck. She unfastened his jacket buttons one by one, touching his bare flesh with her nails.

"What a strong heartbeat," she whispered.

His chest rose and fell even faster.

"There you are."

Her hands lingered over the final button near his waist. She looked him in the eye with a wry grin.

Xan eyed her back. "Do it," he said.

She undid the last button and brought her hands inside his jacket. Her hands slid around his shoulders and pushed the jacket off his arms, dropping it to the floor. She slowly backed away from him as she unfastened her collar.

"Take off the rest," she said.

Xan looked down at his pants. "What if someone comes in?"

"Take off the rest. Stop being coy."

Slipping his pants off, he glanced between her unbuttoned jacket at her black bra. His heart raged out of his chest. His breath couldn't move fast enough. He stood in the middle of the room with one last piece of garment on, waiting for her to come back and touch him again.

"Here," she said. "Now."

He stepped closer to her.

She placed her body upon his, skin to skin. "Have you ever won at anything before?" she said.

"Just once, a silly game."

Her lips slid past his cheek. "The rush," she said, "is beyond this world."

"I bet."

"I expect to win again and again."

Her nails ran down his back, tracing the soft waves. He shook with pleasure at the touch of her hands.

"You want to touch me?" she asked.

"Yes."

She pressed her body further into his. He felt his sweaty chest bumping into hers with each thrash of his heart.

Xan took his hands from his side, shaking involuntarily as he reached towards her waist. He rubbed along her hips, feeling through to the small of her back. He moved his hands closer to her navel. His hands continued travelling up towards her breasts. He reached right under them.

She backed away and refastened her uniform. "Oh," she said. "The crew is coming back. My mistake. Might want to get dressed." She fastened her uniform in a moment and laughed out the door.

Xan stood stark naked in the room, looking at his clothes scattered on the ground. He picked up the pieces and threw them over his legs and arms.

"You idiot," he said, tripping over his pants.

He threw buttons inside their loops as quickly as he could. "Come on," he told himself. "Come on. Don't get caught like this."

As he fixed his last button, the door slid open, and one of the flight crew came in. Pointing out, he watched Xan leave without a word.

Room Cleaning Request, flashed across his Vlex.

"Give me a break," he said. "God damn it." Xan went down the halls and to the empty suite.

He went about cleaning with so much anger that he dropped the cleaning tubes a few times and almost smashed one in half. The butler was not around, leaving him alone with his thoughts. When Xan reached the kitchen, he saw two pieces of cheese up on the counter sitting on a plate. He glanced around to see if the butler was there so he could ask him what to do with them, but no luck.

Xan opened the fridge and saw the giant mounds of cheese inside. White-golden ridges peeked along the fridge box like a mountainscape. His eyes trekked along those tantalising pieces. Saliva formed on the underside of his tongue.

If anyone deserves a piece of this, it's me.

No, don't think like that. That's what she wants. That's what the butler wants too. Any excuse to send you to confinement.

He touched the cheese with a slight print but resisted further to keep himself in check. He then placed his finger into his mouth. Nothing more than a fleeting scent on his tongue. He wasn't sure he even felt it.

Remember what grandpapa said when handed you a piece. Think about it. Don't get lost in this moment.

Xan stopped. "It's not worth it." He picked up the plate with his unsteady hands and placed the leftover pieces inside the box, and gently closed the fridge.

Xan looked up as if he might see his grandfather's spirit. "I promise," he said.

CHAPTER 12

The days bled like coagulated lumps. The nights screeched from the metal door. Evaluations approached them once more.

Xan went to start his day in the cold showers. He heard someone entering the bathroom. He kept the shower on with his towel at his waist. The little panel slid back, revealing the cleaner he'd met before.

"Morning," he said.

The cleaner nodded. "Still creeped out?"

Xan looked around the stall. "It's a prison in here." His face flushed red with anger.

The man nodded with a helpless gaze. "Could be worse."

Xan shook his head.

"It's not permanent," said the cleaner. "It'll be over before you know it."

"I've been keeping a countdown."

"What day are you on?"

"Eighty-six," he said. "And you?"

"I stopped counting long ago."

The shower drizzled water on the side of the wall, masking their conversation. Xan strangled an imaginary neck in his hands.

"Do you know anything about the managers around here?"

The man watched his fists. "I've heard stories," he said. "You never know anyone on a personal level though. Why?"

Releasing his fists, he grunted to himself. "Never mind."

"Who do you have?"

"Who knows her name? I'm only allowed to address her by ma'am."

The man touched his chin with one forefinger. "Anything particular about her? There's a lot of managers like that here."

"I don't know. She's very..." He held his mouth open. "Aggressive?"

"Electric collars?"

"Yes! She loves those things! You should've seen her when she introduced them. Like she's holding a small child."

The cleaner looked nonplussed. "That's what they all do here pal," he said. "It's the way things are run... Can you give me a specific example?"

He reluctantly told his story with as little detail as he could. It left him feeling even worse than before.

"Whoever she is, she's delicate in the head. Do what you're told. Believe me. Some people have it much worse."

Xan punched the side of the wall.

"I know how it feels."

Xan punched the wall a second time. "You know her? What have you heard about her? I need to know."

The cleaner sucked at his teeth. "Honestly, there's not much to say. Stories are stories, and some can be fake. But if she's the one I'm thinking of, then please, don't test her."

"That's mental. Can she really do this? I mean, even if I've done nothing wrong?"

"Nobody knows for certain who's on board this ship," said the cleaner. "Have you ever spoken with your roommates?"

"No."

"A year ago, I stumbled into a suite and tripped over my manger's body and three guests within. They were all stabbed violently to death with a makeshift knife."

"Maybe they pushed them to it."

"Maybe, but who can say? You remind me of another cleaner I knew. He took a great deal of grief aboard until it got to his head and he attacked a butler with a cleaning tube."

"Good for him," said Xan.

"Yeah and good on him when they rushed in and shot him point blank, no questions asked?"

Xan kept quiet.

"Everyone has their own story in life and a reason for their behaviour. Even if it doesn't seem that way."

"So there's nothing I can do?"

"Wait it out," said the cleaner. "I'm not saying any of it's right."

A door opened inside the room and the little panel slid shut. Xan turned off his shower.

* * *

The day rolled by like any other.

He enjoyed his time in the flight deck watching the endless stars in the sky. The placid robots sang their songs in soft whirs. The air tasted fresher; it wasn't as stale anymore.

The doors slid open, and a large captain stepped into the room. He walked right past Xan without a second glance and plopped himself down in his seat. The rest of the crew piled into the room. One of the last members said, "Out," pointing towards the door.

Xan complied and scurried away. He went to tend to the other rooms on his daily track. He followed their order. Then when he was called, he went back to the suite and began his standard cleaning pattern.

As he was freshening the ceiling, the butler entered without looking at Xan.

"There is a stain in the master bedroom," he said. "On the rug. Clean it."

"Can I get to it after this?"

The butler's face dropped. "What filth," he said. "When a superior asks you to do something, you are to comply, without question."

The butler shook his head and fixed his jacket. "What sort of trash do they allow on this ship? No manners. No class."

The butler turned away. He started talking to his masters as if they were there. "Yes sir, I remember the cleaner watching me when I stored your wife's jewellery in the safe. He must've been the one who took them. How much did they cost sir?"

The butler straightened his jacket and pulled at the base of his gloves. "Yes sir, he was always looking in your fridge. What? He took some of your cheese too? I'm appalled. Maybe he's from the underground."

Xan put the cleaning tube away. "I'm sorry," he said. "I meant no disrespect. I'm so sorry sir."

The butler refused to look at him.

Xan dropped his head and rushed to the master bedroom. He attacked the stain with a ferocious will. He kept his head down in his work and pleaded with every breath. "God let me off this ship."

The butler left the suite without a word.

"Please don't tell her," he said.

He finished his chores and headed off to the dreaded nightly crew session. He slipped inside the crowd and waited for the manager to come out and yell. She stomped into the room and started a rant that lasted for the next twenty minutes.

"That's all," she said. "If you get the green light, you can leave. The rest of you know what to do."

The crowd blinked in green light. Xan looked down in horror. His Vlex hadn't changed. The room emptied. He was the only one left. He waited before approaching her, dragging his feet all the way up there.

"What the hell took you so long in the flight deck today?" she said. "I heard that one of the crew members had to tell you to leave?"

"I wanted to do a perfect job," he said.

"IF YOU WANTED TO BE PERFECT THEN YOU WOULD'VE FINISHED ON TIME. DON'T GET IN THE CREW'S WAY. DO YOU UNDERSTAND?"

"Yes ma'am."

"WHAT IS WRONG WITH YOU?"

"I don't know," he said.

She slapped him across the face. "YOU DON'T. YOU'RE MAKING MY JOB A LIVING HELL. GET YOUR SHIT TOGETHER."

He put his head down. "Yes ma'am. It won't happen again."

He watched her tap her foot for what seemed like hours. Fast and slow then faster again. She let him sit in his shame, and let the guilt seep in. Her foot stopped tapping on the floor.

"Look at me," she said.

He looked into her eyes as she touched his collar.

"One last thing." She continued to fix his collar. "Keep your uniform tidy." She brushed the shoulders of his jacket. "I won't have any sloppy crew members working for me," she said, holding onto his arm.

"Yes ma'am," he said.

She looked him in the eye then pulled her hand away. She brushed a soft wave. "Scram."

Xan bowed and left the room.

CHAPTER 13

Her body rocked on top of his in a blaze of passion. They inhaled and exhaled the sweat-filled air, lost for a moment in time. Xan held onto her hips as she moved up and down at her own pace. Then a surge pushed his system over the edge, releasing all tension from his body, where nothing mattered and life no longer existed.

He growled a deep breath then looked up into her eyes. She stared down at him with a vicious grin that didn't quite match his. He felt insecure and embarrassed that he'd let himself lose control on the ship again.

She hopped to the floor, buttoned up her clothes, and put on her cap. She laughed at him lying on the bed.

"Stop lazing about," she said. "Get up and clean the place. For gripe's sakes."

Xan rolled off the bed, feeling ashamed as he put his uniform back on. *It's not worth it,* he thought. *Not with her.*

He glanced at her for a moment and then went back to buttoning his uniform. *You're an idiot. What did you think they meant by a free trip to Mars? What a happy company they are. Recruiting dumb kids like myself to go slave away on the red planet. Idiot. Reject her next time. Tell her to piss off. Then go and report her.*

He laughed to himself. *That's right, and get yourself a nice electric collar. Go on and tell. See how quick they throw you in that prison.*

She fixed her cuffs, looked at him, and then said nothing when she left the room.

That's your exit, isn't it? Always the same. Hop up on me and rock around for a bit then dart off as quickly as you can.

Xan took out the cleaning tubes, not fully aware of his actions. His thoughts, those that still lived, were small ones that made him forget why he even came aboard the ship in the first place. Mars? What was that to him anymore?

Deep Laundry Cleaner: Grab the tube firmly and press...

He cleaned the bed they had used. His eyes were blank, and he felt numb. Over time, he'd become a shell. A hollowed-out shell with one tiny light flickering inside. The only way to see that faint light was for the darkness to surround him. Inside him, a tiny eye watched through this hollowed case. Nothing excited that eye anymore. The only moment he felt moved was when he was in the flight deck. Comforted by stars, he could never touch.

Xan went around the bed, double freshening it with two different cleaners. The rooms felt recycled no matter how much he cleaned them. Nothing ever tasted new on the ship; everything felt vacuum-packed with everyone else's recycled filth.

He looked at the sad room, thinking of the flight crew member that lived in it. He thought himself sick wondering how many privileges this person had compared to him. His gut burned.

The door slid open, and the owner of the cabin walked in, pointing him out the door. Xan put away his cleaning supplies and shuffled towards the door, watching the crew member sniff the room. "Smells better than usual," he heard the crew member say.

Xan often thought of those androids inside the flight deck. He wondered what drew the lines between him and them. They had a faint blink inside them, the same as him. They twitched too, even if it was considered insignificant.

He headed back to his tiny room and lay upon his bed. Something hooked inside his shell, holding that hermit's tail. The tiny light inside him couldn't get the attention from above – it was too painful a truth to recognise. Xan cried, and he didn't understand why.

Giant beads washed down his cheeks as they normally did this time of night. A thought that couldn't be spoken, right underneath his breath. The one thing he couldn't bring to himself to think.

He hopped out of his bed, checking in the showers for his only friend who hadn't shown his faces in ages. Their last talk was so long ago he couldn't even recall what they'd said.

Something about a crazy woman, someone who'd lost their head? No, it was cogs missing from someone's head? He couldn't remember anymore, all he knew was he could use a friend right now.

Room Cleaning Request. Room Cleaning Request.

Xan had no power to care. This was his life now. This might be his life forever.

He walked like a worn out phantom drifting through the same ghosted halls, night after night, never breaking its pattern. He entered the suite – there was no butler in sight – and went about cleaning, freshening, and spot checking everything.

When Xan went into the kitchen, he cleaned the counter where he bumped against an old plate sitting on it. Xan put his cleaner down and slowly lifted the crumb-filled plate. He paused over those crumbs, feeling unsure. He couldn't put the plate down; he could only stare at the crumbs like he did not have a choice.

"Cheese," he whispered.

Should I throw them out or place them back? If I have to throw them out, I might as well have a taste. Surely they wouldn't notice that I took one little taste. One little crumb might be, all right?

The flame inside his shell glowed. The old pile of grey ashes stirred bright red coals that'd been left forgotten. He wanted to remember what cheese tasted like. He wanted to know what delicacy lay in sight. A simple taste couldn't be so bad. One small bite for him.

He held the plate closer. Salivation. Those little pieces of white captivated his eyes. They were crumbs he could pinch – no one would know, if only he pinched. His heart pulsed with a joy he'd not felt in a while.

"Take it," he heard. "I see the lust in your eyes."

The butler leaned against the doorway with only the whites of his eyes shining. "Are we going to act noble now?" he said in a low voice. "The masters plan to throw it out. Why let such a delicate treat go to waste?"

Xan looked down at the welcoming plate. *One little crumb won't hurt? One tiny bite won't be noticed. They'll throw it out anyhow. He's giving me the green light. Think of him as the station manager, green light go, red light stop.*

"Cheese is a privilege," said the butler. "A privilege that less-fortunate souls will never have. When would an opportunity like this ever arise again? It's not every day a poor man mingles with such wealth."

The white smile shone underneath gleaming white eyes. Xan looked back between the plate and butler's smile.

Will it happen again? What if it's my last chance? I should take it. It's one tiny crumb. How long have I cleaned this place for? It's the least I deserve.

His thoughts ran wild. The butler kept his hawk eyes on him.

Xan took the plate in his hand. The butler leaned further into the doorframe. Xan slowly put the plate down on the counter and raised his hand over the tiny crumbs.

"You know where the forks are," whispered the butler.

Xan cupped his hand, glanced back at the butler, and then placed every crumb inside his palm.

"That's right," smiled the butler.

Xan held the crumbs inside his palm and used his other hand to open the fridge. With one swift release the crumbs fell back in the chilled box with their brethren.

The butler snorted before vanishing in the dark. Xan felt alive again. He made a choice. His own destiny.

* * *

The night woke him quickly as the entire ship rumbled violently. It thrashed about, smacking him like a helpless doll up against the wall, and back into his bed.

"We're going to crash," he said, gripping at his bed with every ounce of strength he had. "All this shit for nothing?"

Then a giant jolt shocked every bone in his body. Everything stopped, with only the remaining echoes of fear rippling down the halls.

Xan slowly moved out of his bed, looking down at his roommates, each one of them poking their heads out of their bunks as well. A guy with a bony face from two bunks down looked Xan right in the eye.

Xan moved back into his bunk and lifted his Vlex up to see.

Mars Arrival.

He put it back down, thinking he must've misread it, then he lifted it again.

Mars Arrival.

His roommates quickly leaped out of their bunks and sped through the door. Xan was left alone up in his bunk with burning eyes and shivering teeth. After some time, he climbed down his ladder and stopped by his locker, remembering that he'd put his bag in there.

He opened it and saw a jacket, boots, and leather goggles. His eyes stung through his sights. He held the items in his hand like precious friends. He didn't feel so lonely anymore. He touched the coat and rubbed the boots, remembering those who cared for him. People who gave him parting gifts.

People who sent him off with a piece of themselves.

He held the goggles in his hand and closed his eyes. *The cook was propped up on his crutch, patting him on the back.*

He touched the boots. *His mother smiled at him with a tear in her eye.*

* * *

He sank into the back of the crew deck, looking at the people he had worked with. Some of them wore metal collars on their necks, and it was possible that some were missing, never to return.

The nightmare seemed to be in its last phase. The people around him kept their wakefulness to a stupor. Hidden behind those watchful eyes crouched lives that were ready to burst. He knew it. He felt it too. But they were all careful. They'd come this far.

The manager paced up at the front with wide eyes and a frantic breath. "This is your last cleaning, and you'd better not mess it up," she said. "We don't have to let you off here. We can keep you, and no one'll think twice about it. Don't push it. Do your job right until your tasks are done! Remember, I'm the one who does the final checks. Remember that."

She looked around with a helpless gasp. Her power waned with every breath. "When I say do your jobs right, I mean it. We still have the collars on some. You know who you are. We all see it. Do you think you'll be in the clear if I get a bad report or spot a sloppy job?"

Nothing moved inside the room, only dormant hopes simmered below.

"Get moving now!"

Xan rushed out to his suite to give it its final clean. He approached the door with glee then stopped in his tracks when he saw: *Occupied. Please enter.*

"Huh?" He stood outside the room, confused. He looked at his Vlex again. He didn't understand the message. It said occupied. How could he go in?

The door slid open. The butler looked at him and turned over his shoulder to speak. "He's out here sir," he said. "As expected."

A voice echoed from inside the room. "Bring him in."

The butler turned back to Xan with a polite wave of his hand. "Please enter," he said.

Xan stepped into the room hesitantly. A man with grey hair was sitting in one of the white armchairs with his wife in the twin chair beside him.

The older lady raised her eyebrows and gave Xan a condescending look. "This is him?" She almost laughed.

Her husband let a grin linger on his face. "Would you look at him?" he said.

They shared a snicker with each other as if Xan was invisible. When they regained their composure, the older man looked at Xan. "You're a cleaner right?"

Xan glanced between the two of them. "Yes," he whispered.

The couple couldn't keep the smiles from their faces. His wife kept her lips pursed with suppressed amusement. The man smiled at her, then he looked back at Xan.

"Let me ask you a question," he said. "What do you think about cheese?"

Xan shrugged his shoulders and felt his palm dampen. "Uh - I don't know?" he said.

The man leaned back and raised one eyebrow. "Do you crave it?" he asked. "Do you desire its taste? Come on now. Even someone from the underground knows of it."

Xan looked back and forth between them, wondering what answer was expected of him. *I'm not from the underground,* he thought. *I've tasted cheese before. My grandfather used to work -*

The grey-haired man raised his eyebrow higher. "Well?"

Xan shook his head. "I guess," he said. "Yes."

They laughed. "Oh, listen to his modesty," she said. "I guess."

The man stopped laughing and rubbed under his eye. "You're being bashful," he said. "We heard about your little ordeal last night."

The man then looked at the butler. "I thought it was a joke when I heard." He raised his eyebrow. "A crumb? A tiny crumb?" He pointed towards the kitchen. "Then I went to the box and saw it for myself. Those sad little pieces lying there beside the bigger blocks of cheese. It was pathetic."

"I didn't eat any of it," said Xan.

The grey-haired man held up his hand. "You're in my room," he said. "Don't interrupt me while I'm talking. Right? Show a little respect."

Xan lowered his head. "Yes sir."

The grey-haired man rubbed his hands together and looked back at his wife. "So," he said, "we decided, if you crave such a small taste, then why don't we watch you eat an entire piece?"

He snapped his fingers at the butler who then picked up a silver tray and opened it to reveal a slice of cheese inside.

"Go ahead," said the man. "Indulge us. We'd love to see your reaction. Go on, take a bite."

Xan looked at the slice of cheese on the silver tray. He saw the eyes in the room watching him. It wasn't what he had wanted. Not like this. Cheese was to be enjoyed with loved ones, with friends, not as a joke.

The man cleared his throat. "You're being rude," he said. "We've offered you something you'll never get a chance at in your lifetime. So drop this act of dignity and take a bite."

Xan took the slice of cheese in his hand and brought it under his lips. The smell trailed through his nose, tickling the fine hairs inside. He opened his mouth and placed the fragrant piece within.

Graceful scents carried throughout his mouth. Small lifts within his head brought him into a clouded den. Soft laps pattered warmth inside, tickling every little bud it could with fragrances unknown.

He closed his eyes.

His grandfather handed him the last small piece of cheese. The young boy glanced up at him.

"Why don't you take it?" he said to his grandfather.

The old man pushed the cheese towards the boy. "Go on," he said. "It's for you."

Xan saw his child-like hands taking hold of the cheese. He looked at his grandfather with earnest eyes.

"I'll buy you cheese when I grow up," he said. "I'll buy you more than you can ever imagine. I promise."

His grandfather let out a pleasant laugh and kneeled down beside him with a smile.

The memory dissolved from his mind. His eyes cleared to the room and his ears perked at the laughter. The fragrance no longer mattered. His memory was left to ferment even longer in his gut.

"Did you see his face?" said the old lady between laughs.

"I know. Like a child on drugs."

She reached out to hold her partner's arm to laugh with him. "This happens when you introduce some classless runt to an elegant taste."

Xan went back into his shell. He crawled through his mind once more. The butler laughed with them. He knew he didn't have to stay. He turned to the door as their laughter built up.

"Awww, we hurt the little guy's feelings."

He could hear their banter ringing down the furthest hall. It didn't leave at once but continued throughout.

"Let it go," he said. "You're here now. Let it go. You've made it." But that thought didn't take the pain away – it only numbed it. A steaming volcano built up deep within, bubbling acrid clouds with static charges.

Xan went back to his room and gathered his things. *Final Check Out Required,* his Vlex said. He went to the bathroom to look for his friend, but he wasn't there. So he ripped off an extra button from the underside of his uniform and left it in the shower stall as a farewell to him.

"Good luck," he said to the empty stalls. "Don't let them beat you down. You'll make it too one day."

He clenched his fists around his bag and touched the sliding square inside the stall and turned away from it. He left the bathroom and made one last trip down the hall. He arrived at the crew's deck, where he saw a line of people waiting to be cleared for disembarkation. He waited until it was his turn to talk with the manager.

She watched him approach. Her eyes looked defeated. She couldn't keep him. There was nothing else she could do, except to wait for the next batch of victims. She took his Vlex and placed it on top of the large one she held. The two devices illuminated in a blue-green glow, and then went blank again. She kept her head down, and her tone was lower than a mumble. "Everything's checked out," she said.

Xan kept his head low, waiting for his release.

She looked him in the eye. "I'm the best manager here," she said in a soft voice. "People are grateful to have me. They've told me before. I'm the best."

He lowered his gaze.

She bit her lower lip, looked around him at the rest of the line, and then held out his Vlex to return it to him.

"You can go," she said. "But you won't ever find a manger as kind as I am."

He looked at her, then snatched his Vlex. He wasn't sure what he felt at that moment, but he knew he was ready to leave. Xan smiled to himself and then turned out of the room.

Her eyes followed him, hoping for something to give her power again.

ChAPTER 14

An older lady examined him, then checked at her desk, then studied him once more. With a sudden jab of a button, the small glass barrier slid back, and the Martian spaceport lay open to him.

"Welcome to Mars," said the immigration officer.

His eyes widened as he stepped through to the other side. His hands trembled and his arms felt weak. Then he caught a glimpse of red sand at the end of the narrow tunnel.

He walked towards it, and before he knew it, his legs broke into a run. Dropping his bag, he lost sight of everything as he raced to the gigantic window. It was better than he had expected. In the distance, he saw circular buildings towering over the red lands and a ridge of high mountains trailing up and down behind it.

His palms were glued to the window and his nose pressed upon the glass. A few sandrovers bustled through the dust, and a line of workers walked towards the city limits. He could not move from his place. He stretched his time until he knew he had to go. He returned to his senses and looked around as he picked up his bag. A few other cleaners were beside him, their faces smashed to the windows as well.

He saw the exit and noticed that everyone else had changed out of their uniforms into Martian clothes. He found a bathroom and changed into his new attire. As he looked into the mirror, he thought he looked like a legitimate Martian resident.

"One sandrover please," he said to the mirror. "Oh, yes, I do enjoy Martian cheese from time to time." The mirror listened to him with patience as he flattered himself.

Xan went back out to the exit. He took his first step onto the Martian sands. The warm ground crunched beneath his feet. He took a breathful of manufactured air. The open skies sure tasted better than any vacuum-packed ship.

He lowered his sights and watched the sandrovers trickling by. They were coming from a garage in the Martian spaceport. Xan went over to get a ride. He walked to the glass doors that lay between him and the sandrover garage. He tapped his Vlex on the transparent pyramid outside, and it flashed red.

Access Denied: Insufficient Credits.

"Hmm," he said. "I guess I'll need to wait until I've been working a couple of weeks or so."

He followed the trail of humans marching towards the city. The winds pelted fine sandy grains at his skin. He quickly put on his goggles to protect his eyes.

"How far away is this place?" he wondered, looking ahead at the city.

His feet felt like they sank deeper into the sands with every step. After much of his energy had been expended, he finally reached the outskirts of the city and gave thanks to the paved roads.

Veils of sand danced over the streets while the winds cooed between the buildings. Xan took another lungful of fresh air and continued on searching for his place of work.

It was tough to tell who might be from his ship as everyone was dressed similarly: long coat, boots, and a pair of sand goggles on their face. He did notice one small difference: long-time residents of Mars had more of a reddish complexion.

Sandrovers zipped through the streets at their own pace while pedestrians walked in the breeze. Xan consulted his Vlex, trying to look for the factory. His piece of glass didn't work the way it did on Earth. The best it could do was to show him an archaic map. No movement, no pinpoint turns, no outlined doorways. Just a red trail showing him where the spaceport was and the factory at the end.

He did his best to follow the map but ended up taking several wrong turns. He had no clue how to use this thing. As he stumbled through the city, he noticed others doing the same. They were looking down at their Vlexes in confusion too.

Each of them followed the others in front, as those in front of them followed those in front of them, with the person in the lead having no clue where the red line ended. A lost and confused group piled at the opposite edge of the city and consulted their maps again and again.

A trickling line of people emerged from the large domed buildings in the distance.

"That must be the factories," said Xan. "Ahh, that's what that is." He touched the oval-shaped markers on his map.

The rest of the group had already made this conclusion and were on their way to the factory. Xan followed behind them.

The factories were large with rounded structures to withstand the fierce Martian storms. The first building looked like where he was supposed to go. A small plaque carved at the side affirmed this: *GH1 Factory Inc. Mars' First Established Manufacturing Centre.*

The factory had a large round entrance that opened to a long hallway. Xan walked in, marvelling at the tall ceilings and the artificial light at the end. When he walked into the main lobby, he saw a giant statue sitting in a chair, pointing his finger into the distance. The man in the chair had a stern expression and was wearing a well-decorated military uniform.

Xan watched the Martian residents buzzing through the circular lobby, heading in and out of the various hallways. He felt lost. The giant lobby held no answers within, with the giant statue pointing back out of the door.

He watched another worker going behind the statue for a moment then continuing on their way. He moseyed over there and saw a pedestal with a glass pyramid sitting on it. Xan tapped his Vlex against the pyramid and received a set of directions. It had the same archaic layout.

From the entrance hallway, find the seventh entrance from the left, then take...

He proceeded into the building, soaking in the sounds of giant welding machines welding and the random shouts back and forth. Xan slinked by a line of workers who were pressing buttons, moving the cargo from step to step.

He slipped into a small room and was approached by a tall, androgynous employee with dark locks of hair tied up.

"Just arrived?" she said in a low but clearly feminine voice.

Xan nodded. "Yes."

"Lucky you made it off the ship," she said. "Let me see your Vlex."

She held out her muscular hand. He handed over his Vlex, and she tapped it on the pyramid behind her. Then she brought out a larger Vlex and placed them together.

"I'm your manager during your time here," she said. "Your work schedule is already on your device. This will be your home station, and I expect you to report here every day."

She pointed behind him and started walking. "Have you done any factory work before?"

"No," he replied.

She nodded, keeping her expression neutral. "That's fine. You'll get the hang of it."

She walked him over to one of the yellow squares near the factory line and pulled up a rectangular box from the ground. She tilted the box so that Xan could see better. There were two buttons on it, a red and a green one.

"You'll push the red button when the container has been loaded onto your station." She pointed down the ledge to a container slipping onto the track below him, heading towards his station. They waited a while for it to reach the station.

"Wait until you see the red light down there, then press." She pressed the red button, firing up the surrounding machines. Bright sparks lit up around the container as the machines welded it shut, and then the light below turned green.

"If you ever see a flashing yellow light, it means something's jammed, so don't press the red button. Otherwise, you could screw up the machine. Now, once you see the green light down there, press the green button to send it off to the ship. Questions?"

Xan scratched the back of his head. "No... I think I understand."

She put the rectangular box back to the ground. "Good. If you have any questions come and find me." She pointed to a small door behind them. "That's my office. I'll be inside most of the time."

"Okay, thanks," he said.

"We'll see you tomorrow."

CHAPTER 15

He pressed a button beside the oval-shaped door, praying that he had finally found his new home. Xan felt exhausted from the immense amount of walking he had done earlier in the day. He thought it was bad enough going to the factory, but then searching for his home up a hill took more breath out of him than he had expected. Every dome he passed on the sand looked the same as the previous one, each one scattered amongst the rest. He hoped this was the right one.

A large man with a giant beard came out of the dome. "Where's your Vlex?" he said.

Xan held it up.

The man tapped their Vlexes together and saw a green light. "Come in," he said.

Xan took one look behind him––down the hill at the city turning grey in the fading light––and went through the little door into a rounded room. He saw a cozy living area with two bedrooms in the back.

The bearded man walked around him and pointed towards one of the room. "You're in there," he said. "Some of your friends have already arrived."

I don't have any friends, thought Xan. "Thanks."

Xan stood in the main room, waiting to see if the other man would say more but he simply walked away into the other room.

Xan went into his room to unpack. He saw four beds bunked inside the room, with three occupants already there. He placed his bag on the vacant one and threw his body down. He didn't talk with any of his roommates as sleep took him in an instant.

The night went by without any metal doors yelling at him or lights shining into his bunk. He woke up feeling mentally relieved, but his body was sore from all the walking. His life on board the narrow ship had not prepared him for the strenuous treks on Mars. He tried to stretch, but his stiff muscles clenched tightly to his bones.

He had slept in his clothes. It seemed all of his roommates had done the same. Each one of them prepared silently for the coming day and went out into the red Martian world. Two of his roommates grouped together as they went down the hill, off towards the city, leaving Xan and another behind.

The roommate walked faster to catch up with Xan. "From the ship?" he said.

Xan nodded. "That's right." Then he stopped to take a better look at him. The other young man had blond hair that matted to his head and a bony face. "We were roommates, no?"

The blond man squinted his eyes and then grinned. "I guess we were."

Xan felt a sense of camaraderie for a second. "What was your job on the ship?"

The blond young man bobbed his head. "Room maintenance," he said. "And you?"

Xan sighed. "Same."

They walked down the red hill towards the giant circular city below. A few other workers were leaving their domes and weaving down the various paths.

His roommate glanced at the others, then up at the sun, and then back to Xan. "What's your name?" he said.

"Xan."

He held out his arm. "I'm Sven."

Xan stopped and grabbed him by the forearm as Sven did the same. They held on for a moment as was custom when making new a friend and then released each other's forearms at the same time.

They continued walking down the hill and reached the city outskirts. A few sandrovers glided between the buildings as they walked towards the factory.

"You think this world is just?" said Sven.

"I'm sorry?"

"What brought you to Mars?" Sven said.

"Space?"

Sven's face turned serious. "They say you can make something of yourself here."

"That's what it seems like."

"Maybe people get what they deserve on the red planet," he said. "Sounds nice when you say it out loud."

They reached the factory and walked past the statue of the man pointing outside. They both looked at it for some time.

"What do you think he's pointing at?" said Xan.

"Where he buried his workers' bodies once they finished his statue."

Xan laughed then slowly felt his laughter fade away. "Who knows?"

Sven pat him on the shoulder. "I'm glad we talked."

"Me too."

"See you around."

"See you."

They both moved away and went to their own workstations, where the green and red buttons were waiting for them.

* * *

His muscles soon grew accustomed to the strains of the Martian climate. Even his skin colour seemed a little redder than before. His communication access to Earth was limited because of his factory's regulations. Full Vlex privileges were reserved only for those who had spent years working for the company.

Xan looked at his Vlex, keeping his eyes on it. He exhaled and shoved it back in his pocket. He went to the entrance of the factory where he heard a group of people gathered in an argument. Xan stepped closer to see what the commotion was about.

"We wouldn't advice anyone to go out," said a manager to the group. "If you want to wait here until the storm passes, that's fine. There's plenty of room in the worker's lounge."

Xan climbed to the front to listen to another group of men. "We can't make it in time," one of them whispered. "Let's not risk it."

One of the other group members looked outside. "Would you look at that? Poor guy's heading straight for the desert."

Xan peered outside and saw a man walking further from the city, fighting the winds.

"Oh shit," he said. "Sven?" Xan stepped outside.

The manger at the entrance turned to him. "The risk is on you if you leave," he said. "We won't be held responsible for any accidents that happen."

Xan chewed his lower lip and stuck his head out further. The winds increased. He lost sight of his friend in the storm.

"Don't do it, kid," said one of the other workers. "People die all the time in those storms."

Xan felt a sense of pressure building within. Then he threw on his leather goggles and took a leap outside and rushed towards Sven. The strong winds pushed him to the side. Xan pulled his coat tightly across his body as he headed towards the last place he saw Sven. The city limits looked further than he thought.

The rushing winds whipped his coat behind him, and little pelts of sand smashed into his skin. Tiny drops of blood formed from the pelts. Xan rubbed his face and kept trudging on.

In the distance, a great cloud loomed. The sky flamed with orange, yellow, and red crests. Xan panicked and caught a glimpse of Sven's figure in the storm, holding his hood over his head, turning in circles in search of the city limits.

Xan cupped his hands around his mouth. "SVEN? SVEN?"

Mustering all his strength, Xan plunged into the sand. He lifted himself up and kicked his feet to get closer to his friend. Stumbling through the powerful winds, he reached out and snatched Sven's wrist.

Sven looked terrified.

"You're going the wrong way!"

Sven trembled. Xan dragged Sven towards the edge of the city. The winds hit them harder, punching into them, one blow after another until they landed on solid ground. They both jumped into the nearest building. They held their chests as they looked back outside, where sand poured like a dense fog before a torchlight.

A few people in the lobby walked past them with strange looks. Xan pat his coat down, showering grains of sand to the floor.

"What the hell are you thinking? People die out there all the time!"

Sven removed his sand goggles and spit in the lobby.

"You were headed straight for the desert! What are you, stupid?"

People stopped to watch them. Xan picked himself up and helped Sven, then pushed him into a nearby stairwell.

"You would've died out there. What are you thinking?"

They walked downstairs and entered a large circular library that was filled with shelves of books in thin metal cases. Sven tossed himself in a chair and buried his face in his hands.

"I can't stand working in that place."

"Don't talk to me right now," snapped Xan. "You almost got us both killed."

"What do you want, a medal of honour?"

Xan turned away from him and went deep into the library. He paused by a glass display that held antique paperbacks inside. Drumming his thumb on the glass, he grit his teeth as he read the titles. *2001 More Jokes for the Office Party. Remedies for the 21st Century Soul. Tomato Soup for the Heart.*

Xan growled and sighed. He stepped away from the glass case and checked his Vlex for the weather forecast.

"It's gonna be a long one," he said, looking at the satellite images.

Xan pushed through the different sections in the library, feeling his emotions settling down. He passed by a section titled *Martial Arts*, and saw Sven perusing the books within. He whipped out of sight, moving down the sections until he came to one that caught his eye: *Local.*

He slid in and scanned through the titles.

Terraforming Mars: The Theory, Realities, and Mishaps; Taming the Martian Soil; The Tak Family Murder Case; Systematic Frequencies and the Martian Harmonic Cipher.

Xan remembered why he avoided libraries.

Varieties of Cheeses Within the Solar System. He picked up the metal book and flipped through the thin film-like pages to read about the different types of cheeses. He noticed that most of them seemed to come from Switzerland. Then he read that all of the mountains and farms on Earth were owned by a single tycoon who has effectively monopolised the cheese industry.

...The last known human to own a cow, Mr. Sioux, failed in his several attempts to save the species by cloning his cow, Vern. After the devastating loss, the price of cheese shot up and the price of goats rose three-fold. Rumour has it that Mr. Sioux has stored away a precious reserve of sheep, cow, buffalo, and yak cheeses in one of his hidden cheese caverns. The price of these cheeses has been estimated to range from...

Xan read about a man who stole goats and made cheese in his government flat. He sold it to different markets around the world, making himself a fortune until the government discovered his operation and contacted Mr. Sioux.

To this day no one knows for sure what happened to him as he disappeared when his government flat was re-possessed and all of his goats taken.

Xan flipped on to the next section: *Cheeses of Mars.* There was only one cheese farm on the planet, located in the northeastern outskirts of Meridien City. It was originally designed by scientists who claimed it was for academic purposes and not for commercial use.

Cheese varieties produced on Mars: Ancient Garrotxa, Brunost, Castelo Branco, Chabis, Aged Cheddar, Crottin de Chavignol, Gevrik, Mato, Racamadour, Tesyn, Tulum, and Valencay. All cheese varieties produced on Mars have been...

The room spoke with a gentle voice. "Outdoor conditions have returned to safe levels. Normal operations may continue. Thank you."

* * *

Xan took his metal-cased book up the stairs and out into the sand-filled lobby. He saw a cleaner coming out with a tube, vacuuming up the grains and cursing under his breath.

"Every damn time. Fucking storms. People can't leave the doors shut..."

Xan slipped outside of the building, taking care to avoid the cleaner, and then looked at the horizon where the sun was setting. He stood outside the library for some time, staring at the sunset. Then he started his trek back home.

Sven appeared beside him and ripped Xan's book out of his hands. "What's this?" he said.

Xan cleared his throat. "A book."

"The storm picked up faster than I expected."

Xan looked ahead of himself.

Sven flipped through some pages. "Cheese?"

"Yes. They have a farm up here."

Sven flipped to the next page. "I've heard of it. One of the miners said something about it a few weeks ago, but I can't remember what."

Xan slowed his pace. "Have you ever seen it?"

Sven scrunched his face. "No. Why the hell would I waste my time with a cheese farm?"

Xan pursed his lips and carried on.

Sven closed the book and thrust it back to Xan. "You could come to one of the meetings I've been telling you about," he said. "The miners might know something about cheese."

Xan eyed the road.

"We're holding another meeting next week," said Sven. "It's a celebration. Phobos will be full then."

Slowing a little more, he walked alongside Sven. "This group of yours, do you think they really know anything about the cheese farm though?"

"You could ask."

Xan stared at the setting sun. "Isn't it dangerous to have so many people gather?"

Sven let out a dry laugh. "They're practically family," he said. "Let me repay you. You saved me from the storm. I'll bring you along to one of my secret gatherings."

"Don't need to repay me," he said. "Just think next time."

"Does that mean you'll join us?"

Xan gazed out to the veiled sunset. "Why are you always bringing this up?"

"It's a good time," he said. "Plus you're the only real friend I have."

Xan sighed. He flipped open his book and read a small paragraph. *Visits to the farm is by invitation only. Those who wish to visit should wait for a notification instead of sending in their enquiries. The farm is heavily guarded, and they mandate that all visitors read their code of conduct before their visit.*

CHAPTER 16

"You can see it from here," said the miners. He held out his blackened finger and pointed into the distance. "The little dome out there, that's it. You wouldn't know it though, unless you were looking for it."

Xan gazed into the distance, spotting the farm. It looked like a factory sitting all on its own. He was glad to see it before the sun had set. "Have you ever been there?" he asked.

The man chuckled. "Not a chance. Those bastards would shoot me dead before I even said hello. They know who's rich and who's not. It's like any other farm on Earth, just stay away from the place."

Xan nodded his head but kept glancing back at the farm.

The man squinted his eyes at Xan. "Why do you ask?"

"I wanted to try some cheese."

"That's rich," he said. "Don't waste your time with those guys over there. They're all assholes. If you really want to try the stuff, talk to some of the guys around here. They manage to get quite a few goodies smuggled out. Especially in the village over there."

"Is there a hidden farm there?" Xan asked.

"You're funny, kid."

"Then it's from the farm?"

The miner picked a black chunk out of his jagged nail. "I'm not saying where they get it. But that is the only farm on Mars."

Xan closed his mouth and glanced at the farm. "I see."

The miner looked at the group slowly growing behind them.

Sven slapped him on the back with a smile on his face. "See?" he said. "I told you they're nice here. You should join us more often now that you know."

Xan nodded. "Yeah everyone's real nice."

"That's a lie," said the miner. "I'm sure there are some assholes among us."
He glared at the group behind them with a faint growl.

"Talking about yourself I assume?" said Sven.

The miner nodded his head with a serious expression. "Probably."

The crowd behind them moved as a large man in the centre waved his hands high in the air. "Everyone. It's time," he called.

Xan went to join the circle with everyone else.

"This is the guy who started these meetings?" whispered Xan.

"He's somewhat of a leader to us. Niall Salukkius, but most people call him NS," Sven replied.

Xan looked at the large man with broad shoulders, and his thick arms raised high in the air.

"I'm glad to see everyone here tonight," said Niall. "It seems as if we've grown again since last week." He grinned. "Soon we'll have to rent our own factory."

Xan glanced at the others in the circle and then back to Niall. The man had a certain presence to him. Maybe it was the fact he could easily go toe-to-toe with anyone in the circle and leave with nothing more than a pair of sore knuckles. Or maybe it was that he seemed kind, not unaware of his strength, but rather sharp enough to be diplomatic when he didn't have to be.

"Tonight, we celebrate the moon's return," said Niall. "For the next three days, we will have Phobos' full energy graced upon us."

Niall paused for a moment, holding his hands over his heart, and looking each person in the eye. "When we allow the celestial vibrations into our cores, we become the channels of energy we were made to be. So tonight, I ask every one of you to reaffirm within yourselves what that purpose is deep within. For some of you, it may be dedicating yourself to the betterment of your friends."

He stopped to wave his hands around the circle of people. "For others, it may be opening your mind to new ideas and experiences. But no matter what it is, it's important that we recognise and acknowledge our purpose within ourselves, as Phobos appears to us in her full lunar glory."

He shot his hands high into the air, clasping them together and bringing them back down over his heart again. His eyes caught Xan's and lingered on them.

"I notice that we have some new guests joining us tonight," he said. "We are always glad to invite our comrades into our family events. If this is new to you, please don't feel flustered by what I say. The key point I want to make is that we should try to be aware of, and feel, a greater power at work.

"This power exists not only in the minutiae of life—what our bosses are like, how we stack up in the hierarchy where we live on the hill, or how long we've done something. But the power I speak of is greater than all of that combined if we can only remove ourselves for a moment to see it clearly."

He looked into the sky again as little blinking stars came to join in the ceremonies. "The stars hold more power than any of us could ever fathom," he said. "Inside each blazing being is an incalculable mass of energy that smoulders every moment of their lives until they explode their radiant bodies into the vast expanse of space.

"How then can we fleshy humans compare to them? We can't. But if we watch them, listen to them, call out for their guidance, and give of our lives to their causes, then can we align our purpose with them. This is how we take control of our destinies. Can you see it now? The great power that's at play around us?"

His eyes scanned the crowd. Nothing moved but the whistling breeze. "How often have you been thrust down into the trenches of life? Are these the same things our brightly burning fathers would have for us? To be held as slaves? To keep us beaten in the fullness of our lives?"

He held his hands out in question for the group and waited for no response. "This is what I ask of every one of you," he said. "Open your eyes to the wonders at hand." He touched his ear, and then lowered his hand to his chest. "Listen not only with your mind but in your heart."

Xan had never heard a person speak with such passion before. For a moment, he felt glad he agreed to come. There was something about the way he talked and the things he said that made him feel there was truth within his words. He had felt held down his entire life. At the station, the ship, and now the factory. He wanted to do more with his life.

The man continued to talk about the stars and coming together as a family, but Xan could only think of the farm. *They shouldn't keep it from the masses*, he thought. *What makes it so damn expensive? How can they tell me I can only visit by invitation? They don't even know how much I want it. It's not fair to run a business like an ancient country club.*

Xan looked over his shoulder back at the faint silhouette of the farm in the night. He now knew where it was. They couldn't keep him from looking. They couldn't keep him from visiting. How much of the Martian terrain did they own before it became farmland?

"Now, lets take the time to hold our visions within our mind's eye," said Niall. "Look to Phobos shining above us in full light. She is here to offer her knowledge. To unlock those doors, we've found. Let us open them now. Let us hold that vision tightly in our minds and see them growing in fertile grounds."

Everyone in the circle closed their eyes and held their hands up in the air. Xan felt strange, but he felt even worse to not do the same. His breath slowed as he thought about cheese. Partaking of it without being a puppet or listening to mocking jibes.

The speaker started humming. Xan opened his eyes to see the group bellowing a strange chant. He wanted to laugh, but he knew it was inappropriate. Instead, he tried to sing with them. The song took off, and the group swayed. Xan moved with them and tried to catch the lyrics but found it difficult.

The group's pace quickened, and Niall's voice heightened. In no time, his notes turned into ghoulish screams. Xan opened his eyes to make sure the man was okay. The others in the group shouted until the entire group gave in to their animal shrieks. All the members shook and screamed, throwing their hands in the air. Niall went into the middle of the circle with his seizure-like grace and yelled so loud that Xan felt his chest rattling.

Xan clenched his teeth and slowly realised that the shouts were made up of actual words.

"TAKE BACK. HOLD THE LAND. GOD IS GOOD. HE IS IN OUR LAND. TAKE US HOME. GIVE US STRENGTH. GIVE US YOUR HAND."

Xan watched the group break down into more convulsions. He wondered if the small villages nearby them heard this madness or if they would think to call emergency services. He looked down at his Vlex and saw the time: *12:34.*

Xan sighed and nervously tapped Sven who was mid-tremor and said, "Sven... Sven... Sven?"

Sven opened his eyes like a man waking from a night's slumber. "Yes?" He grabbed Xan by his upper arms. "You're seeing it, aren't you? The vision?"

Xan faked a smile. "Oh, yes," he said. "But I think I might need to head back. I've a long day tomorrow with an extra shift. It's the only way I can talk with my family."

Sven stopped his dance and loosened his grip. "Okay. Sure." He turned his head to look at the group and then back at Xan, bewildered. "Well, thanks for coming."

Xan left his fake smile upon his face. "Thanks for inviting me."

Sven grabbed his arm before he turned. "Remember we can always be your family," he said. "And you never have to work extra shifts to be with us."

Xan glanced at Sven's hand and then nodded. "Okay. Thanks. I'll see you later."

Sven let go of him and worked back into his dance. Xan slipped away quickly and hurried up the hill. The group seemed innocuous enough, but he knew after a few moments of peace that he didn't want to return. Something strange had happened out there in the sands, something interesting, but nothing he needed to try again.

Xan kicked rocks along the way as he watched the tiny moon hanging in the sky. "Phobos," he said. "Can you help me get some cheese? I'll even have a stroke if that's what you want." He laughed as he kicked the rock further. "Right here and now," he said. "I'll do it. If that's what you need?"

Phobos did not respond. It did as a satellite and hung itself in Mars' gravitational pull.

Xan laughed his way back up to the dome. The lights were left on, but no one was home. He walked into the silent living room and crept into his bed. The moment he lay down, he fell into a hypnotic trance, diving straight into his dreams.

CHAPTER 17

Xan left the factory line and went out to the entrance hallway. He felt a hand patting him on the back and knew who it was before he even turned around.

"You missed out last night," said Sven. "That was only the beginning you saw. Look at me now. Go on, take a good look."

Xan examined him for some time. "What is it?"

"Can't you see?" Sven pounded his chest with one fist. "Look how energetic I am. I'm full of Phobos's energy. No full night's rest could do this to a man!"

Sven then stepped outside, shouting at the top of his lungs and raising his hands in the air.

Xan grabbed hold of Sven. "What are you doing?" said Xan, looking at the people turning their heads.

Sven smirked with a large grin. "Living," he said. "Living life to its fullest. Not allowing anyone to stand in my way. I've found a family, and we're growing every single day! Doesn't that make you feel alive? To know what you're doing will change the way we humans live?"

"Yeah, it's... great."

Sven put his arm around Xan and pushed them both away from the factory out towards the city streets.

"Everyone asked about you after you left," said Sven. "Niall even said you could come talk with him one-on-one if you wanted."

Xan did not respond.

"Did you hear what I said?" Sven pressed.

"Oh."

Sven slowly took his arm off of Xan's shoulder. Xan was gazing in the distance. Sven looked in the same direction, and a great smile spread across his face. "You feel it," he said. "You feel it?"

Xan shook his head, regaining his focus and glancing around them quickly. "You feel a storm?" He panicked a little.

Sven rolled his eyes with a laugh. "No." He threw his arm over Xan again. "You're feeling the energy from last night." He poked Xan's chest with his forefinger. "That's what it is. Do you even know where you're looking at right now?"

Xan shook his head.

Sven pointed into the distance where Xan had been gazing. "The same place we held the meeting last night! You've had a taste of it. You're coming into the realisation. This happened to me too. The same exact thing!"

"I'm not looking there," said Xan. "I was looking at the farm." He nodded his head toward the lone building in the distance. "I've never seen it in the day."

Xan felt some kind of energy drawing him to the farm. It quietly whispered to him.

Sven took his arm down again and tried to break Xan's gaze. "Don't waste your time," he said. "They don't care about you, and you shouldn't care about them. Why would you even go there? Listen, let me ask you something. Would you be accepted into a place like that, the same as you were last night?"

"Maybe not?"

"That's the difference, right? We're family over there but the people in that farm... Think about it."

Xan let out a sigh. "I don't expect you to understand," he said. "But I have to go. There's an energy I felt last night, and that place was all I could think about."

Sven shook his head. "You felt the wrong thing. Phobos wouldn't send you that kind of message. If you read some of the literature we have, you'd see what I mean. It has nothing to do with our plans."

Xan interrupted his speech. "When I was a kid, my grandfather..." He looked at Sven, whose face had gone sour. "That energy, maybe it was - "

Sven pounded his fist into his palm. "Wrong. You don't get it. They have laid these plans down for generations. Since before your grandfather was born."

Xan rubbed his eyebrow. "My grandpa was pretty old."

Sven wasn't listening to him. "They channeled these plans through the same energies you felt last night. I can tell you with a hundred percent certainty that that farm over there wouldn't be a part of the plan. Do you want to talk with Niall about this? He knows more than I do."

Xan lowered his head and looked at the point where the city's paved streets ended and the red sands began. He turned back to look at the factory they'd left, now resting in a heated mirage.

Sven tried to push Xan in the other direction. Xan threw his shoulder out of his grip.

"Your friends are great," he said. "The energy is fine but would you let me do what I'm going to do?"

Sven was shocked. He glared at Xan, his fists clenched. "I'm trying to help you," he said darkly. "Don't be stupid."

Xan looked at the factories again, cut off from the paved city, and then off to the northeastern corner where the farm sat. The energy was different. He felt it. When he looked at the factories, he felt nothing––not anger, not even bitterness, but nothing. Yet when he looked at the farm...

"You need to speak with Niall," said Sven. "I've heard them mention the farm before and maybe that's what you're feeling. But you need guidance right now on how to properly process those feelings and if we - "

Xan took a step off the paved street down into the sands. Sven watched him with horror.

Xan turned to Sven. "I'm going to the farm," he said. "Today."

Sven reached his hand out. "Hold on."

Xan took another step towards the farm.

"Seriously. Come with me. I'll take you to Niall's house right now. You don't have to go there. He'll help you straighten all of this energy out. You're making a mistake!"

Xan stopped and gave Sven a wistful smile. "Sorry," he said. "It's nothing personal."

Sven stood on the pavement while Xan stood fully in the sand. Xan took another step towards the farm. Then another. And another. He refused to turn back for some time as he ploughed through the terrain. The winds moved around him as he turned back over his shoulder.

Sven was still standing there, his fists to his side, staring right at Xan. "IT'S YOUR MISTAKE," he yelled. "YOU'RE MISSING OUT ON SOMETHING GREAT. SOMETHING BIGGER THAN YOURSELF. DON'T YOU WANT TO BE A PART OF THE CHANGE?"

He listened to him with his head down. *He's your friend*, he thought. *Your only friend.*

It's not him though. It has nothing to do with him. I want to visit the farm today. There's no harm in that. Why is he being so obstinate?

Sven waved for him to come back. Xan opened his mouth to say something but felt it pour into nothing.

Sven waved again.

Xan cupped his hands around his mouth. "I'm just going to see. It has nothing to do with the group... Or their plans..."

Sven stood like a statue. The winds pulled at his jacket, and then after a while he gave up and turned away, walking through the city streets up towards the hill.

Xan watched him leave.

* * *

A few sandrovers drove by as he dragged himself towards the farm. He looked over his shoulder to see how far the city lay behind him. Everything always seemed closer than it actually was on Mars.

The winds tugged even more at his jacket. He looked down at his Vlex and saw another sandstorm brewing close to the city. He bit his lower lip, glancing between the farm and city.

The city whistled while a cloud of dust surrounded him. Xan strapped his sand goggles over his face and quickened his pace towards the farm.

The winds picked up its chorus, howling with speed. Xan pulled his jacket closer to his body. He looked at the hazy dome in the distance and pushed himself on.

"You will make it," he told himself. "You can do this."

The winds flexed their strength, pushing him around, testing his strength and balance. His breath increased. His heart rate fluttered. His eyes bounced back and forth for anything that might save him.

He approached the farm as the winds whipped around angrily. A guard came outside the entrance and talked to two other guards who were standing watch. The two guards ducked inside the building while the other stayed out, poking at a control panel.

The guard caught sight of Xan walking towards the farm and stared at him in the rounded archway. Xan saw the guard's hand lingering over his side, right over his gun. He pushed through the winds, holding his jacket closed, trying to reach the dome.

The guard took a step outside, holding his arm over his face to block the sands from hitting him. "Hold it!" he yelled.

Xan held his jacket as the winds raged around him. The guard wagged his finger in the air back and forth. "We can't let you in here!"

Xan reached the entranceway. "I can't go back," he said. "I walked all the way out here. I don't have a sandrover or anything."

The guard bore his teeth at him. "Tough."

Xan raised his voice over the winds. "Let me in! Please? I can't make it anywhere else in time!"

The guard eyed the storm that was building, his body swaying against the powerful gusts. "What the hell are you doing out here anyway? This place is by invitation only."

Xan grabbed the dome, bracing himself against the winds. "It was the only place I could see when the storm came."

The guard looked down the hallway and then back at the young man. He growled a sigh them jabbed his thumb over his shoulder. "Get in!" And then pointed beside himself. "Stand right there and don't you fucking move!"

Xan rushed into the hall and stood exactly where he was told. The guard finished tampering with the control panel on the wall and closed the entrance shut. He looked down at his Vlex and tapped a few things on an interactive map that rose above his display.

"You're lucky this door broke down," he said. "The whole building gets locked up with a simple click." The guard held up his Vlex.

The winds picked up outside. The doors trembled, and the lights flickered overhead.

The guard finished tapping on the map, then turned to Xan and grabbed him by the collar. "Do you know what this place is?"

Xan shook his head. "No, sir."

The guard spoke through his clenched teeth. "It's a farm. Government-owned. They loathe uninvited guests. Do you understand?"

"Yes."

The guard looked around him again and then brought his focus back. "I want you to stick close. Don't you leave my side. Got it?"

Xan nodded. "Okay."

The guard released him. "And don't you talk to anyone."

Xan shook his head fast. "I won't."

The guard looked down the hall again with a deep breath. He refastened the strap over his holster. "Let's go."

Xan walked beside the guard through the hallway. They reached a second door that blew a fast gust of wind over them. He noticed all the sand that got caught in his clothes had fallen to the ground as streams of vacuum along the base of the walls inhaled the grains into their vents.

The guard waved his Vlex, opening the door to a beautiful lobby. The circular lobby had a few people drifting about at a leisurely pace. Their heels clicked softly on the white-tiled floors, echoing up to the top of the round dome and back down to the grounds.

Up on the wall hovered a massive hologram of a man shaking the hands of other individuals. They all stood outside the farm, then in a storage cavern full of cheese.

"Who is that?" said Xan.

The guard glanced to the side. "What are you doing? Shut the fuck up."

Xan closed his mouth and carried on through the lobby. They passed by a circular desk with a few people behind and walked underneath a colourful orb hanging from the ceiling. The orb shifted patterns, colours, and shapes in a brilliant display. Inside shined a bright blue sun that melted into wisps of orange smoke.

"Sioux," the guard whispered. "You know him. Owns all the mountains on Earth. Sioux Air. Sioux Water. He might overtake the government soon. I thought everyone would recognise him."

"That's him?" said Xan. They turned down another hallway, leaving the lobby. "He's one of your investors then?"

The guard laughed as he motioned for the Xan to follow him down the hall. Xan couldn't place the smell drifting in the hall, but he knew its scent was familiar. The guard looked through a little window and then tapped on his Vlex, checking something off a list.

"Sioux owns the place," he said.

"With the government?"

The guard grunted. "You think they could afford something like this?"

Xan paused for a moment.

"He lets them keep up the speculation that they own it," said the guard. "He's letting the government keep face."

Xan continued walking alongside the guard when his attention fixed on something through the window. He glanced inside at a giant storehouse full of browns packages.

The guard gave him a nudge. "I wouldn't do that," he said. "Keep walking."

Xan moved on. *That was cheese in there*, he thought. *They're fermenting it.*

The guard kept Xan close to his side. As they passed by a group of scientists, he grabbed him by the elbow and pushed him into a vacant hall.

"How" you land a job here?"

The guard licked his lips and left his mouth parted. A voice spoke throughout the building before he could respond.

"Wind levels have returned to normal. It is safe to resume outdoor activities. We repeat, wind levels have returned to normal, it is safe to resume outdoor activities. Thank you."

The guard closed his mouth and legged it to a large control panel in the back. The doors in the building opened with a loud whinge while the building quivered.

The guard came back to Xan and grabbed him under the arm. "Time for you to go."

Xan nodded. "Sure."

They walked back to the main entrance and stopped outside behind a few men carrying large boxes. The guard slipped in front of them and opened the door. The sands were calm and the winds low.

The guard thanked the men for coming and then went back to Xan. "All right," he said. "There you are. Find another path next time a storm comes. Yeah?"

Xan nodded. "Sure."

The guard took in a deep breath and let it out, waiting for him to leave. Xan went out of the entrance and to the side of the building. He overheard the conversation between the men carrying boxes as they loaded their sandrovers up. They complained to one another about the journey from the city out to the farm.

Xan felt angry that these men were complaining about something he'd be happy to do. He didn't care if he found himself stuck inside the farm during a storm. He wouldn't care if he had to commute from the city, what difference was it to him?

Then a thought came to Xan, and he ran over towards the complaining men. "Excuse me?" he said.

The men turned back to look at him, their eyebrows raised. "Yes?"

Xan glanced between them for a moment and then cleared his throat. "You feel that it's a burden coming out here?"

They measured him. "What are you, some miner?"

"No. I'm a businessman."

They smirked to one another. "Okay. Well, would you then take your business somewhere else? Check out those manmade caves over there." The man pointed to the mining plant along the ridge.

"What if there was a service that would do this for you? Deliver it right to your door. Would you pay for it?"

Their smiles were small and then their eyebrows arched. "You think we'd pay for that? You realise we're butlers? This is our job."

Xan's mouth stayed open, saying nothing. The men snorted and then turned away, and continued to load their sandrover.

Xan stepped closer. "But wouldn't butlers be willing to pay for such a service?"

One of the butlers turned back and sliced his hand through the air. "No. Plain and simple. No."

The other butler turned from loading the last box. "Let me hear this again. Butlers paying a miner to do their job?"

The first butler sneered at Xan. "Go back to your dome. You've embarrassed yourself enough for one day."

They cranked up the sandrover and kicked dust in Xan's face. Xan squint his eyes shut and spat out the grains of sand.

CHAPTER 18

The sun rose and set. Winds covered the hill in sand, and the factory still needed buttons to be pressed. Xan did his usual work, took the same route, pressed those buttons, and finished his daily shift. He couldn't resist the urge to look at the farm standing alone in its corner along his way back home.

"They want to meet with you again," said Sven. "They liked having you there. Can't you feel it? I know I did the first time I went. Something big is happening in that group. We all know it too. If you come to more sessions, you'll get it soon enough."

Xan nodded as they walked the city's outskirts towards the hill. "Oh, okay."

Sven glanced at him. "They tell me I'm inner circle material," he continued. "They say I really know how to channel the energies. You should come join us again. Imagine me and you being a part of the bigger plan. The big change. We're at the front of it Xan. First Mars and then Earth!"

Xan had listened to these talks for over a month now. Ever since he came back a failure from his farm visit, Sven had pushed the group more and more upon him. He even went to another of the trance-induced gatherings.

Sven held both hands wide open. "If only you could see what's happening right in front of us," he said. "I wish you could hear the full message. The way they talk about it makes it so clear. It's right under your nose, and until you put your faith in the group, you won't be able to spot it."

Sven stopped walking when he noticed that Xan had slowed down behind him. "What are you doing?"

Xan stopped in the northeastern corner again. He stood against the pavement, looking out at the expanse between him and that lone building.

Sven looked in the same direction. "The energy?"

Xan shook his head. "No."

Sven looked to the farm. "What is wrong with you?"

Xan said nothing.

Sven sighed. "They almost let you die outside and then pushed you out as soon as they could. These are the people you want to be with?"

"It's not the people," said Xan. "It has nothing to do with them. It's the product... It's a promise."

Sven eyed him. "I get it now," he mumbled. "Why don't you come talk with some of the members about it tonight? I know there's someone who can get you a chunk if you have to try it."

Xan stared at the farm. He didn't answer for some time. "It's not about eating the cheese," he said. "I can't explain it. There's an energy there. I can't put my finger on it, but I'm drawn to it."

"You're sensing the wrong thing," said Sven. "You're not ready to practice energy like this. Let's talk with Niall tonight. Then it'll all be clear - "

Xan threw his hands up near his head and then stomped his feet on the ground. "Stop! Just stop!" His face reddened. "I don't want to go the damn meeting. I can sense my own goddamn energies all I want! Stop wrapping me up in someone else's plans!"

Sven's lips flickered. Xan felt his stare, but he would not look back.

"It's nothing personal," repeated Sven, "it's not about the people working there, and it's also not about the cheese. Then what is it about?"

Xan shook his head, exasperated and at a loss for words. Sven walked away, saying nothing more.

Xan watched him leave. "Even I don't get it myself," he shouted.

Sven stopped, his back facing Xan. "That's what I'm telling you," he said. "There are people that understand this stuff." He looked over his shoulder. "And you just slapped them in the face."

Xan didn't move.

"It's all about you, Xan. You bounce whenever you want from the meetings. Ditch your friend on the way home only to get snubbed at a stupid farm. I offered you a place to better yourself. To be a part of something other than your own promises."

Xan lowered his eyes. Sven marched on his path towards the red hills.

Xan opened his mouth to say sorry but he could not. He had grown tired of hearing about the group. His gut churned from what he had said. *You can't control me,* he thought.

Xan waited until he lost sight of Sven before he took his first step onto the sand. The winds were nice to him as he made his trek and the skies remained pleasant.

I'm selfish? For following a dream? Every time I ask you to join me, to take a slight interest, you swish it off, and yet I have to slit my wrists for your stupid group of lunatics?

He kicked a patch of sand.

Inner circle? Give me a break.

His face tingled when he reached the farm. He shut his eyes, and for a second he saw a vacant building, wind-torn and derelict from age.

Xan kept from going further. He saw two guards standing watch near the entrance. "Get it together." Xan threw his hands through his hair and straightened his coat as he approached them.

One guard stepped over the threshold of the entranceway. "Do you have an appointment sir?"

"No."

The man left his palm open and pointed towards the opposite direction. "We must ask you to leave then."

Xan looked at the man's palm and then up to his eyes. "I need to talk with someone about my business," he said.

The second guard jumped in. "All business matters are required to go through the head scientist. We do not accept unsolicited business proposals or allow anyone to enter without an appointment."

Xan looked down the hall where he had once walked before. He did not like feeling barred from it. He was in there at one point. He'd stood right where those guards were. "Isn't there someone I can speak to?"

"Sir, please leave."

Xan didn't move. He stood there watching them. The guards turned their sights elsewhere, ignoring him.

Xan stayed outside. He sat on the ground looking at the city before him. The sun kept its heat upon his skin. He caught the speckled glimpses of sandrovers weaving through the glass towers. He looked back at the farm and saw a woman loading her sandrover.

"Are you pissed about coming here too?" he asked himself, dropping a handful of sand.

Xan jumped to his feet. "Excuse me, ma'am?"

Fear ran over her face. "What?"

"May I ask you a question?"

She turned to the guards and then back to him. "I'm running late," she said.

"Do you enjoy coming all the way out here to collect cheese?"

Her eyes narrowed. "It's not my favourite thing to do."

"Well, I operate an independent delivery service in the city for those wishing to cut this hassle out of their daily routines - "

She cut him off. "I'm not paying you," she said. "And my employer wouldn't either."

"Wait, don't you want -"

"No."

She hopped into her sandrover and sped off. Xan heard the guards laughing behind him. He went back to his seat in the sand and refused to listen to their murmurs drifting through the winds.

Every day after work, he went to the farm to promote his services and returned with no takers. The guards enjoyed watching him fail time and time again.

A month went by, and nothing happened.

Xan pressed the button, sealed the containers, and went back to his place in front of the farm. The rejections remained constant as well. Now, the customers even avoided him when they left the building.

More months went by. Sven stopped speaking to him and went to live in another dome with *other* like-minded people. He never told Xan about the move; he just upped and left one day, and Xan only realised what had happened when a new roommate took Sven's place.

He couldn't find Sven after work to talk to him. After a while, Xan wondered if Sven had found a new job. Maybe Sven wanted to work with more like-minded people too.

Whenever Xan got the chance, he would speak with his family. He even built up enough overtime to extend his conversations with his sister. All she had to say was that Mars sound very similar to Earth, which made him angry as he sat in front of the farm that day.

Xan went about his daily grind. "Excuse me?" he'd say. "No. Never. And get out of my face," is what he'd hear.

The guards no longer laughed and had started to take pity on him. "Let it go, kid," said one guard. "Why don't you go back to your job, this is how life is."

Xan turned away from them, sitting in the sand and looking at the city in the distance.

"Easy for you to say," he said. "Look at where you stand every day. Look at what you get to do every single day. Do you know what it's like working at a factory or in a train?"

The guards didn't respond. They went back to where they stood and kept their eyes ahead of them and their faces stern.

A sandrover pulled up beside the building. A beautiful woman, who looked to be only a few years older than himself, stepped out with her butler at her side. Xan pushed himself up and went to approach her.

"Excuse me, ma'am?"

She was tempted to ignore him for a second. "Yes?" she said, glancing out of the corner of her eye.

Xan stepped an inch closer. "Do you find collecting cheese to be a hassle?"

Her soft hazel eyes measured him over. "Not at all." On her shirt, Xan noticed a small broach in the shape of a tropical bird. Her butler stepped up beside her. He had a golden earring in one of his earlobes and a shiny bald head.

Xan swallowed his breath and opened his hands to them. "I would like to extend an offer to you," he said, "as an independent business that delivers cheese to the entire city."

She looked around him for a moment and creased a smirk. "How long have you been doing this for?"

He thought for a moment, not sure how long it'd been. *Ten? No - twelve?*

She pivoted.

"Fifteen months," he said.

She measured him and then turned to her butler, whose expression remained stoic. "And how would you transport the goods from here to your customers?" she asked, glancing back at him.

Xan flattened his palms before himself. "By hand."

The woman and the butler smiled at each other. "You can't be serious. You have a business dedicated to cheese delivery, and you do it by hand? Do you know how far this farm is from the southernmost point of the city?"

He left his mouth open and his eyes soft. She lifted her nose an inch and pushed her dark wavy hair back.

"Now if someone like me were to engage your service, how do you think I'd feel on a hot day like this? How do you think my cheese would arrive? Melted, that's how."

Xan looked off to the mountain ridge and away from her eyes. She turned towards the entrance and walked with her butler at her side. Xan went back to his little seat in the sand, burying his head inside his knees. He could hear footsteps crunching closer to him and then a guard cleared his throat behind him.

Xan turned to the guard. "What?"

The guard scratched the back of his neck awkwardly. "You've done a strong round here," he said. "But it's not going to work."

"Thanks. I see that."

The guard hissed as he continued to scratch his neck. "Time to pack up and go home."

Xan shook his head.

"Come on. You've had your shot," said the guard.

"I'm not leaving."

The guard snorted. "Leave. I'm not mucking about."

Xan refused to look at him.

"I've asked you nicely for the past month. We've received too many complaints." He pointed his thumb over his shoulder towards the farm. "The big guys ordered me to take care of this situation, today."

Xan didn't move. He kept his gaze on the city and his back to the guard.

"Listen, damn it! Get out of here. I've asked you nicely, and I won't do it again!"

Xan didn't answer. He put his face lower into his knees. He could hear the guard unlatching his holster.

"I don't want to shoot a man with his back to me. Would you listen?"

Xan heard the guard stepping closer. "Go ahead," said Xan, lifting his face up. "What does it matter anyway? Throw me in the sand behind the farm, no one will ever know. Just do it. What does one more factory worker matter?"

The guard stomped his foot. "Stop being a damn fool and go home!"

Xan stood to his feet and turned around to face the guard. The man had his gun drawn. "Do it," said Xan. "No one'll notice. I can assure you that."

The guard curled his lips back and let out a pinched noise. "Twit," he said.

Xan let his tears roll down his face and did not bother to wipe them away. "I won't care either," he said.

The guard jabbed the gun at him. "Come on," he said. "Stop this nonsense. Go home."

Xan looked him in the eye. Tears were running down his sand-crusted face. The guard straightened his arm and aimed the gun dead centre at Xan's chest. Xan stepped closer, putting the steel barrel right at his heart.

"What are you doing?" came a woman's voice from behind.

The guard glanced at her. "I'm following orders," he said.

She marched over towards them both. "Oh shut up," she said. "Stop acting so noble. Put it down."

The guard did not move. "I have my orders lady."

She pushed the barrel of the gun away from Xan and pointed to the entranceway. "Go to your post," she said.

"It's not my call," said the guard. "You think I want to do this?"

Her eyes went black with rage. "It's always your call."

The guard looked at Xan then back at the woman. He held the gun to his side. "How else are we to get rid of him?"

The woman glared at the guard. He put his head down and hesitantly returned his gun to its holster.

"Go back to your post," the woman said. "I'll deal with him."

The guard looked around before he slowly walked back to the entranceway. He kept his eyes away from them both. The woman took her time to examine him.

"You don't know shit, lady," said Xan. "What difference does it make if he kills me or not? You've never worked the sands like I have. So don't come here telling me how to live."

The woman remained stern. "Come with me," she said.

"No."

"I said, come with me."

"Fuck you."

"Stop being stubborn," she snapped. "I'm not taking you away from your business. If you want help, then I suggest you take my offer."

Xan looked at her and the butler. There were no grins or smirks. Their eyes were honest. "You're lying," he said.

"I'm serious," she said. "Come with me, and we'll talk it over."

Xan looked back at the butler and then at her again. "No more jokes or pranks," he said. "I'm not in the mood."

"No one's laughing."

Xan watched them cautiously. The woman stood firm as she extended her hand towards him.

He looked at it. "I'm serious," he said. "I'm not some jester to laugh at."

She drew in a deep breath and stayed still, only moving her hand to reaffirm her offer. He glanced at the butler standing behind her. His wore a dignified expression, and his eyes seemed trustworthy.

"All right," Xan whispered. "Fine."

The woman linked arms with him and brought him to the sandrover. She and her butler hopped in, and Xan climbed in behind them. He glanced back at the dome and then at the city ahead of them.

The butler started the engine, and the machine took off. It was exhilarating to watch the sands move rapidly beneath them. The city approached in no time.

Xan stuck his hand out of the sandrover to feel the rush of wind between his fingers. When the sandrover hit the paved roads, it picked up speed with a smooth glide and precision. They zoomed past pedestrians slogging on foot. A few other sandrovers drove alongside them, eventually breaking away onto their own path.

They approached a circular skyscraper in the southern edge of the city and parked the sandrover close to it. A middle-aged man stood outside, waiting to help them park their rover.

Xan stepped out and watched the valet hop in the sandrover and drive it off. He scanned the building up to its peak. *It has to be the tallest one here*, he thought.

"This way," the woman said. "It's easier to talk inside."

Xan followed as they entered the building lobby. In the middle of the lobby stood a circular desk with staff members behind it ready to assist the residents with their queries. There were four circular lifts inside, their columns rising at equal distances from each other.

Xan followed her into the lift and got out when they did. They reached a beautiful faux wooden door, and the woman slid it open with a swipe of her Vlex.

The flat was like none he had ever seen before. Tropical birds swooped from the ceiling down to perch on the staircase railing. There was no wall on the opposite side of the room, just a giant window stretched from end to end. The view of the clustered buildings and the Martian landscape looked like a hyper-realistic wall painting.

He had never seen the city from this vantage point. He nearly tripped over the rug as he moved closer to the window. He caught himself and checked to see if the others noticed. They did, but they didn't care.

"I like your idea," said the woman. "I know delivery services are quite popular on Earth. It's never taken off on Mars though, due to the lack of hovercrafts and androids."

The butler patted the couch with his hands and then smoothed it out. The lady sat down and waved for the Xan to join her. He sat on the couch, and felt like he had sunk into a heavenly cloud.

"Oh my god," Xan whispered, sinking further into glorious comfort. He looked over at her and noticed she had a faint smile on her face. He straightened his posture, trying to look more dignified in his factory attire. He cleared his throat and crossed one leg over the other.

"No one thinks my idea's any good," he said. "And to be honest, I'm wondering myself."

A large toucan sat on the couch behind her. "That's because you're marketing to the wrong crowd."

"Who else is going to buy cheese?"

She lifted her Vlex and gave it a tap, then looked at his legs. "You might want to put your legs straight," she said.

Xan straightened right before the couch moved up and over towards the giant window. Soon the couch hung up above the floor, angled in such a way that he could only see the world outside.

This was it. This was the view he wanted all along, he just didn't know it. His eyes caught on the beautiful city below. He felt like a bird in a nest watching little bugs crawl upon the ground. Tiny sandrovers were like little robots, and the people seemed to be scurrying about like ants.

"I thought you were joking at first," she said. "Then I kept turning the idea in my head. I've already had a similar discussion with a co-worker of mine. He doesn't want to walk all the way out there, he doesn't have a butler, and also doesn't own a sandrover. But I'm certain there are more like him."

Soft billows of sand dragged into the winds below. The woman reached a hand back to pet the bird. "You can see how the problem isn't with your idea," she said. "It's your approach. You can't go offering your services to those who already have sandrovers or butlers. We need to come from a different route."

Xan looked over the edge and saw the butler preparing a warm meal on a table below. The woman turned her body slightly towards him. "I don't mean to pry into your personal life but what is your situation exactly? Is this a side hustle for you or a project for someone else?"

"On the side," he said. "I'm the only one."

She glanced over at his sandy clothes and the crust upon his cheeks. "And are you working somewhere right now?"

"Yes, at a factory," he said.

"How much longer do you have left on your contract?"

"Three years left."

"There'll be a penalty if you break your contract."

"Yeah, I know."

She paused for a moment, leaving her tan lips parted. "And I assume you'll need accommodations as well?"

"I have a bed in my dome."

"You won't if you break your contract."

Xan did not know what to say.

"Look, if you're serious about this business, then I'm wiling to invest in it as a full partner. I'll pay the penalty, and we'll split everything right down the middle. You can stay here while we're setting up. And in return, the groundwork is fully on you. I can only support your basic needs until the business takes off."

Xan felt his palms grow cold.

She looked him over. "What do you think?"

A parrot picked at the back of his shirt. "I don't know where to begin," he said.

"Do you think it's a fair split? That's the most important part. Everything else can be worked out later."

Xan tried to swat the bird away. "Sounds fair," he said.

"Then should we make it official?"

"What do you mean?"

She held her Vlex in the air. "We register the moment together?"

"What about my job?"

"You can't keep it and do all the legwork. You'll need to choose one."

"Oh."

"I mean, if this is a whim then keep your job."

"No, no, that's not what I'm saying. Give me a second to think here. This is big."

"What's holding you back?" she said. "You let that guard put a gun to your chest."

"What if I get used to this lifestyle and fail in the end?"

"It's a risk you'll have to take."

The winds sailed throughout the city, stringing along a trail of orange and red sand. Xan watched the pedestrians marching on below. He felt the distance between them and himself grow smaller.

There's no turning back if you do this, he thought. *What have I got myself into?*

CHAPTER 19

Xan tapped his Vlex on the pyramid behind the statue and slugged his way out of work. With his hands in his pockets, he walked through the sands to the city's edge. He waited for some time, hoping to see a familiar face, someone to talk with to clear up his head.

Kicking his toes before himself, he walked to the outskirts and went round the northern section, stopping only to look out at the farm. "What if this doesn't work? Not only will I be forever banished from my dream but I'll also have nowhere to go."

He soon found himself in the library, searching the books for an answer. None of the books had any advice on what to do if you found yourself in a situation like his. Everything he read put the weight back on his shoulders.

"Make your own decision." He chewed his lip as he thought of his parents and sister.

Fail, and no one will ever know, he thought. *Succeed, and you can save everyone you love.*

A big hand grabbed him by the arm. Xan whipped around to face Niall staring down at him. "I remember you," he said. "Sven's friend?"

Xan held his tongue and nodded.

"We haven't seen you in a while." Niall loosened his grip. "The thing about family is that you're always welcome back."

"Sven told me I don't fit the vision."

"I'm sure you do. Come for a few more sessions and have a real taste."

Xan looked up at the large man.

"We have another gathering tonight. Why not join us to clear your head?"

* * *

Xan raised his hands to the sky, screaming to the moon above. "Take back! Hold the land. God is good. He is in our land. Take us home." When he finished yelling, he swayed with the rest, dulling his mind and leaving a small glimmer of thought inside.

"I'll buy you cheese when I grow up," he said. *"I'll buy you more than you can ever eat! I promise."*

Xan stood still. The group swayed around him. "He's dead," he whispered. "Why do you hang on to this promise? For what?"

He saw his grandfather smiling down on him, and for a split second, he felt warmth. His arms uncrossed as he glanced up at the bright moon hanging in the sky and took a step back.

A shoulder bumped into his. He saw Sven standing beside him. Sven stopped swaying for a moment and offered his arm. Xan grabbed his forearm as Sven did the same.

"I'm only months away from the inner circle," Sven said. "I can tell you that the visions are things we've always talked about. Having no voice in this button-pushing world."

"Can't I be a part of both? The farm and here?"

Sven looked down and shook his head.

"I could bring fortunes to us," Xan said. "No more sad tents in the desert. I could build a proper facility."

"And if you forget all this when your credits overflow? Don't you see how selfish that is?"

"Not when I think about it. Not what I have planned."

Sven remained beside him for a few minutes longer. He then faced him before he left. "Choose one or the other," he said. "Family or rich snobs?"

Xan bowed his head and kept it there for some time.

***

The darkness faded under the pale moonlight. Xan's steps carried him out into the desert. He stumbled over a small mound and threw his arms out, but failed to catch his balance.

"You all right?" said the miner.

Xan brushed his legs. "Fine."

They both stopped when they reached the farm.

"I've never met anyone as obsessed with cheese than you."

Sven stood beside them with his arms crossed. "It drives him nuts," he said. "If you have to have a piece, then do it. Go take what's yours."

Xan hesitated.

"This place is easier than others," said the miner. "Still gotta be careful, but they're not nearly as strict as Earth."

"You want it so bad," said Sven. "Now's the time to get it."

"Sneak along the back there, you'll find the opening I told you about."

Xan inched forward, then looked back.

"Go for it. This is what you want." Sven gave him a push ahead. Xan stumbled at the first few steps and then continued on. He ducked over to the building and crawled along the side. He reached the back and found the small opening, just like the miner said he would.

Getting to his hands and knees, he slithered towards it and started digging a larger hole for himself to slip through. He put his hand in the opening, then pulled it back out and sat down in the sand.

What am I doing? This isn't it. Why am I sabotaging myself? I'm so close, and here I am, chipping away at everything I've done.

Xan pushed himself up when he heard a loud shout behind him, gunfire, then a thick arm wrap around his neck.

"You stinking thief!"

His airway constricted as the arm tightened around his throat. Gurgles spewed from Xan's mouth.

"Think we don't know our buildings? Think you're smarter than us?"

The guard shoved Xan's face into the sand and wrangled his arms behind his back, cuffing his wrist and feet in one smooth motion. "Stay there, I've got a call to make."

Xan squirmed. He rolled in the sand and managed to get up on his knees. Xan scanned the area and saw no one around. Getting to his feet, he shuffled as far as the chains would allow, making little ground.

He heard two guards rushing back, yelling as they approached. Xan hopped towards a large mound behind the farm. Torchlights searched the area behind him. Xan made it to the crest of the hill.

"I think I shot one, but good god are they fast."

Lights nicked at his feet while he stood at the peak.

"I smashed him up nice, where the hell did he slip to?"

Xan threw his body over the other side and tumbled all the way down the hill.

The sun rose as he scraped through the desert in chains. He stayed behind the small hill, up near the top, edging towards a village of domes. He watched the city but couldn't see the farm anymore. A sandrover full of officers sped along the street below.

Xan waited for it to pass. When he reached the back of the village, he crawled over the top and scuttled down to a nearby dome. Resting upon it, he closed his eyes and let himself drift for a moment.

The sound of voices awoke him. A door slid open, and the voices got louder outside. Xan kept still. He listened to their conversation about work and how their colleague lost his arm down in the mines.

Xan swallowed hard. Then when the voices vanished into a dull whisper, he curled his body, flinging himself upside down and onto his back. He did this three more times, but he was no closer in getting his Vlex to slip out of his jacket pockets.

He stood to his feet and tugged at his jacket, trying to bring it close enough to his hands behind him to dig inside the pockets. It remained stuck. Then, using his mouth, he pulled at the jacket and held the pocket in his teeth, but was unable to do any more. He thrashed his head and turned upside down, shaking the pocket like an animal.

Refusing to let go of the pocket, he started jumping up and down, then flipped himself over until the Vlex peeked out. Xan froze, afraid to move. He released the pocket from his teeth and slowly moved his mouth, then clamped the Vlex between his front teeth. With a quick snap, he flung the Vlex out onto the sand. Turning his body over, he tapped the Vlex with his hand, pressing his contacts for Sven's name.

A dial tone blipped. He twisted around to place his ear on it. "Sven? Sven?" he said. "You rotten bastard, pick up, you're the one that got me in this mess!"

"I'm sorry?"

"Sven?"

"No, Razan."

A cold knife ripped into his gut.

"Xan? Have you second thoughts on the offer?"

No words came.

"Hello?"

"Razan," he said.

"I know asking for half is a large stake, but think about it from my point of view: either I have to rent you a lodge, or keep you here, while the both of us wait and see if the business takes off. That could be years."

"Razan?"

"Though, and I mean this, I don't believe the business will take off unless we work together. I have the resources, you have the grit. Fifty-fifty is the best split I can offer."

His dry lips quivered. "Razan..."

"Yes?"

"I'm in. I'll do anything it takes."

"Should we make it official then?"

"Yes."

"How's tonight? I'll ask Zola to help you move your things."

"Can you do it any earlier?"

"How early?"

* * *

The engine shut off with a strong hum. Footsteps pattered over the hill and Zola appeared around the peak, wearing in a thick pair of boots. He rushed over to Xan, got him off the dome, and, with great ease, lifted him onto his shoulders.

Zola ran up the hill to the other side and slung him into the back of the sandrover. He looked down at Xan, sweat running down his clean-shaven head.

"Zola..."

"You haven't hurt anyone?"

"I'd never - "

"Then you need not tell me."

Xan's eyes welled up.

Zola threw a blanket over Xan and hopped into the driver's seat. "One thing though, try not to move until we reach the flat."

CHAPTER 10

Zola kneeled down and tinkered with the ankle binds, trying out a variety of tools on them. "You should be grateful to whoever clamped these on you. They forgot to switch them on fully." Zola put a thin metal piece in his teeth.

"They must've been in a rush, or they're just very sloppy. Most cuffs have trackers inside and an electric stunner to keep a man from running."

The first bind snapped open. Xan sighed with relief. Zola raised an eyebrow and raised the open cuff.

"They're broken," Zola said. "See right here, that's your tracker, and this is your stunner. You, sir, are one lucky man."

A mixture of fear and gratitude washed over Xan. *I should be in prison right now. I got lucky. God, I got lucky.*

* * *

After a deep scrub and a clean shave, Xan fumbled into his new room and found a set of new clothes waiting for him. He had never worn such nice clothes before. In fact, he'd only wore uniforms up until now, in his various roles as a student, conductor, cleaner, factory worker.

He put his new clothes on and looked at himself in the mirror. "You're not a kid anymore," he said to the mirror. "No more acting like one."

In the corner of the mirror, he saw Zola standing behind him. Xan turned around, feeling embarrassed.

"Speaking to oneself is one of the earliest signs of mental illness," said Zola, entering the room. Zola walked over to Xan and fixed his attire.

"These sleeves are all wrong. And why would you fasten this here?" He continued to readjust Xan's new clothes.

"Do you think I'm mentally ill?" he asked.

Zola straightened his back and drew in a breath. "If you are, it might be a good thing," he said with a smile. "A normal person rarely achieves greatness in their life."

When Zola was done, he smacked Xan on the back of the head. "See how it's done?" he said. "When you can do this properly yourself, then you'll be a man."

Zola grabbed the lining of his own coat and then walked out of the room. Xan looked back at the mirror.

"Give it time," he said, "I'm on my way."

* * *

Xan went downstairs and saw Razan sitting at the table. A few birds were chirping on their perches.

Razan held the binds in her hand. "Glad to see you're feeling better."

Xan blushed. "It's not what you think."

Razan smiled as she set the binds on the ground. "By the looks of it, these cuffs came from the farm."

"You can tell?"

"There's a name on them."

"Oh."

"You must be hungry?"

Xan shuffled to the table, waiting for a bird to move so he could sit in his chair. "I'm starving," he said.

"Come and eat then."

They sat and took the lids off their meals. The sun set behind the mountains outside. Xan looked across the table at Razan, thinking about how little he knew of her, and of how little she knew of him. After every few bites, she would pause to caress one of her birds or to look up and smile.

"These birds aren't real?"

"No, could you imagine the mess?"

He twirled his fork. "Thanks for picking me up," he said. "And for not thinking the worst of me."

Razan placed her knife down on her napkin. "Maybe I'm being polite?"

"Eh?"

"I'm taking a gamble here," she said, "but something tells me you have a good heart."

He stopped twirling his fork and set it down on his napkin. "Is it common to invest in this way?"

She looked at him for a moment. "I don't think so. But I'm not the typical kind of investor."

Xan curled his cloth napkin. Razan smiled with slight concern and then continued eating.

Xan picked up his fork and tapped it on his plate. "You've invested in others before me?" he asked.

"Sure," she said. "Not related to cheese though."

Xan stopped tapping his fork. "What exactly happened with them? They became rich and successful?" He let out a nervous laugh.

She looked to the side, nonplussed. "Some were successful."

"Some?"

She eyed him. "Yes."

Xan tried to keep eating.

"I find birds so calming," she said.

"I've only seen them in zoos."

"You'd be amazed what an animal do can do for you," she said. "I always wanted birds growing up. But they're so expensive. And messy."

Xan tried to go back to his dinner. "I quit my job for this," he whispered. "I'm just like one of these birds."

"Excuse me?"

Xan looked up, his mouth agape.

"You think I'm a princess?"

"I never said that."

"You think you're the only factory worker to rise out from the belts?'

A tingling sensation ran over his head.

She pushed her chair back and stood. "I won't lie to you," she said. "Most businesses fail."

A few birds flew off as he stood up too. "I'm betting my life on this."

She touched his upper arm. "That has to be your own choice,' she said. "I can only invest. You understand?"

Xan chewed on his lip.

"You have a long road ahead," she said. "Most people will never leave the factory or even get this far."

"I know," he said. "This business isn't just for me though."

She left her hand on his arm. "They rarely are."

"What makes me any different?"

"You must discover that yourself. I can't tell you."

"And if I fail?"

She took a breath and let it slowly out. "Take it one day at time Xan. Don't expect to do everything at once."

Xan looked into her eyes. "You weren't always rich?" he said.

She shook her head, lowering her fingers from his arm. "Money can come and go quicker than you'd think."

He watched her hand leave his arm. "You took a sponsored ship up here as well?"

"There's no other way."

Xan's shoulders rounded. "They treated you like filth?"

"That was so long ago... I try not to think about it."

Xan bowed his head.

Razan lifted his chin. "But then again, there are certain things I'll never forget."

CHAPTER 21

A bunch of files flooded into his Vlex. Xan stared, intimidated by each of them.

"Access codes... Xan? Xan?" Razan stood in the doorframe.

Xan nodded without looking at her. "Yes. The files. I have them here," he said.

"Not the files. I said, do you have the access codes?"

Xan looked through the myriad of files on his Vlex. "Right. I've got them." He waved his Vlex in the air with a strained grin.

She blinked a few times. "Are you overthinking it?"

"No."

"Zola will be with you. You'll do fine."

"I'm not overthinking it."

She took a step back in and touched his arm. "Confidence is your greatest resource when starting out. Even if you're putting on a show."

"This is so new for me."

"It'll feel uncomfortable for a while."

"I'm not supposed to be here. I should be out at the factory. Pushing buttons."

She squeezed his arm then let go. "You'll do fine," she said. "Zola will be there. I'm sorry I can't join, but I have to run."

"Thanks."

"Don't over think it." She backed out the door and waved goodbye. The door slid shut behind her.

Xan sat alone in the giant flat. A terrifying scenario screened inside his mind.

He was in a dark farm. He walked across the floor, hearing nothing but seeing a blinking pyramid waiting in the middle of the darkness. He walked closer and closer. He looked behind him to see if anyone else was around.

"Hello?" he called out. No one answered. Then, as he pulled out his Vlex to tap it on the pyramid, a hand grabbed his wrist. He saw a pair of handcuffs weaving over his arms and a muffler coming over his mouth.

A large group of people beat him until he fell to the floor. Then they dragged him into a pitch black room as they talked amongst each other, saying things he couldn't understand. He heard them pulling lasers out from their holsters. He watched a single barrel charge up in the dark.

"What a pest. We were wondering how to get rid of him. Guess they granted our wish."

The man laughed and the trigger -

"Sir?"

Xan jumped from the couch, grabbing Zola in a single bound. Zola raised his eyebrows high up into his bald head. "Are you all right, sir?"

Xan's eyes were wide. "I'm fine. I'm fine. I didn't know you were here. I thought I was the only one." Xan slowly let go of the butler.

Zola fixed his jacket. "I called your name from the door," he said.

"Really? Maybe I'm going deaf."

Zola fixed Xan's coat, then brushed Xan's shoulders and the top of his back. "It'll be fairly simple," he said. "I can assure you of that."

"They'll remember my face," he said.

Zola closed his eyes slowly.

"Listen Zola, you won't want to hear this but - "

Zola opened his eyes and looked at Xan straight in the eye.

"The last time I was there," he said.

"Human beings are visual creatures. One glance can weave an entire narrative within our heads. Keep in mind that no matter how long you hustled outside there, the man I picked up on the mountain looks nothing like the one I see right now."

Xan inhaled a deep breath.

"No guard will embarrass themselves by pointing out who you look like, especially not when you are dressed this way."

"It feels fake."

"Eventually you'll discover that we're all fakes."

They glided through the city, passing the sun's reflection on the silver windows as bits of sand flew around with the winds. The little farm grew larger in the distance.

As they reached the outskirts, they spotted a group of workers digging in the ground with heavy machinery. Xan watched the group sweating away, seeing his old self out there.

As they drove by, Xan picked out a few familiar faces among them. He knew them from the Moon gatherings, but the sandrover zoomed by too quickly for him to recall their names. They sped on and continued off towards the farm.

Xan sat back in his seat and squinted at the red sands before them. "Do you know what those men are building?" he asked.

"I believe they're breaking ground on new tunnels underneath the city," said Zola.

"They're putting in a hovertrain up here?"

Zola tried to speak with poise over the rushing winds. "I don't believe it's a hovertrain," he said. "I heard it will be an intercity tunnel for pedestrians. Did you miss the news about it?"

"When did they announce it?"

Zola projected his voice over the winds again. "Last month while Mr. Vlex was here. He's leading the project."

"Why? He makes Vlexes, not tunnels."

"He's not the only one they mentioned," said Zola. "Mr. Sioux is also a part of the project, and the Earth's government as well, but in name."

"I see," said Xan. "My Vlex's access has been patchy over the past year. I think I might've missed a few important notifications along the way."

Zola turned into the farm. "That's over now," he said, parking beside the farm.

Zola killed the engine and sat waiting for Xan to get out first. Xan stepped out and looked at the farm with apprehension. Zola exited the vehicle and stood beside him in silence.

"Zola?"

"Yes, sir?"

Xan said nothing as he rubbed his wet palms inside his pockets. He looked at the entranceway again.

Zola tapped him on the back. "Sir, don't walk with your hands inside your pockets."

Xan took them out. "Right." He waited for a sign to tell him to go. He wanted his Vlex to flash a green light and say: *Please enter the building. They are ready for you now.*

"What if they know I'm not well off?" he said.

"It doesn't matter," said Zola. "Don't note what any of them think. You have the invitation to collect and use their services. They can't discriminate against you."

Xan looked back at the sandrover.

"You want my advice sir?"

Xan looked at Zola.

Zola straightened up and brushed sand off the young man's arms. "Stop thinking and start doing," he said. "Thoughts can lead you down a maze with no exit."

Xan took in a deep breath and nodded. "Thanks Zola."

Zola straightened his neck and eyed the young man. "Something, my first employer, told me," he said.

Xan turned towards the entrance and walked along the side. As he approached, he felt the urge to put his hands back inside his pockets. A gentle tap reminded him not to. The guards glanced at them both as they entered.

"Good morning," they said.

It was as if the guards didn't even recognise him. They moved away from the door without a second thought. Xan felt as if a cloud had shrouded him with a protective haze. He didn't feel comfortable in it, but it had gotten him past the first round. At that moment, he caught himself instinctually lowering his head and realised he did not need to do that anymore.

As they walked in, one of the guards took a second glance at Xan, but quickly averted his eyes. Xan and Zola emerged from the hallway into the open lobby. The giant orb above them shone a bright display of green wires stretched inside. The wires slowly dissolved into red electric beams that mixed with flames that appeared around the edges.

A female employee with a glass pyramid in her hands walked over to meet them halfway to the lobby desk. She stopped before them and held out the pyramid.

"Good morning. Here for pick up?"

"Yes." Xan held out his Vlex. A swollen lump jumped into his throat as he waited for the moment of truth. *Let it work*, he thought as he brought his Vlex to the pyramid. *Don't let them think I'm a fake.*

His Vlex touched on one side of the pyramid, igniting it in a yellow flash. The lady looked down at the pyramid for a moment and then squinted her brow. "Can you do that once more?" she asked.

Xan felt his face burning red. "Sure."

The same yellow flash appeared. The lady pulled out a thin transparent square from underneath the pyramid and tapped on it. Her brow went further into a squint. Xan clenched his teeth with his mouth open at the corner.

"I'm sorry sir, it seems you're picking up an order for someone else, but you're not the butler?" She looked up at him in confusion.

Xan tried to swallow the lump in throat. "Yes," he said in a mixture of tones. "We're an independent delivery service. I'm here to handle the pickup for my customer."

The employee glanced at Zola beside him. "Delivery service? I'm sorry, but we've never dealt with a delivery service before. In order for this transaction to go through, we'll need the access codes and the notary configuration."

"That's fine," he said. "I have those here." Xan felt his Vlex slipping through his wet palms.

She kept her brows clenched, and her eyes darted back and forth from him to his Vlex and then to Zola.

Xan retrieved the access codes and tapped them into the pyramid. This time, the pyramid flashed green. The lady reluctantly inserted the little square back and swallowed her thoughts.

"I'm sorry for the hassle sir," she said. "I'll have the packages brought out at once." She turned away and left them.

Xan watched her gather behind the circular desk with the other employees. She leaned over to her co-workers and looked back to make sure he did not see her there. He knew she was chatting with the other workers about him. Their eyes glanced at him and Zola furtively.

Xan turned away from them.

A man in a pale brown coat dragged out a handcart with two boxes on top of it. He pulled the cart to them, gave them a pleasant nod with a little tap at the brim of his cap and left.

The employees behind the counter tried to act busy as they watched the transaction take place. The employee who verified them peeked her head over the counter while Xan picked up one of the boxes and Zola grabbed the other. She murmured again, but Xan turned away. He walked down to the dimly lit hallway, and out into the bright Martian landscape.

"Thank you. Have a nice day," said the guard.

"Thanks," he said.

The guard twisted his head in a flash of recognition at the voice, but decorum took over and kept him from staring at Xan.

Xan loaded the box into the rover and hopped inside. Zola turned on the engine and drove them away from the farm.

"That lady didn't want to give us the cheese," said Xan. "Are they going to ban us from doing this?"

Zola turned the sandrover towards the city. "I don't think they can," he said. "You're not doing anything illegal. If they implemented a rule against it, there'd be no customers. Most of their sales go to people who have butlers, and we're no different from that."

They passed by the groups of people digging in the outskirts of the city. He wondered if he'd be doing that right now too. Xan then noticed one worker from the moon group. It was the same man who had taken him to the farm the other night.

Xan smiled, nodding his head at him. He almost put up his hand when the man spat towards the sandrover.

Xan eyes widened. "The hell?" he said. "Zola, that man just spat at us."

Zola drove the sandrover onto the paved streets and weaved through the city. "I don't pay attention to these things," he said.

"How could you miss it? He did it on purpose!"

Zola focused on the road, keeping his thoughts to himself.

Xan turned back to look at the group working at the outskirts of the city. He couldn't let it go.

"You can't do that," his father said. "Nobody does that. What are you thinking? You'd better go back to the factory and beg for your job back right now!"

Xan looked at the projection of his family on his wall. His father dug into his eyes and grit his teeth.

"What about Mr. Vlex?" said Xan. "He started something too. He didn't sell many of his products for over a decade, and then one day he gets a government contract to supply every citizen with one."

"No," his father said. "No. I'm tired of hearing this. You're not him. People like him have nothing to lose. It's not like he had to work in factories or train stations. They handed him everything he wanted. There's a reason he got that government contract. He knew someone working there. Guys like that already have all the contacts, credits, and time they could ever need."

Xan wanted to cut the feed. The people he expected to encourage him the most seemed determined to undermine his success.

"You're meant to work in the factory," his dad continued. "That's what our family does."

Xan couldn't look at them. He clenched his jaw until his teeth hurt. "You don't want me to be successful do you?" he said. "You'd prefer me to stay where I am. This isn't about me being foolish. You're afraid I'll become something. And then what? Then what for you? You'll be stuck in your lousy government flat doing exactly as you're told, while I'm cruising the sand dunes in my new rover. Piss off and go rot in your little hole."

Xan slammed his index finger onto his Vlex. The wall reverted to its original colour, and his family disappeared. He punched his fist into the bed with a growl. The last thing he wanted to deal with was their pessimism. They couldn't see the dream he could. They couldn't see the vision he had. They had travelled no further than the electric park. Experiencing artificial senses made no one an expert on travel.

Xan turned from his room and went downstairs. He saw Razan at the table eating her dinner as she looked out at the cityscape. She turned her head towards him, catching his eyes. He saw a place reserved for him at the other end. She smiled and waved him over. Xan focused on his breath again. He wanted to smile at her but his mouth twisted into a half-scowl.

"The lady you delivered to yesterday recommended our service to her friends," she said. "We've got one more customer because of that."

Xan looked at his meal on the table. "That's great," he said.

"I told you it takes time."

"Yeah," he said, jabbing at the mock chicken with his fork.

Razan sat up with a soft joyous look in her eyes. "You know, one of my co-workers said he'd be signing up for our monthly service. If we can get a few more subscriptions, we'll have a good grasp on the market."

Xan did not feel her smile nor her eyes watching him as he stabbed his meal into tiny fragments. *Fucking bird. You're not even real meat. You're just some plants made to look like the animal that went extinct.*

Razan paused to watch him. "How were the deliveries today?" she asked.

"The usual," he said.

"Okay."

He threw his fork down and looked at her across the small table like a wild animal.

"Some people are real jerks," he said. "They may say they care for you, but when it really comes down to it, they're afraid you'll be more successful than them."

Razan opened her mouth a little, unsure of what to say. Xan grabbed his glass of water to take a sip. He spilled some down his shirt and growled.

Razan put her fork down gently. "It's part of the game," she said, straightening her napkin. "My father refused to speak with me when I grew into my first small business. He thought I'd end up dead or part of a terrorist organisation." Razan held her thoughts for a moment, picked up her fork and knife, and then placed them upside down on her plate.

Xan pushed at his plate with his index finger. "What about your mother?"

"She died when I was fourteen."

"Oh, I'm sorry."

"It's fine."

"I didn't know."

"How would you?" she said. "Yes, we didn't live as comfortably as before, but my father kept us alive. Even if it almost killed him."

"He sounds like a good man."

"I didn't deserve him."

Xan thought about touching her hand. "What happened though after you hit it big?"

She looked up and blinked a few times. "Well, he came around and broke his silence in time... I know he loved me too much to see me get hurt. He didn't know how to communicate it, though, without a power struggle."

Xan moved the mock chicken around on his plate. "At least he loved you," he said.

"Did you talk to them just now?"

Xan laughed. "In my father's expert opinion, I should go back to the factory and beg for my job."

"There might be days you wish you did," she said.

Xan looked up at her face. "You can't be serious."

"There are days that will knock you flat on your tail," she said. "Things you never thought of or expected will burst into your life without warning."

Xan lay his utensils across his plate and tapped the table with his thumb. "Do you ever regret your decision?"

She pursed her lips and shook her head. "Not anymore."

Zola had discreetly placed Xan's silverware upside down on the plate so that the fork and knife were touching at their tips, creating a v-shape.

Xan picked them back up. He looked down at his meal and broke it apart with his fork again. "He eventually came around?"

"Eventually."

"Then what?"

Razan sipped from her glass. She took her time in placing it back down. "I didn't know at the time," she said. Her eyes went down as her tongue touched her lower lip.

Xan quit cutting his meal.

Razan met his eyes. "He'd already registered," she said. "Ready for, well, the next great adventure."

"Euthanasia?" he whispered.

She drew in her breath and her lips formed into a painful smile.

"He couldn't break his contract?" he asked.

"Not at that point."

The table went silent. Xan returned to his food. Their silverware clicked across their dishes as white static hummed in place of their unsaid thoughts.

Razan stood from the table. "I'm going to get some rest," she said.

"Sure."

Razan smiled and then drifted towards the staircase. She held on to the railing and slowly walked up the stairs. Xan stood from the table and walked towards the stairs.

"Sorry for asking," he said. "It was the wrong thing to say."

Razan looked at him. "No," she said. "When I'm with you, I feel connected, ready to move on from the past and into something new."

Xan took a step closer to her. Razan placed her hand on his face. "Goodnight Xan."

"Goodnight."

ChAPtER 13

No calls ever came in from his family. He only received the occasional message from his mother or sister.

Send me a picture of the sandrover. I don't believe you.

He sent his sister a picture of himself inside it. A large bird squawked at Xan. It tried to nip at his finger.

"If I can push my proposal through to the city council," said Razan. "Then one of these days I'll fill the entire city with electric birds."

"The whole city?" he said.

"Sure," she said. "Think of how beautiful they'd look. All variety of birds flying from tower to tower."

"What if people steal them?"

Razan contemplated. "I hope they wouldn't."

Xan shrugged.

"We can put trackers in them," she said.

A falcon landed on the table between them. Razan pet the top of its head. Xan eyed it wearily. "Where did you buy all these from?"

Razan continued to pet it. "From a friend of mine," she said. "He imports fish from Earth, and every now and then he lets me tag on a few electric birds in his shipments."

"Sounds nice."

"He is. I'm sure you'll meet him one day."

Xan didn't realise his hand was curled into a fist. Both their Vlexes beeped at the same time. Razan opened the message and raised an eyebrow. Xan checked the message too.

"They're asking for a lot," said Razan.

"Another one of your friends?"

"No. I've never met them."

Xan returned to the order, scratching the back of his head. "Can the sandrover carry that many boxes?"

"I bought it off an old colleague with four kids," she said. "I think it can manage."

Xan laughed nervously.

"Things are looking good," she said.

"I didn't expect this much."

She smiled at him. His heart ticked. Then she looked at her Vlex. "Oh. Shoot, I'd better get going."

"Sorry, I'm distracting you."

"No, my mind's on twenty different things other than work."

Xan got up.

"Good luck today," she said.

"Yeah. You too."

She brushed his arm and let it linger for a second more, then rushed off to work.

Xan sat in the quiet room for some time, learning more about cheese, and then went to stand in front of a mirror in the living area where he practiced his pronunciation of different cheese-related terms.

"Why yes, this one is milky white with a herbaceous flavour and as you can feel it's moist...moist touch? It's a moist feel. The cheese feels moist..."

God that sounds wrong

" - and you can tell that the cheese is moist just by touching it?"

"Talking to yourself again," said Zola behind him.

Xan glanced at him in the corner of the mirror. "Yes, Zola. I'm practicing my speech."

"What speech are you giving, sir? Is there an award I should be aware of?"

"No award Zola. Sorry."

"Pity." Zola watched him fix his shirt. He shook his head and readjusted it for him. "Now that the speech is out of the way, shall we begin our deliveries?"

Xan gave a sardonic bow. "We shall."

The two men went down to pick up the sandrover and went about their deliveries.

"You know, Zola, sometimes you sound like a poet. Is that something they teach you as a butler?"

"No," he said. "I file away memorable quotes from my previous employers. You never know what'll stick as long as you listen."

"You sound like a children's book."

"If only you knew how many fairytales I've had to read in my life."

They passed by the outskirts of the city where groups of workers drilled into the ground with giant machines. Xan didn't look at their faces nor take heed of the slight gestures they might be making towards him.

"Zola? Do you know what's supposed to make this tunnel so high tech?"

Zola kept his focus on the path ahead. "I believe that's the big secret," he said. "Builds more hype that way."

"So no one knows."

"Except them."

Xan brought his eyes back to the approaching farm. He watched it grow larger as they approached it.

The sandrover stopped at the side of the building. Xan gathered three cartfuls of cheeses and dragged them back out. They drove the sandrover back towards the city.

Xan brought his voice over the winds as he spoke. "You don't think they're planning to start their own delivery service?" he said. "Is that why they're not helping us promote our business?"

"I don't know sir."

"You must know something. How long have you been a butler? Ten years? Let's say if any of your prior employers heard about our business, would they create their own to compete with it? Do you think they'd undermine what we're doing? I'm always asking them to promote our business, but they never want to help. There seems to be something dodgy going on there. What do you think?"

Zola cleared his throat before speaking. "I'm not sure how to answer your question. Each person I've worked for has been vastly different. Should I list them all and discuss them with you?"

"That's not a bad idea," said Xan.

"Okay," said Zola turning the wheel. "From the beginning then?"

"Go ahead."

Zola sighed. "For the first five years, I lived with a family that owned stock in the mining industry. The father wouldn't care about such a small business and especially would not bother wasting his time competing with it. His wife was far too wrapped up in the mirror to see the world around her, and the children weren't motivated to work with anything other than whine.

"The sixth year, I worked for a military official who wouldn't be concerned with a start-up business. The only things that caught his attention were drug manufactures or anything related to terrorism.

"The next year and a half, I worked for an entrepreneur whose company went bankrupt, which resulted in the termination of my contract. The next six months, I worked as a temporary replacement for various vacancies.

"During that time, I helped a politician who'd only be interested if he could exploit your business for his own benefit. I also worked for an android designer who wasn't aware that any other human being existed. And finally, I watched a constantly drunken teen sip his life away while living off his trust fund.

"Then as you know, I was transferred here to Mars to work for Ms. Razan. Do I need to explain her to you as well?"

Zola swerved to avoid a giant rock in the sand. Xan watched the rock pass out of sight.

"Actually, yes," he said. "Explain her to me."

"I was being facetious, sir."

"You can tell me something though. Tell me more about her prior investments or her friends. That's not breaking any ethical code right? If I wanted to look them up, I could."

Zola brought the sandrover in between two giant machines smashing into the ground. Xan covered his ears as they passed through. The city towers slowly dissolved the echoes down different channels.

When they were far enough away from the drills, Xan spoke again. "Zola, back to my question," he said.

Zola raised one eyebrow. "I don't know what to tell you, sir. There were some investments she'd made that went well and others that didn't. This is the same thing she told you."

"Well, then tell me about them. Who were they? Were they women or men? And what happened with the failed ones?"

Zola zigged through the city and whipped around the circular buildings with ease. "Some were women, and some were men," he said. "There were a few who stayed with her. Some minded their own business and others formed what I might consider a friendship."

Xan throat went dry.

"There's one woman she still keeps in touch with," said Zola. "They've become a unique pair of friends. You might meet her soon."

"What about the men? Did she make friends with any of them?"

Zola pulled the wheel around the circular building. The tires skidded.

"Zola?"

He kept his eyes to the road. "There was one that got close to her," he said.

Xan's heart plummeted through his stomach. "Were they closer than friends?"

Zola focused on the road.

A sour hole eroded in his intestines. "Were they?"

"I can't say. The relationship went downhill after the business collapsed."

Xan watched the pedestrians walking slowly around them. "What do you mean downhill? Did she kick him out?"

"Yes. It was quite the ordeal. She quit investing for a long time after that."

Zola stopped the sandrover at a building to make their first delivery. Xan stayed in his seat. "What made her invest again?"

"I'm not sure. It was a surprise to me when we picked you up." Zola stepped out of the vehicle.

"Why me?"

Zola looked up to the top of the building. "She has an eye for business." Zola looked back to study him. "You don't look very lazy either."

Xan sat in his seat.

"Come now. We need to deliver these," said Zola grabbing the first box.

"Sure," said Xan, slowly crawling out of the sandrover.

He picked up the other box and marched alongside with Zola. They walked towards the lobby entrance and a door opened, allowing them in. Xan searched for the lifts. "Does she ever talk with that guy anymore?"

"No," said Zola. "She can't."

"He moved back to Earth?"

"No. He's dead."

CHAPTER 24

Xan stared blankly out of the windows. He sat down on the couch and tried to do more research, but the endeavour turned out to be fruitless. Dusk had fallen. Razan had yet to return. Xan couldn't stop himself from thinking about her meeting up with all of her old business partners.

The evening waned into darkness. Xan snatched his Vlex and plodded up the stairs into his bedroom. He looked into the mirror. "It's business," he said. "She wants money. She probably does this with everyone. You're no different."

Xan turned to his bed and slipped under the covers. "There's a term for this kind of woman," he said.

Thoughts crept into his head like buzzing ants working for their queen. He couldn't stop their marching along the back of his eyes. The night went black, and he hadn't realised that sleep had taken him in.

Xan woke to the light simmering through his window. It nudged him to break from the binds of his covers. He slipped his foot out of his bed and fixed himself up for the day. As he went down the stairs, a lump on the couch caught his attention. The lump lay wrapped in covers, rising and falling ever so slightly.

Xan inched over. Razan's face peeked through the blankets. He shook his head.

"Don't disturb her," said Zola.

Xan turned around. "I'm not going to," he said. "What is she doing there?"

"She had a late night. She couldn't make it back up to her room."

"With who?"

Zola stopped in the conversation to examine the young man.

"With some of her friends," said Zola.

"Previous investments? The fish guy?"

Zola led Xan to the table that overlooked the window. "I wouldn't concern myself with her prior investments," he said. "What you need to do is focus on your work. Not her personal life."

"I'm not focusing on her personal life. I'm curious. I have a right to ask. What if they have some good tips for me or something?"

"Let's get to business. You have the file for today?"

Xan reluctantly pulled out his Vlex. He showed no enthusiasm as he tapped on the files. "It's all here," he said.

"Good," said Zola. He looked Xan dead in the eye. "There's one more item we need to discuss," he said.

"Let's hear it. I'm being kicked out after this?"

Zola raised his eyebrow. "No. It's about tonight."

Xan nodded. "Okay?"

"Tonight is her birthday, and she's placed you on the guest list. I normally would allow her to discuss this with you, but as you can see, her current state makes this difficult. I don't believe she'll wake in the next few hours."

"It's her birthday?" he said. "Oh shit. I didn't get her anything. I can't barely afford anything!"

"She doesn't want a present," said Zola. "She wants you to attend her celebration. As you can see, she's already started celebrating. So, will you join?"

"Yes, of course."

Zola looked at Xan, expectantly waiting for the next question.

Xan lay his palm on the table and opened his mouth. "Are her prior investments going to be there?"

Zola glanced at Xan's hand on the table as if it were out of place. "It's possible," he said. "We won't know until tonight."

* * *

Night arrived faster than he had expected. Xan and Zola drove through the city as Phobos shone high in the night. Xan looked towards the hills, spying for any large tribes praying to the glowing god in the sky. He didn't see them, but he knew they were probably there.

Zola pulled the sandrover up to their building and waited for the valet to take it.

"Is she up there now?" he asked.

"No," said Zola. "She will meet us at the restaurant."

"Restaurant?"

"Yes."

"I've never been to one before. You think this is okay to wear?"

Zola took a moment to look him over. "They won't kick you out," he said.

The two men climbed into the transparent building and entered the lift.

"How many people will be there?"

Zola kept his eyes on the numbers flashing in the lift as they ascended. "Ten or more," he said.

"They'll realise I used to be a factory worker," said Xan.

"What does it matter?"

"They'll look down on me."

Zola smiled.

"I shouldn't go. It's not my crowd. I'll end up getting in everyone's way. Just tell Razan I'm sorry. Tell her I wanted to be there but -"

The lift slid open, and Zola motioned for them to exit.

"No. Tell her I wanted to be there, but I got caught in a storm. No, she'll know that's a lie because you're there. How about you tell her?"

Zola slid open the apartment door and waved Xan inside.

"Tell her - "

He saw Razan standing inside. She wore a long dress with bird prints on it, and a small broach near her collarbone. Her eyes lit with confidence as her luscious hair curled at her neck. He felt a rush of warmth prickle his face.

"I thought I'd wait," she said. "The others won't be there for another thirty minutes anyhow."

She waved him over towards her. He complied.

"I'm glad you're joining," she said, touching him. "You'll like everyone. I've already told them about you."

Xan rubbed his palms together. "Wouldn't miss it."

Razan motioned towards the table. "Something to drink before we go?"

"Sure."

Xan tried to look at her the way he always did when he sat across from her, but something different shone in her eyes. He felt nervous talking around her like someone had tied his vocal chords into a knot.

"Happy birthday," he said finally.

"Thank you."

Zola brought them drinks and set them on the table.

"And you Zola?" she asked.

"I must decline. If the three of us have a drink, then who'll account for us all by the end of the night?"

She nodded her head. "If you insist?"

He gave a serious nod.

She raised her glass towards Xan. "Then it's the two of us I suppose. Cheers!"

"Cheers." They both sipped the red liquid and placed their glasses back on the table. Xan shivered at the metallic aftertaste.

"We should have a little something to eat before we go," she said.

Xan jumped out of his seat and grabbed his delivery bag, pulling a small box out from it.

"We can eat this?" he said. "I picked up some cheese for your birthday. I don't know what you like, but I got Tulum."

"That's so sweet of you," she said. "It's one of my favourites."

He handed her the box as she grabbed his other hand and gave it a thankful squeeze. Xan wondered if she could feel the sweat from his palms or the pulse bursting through his veins.

"You're welcome," he said. "Just a little something." *That cost me a year's salary*, he thought.

She let go of his hand and eyed the box. "Do you want to try it now?"

"It's your gift. So it's up to you."

She handed it to Zola. "Why not?"

She patted his chair, asking him to come and sit down again. He took his seat and brought it closer to hers.

Xan sipped the red wine and placed a lot of faith in that sip, hoping it would take him out of his nervous state. Zola came back out with a stone board and a small wire to slice the cheese.

Razan picked up a piece and handed it to Xan. "Let me know what you think," she said.

Xan slipped the delicate piece between his lips and onto his tongue. A burst of flavour cascaded along his tastebuds. He felt a pulse of elation rise through his brain. He looked over at Razan. A surge of lust drew him closer to her.

"Well balanced," she said.

Xan felt his nerves taking over. Something hooked within his mind. Each beat of his heart told him what he wanted. She sat so close to him. He felt her pulse between them.

She stood from her seat and straightened out her sleeves. "We'll save the remaining pieces for another time," she said. "Are you ready?"

"Ready," he said.

She held his hand again before he could breathe. "Thanks," she said.

"No worries."

* * *

Xan tried to focus on the conversations happening around him. His eyes probed their surroundings, wedging into each nook of the room. A band played soothing tunes on the stage. Soft billows of smoke whispered through the air. The tables had glowing lights underneath them that changed colours according to the mood of the songs.

Razan glimmered in blue light, laughing with the other women, talking with ease. No knots or kinks were throwing them off their muse. Laughter came and went at the appropriate cues. Xan wanted to be over there with her. He wanted to be a part of their conversation, laughing and gliding along.

"Another one of her investments?" asked the large man beside him. He had made two friends. They seemed similar enough to himself. The larger man's name was Mick and the tall skinny one's Kane.

"Yeah," said Xan.

Mick scratched his reddish beard a few times. "She hasn't taken on an investment in a long time," he said. "You're the first in a while."

"Why is that?"

Mick spat a laugh. "If you knew the last guy, you'd be burnt out too."

Xan sat up straight. He took another sip of his drink. Liquid courage spewed in his mind. "What was the story? Does she pick these people up at random?"

"She's good at choosing her investments. The last guy was a flake though. His inconsistency drove her mad. One day he's pumped up and the next he's in a depressive slump."

Xan finished his drink. "She wanted him to be around her more, is that it?"

"I don't think it had anything to do with him being around," said Mick. "She didn't even like the guy. It was obvious he was using her. But it all seemed to work out in the end. The business went down the tubes. Gave her a good reason to boot him."

Xan felt a lining of hope surge within. "Was she upset when he left?"

"Not at all. She had to call me over to help toss him to the curb. He refused to leave and kept screaming about some contract bullshit. Then he saw me walk in the door with a few of my pals. He left quietly after that."

Xan laughed.

Mick shrugged his broad shoulders. "You never know what'll happen with these types of ventures. Lots of people in this world, all thinking different thoughts."

Xan set his empty glass on the table. Mick waved to the waiter and then pointed to the three empty pints on the table, sticking three of his fingers in the air. The waiter nodded, and Mick looked back at Xan. "You're not worried about these other investments are you?"

"I don't know if I should be."

"I wouldn't be concerned. She told me about your business. It'll take off. Give it some time."

A waiter approached with three new drinks.

"I hope so," he said.

Kane, who'd been looking at the aquarium inside the wall, broke his focus to join them. "You know," he said. "I don't think she's ever brought one of her male investments to a party before."

Razan continued talking with the women in her group as the men took more sips from their drinks.

"Cheers," said Mick, lifting his drink.

"Cheers." Their glasses clinked.

* * *

Zola drove them home. Their words were slurring, and their voices were raised in the back of the sandrover. Razan's hair kept whipping around her face and then behind her head. Xan occasionally stuck his hand up in the air to feel the winds.

"Kane's not so quiet once you get him talking," she said, holding her hair. "Ask him about aquariums, and he won't stop."

"He was watching the aquarium the whole time," said Xan. "I thought he'd never seen one before."

"No. He owns the only aquarium business on Mars. Mons doesn't even have one."

"He's the guy who shipped your birds?"

"I thought you realised that."

"No. He owns aquariums?"

"Tons."

"No wonder. How did he get into that line though? And why set it up here?"

"It's a family business," she said. "He's the youngest of seven kids. His grandfather owned the last few remaining stores on Earth. By the time he left college, his siblings had claimed all the other shops. So he invested in one up here."

"You like Kane?"

Razan laughed. "He's nice and never puts on airs."

Xan threw his hand out of the side of sandrover and cupped the wind within his palm. "How'd you meet?"

"Through a friend years ago," she said, nudging her body into him.

"Ah."

Razan pinned her wild hair down. "The Earth's government gave him a larger grant for opening a business on Mars," she said. "They want business owners to invest here to get more humans up here."

Xan looked into the star-filled night. His eyes tried to look out for a blue star as he thought about his home planet. He put his head back down and saw Razan smiling.

"And what about Mick? What's his story?" Xan asked.

"He used to be a miner until his boss showed up late one day."

"What?"

Razan pulled her hand back inside the sandrover. "Apparently his boss had to meet with potential investors from Earth, but he's very shy when dealing with clients or talking face to face with anyone. I think his uncle owns the mine or something.

"Anyway, his boss had been pacing the floors all day, waiting for the new clients to arrive. He stood around, watching over the workers' shoulders and one of those happened to be Mick, who asked why he was so nervous. His boss had a panic attack and hid in his office for the rest of the day.

"Mick felt bad for scaring him and went to apologise. And according to Mick, when he reached the office door, a group of people addressed him as if he were the boss. Instead of correcting them, Mick kept up the ruse and showed the clients around the plant. He could give them a full tour, having worked there for a few years.

"Then by the end of it all, they'd appreciated Mick's personality so much that they signed a large contract that same day. His boss heard how Mick won them over and offered him a job right under him."

"Sounds like the type of smooth talker you'd want to keep around."

"He's helped me in tricky situations before."

"I'm sure you're fond of him."

"He's a good friend to have."

Xan's smile fell as she looked into his eyes.

"Chemistry is vital in any relationship though."

The sandrover stopped. Their eyes broke, and they headed up into the apartment. Xan wanted to touch Razan's hand or brush his hand against her back. The lift door slid open, and she lingered next to him.

"Thanks for inviting me," Xan said.

"I wanted you to meet my friends. It's good networking too."

Xan scratched the back of his head. "Now they can put a face to the business."

The apartment door slid open and dim lights came on, keeping the mood soft. They both walked over towards the window where the city lights flickered within the towers below.

"Do you want another drink?" she asked.

"If you do?"

Zola went into the kitchen as they slowed down near the little table.

Xan put his chair closer to hers. "Razan?"

"Yes?"

"You're confident about this? You think it'll take off?"

Zola brought out two glasses.

"Did someone say something?" She took the glass and held it up towards him.

He brought his glass up towards hers. "Cheers," he said. "And happy birthday."

She nodded her head in thanks, and their glasses clinked. They sipped in unison.

"So?" she said.

"No. No one said anything bad. They all seemed to think it was a good idea."

"Then what is it? I'm no mind reader."

He rubbed his thumb around the wine glass. "I heard about your last investment."

Razan looked down.

"Never mind," he said. "Too much alcohol."

"Are you worried that you'll end up the same?"

He shrugged his shoulders and continued rubbing the glass. "I feel that I know nothing. Everything seems uncertain no matter what path I take."

Razan took a sip from her glass.

"Sorry, now's not the best time," he said.

"No, it's fine," she said, placing her hand on top of his. "I understand."

He felt an electric buzz.

"He was a jerk from the start," she said. "I was too kind and naïve at the time to realise what he was after. Zola watched every little thing he did." She nodded up to her room. "I even installed a second lock on my bedroom door."

"Seriously?"

"He never worked. He wanted someone who could take care of everything for him. Eventually, I asked Mick to help me get rid of him."

"I heard," said Xan, glancing down at her hand on top of his.

She blinked a few times. "I see," she said. "And I'm assuming he told you the rest of the story?"

"He died?"

Razan slipped her hand off. "He didn't want to go back to the factory."

Xan placed his hand on hers and then slipped his other hand underneath, holding them together.

"It takes a while to see things clearly again," she said. "To get your stride back."

"I won't flake out. I promise."

She looked at him and slipped her hand away. "You don't seem the type," she said. "It took a lot that day to convince myself. I'll admit the gun helped." She laughed and then rubbed her eyelids.

"Thanks for that," he said. "I was ready for the worst."

They both sipped the final drops of their wine. Zola swooped in to refill them.

"I'll make this happen for the both of us," he said.

Razan cleared her face as a small parakeet sat on her shoulder. "What do you say we finish off the last pieces of cheese?"

"Sure."

Zola brought the remaining pieces of cheese and laid them on the table.

"This always picks up my spirits," she said, holding a piece.

He smelled its fragrance, touching his memories with a fine comb. Razan took a bite, and he followed her lead. The cheese melted on his tongue, calling up his tastebuds for another rush. This time, he could describe how he felt as he ate it. The way the cheese melted was like nothing he had ever experienced from any reconstructed meal before.

Sharp, slipped through his mind. "Sharp?" he said.

"It is sharp," she agreed. "You already sound like a turophile."

"Sorry?"

She smiled. "A connoisseur of cheese."

"Oh, thanks."

She had a pleasant smile. He did too, but he didn't realise it.

"Last bite," she said, pointing to the two slivers waiting for them.

"To birthdays," he said as he held it in the air. "May they always come once a year."

She snorted a laugh, grabbing her nose. He couldn't help laughing too.

"To birthdays," she said.

Xan savoured his last taste of the night. The lights burned low, and the wine vanished from their glasses. Then silence.

Razan took the small bird in her hands. "Good thing birthdays come only once a year," she said. "Anything more would be tough to manage."

Xan saw that their glasses were empty. Razan stretched in her seat and let out a yawn. She released the bird and stood from her chair.

"Thanks for the gift," she said, leaning down to give him a kiss on the cheek.

His face warmed. There was nothing else to say.

"Good night," she said, leaving the room.

He sat holding his cheek, looking out the window as the city watched him. It didn't judge him, it just let him know it was there. Every light had its own story unfolding too.

He didn't want to move from the moment. Not yet.

CHAPTER 25

The business grew. More people requested deliveries than Xan had anticipated. His life had fallen into a pleasant track. Down to the farm he drove, collecting boxes, and then back into the city he came.

For years he did this. He had thrown himself into the business without keeping count of time. It was different from his prior employments. Now he was making a way for himself.

Customers began asking him for advice. He had built a nice rapport with many of them. He spent all of his credits on tiny pieces of cheese to taste. He had to know them, their taste, their touch, everything about them. This study paid him well.

Over the years, the business grew to a point where he could hire a few workers to handle the deliveries for him. Xan stepped aside from the grunt work and slowly moved into the role of a consultant.

He guided his customers on cheese pairing: which ones went well with wine and which complimented fine whiskeys. He suggested new varieties based on their previous orders. His knowledge grew with every piece he bought.

Xan learned about all the great traditional cheese dishes. His grasp upon the niche put him in a position of power he had never dreamed of. Maybe because he was the only one foolish enough to do it.

The passage of time brought him back into contact with his family. They noted the success of his business but didn't seem to understand the reality of it.

Xan stayed ahead of the curves and pushed his business further with each step. He made friends with some of the scientists on the farm. He learned about the politics that kept the farm running. They told him how their unofficial owner, Mr. Sioux, was regarded as an absent owner. The man was all but impossible to contact.

For years, they had been asking him to expand the farm, but he could not be bothered. Xan saw this as an opportunity and offered to financially support the expansion. To Xan, expanding the farm meant new cheeses, and increasing his client base.

Xan leaned inside a half-dug-out cave. He was proud of the expansion. He could already imagine the new cheeses resting peacefully within it.

Dr. Dupont, one of the scientists, stood next to Xan. He wore a white lab coat and his round glasses hanged off his nose. He touched at one of the installation tubes protruding from the wall and fixed his glasses upon his face.

"We've tried to make Rodoric for years," he said. "If I'm not mistaken, it's been six years. How ridiculous is that?"

Dr. Dupont had a very sharp face. His eyes were calculative yet empathetic. "They never returned our messages," he said. "For over six years."

Xan looked around the cave. The far end was still being dug out. Lines and wires were left hanging unfinished. "He's too busy with Earth," he said. "I don't think he cares about this operation. When you're that rich, what does it matter?"

Dr. Dupont let go of the installation tube and fixed his coat. "Six years," he said. "It's incredibly rude."

Xan agreed.

Dupont crossed his arms up to his chest. "A normal business could pile its credits into these types of things," he said. "Our profits either go towards paying the workers or into his pockets."

Xan stepped inside the cave a little further. He peeked his head around the corners and tapped at the walls. "What do the other scientists think of this?" he said.

"If anything, they're happy. You know Dr. Mikos?"

"I remember her. Bright green eyes?"

"That's her," said Dupont. "Anyway, she approached me the other day with a new list of cheeses she wanted to make. I think some of them think I'm the leader of this project."

Xan smiled. "You're okay with that?"

Dupont cocked his head to the side. "Fine with me," he said. "Everyone hands me a list of cheeses, so I get to choose what's in and out."

Xan pulled out his Vlex from his jacket and looked down at a new message. "I need to get back," he said. "I'll come by in a few days."

"Sure," said Dupont. "See you then."

Xan left the farm and received polite nods from all the workers as he exited. He felt a flash of nostalgia ripple through his skin. *There he was, some years ago, trying his best to break into the place. He was shaking like a nervous child walking through a dangerous storm.* How time had shaped him. The sands blowing in the winds had nicked off the rough edges that no longer served him.

He followed the blazing light that emitted from the farm's exit. He opened his palms to the sun as he stepped outside. The two guards said kind words to him, and he went on his way.

Xan stepped towards the old sandrover he had bought over from Razan and placed a box on the passenger seat. Then he jumped into the driver's seat. The engine hummed, and he shot down the sandy path. The sun whipped brightly in his hair.

He thought about the days approaching. There was something special he had been longing for that still lingering in tomorrow's web. It would be Razan's birthday again. Xan touched the box that lay in the passenger seat. He let out a large breath of worry as the sandrover rolled back into the city.

Xan kept losing his train of thought. His eyes focused on a freight ship hovering above the ground. He had seen it before he left for the farm. They always took a while to land. "Smaller than usual," he noted, watching the ship.

A scream pierced his eardrums. Xan jerked the wheel to the left, avoiding the man he had almost hit, and slammed his foot onto the brake. The machine screeched to a halt. Xan's chest rammed into the steering wheel, knocking the wind out of him. Before long, a curious crowd had gathered.

Xan quickly pushed himself back into his seat, still gripping the wheel with the sense of impending doom. Two men screamed obscenities from across the road. They charged at his vehicle. One man spit on his sandrover, and the other kicked his wheel.

It cranked Xan's nerves like a lithium spark. "Sorry," he shouted, but they didn't care to listen.

"Get your ass out of there," they yelled as they approached the driver's seat. "Let's have a talk!"

Xan looked into the man's face and felt shocked. The man spit again on his rover and reached out to grab him by the shirt. The other man was reaching towards him from the other side of the vehicle. Xan turned the gear into reverse, pressed down on the power, and shot away from them, increasing the distance between them.

The men grew angry and shouted as they ran towards him. "HEY! ASSHOLE! GET THE FUCK OUT OF THERE AND FACE US - "

Xan turned the gear forward and peeled down another street. He increased his speed as he flew through the city. His heart was pounding. He kept turning the moment over and over in his head.

"He didn't recognise me," he mumbled. "He didn't even know it was me."

* * *

He stood at the window, watching the ship touch down next to the spaceport. Zola brought him a warm drink to help soothe his nerves. Xan felt a surge of embarrassment mixed with anger as he thought about the situation. His mind was churning.

It looked just like him, he thought. *I know it was him. I didn't try to hit him on purpose.*

Xan sipped the warm liquid, allowing it to warm his core. "Maybe I should go find him and apologise," he said out through the window.

His Vlex rang, but his mind was in a prior moment that needed to be fixed. "God, if I'd been driving a little faster or my reaction was any slower..."

The severity of the situation weighed on him like lead in his gut.

"Is everything all right?"

Xan turned around. His was expression mixed. "I almost hit someone," he said.

Zola lifted his eyebrows and nodded for him to continue.

Xan rubbed his palms together and let out a strained sigh. "I think it was someone I used to know."

"I'm certain you had no intention to run down your old friend," said Zola. "Did you talk it over?"

Xan glanced back through the window. "No," he said. "I didn't have a chance. He didn't even recognise me."

Zola moved closer to the window near him. "Is this friend of yours from the factory?"

Xan watched the ship out near the spaceport. His Vlex buzzed for his attention, but his mind was wrapped somewhere else.

Zola came to his side. Xan looked up at him.

"How did this friend of yours react?"

Xan threw his hands in the air. "Like an animal!"

Zola nodded. "Well, you did almost kill him," he said. "Keep that in mind."

"No," said Xan. "It wasn't right. He should've known it was me."

His Vlex begged for his attention. It did its best to pull at his consciousness with repeated pleads.

"Put yourself in his position," said Zola. "Would you have recognised Razan in a factory uniform, especially in a life-threatening moment like that?"

"I would!" he said. "I'd know her face anywhere and in any uniform. Even if she tried to run me down!"

Xan put his cup on the table. "I think I need to go back out," he said. "I need time to think."

"It's okay sir. What you're feeling is normal."

Xan walked along the city streets, leaving his sandrover behind. A clouded space in his head wanted the same situation to happen to him. He wanted the chance to act out as Sven did. He would react differently, he was sure. He would be calm, and not try to beat anyone to a pulp.

He watched the few sandrovers zip by him. "Come on," he mumbled. "I wouldn't freak out like that. I wouldn't go around jumping and screaming like some freak. It's so damn childish."

The winds picked up, nudging him left and right as he walked. Xan looked up at the sky. "It's that moon energy stuck up his arse," he said. "All that stupid dancing at night has finally wrecked his head."

Phobos was visible in the daylight. He noticed that it was close to being full. Xan stopped in the middle of the city, staring up at the moon. He leaned against the building behind him and slid his body down to the ground. He sat watching the moon hang silently in the sky. A few pedestrians walked past him without paying him much heed.

His Vlex continued to buzz. Xan finally dug it out and opened the messages. They were all from Dupont.

We need to talk. Please contact me.

We need to discuss something important.

Can you please contact me?

There is something important we need to talk about.

When you get this, please contact me.

There is an important matter that requires your attention.

Hello?

I need you to contact me.

Hello?

Don't ignore these messages.

You've already heard?

Xan typed a message back. *Just got your messages - what happened?*

He sent the message and waited for a reply. His mind wandered around all the dark corridors, searching for any unseen problems. "What is he on about?" he wondered.

A reply came in.

Mr. Sioux is here... His ship just landed.

* * *

Xan sped out to the farm in his sandrover. As he approached, he noticed a few vehicles gathered at the building. Many of them had hardtop covers over them, unlike the retractable glass on his.

He parked his sandrover beside them and took some time to examine the unusual vehicles. They were hovercrafts. Xan hopped out and circled them a few times, looking at his curved reflection in their windows.

"He brought his own hovercrafts?" he whispered.

Xan was in disbelief. He'd never seen a hovercraft on Mars. It made little sense, especially because the infrastructure wasn't built for them. "It can't be good to park them on the ground..."

The doors clicked open, and a few large men stepped out, holding guns at their sides.

Xan backed away, putting his hands into the air. "Sorry," he said. "Just curious. That's all."

The guards stood at the ready, watching him leave their presence. Xan headed to the entrance where he saw the two guards sweating bullets. It wasn't a hot day; there was a nice breeze in the air. One guard stepped out, holding his hand up to his chest. He swiped his eyes back and forth. "I won't stop you from going in," said the guard. "But I'd highly advise you to keep away from here today."

Xan looked at the sweating guard. He moved his head to the side, looking past the guard and down the hall. "He's here?"

The guard nodded.

Xan continued looking down the hall. "What is he going to do?" he said in a low voice. "He doesn't officially own the place. I'll tell him to look at the documents. It's owned by the government, not him. If the government has an issue with what I've done, then they can come deal with me. He has no power here."

The guard shook his head and glanced back over his shoulder. "Don't be ridiculous," he said. "Mr. Sioux is the government."

* * *

Xan sat in his sandrover trying to send a message to Dupont. Dupont was probably trying to explain the caves at this very moment. Xan hit his head against the steering wheel. The large men standing outside their hovercrafts watched him grovel in his own mess. They stood motionless, their eyes on him.

Xan felt a buzz in his jacket. He fumbled to get his Vlex out. As he pulled it up to his eyes, he saw the men raise their guns. He showed them his Vlex, and they relaxed.

Dupont: *He wants to see you tomorrow. I don't know anything more. Good luck.*

Xan put the Vlex down on his lap. He felt numb. He knew the men were watching him, but he did not care. They'd be shooting him soon enough anyhow.

CHAPTER 26

The sun took its time to set. A blue ring circled the white orb as it sank behind the red mountains on the horizon. Xan watched out the window, wondering what would happen to him when it rose up over those ridges again.

Zola brought him more warm drinks, but none of them seemed to open him up. He wouldn't talk. All he did was look out that giant window in front of him. There were no thoughts when he brought the warm cup to his lips. The life he had been living up until now had been sailing steadily on course. All of that seemed to be fading away now. This was the end.

The unofficial owner was the government. The guard was right. If Mr. Sioux wanted someone dead, it wouldn't appear in any headlines. They would finish the job and go off to relax afterward.

"I'm a damn fool," he whispered.

Zola quickly turned back to him. "Sir?"

Xan went back into his shell. He turned off the lights and looked out at the world from within himself.

It was a dream. That's what it was. It's gone now. What a fool. What a goddamn fool you are. Touching someone else's land without their permission. You dumb fool. This is it. No more visits with customers. No more sandrovers. No more Zola. No more Razan. No more Razan? She's done for. You've lost all that. She's gone, and now you're the flake.

You promised her. You gave her your word. You'd do it for the both of you. I've never even kissed the woman. All the god damn moments she waited. All those times were right in my hands. I stumbled, wondering if she'd reject me. I gave into the thought that we might go sour. Stupid. It was so stupid. She was perfect for you. SHE WAS RIGHT THERE!

Xan beat his fist on the window. A few birds fluttered away. Zola lingered beside him.

Xan hid his face inside his palms. "I've failed, Zola," he said. "The business is over. I'm the flake."

* * *

Razan sat beside him, doing her best to console him. "It's okay," she said. "We can do something else. Don't worry about it. Just see what he wants. If he takes all your credits, then I'll hold you over for however long it takes to start something new."

"I never should've built that cave," he said. "I'm an idiot. It was none of my damn business."

"What's done is done," she said. "Don't think about it. That'll only make matters worse."

Xan kept his head buried. "The guy's going to kill me," he said. "He's not going to play any games."

Xan looked up, his eyes wild with streaks of red veins like frayed wires. Razan grabbed his face and kissed him.

Xan straightened his back and grabbed her face too. He drew her closer into his lips, trying to press their bodies into one. Their passion smacked against the night as they intertwined. He grabbed her around the waist, drawing her body closer to his, going back-and-forth, locking and unlocking their lips. Suddenly, the thought of his impending death had taken a backseat. He couldn't think of anything other than this woman.

He brought his hands down to her lower back, gripping his palms against the contour of her hips, then slowly moved them up towards her breasts, cupping them in his hands.

Razan pulled away for a moment. "Wait," she said. "Wait."

Xan withdrew his hands. He couldn't feel anything other than the raging pulse within himself. The lingering molecules between them burnt with embers of magnetic oneness–begging, pleading for them to bind again.

Razan stood up. The space between them faded in the air, leaving a nostalgic wisp.

"I'm sorry," she said. "It's not the right moment. We're not in the right frame of mind for this."

Xan stood up and went closer to her, and held her elbows in his hands.

"It's right," he said. "It's always been. There's no better time. I might not be here tomorrow night."

Razan looked into his eyes. "He's not going to kill you," she said. "I won't let him."

Xan inched his face towards hers. Their lips joined while the city kept its eyes upon them. Razan unfastened his shirt as he removed hers. She pulled away from his lips once more. She looked into his face and grabbed his hand. She brought him toward the staircase and backed her foot up each step. "I love you," she said.

"I love you too."

* * *

Xan drove his sandrover with the calmness of a man going out for a picnic. He took a long route around the city, going off the paved paths and into the sands. With intuitive guidance, he weaved through the larger rocks as if he had already mapped out the route.

Before today, Xan had never taken the time to enjoy the surrounding landscape. He breathed in the fresh air streaming past his head. He turned the sandrover in great wide arches, weaving back and forth. He held the steering wheel all the way to the right, spinning circles of dust out in the sands, and then when he was ready, he broke from the drift and straightened out his path again.

A group of workers had gathered outside one of the plants to watch him spin his vehicle like a madman. Xan turned the wheel a sharp left and then jammed it to the right. The machine skirted its back wheels as the tail whipped into an arch. The group of workers continued watching. Some of them held their hands up and cheered.

Xan felt free this day. He let go of the wheel and threw his hands in the air, cupping the wind inside them. The machine shook, causing him to quickly take hold of it again.

Xan circled around the mining plant in a giant loop and then shot out of its orbit towards the farm. He waved bye to the miners standing outside. "This is it," he yelled.

The workers shouted back.

Xan tore off in search of the farm.

* * *

The farm sat patiently, waiting for him to come and take his medicine. Xan could already see the electric chair inside sparking in a wild fritz of power, waiting for him to sit his soft flesh down and teleport his soul to another realm.

The chic hovercrafts had gathered at the side of the farm. Their dark exteriors absorbed the sun into their shiny coats. Xan knew the army that lay within them.

He parked his sandrover right beside the hovercrafts as if they were just another group of sandrovers. He put up his retractable windshield and hopped out, then fixed his uniform as he looked at his reflection in one of the hovercraft windows. Before any doors opened, he turned and went to the farm entrance. The guards let him in and gave him a consoling nod. Xan walked proudly to his death.

When he reached the entrance, a receptionist brought him a glass pyramid. He tapped his Vlex on it and watched it emit a green flash.

"One moment please," she said, backing away.

Xan waited in the lobby, watching the glowing orb hang from the ceiling. It looked as if it were filled with a dark red liquid flowing along the sides. He wondered if he were to split it now, whether it would drip red dew onto the floor. Then it shifted into orange geometric spikes across the base.

Xan noticed a group of men in black suits walking towards him. As the group reached him, a tall, gangly man held out his Vlex towards him. Xan tapped his Vlex on his, and a green light flashed between them.

"Please follow me. Mr. Sioux is waiting."

Xan walked amongst the group, taking in his few last glances of the lobby. He saw the changing pictures of Mr. Sioux shaking hands with a scientist. *He didn't look so bad*, he thought.

They entered one of the hallways and tapped against the side of the wall. The wall slid away, revealing a hidden staircase he'd never seen before. Xan followed the tall man up the steps and into another large round room.

The spacious room had a long table in the centre and a desk off to the side. Mr. Sioux was sitting at the desk with the back of his leather chair facing Xan. He looked like a giant bear in a suit with his massive body, thick head of hair, and cruel black eyes.

"Sir?" said the tall man as he waited near the door.

Mr. Sioux nodded his head and held up his giant hand, waving them toward the long table in the centre of the room. The tall man led Xan over.

Xan turned to the side where the hidden windows showed them a view of the entire farm from a high vantage point. He could see the lobby and the orb hanging at eye level with him. He had never thought that there was such a place in the farm. All this time, anyone who knew of this room could have been observing him.

Mr. Sioux hovered his chair past his desk and moved towards the long table in the centre. "Please come and take a seat," he said, motioning at the seat across from him.

Xan sat down and looked to the side, out at the goats that were grazing down in their enclosure.

Mr. Sioux studied Xan with his black eyes and a wry smile curled in the corners of his lips. "Good of you to join us today. If I'm not mistaken, you're the one who started the delivery service?"

Mr. Sioux crossed his arms on the table, peering deep into Xan's soul. Xan felt reality sink into his bones again. He felt small in front of the man. He was no longer Xan, the unofficial cheese advisor, but Xan, a child that had stepped out of line. Mr. Sioux waited for him to respond.

Xan wanted to sound confident, but he didn't know if his vocal cords would co-operate. "Yes," he said finally.

"Right," said Mr. Sioux. "And if I'm not mistaken, you've also dug out a new cave in my farm? Without my permission?"

Xan's nerves tangled around his bones. His muscles tensed and his hands began to sweat. "Yes," he said.

Mr. Sioux leaned back in his chair. He looked at Xan and his dark brow furled. Xan sat frozen, feeling weak.

"What are your plans for the new cave?" said Mr. Sioux.

Xan looked down at the table and then back at the giant man. "It was for the scientists," he said. "To make more cheese. They've asked to expand for over a decade now. I wanted to help them. We all wanted to expand."

Mr. Sioux nodded his head but showed no change in expression. "You're an altruistic man? This decision to help the expansion comes from the goodness of your heart?" Mr. Sioux uncrossed his arm to reach for a mug on the table. He picked it up and brought it slowly to his mouth and took a sip as he watched Xan over the rim of his mug.

"Not purely altruistic," said Xan. "My business would benefit from it. More cheese means more customers. It's an investment."

Mr. Sioux kept silent. He gazed down at Xan as if he had found a crack in Xan's skin. A fine little crack that he could rip open with his bare hands and take his heart out.

Mr. Sioux turned his head over his shoulder and lifted his finger towards a man and a woman holding a large box between them. They hurried over at his beckon, dragging the box with them. Then the tall man who had brought Xan in moved behind Xan with something in his hands.

Xan panicked as he turned to the man behind him. He held out his hand, blocking him from coming any closer, and jumped to his feet. "What's this?" he said.

Mr. Sioux's expression remained void of emotion. "Sit down," he said.

Xan retracted his hand and bounced his gaze between them.

Mr. Sioux lifted his brow a little, persuading him to sit. "I want to make a deal with you, if you're willing to take a gamble?"

Xan held the back of his chair and slowly placed himself down in it. "What deal?"

"Well, it's more of a test," Mr. Sioux said. "I saw your little cave, and I won't lie, it pissed me off. Who do you think you are to come in here and rearrange my farm?"

Xan kept his mouth shut.

"Then again," he said. "All the scientists approved of it. That's a hard deal to reject when your whole team is behind it."

Xan swallowed a dry bit of air.

"They told me about your operation in the city. Our sales have gone up because of it. I'll give you that, but I could just as easily destroy your business with my own in-house delivery service."

Xan eyed the man warily.

"What I'm proposing here is nothing more than a simple taste test." Mr. Sioux raised one of his eyebrows. "I've selected different types of cheeses for you to sample today." He waved his large hand towards the boxes on the table.

"If you can identify every single piece of cheese inside correctly, well then, I'll let this matter slide."

Xan sat up in his seat. He thought about his knowledge and the time he had spent gaining it. He probably knew the cheeses better than Mr. Sioux did. He could identify a cheese just by looking at it. This was no challenge for him.

"If you miss one though, I'll ask you to leave, and to cut all your ties with this company."

Xan felt the room contract. The walls seemed to be closing in on him.

Mr. Sioux cleared his throat and leaned back into his seat. "So, what do you say?"

"Okay," said Xan. "I'll do it."

"Good."

The tall man came up behind him and tied a blindfold over his eyes. Xan tore it off his face. He held the blindfold in his hand, examining it. "What's this?"

Mr. Sioux grunted. "It's a taste test, not an eye exam." He shook his head. "Are these stakes too high for you?" He leaned back further with a smirk on his face that told him to back out now before he began the test. *Go ahead kid, get out of here before you embarrass yourself.*

Xan held the blindfold and stretched its fabric between his hands. "Fine," he said, handing it back to the tall man behind him. "I'll play your game."

Mr. Sioux sneered at him.

The blindfold covered his eyes and tightened behind his head. Xan couldn't see anything. He felt the large boxes being thrown open on the table and heard the clicking of locks.

The familiar fragrances wafted up to Xan's nose. He knew there were plenty of pieces for him to taste. He could hear people shuffling around him.

Xan told his grandfather that he'd buy him lots of cheese one day and his grandfather laughed.

"Ready?"

"Yes."

"They will serve the first dish to you."

Xan felt something soft underneath his lips. He opened his mouth and bit into the piece of cheese. A strong flavour swirled in his mouth. He knew it. There was a bouncing freshness to it. *Come on, this one's easy,* he thought. *Think. Relax and think.* Then a word completed itself on a blackboard in his mind. *G-E-V-R-*

"Gevrik," he said.

A large hum sounded across the table. "Yes."

Xan felt the confident pressure sinking in. *Focus,* he thought. *Still more to go. Keep your focus.*

"Ready for the next one?"

"Yes."

Xan tasted the next piece of cheese. *Where have I had this one before? It's so familiar yet different.*

He was sitting at the table with Razan. The meal was ending, and she told him something about the variety of cheese they had just eaten. She spoke to him now like a tape recorder. The words were right there.

What did she say? What had she said?

He heard Mr. Sioux clearing his throat. "Problem?"

"No," he said, going back into his mind.

Zola offered them more white wine. Razan waved her hand, saying no. Then Zola came back with a bottle of red. "Good with red," she said. "Goes good with red..."

Then what? What is it?

"Can leave it to age, it goes good with red..."

"Aged Rocamadour," he said aloud. *I've never tasted it aged this long before,* he thought.

"Hurm. Very good. Ready for the next?"

"Yes," he said.

Good play, thought Xan. *We both know it's usually eaten young.*

The next piece touched his tongue, and in an instant, he found himself on the ship again.

A group of people were laughing at him as he stood in his pitiful uniform. He could hear the old woman's voice, "It's like giving drugs to a child..."

His stomach wrenched. He felt the poison rising from the memory. He knew this cheese. It was the second one he'd ever tried. How could he forget?

"Mato," he said simply.

"Next!"

Xan tasted more cheese and gave all the right answers. He could even identify one that was brought from Earth. It was the same variation as the Martian one, but it had a different texture that gave away where it was from.

"Two more to go," Xan heard.

"Okay," he said.

Xan tasted the next cheese and felt a veil dropping from his mind.

Xan rushed from the table, grabbing a tiny box out of his old delivery bag. He was so eager then.

Xan let out a small laugh, forgetting that he was in the middle of a test.

"Happy birthday," he said with pride.

Razan held his hand gratefully. That moment rippled through his chest like a gentle pebble dropping in a lake.

...my favourite... she said.

Razan was sitting there after the party. They touched each other at every chance they could get. She held his hand for a moment again.

She stood kissing him on the cheek goodnight.

"Tulum," he whispered.

"Say it again? Louder."

"Tulum."

Mr. Sioux waited a moment before responding. "Correct," he said.

The room went silent. Xan felt unnerved. He didn't know what was happening around him.

"You've made it this far," Mr. Sioux said. "Don't screw up the last one."

A piece of cheese landed into his mouth. He tasted it. It was old and nostalgic. It wasn't like any other cheese he would normally eat. It was sweet, almost like a fudge. The hint of salt brought out a caramelised scent. Xan smiled and then laughed.

Mr. Sioux cleared his throat.

A tear bled into the cloth tied around his eyes.

His grandfather handed him the last small piece of cheese. Xan glanced up at him. "Why don't you take it?" he said to his grandfather.

His grandfather shook his head. "Go on," he said. "It's for you."

Xan held the cheese with his little hands and looked up at his grandfather. "I'll buy you cheese when I grow up," he said. "I'll buy you more than you can ever eat! I promise."

His grandfather let out a pleasant laugh. He kneeled down beside Xan with a smile. "I look forward to it," he said. "I bet you'll be the one running the place one day. Never think lightly of yourself, no matter the odds. No matter what anyone else says. Okay?"

The little boy nodded. His grandfather held his shoulder and smiled.

Xan sniffed and dabbed at the blindfold over his eyes. "Brunost," he whispered.

A few moments passed, and no one stirred. Then the blindfold was whipped off his face.

Xan rubbed his red eyes and looked up. He saw the empty trays laying on the table before him, and Mr. Sioux had a large smile across his face.

"Well done," said Mr. Sioux. "You win."

Xan felt a giant wave of relief erupting from his lungs and another tear formed in his eyes.

"I didn't expect you to place the Chabis," said Mr. Sioux. "We brought that one from Earth."

Xan nodded with his head down. "Thank you, sir."

Mr. Sioux bellowed an honest laugh. "You leave no stone unturned."

The workers cleaned the table as they spoke.

"I don't come here often," said Mr. Sioux. "Traveling is fine, but I get so weary of the ship after the first month. I'd been hoping for a while to put one of these scientists in charge, but they're terrible with business. They can tell you how to add the coagulating agents and every other little detail in the process but my god, are they terrible when it comes to sales and management."

Mr. Sioux paused as one of the workers bent down in front of them to pick up a dish. He watched them clean up and move out of the way. "I thought you were some speck hustling my farm," he said. "From the outside, that's how it seemed."

Xan nodded, still in his memory.

Mr. Sioux put his hands on the table. "That's why I wanted to test you to see where your heart was. I'm actually a nice guy. I'm not some paranoid nut, but I had to get to know you better before I made any offers. You understand?"

Xan sighed. "I do."

"I won't waste anymore of your time. What I'm offering you is a head position here. I need someone who can run the business. The last guy we had died about six years back. So I could use someone like you. You already have the contacts and the right vision. Don't worry about your business either. I'll buy it over, and we can merge it with the farm. What do you say?"

The tall man came behind him and showed him a number they were offering for the purchase of the business. Below it was another number: the base salary he will receive to run the operations.

Xan couldn't speak. His throat went dry. "Oh," he said. He couldn't feel his hands. They had gone numb. "Can you let me run this by my partner first?"

Mr. Sioux paused. "I'll need an answer by tomorrow. After that, I'll be at the tunnel opening, and then I'll be heading up to Mons."

CHAPTER 27

"Take the offer," said Mick. "You're not only getting a large sum but also a full-time job out of it. Seriously, take the offer."

Xan swigged his drink and watched the girls talk amongst themselves at the party.

"You know they're talking about the same thing," said Kane.

"I'm sure they are," said Xan.

"Is there something holding you back? What was her reaction when you told her?" Mick placed his empty glass on the table. "Another round?"

"Sure," they said.

Mick waved to the waiter.

"I'm all for it. I have nothing holding me back, other than nerves about the new position. I think I can get the hang of it though."

The men grunted with agreement.

"But Razan seems hesitant for some reason." He paused as a new round of drinks were served.

"Any idea why?"

Xan put his drink down. "No. She said yes, but everything else said no. Her tone was off, her body language seemed defeated, and she didn't even seem excited."

Xan glanced at the group and saw the women looking over at him. They smiled at him and then continued with their conversation. The men let out hums and shot glances back and forth at the women.

Kane smiled as he sipped his drink.

"What?" asked Xan.

Kane continued drinking. He shook his head trying to play it off as nothing.

"You know something, don't you?"

"I know nothing," said Kane. "I can only speculate."

"Would you care to share them with us?"

Kane put his glass down and fixed the coaster underneath it. "What do you plan to do with all those credits after the buyout?"

Xan thought for a moment. "Fly my family up here," he said. "Maybe get a new sandrover. Why?"

"Have you told her that?"

Xan glanced at her. "No. We haven't discussed any of these things. What would that have to do with her?"

"Maybe nothing," said Kane. "I think you should tell her what you plan to do with those credits. Then see how she reacts."

"Okay," said Xan.

Kane leaned towards the glowing aquarium in the wall. He brought his eyes down to a little blue lobster in the corner who meticulously brought food to his mouth with his little pincers. "I warned them against this," he said, keeping his eyes on the aquarium.

Xan leaned over the table to take a look at the aquarium. Mick pivoted from his seat to gaze over his shoulder.

"They'll never live together harmoniously," said Kane.

"Who?"

Kane turned back and pointed at the other red lobster inside the tank. "These two," he said. "One will eventually eat the other."

Xan saw the little red lobster doing the same fervent scavenge for food. "What if they fall in love?"

"They don't fall in love," said Kane. "Even if she lays eggs and they hatch, she'll eat her own children." Kane leaned back. "It's strange they can't even get along with their own kin."

After some time, Kane backed away from the tank, his face lit up by the blue lights. "Not like humans at all. At least we can talk things out over a few drinks."

Mick held his beer out. "Cheers to that."

Kane smiled as he held up his glass.

Xan held out his drink too. "Cheers."

Their glasses clinked together, and the lobsters kept up their night-time scavenge.

They landed back in the apartment a little less steadily than when they had left it. Razan held on to the Xan's shoulder as he walked through the door.

"Okay, careful of the rug," he said. "You never know what it'll do."

She smacked his back with a playful swipe.

"Seriously," he said. "Rugs have been known to attack their owners from time to time." He stopped at the edge of the rug. "Walk around the other way. I'll distract it."

"Get over there," she said, pushing him along.

They both fell down onto the couch, holding each other in a dizzy fit. Xan threw his head back on the headrest.

"So, what did you guys talk about?" Razan asked.

"The usual, cannibal lobsters, and the Martian stock market."

"Is that all you talked about?"

"They asked a few questions about Mr. Sioux and mentioned the new tunnel. But other than that, not really."

Razan rolled her head over his chest.

"That's a lot of credits," he said.

"Sure is."

"What would you do with your share, if we end up taking the offer?"

Razan sat up. She tapped her Vlex to move the couch above the window. It glided across the room and positioned them at the optimum position.

"I haven't thought about it," she said. "What do I need? I'd finish paying for this place, but that still leaves a big chunk."

Xan moved closer.

"What about you?" she said.

"I'd fly my family up here for a little while," he said. "I don't want to upgrade the sandrover. Maybe I'd eat more cheese? Or go on a vacation? We could hike Mt. Tholus? Or see the blue canyons?"

She rubbed her hand along his chest. "You wouldn't buy your own place?"

He paused for a moment. "I could buy one... If you wanted me to?"

Razan moved closer into him. "You could stay here, and your family too, if they don't mind. But there's only one other bedroom up there."

"I could sleep on the couch," he said.

"Might be uncomfortable."

"What other options do we have?"

She wrapped her hand around his waist. "You could share a room with me.”

Xan nodded. “That’d be nice.”

They sat watching the constructed outside world. A small wind created a tornado of dust along the street.

“Do you want to sell the business?” she asked.

“Only if you do.”

“Why not,” she said. “I could use a vacation.”

“Me too.”

* * *

“Yes, yes,” said the small thin man. “They’ve already told me. I guess I’ll be answering to you from now on.”

Xan let out a nervous laugh. He’d seen Quinn before. He knew Quinn was an important man at the farm, but he was never sure of his position.

Quinn shook his bald head. “I’m not so good at the whole expansion process. I’ve never been a businessman like yourself. Everyone wanted me to fill the last guy’s shoes, but I’m not doing that.”

“That’s where I come in then,” said Xan.

“That is where you come in, and I thank god for it. The past six years have grated on my nerves.”

“Was it that bad?”

Quinn raised his eyebrows. “Well, if you were in my position working three different jobs at once, you’d feel the same.”

“True.”

Quinn walked him towards the same hallway he’d gone to meet Mr. Sioux at. He waved his Vlex in front of it, opening the walls to the staircase and walking them up to the private room. “You can use this place.” He stood near the sturdy desk, sliding his finger across it. “Made from actual wood.”

Xan rubbed his finger along its surface too.

Quinn gave Xan a meaningful look. “Oh yes,” he said. “No expenses spared. Mr. Sioux had to have all the niceties for a place he never visits. God forbid he sits at a fake wooden desk.”

Xan let out a polite laugh.

Quinn continued to watch Xan, his nimble fingers still on the desk. “At least you’ll be putting it to good use,” he said.

“I’ll try my best.”

“I’m sure you will. Do you need a tour around the place? You’ve been working around here long enough.”

“I’ll be all right,” said Xan.

“Good,” said Quinn. They stood around the desk with nothing more to say. Xan opened his mouth a few times but closed it back.

Quinn let out a deep exhale. “Well, call me if you need anything. I’m the old bee around the place by now.” The petite man stood by the door and waited for Xan’s response.

“I appreciate it.”

Quinn smiled and then exited.

Xan scanned the empty room for a moment, wondering what to do. He went over to the window that overlooked the goats in their pasture. He then sat at the desk, letting the orb in the lobby shine upon his face.

Xan leaned back in the comfortable chair and looked down at the beautiful desk. He waited for something to tell him what to do next. He stood from the desk and paced around the room, looking through the windows. He stared at the scientists preparing cheeses in one of the storage caves. The men carefully placed the round blocks inside. Another scientist carried a humidity gauge. She moved it all around the blocks of cheese and then held it up in the air.

***

“No. It’s ridiculous,” his father said.

“You haven’t even thought it over. How can you say no like that? I’m telling you that I can pay for your leave and your tickets. You don’t have to do anything other than get on the ship. This is first class transport we’re talking about. For almost two months. When are you ever going to have a chance to be pampered like this again?”

Xan felt exasperated. He contemplated taking back his offer. If they couldn’t be grateful for what he was handing them why should he bother?

“I’ll take it,” his sister said. “I’d go today. Screw this job. I’ll take it even if they don’t let me take leave.”

Her father swung his head around with horror. The veins in his neck were pulsing. “Don’t,” he said.

“Okay,” said Xan. “I’ll fly you up here on the next ship. Consider it done.”

His father looked at his mother for a moment, hoping she would agree with him. She glanced at her husband and gave him a pitiful smile. “I’d love to see Mars,” she said. “I don’t want to be a burden on you though. We know you’re busy and wouldn’t want to place too much pressure on your account.”

"It's nothing," he said. "Trust me. I'd be happy to have you here. All you need to do is get the clearance forms to take off from work and then send me the amount they're asking you to pay."

His father crossed his arms. "It's not that easy," he said. "We can't just go quitting our jobs like this. They won't give us forms to take off that much time. Who do we think we are? We can try, but I'm sure they'll need me at the plant. Same with your mother and sister, they're both too important."

His father put up his nose and turned his face away from the screen.

"Oh, stop being so ridiculous," said Xan. "They'll let you go. People do it all the time. Here are the forms right here."

He sent them through his Vlex right then. "I've already looked up this stuff," he said. "They require you to pay a fee to hold your position until you return, that is if you return. I'll be able to wire the credits to your accounts - "

"We'll be coming back," his father said. "You'd better not forget the return tickets. Got that?"

His mother rolled her eyes.

His sister held her fist in joy. "Can I drive your sandrover?"

"As long as you don't wreck it."

* * *

Xan couldn't wait to tell Razan about his family. He could barely contain his excitement. Time passed slowly as he waited on the couch. His impatience made him fidgety. The clock ticked in his heart but its pace had slowed down to a silent quell.

He stood from the couch and leaned against the window. His eyes caught the slow trickle of pedestrians down below. He tapped on the window with a dulled throb, waiting to tell her the news. "Come on," he said. "Come on."

Xan took out his Vlex but resisted the urge to send her a message. The night seeped through his mind with a poking torment. As the sun set behind the mountains and the little moon shone in the night, he fell deeper into his mind.

The puzzling maze that webbed his fantasies in a horrid spin took him to doors he'd never wanted to open. Where she might be or what she might be doing.

When the door finally slid open, he knew he had fallen asleep. He sat up from the couch and looked over the top of it.

"Hey," said Xan. "You - are you - where have you been?"

Razan slumped inside with a shadow casting weight over her shoulders. "Sorry," she said. "I've been at work the whole night. What time is it?"

Xan held up his Vlex to check the time: 3:07

Razan hung around in the middle of the room and stared emptily at nothing in particular.

"Is everything all right?" he said, rubbing his eyes.

Razan sat down on the couch and dropped her head back. "I hope so." She rubbed her face. "The workers are on strike."

"What?"

Razan rubbed the bridge of her nose. "They're mad about the tunnels," she said. "They're saying they don't reach all the way out to the factories for them."

"Oh," he said.

She moved her head back and forth, stretching out the muscles in the back of her neck. "They want us to bring down the entry fees too. So they can use it."

Xan shook his head. "Tell them to talk to the guys who own them."

Razan sat up and drooped her chest into her legs and let her hands dangle near her feet. She growled.

Xan rubbed her back. "Do you want me to carry you upstairs?"

She sighed and pushed herself back up. "No." She pushed herself to her feet. "I want to focus on the next stage of my bird project. Not this."

Xan followed her. "They can't strike forever," he said. "Give it some time."

Razan paused by the window. Her darkened figure created a silhouette against the city lights outside. Her hand slowly reached up on the glass.

"Can't your company subsidise their fares?"

She hesitated. "Yes. Easily. But the high-ups would never take a pay cut for their employees. That's why the tunnel fees are so high. They don't want workers to use it." Razan moved away from the glass and reached for the railing. "I don't like it any more than they do. Why can't they see that?"

Xan glanced out the window and paused. *The door was wide open, shards of glass edging its frame, and piles of sand building up within the apartment. A hollow wind blew along the opening, catching upon the jagged glass, whistling with a horrid screech.*

He shivered and moved closer to the window, placing his hands on it. A few specks of people were walking on the streets. The night was cool. The streets were alive. The window was fully intact.

"You okay?" she asked.

"Sorry," he said. "Deja-vu I guess." He moved away from the window. "I think I was half-way through a dream. I'd fallen asleep before you came back."

Xan went to join her on the stairs. He saw another old memory filled with dust. A time when he had risked his life to leave the factory before a storm came. The memory felt like an implanted foetus in his brain. His body said it wasn't his, but his mind kept telling him it was.

"Do you remember your dream?" she said as they climbed the stairs.

"It had to do with spiders, I think."

"What were they doing?"

"I don't remember," he said. "I don't even remember seeing any spiders. I just know that I felt their presence. Like a fog over a picture but I knew what the picture was before it was covered? I don't know."

She mumbled something.

"I need to get some rest," he said.

"Me too, or I might be feeling spiders too."

Xan ran a hand up her back like a spider's legs. She swished her hand behind her back.

ChAPtER 18

The group opened fire, killing three officers and injuring four others. Of those killed, two were due for promotion in the coming year. The other officers are currently receiving medical attention at Meridien Central Hospital.

Further investigations are being carried out to find out how these men were able to obtain their weapons. The incident has not yet been reported to Earth as the local authorities are doing their best to...

Xan turned off the screen and moved towards the window. His eyes slowly focused on a bright light hanging in the air above the spaceport. *It's been there the whole day.* The bright light hung in the air as if a strand of wire was attached to it from above. Xan reached out to the table next to him and picked up his beer and finished the last sip.

Xan set the empty glass back on the table, moved towards the window, and leaned his forehead against the glass.

"Perfect day to arrive," he mumbled to himself.

He leaned in deeper, smearing his forehead in the same place. A spot of oil accumulated on the glass as his head smashed against the transparent surface. He tapped at the window, trying to push the little blinking light along.

"Zola?"

"Yes sir?"

"Did I forget to pick up a packet of Chabis?"

Zola slipped into the kitchen and came back out. "No sir, we have plenty."

"Maybe we don't have enough though?"

"Sir, we've a full container in the fridge."

Xan exhaled. The little blinking light taunted him in the night. He then sat back down on the couch and turned the screen on.

"Bloodied bodies flew through the..." He clicked it back off.

"Where the hell is she?"

Zola blinked at Xan, studying him for a moment. "Sir?"

Xan looked up at Zola.

The door slid open, and Razan entered with an armful of wine. "I bought a few more bottles on the way home," she said.

"Great," said Xan. He helped her with the bottles and studied their labels as he took them to the kitchen.

"I don't know if they'll like this one," he said. "Maybe my sister will but dad'll say something about it. Let's open this one when he's not around."

"Whatever you wish," she said. "I saw the ship on the way back. They won't land until morning at this rate."

"Actually, on second thought," he said, "maybe this is exactly the type of thing he needs. It'll give his tastebuds a nice kick. He'll try to act like it's no good, but he does that about everything."

Xan turned the bottle over in his hand. "We should open one of these now. Before they get here."

Razan handed the last few bottles to Zola. "Tonight? Don't you think we should get some sleep before we go pick them up?"

Xan placed the bottle down. "Fine, we don't have to open it."

"If you want to, then go ahead," she said. "I'm not trying to stop you."

Xan waved his hand in the air. "No, I think you're right. We should wait."

He moved over to the window again and spied the blinking light hanging above their planet. "It's getting bigger now," he said. "I wouldn't be surprised if they landed in the next few hours. What if they need us to pick them up while we're asleep? They might think I'm pulling a big prank on them. I don't want to give them the wrong impression. We haven't seen each other in a while, and this is how I welcome them, by leaving them stranded in the spaceport? I'm not comfortable with this."

Razan placed a hand on his back. "Are you okay?"

"I'm fine. I don't want them to get the wrong idea though. You know, maybe we should open a bottle of wine or one of the synthetics? A few drinks won't hurt. Plus, by the look of that ship, we might need to head out in the next hour."

Razan glanced over his shoulder at the blinking light hanging in the sky. She took him by the shoulders and led him to the couch. "Here, why don't you sit for a little while. I'll ask Zola to open one of the old bottles."

She moved away from the couch and spoke to Zola in the kitchen.

When she returned, she walked by the window glanced at the little blinking light then sat down beside him. Silence blew a static wave into the room for a few seconds.

"How was work?"

"Same," she said.

"Nothing new?"

Zola came out with a glass of wine for Xan.

"Thanks," said Xan, taking a large gulp.

Razan laughed.

"What?"

"Do you want a beer?" she said.

"Okay sure. I'll have one after this."

Razan drew in a breath and let it back out.

"They're going to say something about the incident," he said. "They'll get the wrong idea and then act like Mars is a horrible place to live. I know my dad'll say something. He'll say this is why he prefers Earth. You'll see. Just wait."

"Okay, I'll watch out for it," she said.

"He's always finding little things to pick on. It wouldn't matter if I were Mr. Vlex himself. He'd still find something wrong with me. He'd give me crap about Mr. Sioux having more credits. He'd say it's all shoddy work when you really think about it."

Xan finished his glass of wine with a final gulp. "I think a synthetic beer would be nice," he said. "I don't know why I opened that bottle. I should've stuck with a cold one."

Zola had already overheard the conversation and brought him a beer. "Here you are sir," he said, handing over the chilled glass.

"That's great Zola, you read my mind." Xan took a few swigs and let out a small burp. "'Scuse me."

"I thought you wanted them to come?"

"I want them to come," he said. "I'm only having a few drinks before they get here. I don't see what's wrong with that. My dad'll say something when he smells my breath. He'll call me a common drunk or something. Then he'll think that's what all high-earners do.

"He didn't even want to come. It was my mom and sis that finally pulled him onto the ship. He thinks he's too good for Mars or something. I bet he doesn't want to see how well I'm doing up here. That's what it is. He's no longer the alpha male."

Razan rubbed his back with her hand. "Why don't you try to relax and keep an open mind? I don't think he'd come all the way here just to put it down. They're probably more excited to see you in person than anything."

Xan drank his beer while she talked.

"Don't worry too much about how things used to be," she said. "They're going to love this place."

Xan finished his beer with a trailing burp. "Right."

Zola picked up the beer as Xan placed the empty glass down. He asked Zola for another one.

"Do they know we're together?" she said.

Xan jumped up to look out the window again. "The ship's getting closer," he said. "You can almost see the passenger windows."

She joined him at the window. "They know we're living together? That they'll be staying here with the two of us?"

Zola placed the next beer down. Xan moved away from the window to pick up the glass. He took a sip.

Razan laughed. "When were you going to tell them? At the spaceport?"

"I didn't know when to tell them," he said. "They never asked, and I never found a good chance to bring it up. This is the best way anyhow. It's different when they can see you in person, rather than just me talking about you."

He poured more beer down his gullet. "Are you mad?"

Razan moved closer to him. "No, I think you're funny."

He kept his eyes on the spaceship. "It's easier this way," he said.

***

Xan persuaded Zola to take him out in the sandrover for a night drive. Razan was kind enough to tag along. The winds dragged around their heads as the cool smear of night slipped through the air. Xan held his hands out of the sandrover, waving them up and down in the wind.

"Hey Zola, let me drive for a bit," he said, sitting up in the back.

"That's okay sir, I quite like driving."

"No. Come on Zola. Let me give it a spin."

"I can't stop now sir. I'm having too much fun," Zola said with a straight face.

Razan laughed in her seat. Xan threw his head back and looked into the sky. The stars were bright. Each little blink rippled like a call from the past. "Hey Zola?"

"Yes?"

"Let's go near the spaceport," he said. "Let's see how close we can get under the ship."

Zola turned the sandrover towards the spaceport. Xan wanted another drink, but he had forgotten to bring an extra along. It didn't matter that much. He leaned over to kiss Razan's neck. She opened her arms and wrapped them around his shoulders. He slid his hand over her waist as he continued working his lips up to her face.

She moved to meet his lips with hers. "You taste like beer," she whispered.

He kept kissing her anyway. Their lips fastened and unfastened like magnets gripping to the opposite poles.

Xan stopped to look her in the eye. "I'm not embarrassed about you," he said. "I thought it'd be easier this way."

"I don't care," she said. "I might've done the same."

Xan turned his focus to the large ship hovering over the sands. Blue vents simmered with exhaust holding the ship in the air. Tiny windows sparkled around the dark contour of the dark form.

"They're so close," he said. "You can almost see through the windows."

Xan held his hands into the air, reaching for the giant ship. Razan pulled his arms back, holding them down with a laugh.

"Hey! I was about to pull the ship down. You messed it all up."

She put her weight down on him. "Sorry. I like to watch you suffer."

Xan gave her another kiss. They broke apart as Zola swerved to avoid a large rock in the sand. "Excuse me," he said. "Please continue."

"Not while you're watching," said Xan. "Hey Zola, why don't you let me drive? I'm feeling all right now."

"Sorry sir, someone has given me strict orders, above your rank, to keep you far away from the steering wheel. As you can see, it's completely out of my control."

Xan looked back at Razan and then at Zola again. Razan grabbed him down into his seat.

"Zola, turn the wheel to the right and then quickly jerk it to the left and then back to the middle again. It's a lot of fun."

Razan shook her head.

"It sounds exhilarating, sir, but I'm afraid my orders forbid me from flipping the vehicle over tonight."

"Nah. You'll be fine. You haven't even tried it..."

* * *

A powerful quake shook the ground beneath them as the large ship touched down onto the Martian land. Zola turned the sandrover towards the spaceport and brought them outside the entrance.

Xan hopped out while the vehicle was still moving and went up to the exit to wait for his family. Zola looked at Razan, and she shook her head.

"I'll go keep him company," she said.

"That might be best."

She walked up the path towards him and stood beside him, her arms behind her back as they waited. The door slid open, and a mass of people erupted from the gate. Xan scanned the crowd for his family in the sea of faces.

What if he didn't recognise them anymore? Then he saw his mother and sister walking out. He waved his hand in the air, going back and forth in wide arcs. They waved back to him. Xan ran up to meet with them.

"Welcome to Mars," said Xan.

Zola approached Xan's mother and sister and helped them with their bags.

"This is Zola," said Xan. "He's not stealing your bags."

"Thank you," said his mother. She looked around the dimly lit land and then back at him. "You look well."

"You really do have a sandrover," said Ima. "Can I drive it?"

"Maybe."

Razan walked up beside him. His mother and sister looked at her with wide eyes and parted lips.

Razan offered out her hand without hesitation. "I'm Razan."

His mother took her hand. "Nice to meet you," she said as she looked at her son and then back at Razan. "He's never told me about you. Are you two... friends?"

"Where's dad?" said Xan.

Ima cocked her head back towards the spaceport. "He's still lagging behind," she said. "His bag is too heavy."

"I'll go help him then." Xan broke away from the group and rushed to meet up with his father. He saw a man hobbling in the back, struggling with a heavy bag that seemed to be filled with cement.

"This spaceport is horrible," his father said. "It's like they haven't changed it since the old frontier days."

"Welcome to Mars," said Xan. "Here, let me take that for you."

He tried to grab the bag out of his father's hands, but his father jerked the bag away. "I can handle it. I'm not that old. Probably stronger than you think."

Xan stepped back and let his father hobble along with the heavy bag.

"What the hell did you pack in there?"

"You'll find out soon enough."

The two men left the spaceport and caught sight of their group waiting near the sandrover. His mother was chatting with Razan, and his sister sat in the driver's seat of the sandrover, and Zola was pointing out a few of the controls to her.

His father squinted. "Who's that?"

"Razan," he said.

"I'm not looking for a name. You didn't tell us you had a friend?"

"Well, now you know."

His father kept his gaze on her as they approached the sandrover. "Don't mess this up like that sales position. Don't make it all the way to the end and flunk out. Do you even know how to talk with women? What does she see in you?"

Zola turned from the controls and walked over to help Xan's father with his bag. With much reluctance, he handed it over to Zola who let out a sudden wheeze as he took it.

Everyone gathered around the sandrover and Xan introduced Razan to his father. The moment felt like a flimsy knife cutting through a wooden block, a lot of effort was required on Xan's part.

"Let's get back to the apartment then," he said. "We could all use some sleep."

They hopped into the rover and zipped through the sands. Ima put her arms out of the rover, playing with the rushing wind. His father kept his nose up at the entire time, occasionally asking Zola questions about the safety of the vehicle. His mother made small talk with Razan about the Martian climate and living in the city.

As they entered the flat, his sister let out a large laugh. "You live here? It's like an ad from a commercial."

His father lumbered into the flat with his hands wrapped around his heavy bag. He threw the bag to the floor, causing the floors to rumble. "The ship had better colours," he said. "The rugs were nicer too."

"Shall I show you to your room?" said Zola.

"Sure," his father said.

"We'll meet with you all in a few hours," said Xan. "I'm going to take a nap."

Everyone parted into different directions.

Xan fell into his bed and blinked a few times before physical and mental exhaustion overtook him.

Sounds echoed downstairs, and the flat seemed to be full of life. Xan woke up with a throbbing headache, feeling weak. The synthetic drinks had a different effect on his body compared to natural wines.

Razan left a hangover remedy for him on the bedside table. He took the tiny bottle and swallowed the sludge-like substance, and shook with a reflexive twitch as it hit the back of his tastebuds. It was horrible, but its effect was like none other.

There was a glass of water waiting for him as well. He drank it up and tried to rid his mouth of the residue from the sludge. He felt a surge of energy and the storm in his head cleared.

As Xan opened the door, a gust of loud voices broke through. He could hear his father babbling over everyone else downstairs.

"This is all very technical," his father said. "I'm not sure you'll understand it."

"I do," said Razan. "I studied sanitary procedures when I invested in a plant up North."

His father backed into his chair like a child caught in a lie as his speech soon became incoherent.

"So," said Xan. "What would you like to do today?"

"You tell us," his sister said. "You're the one who lives here."

"Okay," he said. "You can check out the city or take a ride in the sandrover while we're at work. If Zola takes you out far enough, I guess you could all have a shot at driving."

His sister clapped her hands with a smile. "Yes!"

Xan's father mumbled something, and his mother nodded her head.

"Great. I guess we'll meet up after work. Then tomorrow I can give you a tour myself. We were thinking about taking a trip to Mons?"

"Whatever you plan will be good," his mother said.

"How do we get up there?" his father asked. "I hope it's not one of those ground transports. You know I read a story about of them breaking down when it got halfway to Mons."

His father tilted his head, looking everyone out of the top of his eyes. "Oh yes," he said. "They found the transport a few weeks later, and all the passengers were dead. There were pictures from that incident circulating around. It's tragic really. I feel sorry for those people."

Xan raised his eyebrow. "Where did you hear that?"

"I read an article. I can send it to you if you don't believe me."

Razan had a strange squint wrinkling over her face. "Are you talking about the terrorist group that stole one of those vehicles almost two decades ago?"

His father mumbled something and then opened his Vlex to check. "There were tourists mentioned," he said. "Same problem could happen again."

"What happened?" Ima asked.

Razan cleared her throat. "They stole the transport to smuggle drugs up north, and along the way, the drug somehow got into their drinking water. Long story short, they all went insane from the effects of the drug, and a few weeks later, a tour group found them."

"Might be the same article," his father said, putting away his Vlex.

"I'll look up their break down rate at work," said Xan. "So we can all decide and travel with peace of mind."

* * *

"Have you ever heard of one of the northern ground transports breaking down?"

"No," said Quinn. "Aren't they well equipped for emergencies? I took one a few years ago and got caught in a sandstorm, but the thing closed up like a dome. The only danger was boredom."

Xan stood near the window, looking down at the goats moving around the different piles of feed on the ground.

"That's what I thought," Xan said quietly.

Quinn raised his thin eyebrow gently into his forehead. "Are you taking a trip up north?"

Xan nodded. "I'm taking my family with me. They're a little nervous about the expedition, so I wanted to make sure it was safe."

"They just came from Earth?"

"Yes."

Quinn closed his eyes and shook his head. "Typical," he said. "We're out of the frontier days, and we have plenty of safety measures up here. People from Earth always think we're living in impoverished huts or something of the sort. Because how could we ever trump the Motherland?"

Quinn let out a snide laugh. Xan watched quietly out the window.

"Do they like it so far?"

Xan shrugged. "They arrived this morning. I'm not sure how I will keep them entertained for a month. You got any ideas?"

Quinn thought for a moment. "You could bring them here," he said. "I don't mind giving them a tour. Let them talk to some of the scientists too."

Xan tapped on the window with his index finger. "Okay. Does it matter when I schedule their visit?"

"Unless Mr. Sioux returns, our daily routine is always the same."

* * *

Xan enjoyed the thought that when he reached his flat, it would be full of people. There was a comforting warmth that came with that thought. As he opened the door, he saw his parents sitting on the couch watching the city bustle.

Ima had the local news up on the screen. "I didn't know it was so dangerous up here," she said as he entered.

"It's not. What are you watching?"

"The news."

Xan turned it off. "Don't watch that," he said. "These kind of incidents are rare. The news loves it when they happen. It gives everyone something to talk about for a while. Don't let it skew your view of the place."

"Sounds bad to me," said his father as he continued to look out the window.

"It's not," said Xan. "Earth is worse. How many bombings happen there every month? How many people throw themselves on the hovertrain tracks every day?"

His father turned his head to look at him. "I'm not sure," he said. "This little fiasco seems more gruesome than what happens Earth. Isn't there some disease that people get from living on Mars for too long? Their brains rot or something? We don't have that on Earth."

Xan thought about the Martian brain rot for a moment. "I don't know what you're talking about," he lied. "There's red lung, but it's more common amongst miners. Either way, what makes this event more gruesome than people being blown to bits down there?"

His mother stood from the couch. "How was work? Did you find out about the trip to Mons?"

Xan rubbed his forehead. "Yeah. I had a talk with my assistant. He said the transport is extremely safe. He took it himself a few years back. They ran into a sandstorm, and not a soul was harmed."

"That's great," Xan's mother said. "It'll be nice to see both cities if we get the chance."

Xan let out a deep sigh. "Yeah. It will be. You know that's where it began. All the historical sights are up there. The first atmospheric station, the first colony, and some new experimental projects too."

"So, it's going to be a science trip?" Ima said.

"Yes, but a fun one."

"I'll be the judge of that."

"Okay. I'll change and then maybe Razan will be back so we can have our first dinner on Mars together."

Xan hurried up the stairs and landed straight on his bed. He rubbed the bridge of his nose between his eyes and let out a low growl.

"All they do is complain," he said to the ceiling.

Xan took out his Vlex and turned his ceiling into a moving picture of flickering stars. "They have no clue how safe it is up here. Can't appreciate the trip I'm giving them."

Xan closed his eyes and opened them as he felt something pressing down on his arm. Razan stood over him, trying to wake him up.

"You're back," he said.

"Yes. You fell asleep."

He sat up. "They're wearing me out," he said. "And they haven't even been here a full day. All they do is complain. Either Mars is unsafe, or Mons is too boring. I don't know why I even invited them here."

Razan sat on the bed next to him. "Well, they're here now. So let's make the best of it."

Xan threw his head back on the bed. "What do you suggest I do?"

Razan fell back on the bed with him. "Isn't it obvious?"

"Kick them out?"

She smacked him across the chest.

"Okay, okay. I'll be patient."

Razan smiled and kissed him on the head as she sat up. Xan lay there for a while more, watching the stars flicker above him. "I act different when I'm around them," he said. "It's like my mind reverts to who I was in that old flat on Earth."

He laid under the ceiling watching the stars.

"Zola's downstairs preparing the cheese for tonight," she said.

"They'll complain about that too."

"They've just arrived. Give them a chance to warm up."

Xan crawled out of the bed and went over to his closet. He let out a sigh.

"It's your family," she said. "Don't let them get to you."

* * *

Dinner went smoothly. His mother and sister complimented the meal, and the conversation lifted with more ease.

"You can't prepare for a speech like that," Ima said. "It's really unfair."

"What did they ask you to speak on?" he said.

"Twenty-second-century political disruptions and their effect on the next development of the next century."

Xan shook his head, thinking back to his interviews on Earth. "Who comes up with these topics?" he said.

"How did it go?" said Razan.

Ima moved her food around with the back of her fork. "Not good," she said. "I didn't even know there were political disruptions in the twenty-second century. Who cares about these dumb things? It wouldn't make me a better salesperson, would it? Who will ever ask me if their purchase will be affected by the twenty-second-century political disruptions?" She dropped her fork onto the dish and snarled.

Xan felt he had just watched an old show about his life some years ago. The things she said and the passion she felt was right where he had been. "At least you got a job at the factory," he said. "It's a big step up from the train station."

His father laughed. Xan ignored him. Ima moved her glass on the table. She looked at the silverware for an extended amount of time as if they were foreign objects to her.

Xan looked at Razan, and she gave him a smile. "Did everyone enjoy dinner?" he asked.

His mother and sister said yes. His father kept stabbing at his food, peeling it open, and glancing at its insides.

Xan stood up from his chair with his hands together. "Well," he said. "I've prepared a surprise for us tonight."

His mother raised her eyebrows. His sister looked up from the silverware with slight disinterest. His father continued mumbling to himself about the food. Razan gave Xan a faint smile to continue.

Xan took in a deep breath. "As I was saying. I've prepared something special for us tonight." He held his hands together with pride and smiled with a bright gleam. "We're going to sample different cheeses tonight. Just like we did when grandpa was around."

His father shot up from the table with a sense of urgency and ran up the stairs. Xan watched him with confusion, wondering where he was going.

"What is he doing?" Xan said to those remaining at the table.

His mother shrugged her shoulders. His father then lumbered back down with his large bag. He placed the bag on the table with a heavy jolt, then huffed as he stood over it.

"Before we do that, I've brought a gift," he said. "Go ahead, take a look."

His dad held his hands out towards the present. Xan went over to the item and opened it with apprehension. He took it out of the bag and placed it on the table. It was a heavy square box that had a sleek shine.

Xan raised an eyebrow. "What is it?"

His father grinned at all those around the table. "It's a Hans-Kaffman safe," he said. "The most advanced safe on the market. You know how much these things cost? I'll keep that to myself. Just know this is a high-end quality piece right here."

His father tapped it, looking around the table with pride.

"Oh," said Xan. "Great, thanks…"

His father continued grinning. Xan rubbed the back of his neck and forced a smile. "What, uh, makes it so advanced? It looks like a normal safe."

His father pointed his finger at him. "It does look that way," he said. "The man who sold it to me knew more about it than I can recall. But from what he said, it's the best of the best. Here, I'll send you a file on it, look it over in your spare time."

His father sent the file to Xan's Vlex.

Hans-Kauffman. The world's safest technology to date. Our safes are rivalled by none other. Hans-Kauffman has been a leading producer in…

"Great… I'll look this over later."

His father held his chin up and went back to his seat with a smirk across his face.

Xan stood, feeling disoriented for a moment. He felt stuck, trying to remember what he was going to do, and then it came back.

"Right," he said. "Okay. Let's have a sample then?"

His family members nodded their heads. Zola came out with a tray full of cheese and then back again with a bottle of wine. He systematically worked around the table, filling everyone's glass and placing two-tined forks on their napkins.

"Go ahead," said Xan. "Take a few pieces."

Each one of them picked up their little forks and speared the cubes on their tines. Xan couldn't hold back the smile on his face as he watched them smell the pieces.

"This can't be safe to eat," his father said. He leaned towards his wife. "Did you smell it?"

She squinted and gave a fake smile. "Yes dear, that's what makes it a delicacy."

His father rotated the cube a few times, giving it a good stare. The mumbling continued.

"Go ahead, try it," said Xan.

Xan wanted to see if they felt the same way he did when he first tasted it. Their faces would tell him. He knew the look, no matter if he saw it on himself or not.

His family members put their pieces of cheese in their mouths. Their faces displayed a different reaction to what he was expecting. His father tried to pretend it was distasteful by wincing and holding back a gag. Xan ignored it.

His mother looked into the air for a few moments and squeezed her cheeks up under her eyes. Xan didn't know what that meant. The only thing he knew was that it was not the face he had on the ship.

His sister had a mess of confusion written across her brow. She chewed on it slowly as she tried to figure out what was happening.

Xan lost his sliver of pride. His face sank in disappointment as he looked at their expressions. He sat down beside Razan and picked a cube up himself and finished it all in one bite.

Tastes fine, he thought. *What the hell is their problem? Maybe they need to try it again. Second time'll help them figure it out.*

"Try another piece," he said.

His father crossed his arms and mumbled, refusing another try. His mother and sister took stabs at the two different pieces, giving them a sniff before they ate them. This time, they knew their faces were being scrutinised from across the table, so they put on a better show. His mother nodded her head as she tried to swallow and his sister did her best to hide her confusion.

"So?"

"I like this one," his mother said, pointing to the one she had just tried.

"Really?"

She put her hands together. "Yes."

His sister looked skeptical at the remaining cubes on the trays. "It's special," she said. "I can't decide if I like it or not though."

Xan waved his hands towards the table. "Try some wine, the flavours will open up."

They tried the wine with a squint. His sister shook after she took a sip.

Is it that bad? Really that bad?

He pointed towards the trays. "Try more cheese," he said.

His mother and sister did as they were told. He knew his mother didn't like it by the affirmative bobbing of her head.

"I guess it's better," his sister said.

Xan tried to keep up with conversation through the end of the meal, but it grew difficult with his head in a different place. He had thought for so long about how they would love real cheese, pairing it with wine especially. It was something to him. He thought they would feel the same way he did.

After some time, his parents left to get some rest, and his sister stayed to talk with him and Razan. Xan couldn't take his mind off the cheese. He wanted to follow the conversation, but the cheese tasting kept cropping up inside him. *They don't know how good it is. Give them a few months up here, and they'll come to appreciate it.*

Razan placed her index finger on the safe for a moment as a blue grid lit up around it. "It only works with a memory?"

"I looked it up," Ima responded. "The owner has to cry a tear to open it or something like that."

Razan eyed the safe. "So you unlock it with a tear?" she said.

Ima shrugged. "I guess? I don't understand how it works."

Xan shifted his focus to the safe. "There's no retina scan on it?"

"No," said Ima. "It locks with a memory of the item and then opens with a tear containing that memory."

"How the hell do you cry a memory tear?" he said. "I'm looking this stuff up. You're pulling my leg."

"Go ahead and look it up," she said. "You'll see."

Xan didn't feel like fiddling with his Vlex right then. Instead, he gulped down the last drops of wine in his glass. Then he reached over to stab another piece of cheese and poured himself another glass of wine.

"You know, dad bought this underground," Ima said. "He wouldn't tell me, but mom did. She said he went down there before we came."

Xan touched the flapping door of the safe. "That's how he was able to afford it. Probably stolen anyhow."

"Don't think of it that way," said Razan.

Ima glared at him. "Be grateful for what he's given you," she snapped. "He went to a great deal of trouble to get it for you."

Xan rolled his eyes. "Sorry. Jeez. I was just joking."

"That's must be easy for you, to treat this as a joke," she said. "Dad probably spent more credits than he has to buy the thing, not to mention risking his own safety down there. Not everyone can live the life you do. Not everyone can go around eating cheese and sipping wine all day."

She picked up her two-tined fork. "We don't all have credits to toss around like handfuls of sand. It must be so nice to own your own private apartment and to have your butler drive you everywhere. While the rest of us go back down to our dying planet with the other pack rats."

She tossed the fork onto the cheese tray and stood to her feet.

"Calm down," said Xan. "If you want to say here, you can. I planned on asking all of you, but I didn't get the chance. There's plenty of room and plenty of credits. If you want to live here, I've no problem with it."

Ima glared at him. "I don't need your sympathy nor your help. I'll go back down to Earth and rot with everyone else." She turned away from him and marched up the stairs, pausing halfway.

"Oh, and Xan, stop acting like you're this noble hero, trying to save us. A month's supply of cheese won't make our reality any less real." She snorted and went up the stairs, out of his sight.

Xan stared for a time and then brought his eyes back to the table. He pushed a few cubes along with his finger and then looked at Razan.

"Am I wrong here?" he said. "I'm trying to give them a good time."

Razan stood beside him, rubbing his back.

"Have I done something wrong? They can't even bother to act like they're enjoying their stay. How many people down there would die to get their hands on a piece of cheese? Or a sip of real wine?"

Razan kept her hand on his back. "I know," she said. "I know. It's all new to them. Keep that in mind. They've experienced nothing like this before. I think everyone needs to give the situation some time. Let it work itself out."

Xan felt like tipping the table over but restrained himself. *How ungrateful. Yet they call me the ungrateful one.*

Razan took his hand.

Offering them all this. All the wonderful things I have. They can't even pretend to like the cheese. Can't even act grateful for one damn second.

Xan glanced back at the safe sitting on the table with its door hanging open. *What the hell am I going to do with a safe? He only got it to show off. Probably the only expensive thing he could afford.*

"Are you okay?" she asked.

"Fine."

"What are you thinking?"

"Nothing."

Razan kept her eyes on him.

Xan saw her watching him and felt annoyed by it. "I'm tired," he said. "I'm not thinking anything. Just tired."

Xan opened the safe door a few times, allowing it to hang open. "I still don't even understand how this thing works," he said.

CHAPTER 29

Time went by faster than he had expected. Xan couldn't believe they were already packing to go back home. To him, it felt as if they had just arrived.

His family had warmed up slowly during their trip. They enjoyed their expedition up north. The ride was safe, and Mons was better than they had expected. The city-bred more research than business. It had a similar atmosphere to the farm. Xan wished that the farm was located up there instead of Meridien.

Xan had taken his family to see the interiors of the oldest atmosphere stations and the first Martian colony. The colony was nothing more than a small three-story city underneath a transparent dome. There was a plaque dedicated to its original citizens.

This plaque was erected in memory of all the brave souls who expanded the reach of humankind. May we always remember the sacrifices they made to bring us what we have today.

Their trip was short, however, and they left without getting to see most of the city. Xan did not want to leave so soon, but their return tickets did not allow them to stay longer.

Their trip north lay behind them as they settled back in. Then the day came when his family was all packed and ready to return to Earth. Xan sat on his bed, staring outside the window. The moment tasted bittersweet. On one hand, he wanted them to stay, and on the other, he didn't mind returning to his previous routine. He tried his best to focus on the new cheese they would be manufacturing by the end of the year.

The trip up north gave him the inspiration to start a supply route there. He wanted to invest in a transport vehicle to take his product to Mons and to bulk up his clientele. Deep down, he knew the only reason he thought so heavily of it was that he hoped to build another farm up there. He liked the idea of living in Mons where something different blew in the winds.

Xan kept his thoughts on that bright future. He would always be able to fly them back. They could always visit again. He had the credits. They could visit again. *They'll stay with me in Mons next time. We can spend the entire month up there. That's the plan.*

Razan shuffled inside the closet as he gazed out the window. Xan focused on the mountain ridges surrounding the city, his eyes trailing up and down the peaks and valleys.

"What do you think about hiking Mt. Tholus?" he said. "The thought keeps running through my head. We could take some time off for ourselves. It'd be fun."

Razan leaned out of the closet. "If you want to," she said.

"Yeah. We deserve it. We can do things, just the two of us. We don't need a whole group to have fun."

He jumped up from the edge of the bed and went over to the closet and kissed her on the cheek as he grabbed his clothes. "You know, I've been thinking about expanding business into Mons."

"Don't we already have exports going up there?"

"Yes, but not a set route. It's rather weak. I'll strengthen it. Did you see how many scientists were up there? They'd love cheese even if they don't know it yet. Who knows, one day I might even build a second farm up there."

Razan continued picking out her attire. "Sounds wonderful," she said. "It's relaxed. They don't run at the pace we do here."

"I thought the exact same thing. I was even thinking of buying a second home up there." Xan fixed his shirt and smiled at his future. He knew there was more to see and do. His family could always visit again.

* * *

Xan saw everyone waiting downstairs with their bags all packed. His father focused on his Vlex, and his mother sat at the table petting a bird. "You all seem ready," he said.

His father looked at him out of the top of his eyes. "Yes, and if we don't leave soon, we'll be late. God only knows when the next ship leaves this planet."

Xan swallowed his breath and then spoke quickly. "You don't have to leave," he said. "I've given it a lot of thought. If you all want to stay, I can help you find jobs and even get you a place to live. It's a good life here. Better than Earth. And I don't mind. I mean it."

His father sighed. He put his Vlex in his bag and stood from the couch. "It's a nice offer," he said.

"But?"

He looked his son in the eye. "We have a life back on Earth," he said. "So do you. I mean, none of us are meant to live up here. Not forever, that is."

His mother chimed in. "We thought you might ask. How can we be sure you'll stay here forever? What if you want to leave and return to Earth one day? We'd be too old to handle such a long trip, and then we'd all be stuck."

Xan felt a shot bursting through his ribs. His heart ticked with misguided intentions. It sank like an old piece of paper falling to the ground. He closed his mouth and said nothing more. His family went back to their bags and busied themselves with straps that had already been fastened.

Xan drifted into the kitchen and opened the fridge. He moved a few bottles back and forth and opened the sliding drawers as his eyes burned with anger. Then he slumped to the ground and beat his fist on the floor. He ripped up the rug underneath him and threw it across the kitchen.

"Sir?" said Zola behind him.

Xan turned to look at him. Zola held out his hand, lifting him up. He brushed the dust off his back and straightened his coat.

"Still haven't figured this out, I see," said Zola, as he fixed Xan's attire.

Xan snorted a laugh.

"I thought about scolding you for dirtying your clothes," said Zola. "But I'm not in the mood today."

"They were always in the back of my mind," he said. "When times were rough, the thought of helping them escape pushed me on."

Zola patted him on the shoulders. "You can offer a man the key, but you can't force him to leave his cell."

"No. Zola."

"People grow used to their situation and will fight to keep the status quo. No matter how much better the alternative might be."

Xan dug his fingers into his eyes then spat an angry growl.

"Everyone's ready, sir. Shall we?"

Xan rubbed his face and went out with Zola into the living room. "We're all ready then?" he asked.

Everyone nodded and went to the door. Razan stopped his mother, handing her an electric bird before she left. Zola drove through the red sands, leaving a trail of dust behind them. The rover stopped outside the spaceport, and they all got out. Xan helped his family with their bags and stood motionless by the sandrover.

"Thanks for having us," his father said, as he picked up his bag.

"It was very kind of you to do this for us," his mother said.

"Thanks for coming. You're always welcome back."

They kept their silence.

His mother and father turned and walked towards the entrance. They walked a few paces and then his father turned back with wide eyes. His head shook quickly. "No," he said. "No, no, no!"

His mother turned back to look. Ima held her bag and was standing near the sandrover with Xan. She didn't follow them up the ramp to the spaceport.

Their mother's eyes glistened. "You're staying?" she said.

Ima looked at Xan for affirmation. Xan nodded. "Of course," he said. "It's no problem."

Ima looked back at her parents. "Yes, I'm staying."

Their father glared at them both.

"There's nothing for me on Earth," she said. "What do I have to look forward to? The chance at getting married? Working in a factory every single day until I decide I'm ready to go? Or wait for the day when you both decided to leave forever."

Their father turned around, waving his hand behind his back. "You make your own damn decisions then," he said. "I'm tired of this shit. I'm so sick and tired of it!" He then whipped back to his son and thrust his finger at him. "You're poisoning this family you know? I hope you can live with that."

He marched into the spaceport and did not look back. Their mother walked a step closer to them. She looked them both in the eyes. "Good luck," she whispered. "Take care of each other."

They had never seen her cry before.

"I will," said Xan. "I promise."

His mother turned, following behind his father and disappearing into the crowd at the spaceport. The winds were calm outside. Nobody moved or spoke.

Xan finally looked at his sister. "You're stuck here now," he said with a fake laugh.

They drove back in silence, and they remained that way as they entered the apartment. Each of them sat on the couch, watching the spaceport from the window. As the hours went by, the ship burst into a fiery lift. The giant machine glided into the sky, and they each said their silent goodbyes. The ship pulled through the atmosphere, leaving a radiant glow behind.

"Bon voyage," Ima whispered.

"Bon voyage," said Xan.

Razan put her hand over his.

CHAPTER 30

Xan sat comfortably in his office, gazing at the shifting patterns in the orb, then at the enclosure below. The goats had started to gather at the door opening in their enclosure. A scientist stepped through, dragging a wheeled cart behind him. Bleats sounded one after the other as they tried to hop on top of the cart.

The scientist threw pieces of food out. They all rushed to the same spot. Xan smiled as he closed his eyes. He allowed his thoughts to drift into the nebulous cloud of sleep before him.

He woke up to a silent room. The lights were off. He lifted his head from the desk.

"Hello?" he called out.

No one answered but the echo from his own voice. Xan rubbed his face. The right side of his face felt numb from where he had slept on the desk. A crust of drool had formed at the corners of his lips.

Xan pulled a towel from the drawer and wiped his face. He peered over the cloth at the door before him. He stopped wiping. He couldn't take his eyes from the door. Xan put the towel down near his chest.

"Quinn?" he said. "Hello?"

A gentle rap sounded. A fleeting thought pattered in his head. He could only see the blue outlines of the door before him.

"Quinn?"

Xan pulled his Vlex out of his pocket. He tried to turn the lights back on. He looked over his head. "What's with this place?"

Darkness prickled at the tiny hairs on the back of his neck. He thumped his finger on his Vlex a few times, but the lights never returned. He glanced out the dark window to the main lobby. The giant orb was turned off. The orb never dimmed. Even at night.

Xan turned to the other window, overlooking the goats stirring in the dark.

"Quinn! Quinn?" Xan rushed to the door, waving his Vlex in front of it. Nothing moved. He put his Vlex up again. Nothing moved.

Xan jammed his fingers in the door crack, trying to pry the door open. It didn't budge. Letting go, he clenched his fists and pounded his fists on the door.

"Hello? Quinn? Hello?"

Xan ran to the window that overlooked the caves. He saw motionless boxes that contained fermenting milk, nothing out of the ordinary. "Calm down," he said. "Calm down."

Xan scrolled through his Vlex while his eyes flickered at the empty room. He couldn't keep his focus in one place. Shadows ran across the private room, tapping his shoulder as they moved.

Xan heard the goats bleat. He ran to the window to take a look. A dark figure sifted within the enclosure. Xan knocked upon the window. "Hello! Hello?" Murmurs crept through the glass as he watched.

"What are they doing?"

Xan grabbed his Vlex and started to message the head security officer. The goats shrieked. He looked down. The goats stirred even more. Xan continued typing on his Vlex. Then he looked at the door. He heard footsteps at the bottom of his staircase.

Click. Click. Click.

"Quinn?" he whispered.

Click. Click. Click.

Xan edged to the door and put his ear on the crack.

The heavy footsteps grew louder. *Click. Click. Click.*

"Can't be Quinn," he whispered.

A laugh bellowed outside his door. Several voices murmured amongst themselves and another laugh echoed through the stairs.

Xan backed away from the door. He raised his Vlex.

A blunt thud hit the door. Xan pressed the emergency button on his Vlex.

Another dull thud hit the door.

"Meridien Police Department. How may I assist you?"

The door shook.

"I'm at the cheese farm, and I think..."

The door broke open with a crack.

"Hello? Sir? Sir?" his Vlex called out.

Several dark figures stood in the sliver of the doorframe. "Hear something?" they whispered.

"Shhhh."

"Someone's in there."

A tube of light ignited. Xan stood, bathed in the light. His eyes narrowed in the beam, and to the side, he saw a man charging up his gun. Xan jumped as a blast snapped across the wall. He crawled on his hands and knees as shots ripped past him. He dove under the desk, listening for the shots to end.

"Put it down!" shouted one man. "You serious?"

Xan curled, trembling under the desk.

"Sorry there fella," a man said, with a snicker. "My pal's a bit dim is all. How about you come over here and have a word with us?"

He heard them murmuring to themselves.

"We can clear the air."

Xan tried to breathe as quietly as possible. He pushed further under the desk, listening to the quiet voices searching for him.

The light scanned over the desk. "Hey friend? Why not come out and answer a few questions for us?"

Their feet shuffled closer to the desk. Xan watched them gather one by one before him. The voices whispered. "Under the desk," he heard.

That voice, he thought. *I know that voice.*

The voice filtered through the silence. The chair ripped away from the desk and fell to the floor. Xan crawled further inside. He saw hands gripping underneath the table. The table flew up, exposing him on the floor. A laser was pointed at his head.

"Tell me something," said the man. "How does it feel living at the top of an unjust world?"

Xan felt a word slip out of his mouth. "Sven?"

The gun backed off his skull. It shook in the man's hand, then swung hard across his temple.

* * *

The sound of explosions forced Xan's consciousness to return. A sudden rush of hot wind blew past him. A pulse of three blasts fired over his head, and Xan threw his arms over himself.

A hand shoved him lower into the sand as another gust of heat exploded near him. A giant man pulled him back up and pushed him to the side of the building, throwing his body before Xan. Four more shots blitzed in the dark. The figure ducked quickly, then fired three blasts in return. Xan couldn't move. His vision could not focus.

Sandrovers roared to a halt as others vehicles peeled away from the scene. Screams of terror echoed in the distant. The figure turned around to face Xan. He lifted Xan's chin and touched his head. Xan spotted small fires dwindling in the sand. He tried to sit up but found it tough.

The figure held Xan's chest. "Try not to move," he said. "They'll be here soon. Hang tight."

Xan wanted to move.

"Stay still," said the guard. "They'll be here soon."

Xan tried to sit up.

The guard looked at him as if he were looking at a dead man. "Trust me, stay put."

Xan tried to sit up again. The guard beside him lifted his upper body and leaned him up against the building. Xan touched his head and felt a sharp pain. He looked at his hand and saw his fingertips covered in blood.

The man held him by the shoulder and moved his fingers away from his eyes, back down to his lap. "It's not that bad," he said. "You're going to be fine."

Xan tried to bring his hand back to his head, but the man pinned it down.

"Best not to touch it."

"Is it bad?"

The man hesitated. "Just needs some simple patching up."

"You're lying."

"What's your name?"

Xan choked up as he tried to speak. The man pushed him back against the wall.

"I'm Marc," said the man. "I've seen you leave the building at night."

Xan tried to look through the liquid that was blotting his eyes. The dark sky weaved into a mesh as he closed his eyes, clearing more drops from them. "Marc?" he whispered.

"That's it."

"Head guard?"

"No." He pulled a piece of cloth from his side and wrapped it around Xan's head. "It might sting, but I need you to stay still."

The guard wound the cloth tightly and then tied it off. Xan hissed at the throbbing pain.

"They're close."

"Sven," he said.

"Your name's Sven?"

"No... No. Sven."

"Right," said Marc. "Looks like they're heading this way now. That's them."

Xan wanted to touch his head, but he was afraid to get another handful of blood. His fingers trembled. His vision faded in and out, and his head bobbed on his weak neck.

The guard waved his arm in a giant arch as a few sandrovers approached. The guard turned over his shoulder, watching them come to a halt nearby. He took hold of Xan and looked him in the eye.

"Hold tight all right? I'm gonna go talk with these guys. I think they've brought medics. I'll be right back."

Xan wobbled. Marc ran to meet with them. People started rushing out of their vehicles. Loud shouts and deep voices howled near the sandrovers. He saw Marc waving his arms in the air and then pointing a few jabs towards him. A medic ran in his direction. They dropped their equipment beside him and drew out a tubular light.

A kind woman came to his side and placed her hands on the cloth wrapped at his head. "I'm going to take this off to have a look," she said. He felt her pulling the cloth back. Her eyes fixed on his wound. She placed the cloth back down and turned to her partner. "We should take him back," she whispered. "It looks serious."

* * *

A nurse entered the room to check the machines that were hooked up to him. She waved her Vlex in front of one them, and it beeped a few times. Then she moved to his bedside and touched the wrap on his head.

Xan grabbed the nurse by the wrist. "Where is she?"

The nurse pulled her arm away and rubbed her wrist. "Who?"

"Razan! Where is she?"

"I'm sorry?"

"Does she know? Did you tell her?"

Touching her lips, the nurse shook her head a little.

"Who else knows? Hurry!"

"I've told no one. Y-your family came by last night, but we couldn't let them in."

"Did you tell Ima?"

"You need your rest."

The nurse patted his chest, laying him back down. "Visiting hours are over, okay?"

"I know who did it."

"Okay."

"Listen! I know who did it!"

"I am."

Xan then wagged his finger at her. "Come here."

She took a hesitant step forward. Xan whispered through his numb lips.

The nurse moved closer. "Can you say that again?"

Xan struggled to get the words off his fat tongue. "Tell them I'm okay," he said. "And that I know who did it."

CHAPTER 31

Razan held his arm, refusing to let him leave. "Why do you need to go there right now?" she said. "Wait a few days. They can figure it out themselves."

Xan tugged his arm, trying to get out of her vice grip. "I'm fine," he said. "I have to check out the damages. They'll need me to approve the renovations, anyway. I don't want to hold us back any longer."

Razan clung tight.

"Seriously. I'll be fine. Zola will take me there. You can go with me too if you'd feel better about it."

She loosened her grip, letting his sleeve drop from her fingers. "The doctor said you should rest a few more days."

Xan struggled to put on his boot.

"You can't even put your shoes on properly!"

Xan fumbled with the strings. "I'm fine," he said.

"Zola. Don't let him out of your sights."

"Yes, ma'am."

Zola went to Xan, fixed his laces for him, then stood him up.

Xan stumbled. "Zola will take good care of me," he said. "No need to worry."

"Don't stay out long. See the farm and then come back here to rest. Otherwise, you might find yourself back in that hospital."

"Okay."

Zola drove Xan to the farm and helped him out of the machine. He stayed by his side, making sure Xan didn't tumble over.

Xan eyed the disheveled farm. Black streaks raced along the exterior of the dome. He touched one of the marks and rubbed the grit between his fingers. The atmosphere was somber as people walked about, assessing the damages.

Xan walked towards the entrance, holding the walls along the way. Inside, he saw the giant orb shattered above the lobby. Black streaks adorned the walls, like remnants of a past war. He felt his heart skip with rage as he walked through the farm. All the workers moved about slowly, not noticing him wobble through the lobby.

His assistant approached him as he entered the hallway that led to his office. Quinn rushed to meet him from the other end of the hall. "Thank god you're alive," he said, holding Xan's hand in both of his. "They're barbarians!"

Xan hummed. *It's not you they want. No one leaves the moon circle without paying their dues.*

Quinn placed another hand on his arm. "How are you feeling?" he said. "Shouldn't you be getting your rest? You didn't have to come here today."

Xan glared at the black marks singed into the walls. "It's more stressful being away," he said though his teeth.

Quinn's eyes bounced up and down, stopping at the medical cloth wrapped around his head. His eyes wanted to peel it back and gaze upon the damage. Xan hissed as his head throbbed.

"Why don't you take a seat?" said Quinn.

Xan waved his hand in the air. "Just help me upstairs."

Quinn looked at Zola. "I'm not sure."

"Just get me up there!"

Zola nodded to Quinn and then fixed his hold on Xan. Quinn slowly opened the passage up to Xan's office and led them upstairs.

Xan's lips quivered when he stepped inside. His desk remained flipped over, with large gashes on its legs. Two windows had been shattered, and small glass pieces lay upon the floors. He stood amongst the shambles of his office, feeling broken with it. He walked over to his desk and saw a giant scar across its surface. He leaned down to touch it, running his finger inside the ridge.

Xan got back to his feet, supporting himself with the overturned desk. He went over to the window and looked down into the goat enclosure. He noticed splashes of blood lining the walls. He almost put his hand on the window seal, but Zola caught him before he gripped the reaming shards in the frame. The goats huddled in a corner of the farm, shaking amongst each other as they watched the door.

Xan ambled to the stairs, and Zola rushed to his side. They went down in silence. When they reached the ground level, Xan continued walking towards the lobby.

"I'm going home now," he said.

"Perhaps that's best," said Quinn.

He left the wrecked building. Zola helped him into the sandrover and Xan took a final glance at the place. Zola started up the engine.

"Wait," he said. "Hold on. Give me a minute."

Xan climbed out. "Wait here, I'll be right back."

He walked towards a guard looking around the perimeter. "Marc," he said. "Marc?" Xan stopped in his tracks and turned.

"Sir?" he heard.

Looking over his shoulder, Xan saw the guard running towards him.

"I told you it wasn't that bad," he said with exasperation. "You're all right?"

Xan touched his forehead. "Yeah," he said. "I owe you some thanks."

"No, no," he said. "We were both lucky that night. If I had stuck to my normal route..." He paused. "God only knows."

"Let me repay you," said Xan. "You tell me what you want."

The guard spouted a nervous laugh. "You don't need to do that," he said. "I was protecting myself too. If I hadn't taken a leak out back..."

Xan rubbed his head. "Still, if you hadn't found me..."

The guard looked up at the wrap on his forehead as he picked at his teeth. "A slice of cheese?"

"Take a wheel."

"Thank you."

The two men stood in silence for a minute.

"They're getting brave these days," said Marc. "Even up north."

Xan didn't respond. *Don't say that.*

Marc turned over his shoulder to look at the sun-weathered domes lining the hills.

Xan glanced that way too. "Did you ever live out there?"

"No, I've always been in a company flat."

Xan exhaled. "You're lucky then," he said.

The guard nodded. "I guess we both are."

Xan pushed sand under his boot, unearthing a fragment of clouded glass.

Marc noticed the heated glass. "You should keep to the daylight from now on," he said.

Xan kicked the glass over. "I can't do that. I leave most nights after dark."

Marc shook his head and squinted his eyes. "It's not smart."

"Duty calls."

Marc cleared his throat. He then spoke in a very low tone. "Maybe you should find a way to keep safe then?"

Xan looked him in the eye and then back at the others moving around the farm. "Bodyguards are too expensive."

"No, not that."

"Then what do you suggest?"

Marc raised his eyebrows. "I'm not suggesting anything," he said, tapping at his side. "You seem trustworthy, but you never know who you're talking with."

"Go ahead," said Xan. "You can talk."

Marc laughed as he kept patting at his side. "All I'm getting at here is that there are ways," he said. "You don't have to bring it all to light, but I'm sure you'll understand."

Xan looked at his nervous patting. He saw the guard touching his gun and thought about owning one for a second. The guard cleared his throat.

Xan felt a hot surge burn through his face.

"Oh," he said. "Oh?"

The guard gave a slight nod.

Xan rubbed the wrap around his head and then put his hand over his eyes to block the sun. "You know how to make it happen?"

The guard turned over his shoulder again. "There are circuits within the city," he said.

"How do you know?"

"Old tick of mine from the war," he said. "Everyone has things that make them feel safe, right?"

Xan scratched at his nose and glanced over at Zola watching him. "I can't be seen with any of this," he said.

The guard put his head down and then looked back up. "I have access to the entire building," he said. "Just check the bottom drawer of your desk one day."

Xan bit at his upper lip. "I'll make sure you get a nice bonus this quarter," he said.

"That sounds fair."

Xan made a pivot. The guard stopped him. "It's tough to get anything modern," he said. "Plus you don't want that kind of thing around. An older model works just as well."

"I don't care," he said. "I'd like to feel safe is all."

Marc nodded his head and shook Xan's hand. "Take some time to rest. Everything'll be in order by the time you're back."

Xan shook his hand. "Thanks."

The guard turned away and went up to the farm where some other guards congregated. Xan slowly walked back to the sandrover and pulled himself inside.

Zola watched him with caution. "Who was that?" he said.

Xan grit a piece of sand in his teeth. "The guard who saved my life."

CHAPTER 32

The investigator drained his cup of coffee, set the mug on the table, then reached in his jacket for an electric cigarette. Holding the stick near his lips, he paused.

"I'm sorry," he said. "I'm having a difficult time understanding. You had a nurse send a message saying you knew who this person was? You even told the guard who saved your life the person's name."

"I was heavily drugged at the time," said Xan.

The investigator kept his eyes emotionless. "Why would you tell these people you knew who did it?" he said. "Even if you were drugged or knocked over the head?"

Xan shook his head with his mouth tightly knit.

The investigator sighed out a cloud of vapour. "There's no point in covering anyone's ass here. We'll find out."

You'll kill him, he thought. *He couldn't even do that to me. I know how you people are.*

Xan rubbed the wrap on his head. "I'm not trying to stick with anything," he said. "Like I said before, I don't remember it very well."

Xan pulled the wrap up, showing the investigator a large mangled scar on his head. "Tell me that you could take one of these and still think straight. Tell me you wouldn't say nonsense on pain killers or in the midst of gunfire? There was someone I'd held a grudge against for a while, and I'm not sure if I made him up in that moment or not."

The investigator sat up straight and looked Xan in the eyes. "Let's have the name then? I'll check him out. If he's innocent, then you've got nothing to worry about."

Xan stared into his eyes and then back at the floor. *They'll find something on him*, he thought. *They'll kill him anyhow. Even if he's innocent.*

He shook his head. "I can't."

The investigator shot a mist out his nose. "You won't," he said. "Come on. One of your workers? An old friend or something?"

"A figment of my imagination."

The investigator laughed. "Being tight-lipped only makes an investigator bite down even harder. It only incites more curiosity." He caught Xan's eye. "I'm trying to be nice here. I get who you are."

Xan stayed silent. *I almost hit him with my vehicle*, he thought. *He wanted to beat me, but he didn't know it was me. He didn't even realise it was me the other night either until I said his name.*

The man rubbed his forehead wrinkles. "You're putting more work on me," he said. "But at least I know where to start now."

The investigator put his cigarette back and went to the door. He paused in the middle of the doorframe, tapping his fingernails on it, quickly and then very slowly. His eyes turned to Xan with a sly look and grin.

"I'd never thought about it," he said. "Cheese would be a perfect cover. You've got a lot of caves in that place. What couldn't you hide there?"

Xan drew in a deep breath and let it back out with annoyance.

The investigator narrowed his eyes on him. "Do you know what people have done in those shoddy domes up the hill?"

Xan didn't look at him. "What?"

The investigator smiled even more. "They dig out caves inside them," he said. "To store things they don't want others to see. Let me tell you, the other day we found one filled with everything you need to make a strong batch of Vasitinmine."

Xan shook his head. "I'm sorry?"

The investigator stopped again, fixing his eyes on Xan. "It's a new drug," he said. "Thought you might've heard of it."

"Please leave me alone," said Xan. "I'm trying to pull my life back together and fix up my business. We lost a huge portion of cheese, they destroyed our lobby, and they killed two of our best goats. So if I'm not in the most friendly of moods, then draw your own conclusions."

The investigator went through the door frame into the hall. He turned back to smile at Xan. "See you around," he said.

Xan sat stiffly in his seat for a few moments. He stood up, shaking from the nervous tension that had dammed up within himself.

"Bastard."

They sat on the couch watching a mild sandstorm rustle the world below them. The sun reflected its rays off each little grain of sand.

"Why didn't you tell him?" Razan asked.

"I couldn't do it."

Tiny pelts of sand hit the window and slid around the circular glass.

Razan eyed him from the other side of the couch. "You saw him," she said. "You were so certain in the hospital. I believe you, and so does everyone else. What good do you gain from lying?"

"Sven's a hot-head. He's dumb, impulsive, bitter. They all acted that way when they broke in. What if I merely filled in the blanks in my head that night?"

"You don't believe that. You told me."

"But what if it wasn't him?" he said. "If I sent that hound after him and he came out clean, then he'd really come back for the kill."

Xan held an imaginary gun to his head and pulled the trigger.

Razan glared at him. "Don't," she said. "He didn't spare your life."

Xan touched the wrap on his head. "The gun was right in my face," he said. "And when I said his name, that hot barrel lifted off my forehead, and well, it felt like I was being spared."

Razan looked out the window with her brow furled.

"You don't know how they treat people who have been suspected of crimes," he said. "I told you about my drug test. Imagine if someone had suspected that I was a real terrorist?"

A goose waddled at Razan's feet. She crossed her arms and stayed silent. The sands built into a giant plume outside. The winds covered the glass before them like a kaleidoscope turning over and over.

***

The farm slowly reverted to its original shape. The orb hadn't been replaced, but the remaining glass shards hanging from the ceiling were gone. Xan was happy to see the scientists wasting no time in replacing their lost goats. Two of the surviving females were now pregnant, and it was only a matter of time before the farm was whole again.

Xan no longer wore the wrap. He displayed the scar without shame. Ima told their parents about what had happened. He didn't care to hear what they had to say, so he asked her to keep it between themselves.

His sister grew weary of living on Mars after the incident. He and Razan did their best to reassure her it was a fluke. Mars was a safe place, safer than Earth.

Xan settled into his office at his old desk. He couldn't get past the large scratch they had left in it. Every time he sat down, he touched the deep groove, and then pulled away from the desk, feeling the scar left on his head.

He took his hand away from the mark and went back to the desk. He tapped on it for a few moments, trying to gather his focus into a plan of action, but found it difficult to regain his old steam. Every time he tried to get into the flow, he ran into a still lake of death. He didn't know why his mind had become an obstacle course to him.

Xan opened his drawers with little thought. He opened them as if the answer to his problems would sit there, like a bag of magical energy he could rub on his hands to get work flowing again.

Xan opened the bottom drawer and quickly shut it back. He waited. His hand remained on the drawer's handle. He looked around his office for a second then hopped out of his chair and kneeled to the floor. He cracked open the bottom drawer again to reveal a silver weapon inside.

Xan felt a surge of power as he had never felt before. A lustful desire took over him, making him weak to it, yet strong with it. His pulse increased, his mind telling him to pick it up.

Xan touched the old handle and then looked around his office again. He kept the weapon inside the drawer, not daring to pull it out into the open. The gun slipped into his hand like how an old friend slips into one's life again. There was no awkward song and dance—they both knew their places.

He turned the weapon over in his hands, giving it a good scan. It was like no gun he had ever seen before. He knew it couldn't be a laser from the design. Xan placed it back into the drawer and ran his finger along the barrel to the cylindrical midsection. Xan lifted it just enough to spin the round cylinder, listening to the metal clicks.

His heart raced out of control as he finally pulled away from it. He shut the drawer and sat back in his seat. His face was flush as he looked around like a nervous man returning home after an illicit affair. It felt so good, but he was well aware of the consequences of what he had done.

He tried to focus on something else to keep his mind occupied. An item of business came to him. He clicked away at his desk, flashing a large projector on his wall. He looked at the list that he made a few days prior.

Expanding to Mons.

Possible Cheese farm up north.

Apartment prices in Mons City.

Xan felt that desire surging again. His focus dripped through the crack left in his skull. The small drips accumulated and soon drowned out his mind. It felt safe again.

CHAPTER 33

Xan entered the apartment to find his sister and Kane discussing aquatic creatures around the most recent installment in the flat.

"Hello," said Xan.

His sister kept her face near the blue aquarium as Kane pulled back to say hello.

"Did you know your Astacoidea is moulting?"

Xan shook his head with a bewildered stare.

"Moulting," said Kane. "Shedding its old exoskeleton."

Xan went over to the aquarium to see what he was talking about. He saw his little blue crayfish shedding out of his old pale-brown shell. "Is it okay?" he asked.

"Sure. Your water is soft enough so there shouldn't be any problems."

"This is normal?"

"Yes," said Kane. "They all do it. When they grow, they shed their old shell to harden into something new."

Xan bent down further to look into the aquarium. "So he's getting a new set of clothes?"

Kane raised his brow. "It's not that easy for him," he said. "He must be careful when he leaves his old shell. His new one won't harden for a few days, and during that time, he'll go into hiding until he feels safe in his armour once again. It's all very serious for him. Equating this process to changing into a new set of clothes is belittling, considering how important this new exoskeleton is to his survival."

Xan watched the little crayfish work out of its shell. Kane tapped on the tank near the crayfish. Xan backed away from the aquarium and fell into the couch.

"Did they ever find the people responsible for attacking your farm?" Kane asked.

"No."

Xan took out his Vlex and opened up the news.

"Did you hear about the wine store being robbed up north?" Kane asked.

"No."

"It sounded very similar to your incident."

The news feed spoke to the room with a monotonous hum. Xan caught a few words during his conversation with Kane. Something about Mons and a wine store.

"They killed your goats," said Kane. "Do you think they planned on eating them?"

Xan thought about the poor goats crying out for help, squealing for someone to save them.

"They left them to bleed in their enclosure," he said.

Kane hummed to himself as he thought. "It doesn't seem to be about money then. It's more like spitting in someone's face."

Xan thought of the man who spat at his sandrover as he re-entered the city years ago. He knew that man too.

"...killing the store owner," said the news feed.

Xan turned it off and let out a large bitter sigh from his chest.

"Everything looks to be in order," said Kane. "Mick and I are going for drinks later. Would you like to join?"

"No," said Xan. "Not tonight. I've got a lot on my mind."

"Could be the recharge you need."

Xan sat up to look at Kane. "Nah, the only charge I need is rest."

Kane nodded. "Okay then."

After some time Kane slowly went towards the door. Xan turned away and looked out the window at the twinkling city lights.

Kane stopped to chat with Ima before he left. The two of them spoke in a low whisper near the door. Xan tried to catch bits of their conversation.

"Might be able to teach you," said Kane. "I could use another assistant, even if it's for a season. I'll let you know when the next shipment arrives. My brother sent me a rare species of fish that's said to be extinct."

Ima eyed him. "How did he find it?"

Kane smiled as the blue light shone upon his white eyes. "They found an old fossil in one of their excavations and took it to their research lab in Kofu."

Xan let out a cough as he watched more lights switching on in the city.

Ima looked back at her brother and then to Kane.

"I'd like to hear more later," she whispered. "Thanks for coming over. I didn't know about the moulting."

Kane hesitated for a moment and then opened the door.

"Shall I ask Zola to drive you back?" said Xan.

"No. I'll use the tunnel."

"It's safer than walking alone at night," said Xan, sounding more abrasive than he had meant to. He quickly looked at his sister and saw her reaction. "I mean, until all these things blow over," he said. "As they always do."

Kane held his hand on the door frame. "I'll be fine," he said. "I don't believe any of our terrorist friends will be down there, unless they're high earners."

"If you're sure," said Xan.

"Positive."

Kane looked at Ima and said something more before he slipped out of the house. The room basked in the gentle patter of the aquarium's filter babbling on top of the water. Ima shut the door and went towards the stairs. Xan continued staring out the window.

"Are you interested in aquatic life now?" Xan said without looking at Ima.

She paused on the steps. "I'm curious about it, sure."

"It's safe working at the farm you know? Don't let that random blip throw you off track."

She moved down next to the aquarium, bathing herself in the low blue light.

"I'm not worried about that," she said. "I happen to like sea creatures. There's something cute about them."

Xan glanced at the moulting lobster in the tank. "You might take a pay cut if you work over there," he said.

She touched the aquarium with her finger. "I'll just bum off you then."

"What if you don't like it?"

"Then I'll ask you for my old job back."

Xan let out a large sigh and lay down on the couch.

* * *

The night ran long as he waited for Razan to return. Every moment felt like a needle in his back. She had sent him a message an hour ago that she would be late. Zola left to pick her up, but it was taking too long.

The door slid open to a bright hallway. Razan slipped through the opening.

"What happened?" he asked.

"Another strike," she said.

Zola closed the door behind them and clicked the extra lock up near the top.

"What do they want this time?"

"Same thing," she said. "They want a tunnel dug out so they can crawl under the city to work. There was another worker killed in a sandstorm last week. He didn't want to wait it out at his factory, and well…"

"It was their choice," he said. "Not much you can do about that."

Razan shook her head, guilt glistening in her eyes. She stood in the blue light of the aquarium looking at the tank and then moved over to the couch with him.

"The owners won't allow us to build them a tunnel," she said. "It's not that I'm trying to punish them, it's just a fact. They won't give me the budget for a tunnel. And I don't have enough to pay for their fares."

The aquarium hummed in between the silent notes with its soft laps. The little crayfish was gone, now that it shed its shell. Razan pinched her eyes shut. A parrot landed on her shoulder, and she rubbed its chest.

"I want both sides to sit down and chat," she said. "Not tug me between them."

"If only it were that simple."

"It is that simple," she said. "Invest in your workers. Stop pinching from people who earn nothing!"

Xan watched her.

"I'm getting sick of this. From both of them!"

"Is there anything I can do?"

Razan sighed. "Talk with Sioux or point that investigator in the right direction."

* * *

Xan sat in his office overlooking the goats in their enclosure. Mick sat at the large table with him, sampling cheese.

"They won't put up with it for long," said Mick. "The government's getting tired of them. One of the murder stories reached Earth, so now they're really locking down. They don't want their Martian colony to look bad."

"Try this one," said Xan, pointing to a cube of cheese.

Mick stabbed it with his little fork and threw it in his mouth. He looked through the window down at the goats. "Is that the pregnant one?"

Xan followed the finger that was pointing to a goat with a larger belly.

"That's her," he said.

"Sorry to hear about your other ones."

"Nothing we can do about it now."

Mick coughed with his fist over his mouth. "They haven't caught the guys yet?"

"No."

Conversation grew flat. The dull drumming of sour topics slid their words across the room.

"Have you had any problems with your sandrovers?" Xan asked.

"No. They're fine. Not a tyre stolen."

Xan smiled, then glanced at his Vlex. No return message from Sioux.

"Have you seen the latest model?" said Mick.

"No."

"They've brought back the old vintage look with upgraded traction," said Mick. "You should have a look. It reminded me of the advertisements I used to watch as a kid."

"I'll check it out."

"You should think about getting one," said Mick. "They're a lot of fun out by the sand dunes."

"Our flat only allows us to store two at a time," he said.

"You can use our storage house," said Mick. "We've still got plenty of space. It's not that much to keep it there. It looks like an old shoddy dome, but it does the trick."

Xan looked at the pregnant goat digging in the sand with her hoof. "How about you let me try it out first? Then I'll decide."

Mick laughed. "I already know your decision then."

Looking at him, Xan grinned. Then after glancing at his Vlex again, he sighed.

* * *

Xan ate his dinner as he watched the pedestrians struggle with the winds. Tiny people swayed back and forth, grabbing their coats around their chests.

"They found a bunch of them about two kilometres out from the city," his sister said. "They had weapons too. A few people died. All over some stolen vehicles."

Xan heard the trepidation in her voice. He knew her true thoughts no matter what she said. He suppressed a lump of guilt that was rising in his throat. Mars wasn't a dangerous place. He wouldn't tell her to stay if he thought so himself.

"People die every day on Earth," he said. "They have monthly bombings. It's overcrowded with miserable people. And not to mention the perpetual smog that hangs in the air."

Ima went quiet as she poked at her food. Razan glanced up from her food, looking between them, and then focused on Ima.

"It's not a normal occurrence up here," said Razan with a soft voice. "Even I'm a little concerned."

Xan swished the back of his hand in the air. "It'll blow over like it always does," he said. "There's no need to worry. If it should bother anyone, it should be me. I was attacked. But I still go about my business like normal. Either the high-ups will cave, or the government will handle the strikers. Let it work itself out."

I could've pointed them in the right direction, he thought. *Go check out what happens when there's a full moon out. You might get whiffs around there.*

Xan tossed his fork onto his plate. Ima looked up at him. Razan did the same. Xan wiped his mouth and turned away from their stares. They all went back to their meals, and Xan picked his fork back up and wiped it on his napkin. Ima took small bites from her dish, and Razan stayed quiet.

Why didn't you tell the authorities about them? floated through the air.

I ask myself the same question, he thought. *But I can't be sure it was him.*

"Safety is such an important thing," said Razan. "If the plant owners won't cave, then the other side should. For everyone's sake."

CHAPTER 34

Xan ignored his Vlex as he grew tired of hearing the news it brought him. If it wasn't another crime taking place, it was a new government regulation being introduced. He sat inside his little office, pent up with frustration. The name sat at the tip of his tongue. Saying the name was all it took. Sven. That's the guy.

A knock sounded upon his door.

"Yes?"

Quinn entered and stood pulling at his coat nervously. "You're not checking your Vlex?" he said.

Xan shook his head like a miserable old man. "No, not right now."

Quinn raised his eyebrows and his forehead wrinkled. "The authorities are coming here to check the building today," he said.

"Let them."

Quinn refused to move. His face held a twinge of frustration.

"Is that fine?" he said. "You're certain the authorities can come into this building and search every room right here and now? Nothing out of the ordinary?"

Xan stopped what he was doing to look at Quinn. He didn't know what this was about.

"Quinn," he said. "Is there something you want to say?"

Quinn looked at his fingernails for a moment and then straightened his sleeves along the cuff.

"No nothing wrong," he said. "I just wanted to make sure that you're okay with a thorough inspection of this building."

"Yes. I've already said so. What time are they coming?"

Quinn took in a deep breath and let it slowly out. "Any time now."

Xan went back to his business and tried to ignore him standing there.

Quinn walked closer to his desk and touched his index finger on the edge. Xan looked at the finger. Then Quinn slid his finger along the scar in the desk.

"I'm not one to pry in anyone's business," he said. "I don't know how I'd feel if someone burst into my office and left a giant gash upon my head."

Xan looked at Quinn's finger running along the desk. The recollection of that night was still fresh in his mind. He felt paralysed in his chair. His breath contracted in small waves.

"Quinn, I don't know what you're getting at," he said, putting his hand up. "But please stop. You're making me uncomfortable."

Quinn looked at Xan, trying to speak through his eyes. Xan closed his eyes and clenched his teeth.

The men breaking into the room. The table flipping over. His heart slammed against his ribs. Xan touched the bottom drawer, reaching for the shiny weapon. He felt safe again.

Xan took a large breath and looked at Quinn and then the illegal weapon in his desk. Quinn nodded to him.

"Oh," he said.

Quinn took his finger off the gash and then moved away from the desk.

Xan pushed his chair back. "Quinn," he said. "I'm going to take the day off. Can you handle the inspection?"

"I understand," he said. "I'm only here to help."

Xan kneeled to the floor near the bottom drawer.

Quinn gave him a smile and walked to the door. "We'll see you tomorrow then," he said.

Xan nodded as he pulled the gun out of his drawer. He felt the destructive power in his hands. An image flashed in his mind of his leg being blown apart by an accidental trigger pull. He stopped and moved with purpose and caution. He held the gun with care as he placed it in his bag.

Xan rushed out the door and down the stairs. As he entered the main lobby, he saw the workers bustling in preparation. He left the farm and cranked up his rover, casting sand into the air as he drove off.

Xan spotted a few sandrovers crawling towards the farm as he drove in the opposite direction. A wave of heat overtook him. He felt the weapon in his vehicle sending out a beacon of its presence. He felt that every person he passed somehow knew the power lying in the seat beside him. It taunted him with its strength, gloating to all around him the damage it could inflict. That tiny little trigger easily pulled by a small hand could take down a giant.

Xan touched his bag and felt its aura consuming him. He did not dare to think of what would have happened if the investigators found it in his desk drawer or on one of his workers. The possession of such old weapons would make him a suspect of terrorist activities.

Xan took his bag into the apartment.

"Back so soon?" said Zola as he entered.

Xan patted his bag a few times then moved his hand off it. "Yes. We're having inspections at the farm today. I have an item they might not like to find."

Zola lifted his brow as he scanned the bag. "Will it be any safer here?"

"Yes. No one will check here. The farm is a big operation. They won't bother with our flat."

Xan turned to go upstairs into his room. His Vlex buzzed all the way up. He went to the closet and gently placed the bag down near a lump in the corner. Xan pulled out his Vlex to see the messages from Quinn pleading for his attention.

Head investigator wants to speak with you. Told him you went home. He is headed there now. Bringing a team with him.

"Shit."

The doorbell rang downstairs. Beads of sweat heated his body as he froze in place. He rushed to the top of the stairs and motioned towards Zola, approaching the door. Zola stopped and gave him a nod and then a look of frustration.

Xan rushed back into the closet. He heard the bell ring again. He pulled out the gun and looked around the closet. He felt his neck slipping into a noose. Drifting one step into jail with every second that passed.

The door opened downstairs. He heard the voice of the investigator that he had spoken to earlier mumbling to Zola. Xan noticed the lump in the corner. It was the safe his father had given him. He opened its flapping door and placed the weapon inside. He kept pushing on the door, trying to close it. Every time it shut, the door slipped open again.

"Just shut you bastard!"

"He's upstairs," he heard Zola say. "Not feeling well..."

Xan tried to look up the instructions on his Vlex, but there was no time. He did all he could to hold the door flush and make it close. Footsteps were echoing up the stairs towards his room.

Xan held the safe with tears welling in his eyes. He held his hand on top of the safe as he imagined everything he had worked for being taken away, all because of the gun.

Then a bright blue grid flashed across the safe in a maze of lines, blinding him as it illuminated the dark closet. Xan watched in awe as the door shut itself. A few clicks sounded and then the blue grid faded. The safe went silent. Its doors were shut tight.

Xan heard the voices coming closer to his room. He rushed out of the closet and into the adjacent bathroom.

"Hello sir?" said Zola. "There's someone here to see you."

"Okay. One moment. In the bathroom."

"One moment please," said Zola to the investigator.

Xan made noises inside the toilet and then headed out to meet with the group. He saw the investigator he had met with before. The man's eyes had grown darker since their last meeting.

"Taking off from work?" he grumbled.

Xan touched his forehead. "My head gave me some trouble today."

The investigator scanned the room. There were two people behind him, carrying small devices in their hands.

"Convenient day to take off," he said. "How's your memory recently? Anything come into focus?"

"Still a blur."

The investigator nodded his soulless face.

Xan didn't like standing in the doorway between his bedroom. "Should we take this downstairs?"

"Sure," said the investigator, turning to his assistants behind him.

They all went down the stairs and sat at the table.

"You know we're searching the farm today under our recent stipulation," said the investigator.

"I'm aware of that," said Xan.

The investigator linked his fingers together. "You haven't always worked at the farm have you?"

Xan swallowed his breath. "No."

The man grinned. "That's right," he said. "I had a look at your record the other day. It's interesting you know? You used to work at one of those factories. Used to be with all the others. Probably made a lot of friends while you were out there?"

"We mainly kept to ourselves."

"I don't believe that. You're telling me you didn't make any friends? That can't be right. You worked there for more than a year. That's hard to believe."

"Have you ever worked in a factory?" said Xan.

"Well, no, but where there are people, there are friends to be made."

"Then you wouldn't know."

The investigator raised his eyebrows and went back to his comfortable position. He watched Xan with a cold stare.

"The farm's a nice place," he continued. "From a criminal standpoint, it'd be the perfect cover for almost anything. Especially if the head of the place has his roots in the factories."

Xan moved to the edge of his seat and sat up straight. "Do you have something to say? If you want to be a bigot, then that's your business but don't confuse it with your duty. Give me the same respect you would anyone else."

The inspector grinned even more. "Touchy today," he said. "You wouldn't mind if we scanned this place? If you've nothing to hide, then there'll be no issue."

Xan looked at the assistants waiting to search his home. Zola kept his face blank as he watched the events unfold. "And if I said no?"

"Then we'd do it anyway. We have the right."

"Fine. Go ahead."

The investigator gave his assistants a nod, and they went about scanning the room.

"For my peace of mind," the investigator said.

"Sure."

The assistants scanned blue beams over the rooms, leaving no nook or crease untouched. Their instruments rang with tiny beeps as they went along the different areas. Xan watched them search his flat.

The investigator kept his eyes on him. "Did you hear about the latest incident?"

"I'm sorry?"

"The factory you used to work for - you haven't heard? One of their housing domes had a cellar full of weapons. The police found it yesterday."

Xan pursed his lips and crossed his arms with disinterest.

The investigator scratched the side of his head. "Now why would these factory workers need such weapons? Can you tell me? Maybe they're some of your old chums?"

Xan shook his head in the most casual way he could. "I wouldn't know," he said. "There's a reason I wanted to move up in life."

The assistants were going up the stairs leading to his room. Xan eyed them and brought his gaze back to the investigator.

The investigator raised his eyebrows. "No dirty laundry up there?"

"Zola keeps the place clean."

"You never know. There are plenty of people who don't know how to wash up."

Xan kept quiet.

"You ever seen a place consumed by mould?"

Xan looked upstairs again. "No," he said.

"It always catches you by surprise. It doesn't grow well in the sunlight, so it flourishes anywhere that's dark and damp. Disgusting stuff, like a festering moss."

Xan nodded his head and tried to look him in the eye, but his vision was not his priority. He focused on listening to every step they made upstairs.

"The places no one goes is where it'll be," said the investigator. "That's how it builds up right under your nose. Nobody thinks to look there."

Xan listened to their footsteps coming from his bedroom. He held onto every little noise, thinking each one meant something grave. The footsteps stopped.

"If you don't catch it quickly, it'll spread like a disease," the investigator said.

The footsteps started again. He heard them moving towards the stairs. The investigator stopped talking for a moment and glanced at the top of the stairs. He waved for them to come down and stood from his seat.

"Let's see what we have here," he whispered.

Xan saw them carrying his safe down the steps, each holding onto one end. His heart fell through the ground. Poison seeped into his bones, filling his innermost marrow with ice. His mouth was dry as he watched the assistants set the safe on the table.

"We can't get a reading on it," said the assistant. "I've never seen one like this before."

The investigator circled it like a buzzard. He grunted from every vantage point. Then he stopped to stare at Xan. Xan shrugged his shoulders.

The investigator tapped on the safe. "Let's look inside," he said.

"I don't know how it works," said Xan. "I accidentally locked it with nothing inside."

The investigator's eyes turned into slits. "Rubbish. Get over here and open it up."

Xan marched over to it and tapped on the safe. "I'm telling you, I don't know how to use it. My father gave it to me as a gift."

The investigator held out his hand for the assistant to give him the scanner. She placed it in his hand, and he moved it towards the safe. The scanner shone a bright blue light over it and then let out three fast beeps. The investigator looked down at the scanner and growled.

"Find out how to open this thing," he yelled at the other assistant.

Xan could feel the gun inside. He could hear it talking to him through the safe. They must have felt it too. The power that radiated from its hollow core.

"Hans-Kauffman safe," said the assistant. "Using the latest in cutting-edge technology, making the safe impossible to crack."

The investigator scratched the side of his face. "Excuse me?"

"Impossible to open."

"Bollocks, every safe has its crack. Now tell me what is it? Retina? Fingerprint? Come on!"

"A tear? Hold on," the assistant paused as she looked through her Vlex. "Okay. So the safe is locked by a memory of the item? Wait. I'm not sure how this works. Hang on. Then it says to open it, you have to cry a tear containing the memory of the item?"

The investigator sighed. "Is this a joke?"

"No," said the assistant.

"Not you," he said. He pointed at Xan. "You!"

Xan held his hands open. "No. I told you I don't even know how it works. It closed on its own. There's nothing inside."

"How about you give us a tear then," said the investigator. "I want to see this nothingness with my own eyes. Come on now. If nothing's in there, then any kind of tear will be fine."

Xan looked at the safe, shaking his head. The investigator grabbed Xan above his elbow and brought him closer to the safe. Xan whipped his arm out and nudged the investigator.

"Back off," he said. "Back off."

The investigator growled at him.

Xan stood his ground. "Don't you dare treat me like that," he said. "Don't you dare push me around like some criminal. You have nothing on me. Nothing. Do you know who my boss is? Do you want me to contact him and let him know how the government is treating his employees?"

The investigator let his anger drop as his eyelids quivered in pain.

Xan clenched his fist into a ball and stood before the group like a centurion guard.

"This little circus act has gone far enough," said Xan. "I've been more than accommodating, and I'm getting sick and tired of your attitude. Yes, I used to work at the bottom. Yes, I remember people there. But don't you dare treat me like that!"

The investigator eyed him for an unbearable amount of time. The silence between them was heavier than the safe that sat upon the table.

"You won't mind if we take this with us then. I'll open it myself."

His assistant held open her mouth and made a faint noise.

The investigator turned to her. "What?"

"There are no current methods or technologies available to break into the safe," she said. "They're built that way on purpose."

The investigator stared at it. Xan bore down on his teeth and glanced between the three. The investigator grunted then stomped towards the door. His assistants looked at each other in confusion and then followed him. The door opened, and the investigator left. The last assistant closed the door behind her.

Xan let out a huge sigh and sat at the table with his face inside his hand.

"Oh my god," he said. "Oh my god." He looked up at the safe and kissed it. "Thank you, thank you, thank you."

CHAPTER 35

"Can't be too sure now," said the shopkeeper as he clamped another lock over his door. "Did you hear about the recent scrap up north?"

Xan didn't want to talk about the restless atmosphere. He picked up a bottle of wine and turned it over to check the label: *Premium Blend of Synthetic*. He placed the bottle back on the shelf.

The shopkeeper kept talking nonetheless. "They trashed three different stores and killed one of the owners," he said. "Killed the guy. For what? They might've gotten off with a few credits but is that worth a man's life? This isn't Earth for god's sakes."

Xan picked up another bottle of wine and read the label.

"It's madness, what we have to do now to keep safe. I never thought I'd be the type to install a credit scan, but you see?" The old shopkeeper pointed to the little box near his door. It would only unlock the door if the person trying to enter had a base level of credits in their bank.

Xan coughed and looked at the scanner. "Did it cost much to install?"

The old man moved his hand. "It's not the price I'm upset about. It's the principle. That's what gets to me. We've been living here peacefully for decades, and now these underground mutts wanna mess everything up."

Xan squinted his eyes on the wine.

The shopkeeper pointed towards the bottle. "That one's nice. Goes great with a bit of cheese."

Xan nodded.

The shopkeeper moved closer to Xan and tapped the bottle of wine. "You know what baffles me?" he said.

Xan shook his head.

"That these guys have weapons. How in the hell are they getting their hands on these things? We don't have a weapon manufacturer up here. We don't have a giant stockpile for an army, and still, they get loads. Like it was nothing."

Xan kept his eyes on the bottle. "Who knows, right?"

The shopkeeper stopped for a moment to look him in the eye. "The pipes are leaking around here somewhere," he said. "I'm not entirely convinced the government is doing everything they can to stop these skirmishes. If we were down on Earth, they'd know all the right people to question. It's not like we can't take a few months to sift through all the domes up here."

Xan handed him the bottle. "I'll take this one," he said.

The shopkeeper snapped out of his trance and held the wine. "Anything else? Don't ask for a security guard, they're all taken."

"Just the wine," said Xan.

"Sure," said the shopkeeper. He then jerked his head towards the counter as if to tell Xan to follow him.

Xan went to the counter and put his Vlex on the small pyramid. The pyramid flashed green. The shopkeeper wrapped up the bottle, tied the ends, and then placed it into a box. He went around the counter and handed the box to Xan. Then he walked towards the door and looked out.

"How did you get here?" he said.

"The tunnels."

A group of workers passed by the store. The shopkeeper turned to watch them go by. He waited for them to leave his sight before he turned off the door locks.

"The tunnels are safe," he said. "You'll be all right in there."

Xan made a move to leave, but then he stopped as the shopkeeper still held the door closed.

"You're not a government worker are you?" he asked.

"No."

"Business owner?"

"I manage the farm."

The shopkeeper took an interest in Xan, scanning him up and down. "God damn," he said. "You guys were one of the first places to get hit. Were you there when it happened?"

Xan drew in a deep breath and rubbed the scar on his head. "Yeah…"

The shopkeeper looked up at the scar. "Oh," he said. "I - didn't mean - "

Xan brought his hand back down. "It's fine. It could've been much worse."

The shopkeeper moved away with a jump. "One second," he said, going behind the counter and moving bottles around. He came back with another bottle in his hands.

"Here, take this one with you."

"Oh, no. I'm okay."

The shopkeeper pushed it into his open hand. "Just take it."

Xan looked at the box and then back at the counter. "Let me pay you for it."

The shopkeeper patted the box. "Take it," he said. "My treat. Just think of it as an investment on my part."

"Investment?"

The old man laughed. "Sure. I wouldn't have half the clients I do now if it weren't for that cheese farm."

Xan rubbed it with his thumb. "Thanks."

The shopkeeper smiled and unlocked the doors, peeked his head outside, and then craned back in. "Coast is clear. Don't stay out too late."

Xan stepped through the door. "I won't," he said.

The door slid shut behind him, and a few beeps sounded as the locks barred within. Xan looked around the streets while dusk followed close at his heels. A swollen wind carried a spiral of dust through the city's scrapers. Few people walked the streets at this time. The new curfew was about to keep everyone in for the night.

Xan carried on, heading for the tunnel passage. He saw the entrance across the street, but was hesitant to go over. A group of workers was gathered at the entrance, speaking amongst themselves.

Xan wanted to turn towards the entrance, but his feet kept him going along the sidewalk. *I used to be one of them too*, he thought. He wished they had heard it. He wanted them to know he understood. He wanted them to know he thought they were harmless, just like him. But he kept walking.

He thought to take the next available tunnel entrance. It was only a few blocks away. His nerves opened him up to the world. It felt as if tiny ants were crawling up his calves without permission. Xan scratched his leg for a moment and then stopped to look back. The group was gone.

"Just go to the next one," he told himself, but the entrance was right there before him.

Xan turned his head back and forth, peering through every nook of the city. He saw no shadows lingering. So he walked with a slight jump as he sped across the road. Xan paused at the entrance and searched his coat pockets. He felt someone approaching. He turned over his shoulder, but no one was there.

Xan retrieved his Vlex and flashed it near the entrance, granting him access. He shot through the door and felt them close behind him. The tunnels were quiet. Soft echoes pattered the walls as he walked through the still night.

Xan hurried his pace along the walkway. A few ads distracted his focus, edging his nerves on even more. The artificial sounds of prerecorded tracks couldn't edge out the stifling atmosphere. It pissed him off more than he thought it would. The sounds blurred his attention, keeping him from watching his surroundings.

"Staying up at night will never make you feel tired again," the advertisement said.

Xan tried to laugh at the ads popping up around him. Every step he took activated a perimeter of screens to bother him. He turned down an intersecting passage and stopped at the lift waiting to take him up to his apartment. He held out his Vlex, and the door opened. Xan stepped inside, leaving the sounds behind. He placed two fingers on his neck to check his pulse.

"I'm being paranoid," he said.

The lift started its ascent. He felt a gravitational pull as it stopped. The door slid open, letting him out. Xan scurried into the apartment with the boxes of wine tucked under his arm. The living room was silent. He placed the boxes of wine down on the nearest table and took off his jacket.

Razan was still at work, and Zola was likely on his way to pick her up. The fish tank hummed its rhythmic gurgle in the corner of the room.

A wall crashed.

He felt a heavy throb throw him into the arms of the couch. His mind spiked with thunder, and his pulse raged. His breathing constricted under the weight of his lungs.

The walls came undone. There were cracks in the windows. The sky was black. Fiery corpses filled with tar. Hanging bodies laying over broken glass.

Xan held his head and screamed. These visions had plagued him for weeks. Dreams of a collapsing sun. Dreams of the world he knew coming undone. The feeling burst within his chest like a horrid bomb full of poisonous sin.

Xan gasped for air. He wanted the visions to stop. He wanted to be rid of these terrors. They were only dreams in his mind. Nothing more than fantasies buried inside.

A warm hand pat him on the back, causing him to jump.

"Are you okay?" Ima asked.

"What?"

She stood behind the couch with Kane standing in the distance.

Xan held the bags under his eyes. "Huh?" he said.

"I said, are you okay? We heard you screaming outside. What happened?"

She and Kane watched him.

"I was screaming? I don't remember that. I didn't scream, did I?"

Kane moved closer to Ima. "Don't push him," he said. "He's gone through enough."

Ima nodded. Kane walked over to the couch where Xan sat quivering with cold tremors.

"Do you want me to take you to the hospital?" he said.

Xan tried to look at Kane but found it difficult. This was his friend. He did not want to be seen in this state.

"No," he said. "I don't need a hospital. I need rest. That's all."

Kane nodded his head and looked over at Ima as they seemed to be telepathically communicating with one another.

"Could you get me some water?" said Xan.

"I'll get it," Ima offered.

The room filled with the babble of the aquarium. The blue lights drafted into a somber glow. Kane sat in the seat near Xan. Dim lights came in through a window. The city saw him weakened. It knew so many of his secrets but kept them all within.

Xan reached over the back of the couch, pulling down a blanket to wrap himself.

"Do you ever get the feeling like something bad is about to happen?"

Kane glanced out of the window. His mouth was open, and his jaw moved without touching his teeth.

"Sometimes," he said. "Rarely though."

"Do you still feel safe up here?"

"Safe?"

"On Mars."

Kane looked at him. "I have no reason not to. It'd be a different story if I were a scientist at your farm though."

"What about the recent stories? You're not concerned? What if they get tired of wine shops and want to wreck aquariums next? Don't tell me it's never crossed your mind."

Kane shifted in his seat, his lips twitching. "I've put in new locks," he said. "We all have. They're fairly safe."

"They can break locks," said Xan. "Windows shattered."

Kane shook his head as he rubbed his hands. "I expect nothing that extreme. What kind of person would be that angry? These people are nothing more than petty thieves. They'll get what they deserve. Just wait. You'll see."

Xan saw the shattered windows in his mind.

"And what if they don't?" he said. "Then what?"

Kane tried to relax in his seat. "We'll call home. Mother Earth would never let its little nest become infested with worms."

Ima walked through the kitchen with a glass of water. Kane caught sight of her and then looked back at Xan. She handed him the glass.

"I'd better get home before curfew," said Kane.

"Be careful," said Xan.

His sister looked at him. "He'll be fine," she said. "We'll all be fine."

Kane paused for a moment and then continued. "See you tomorrow," he said at the door.

Xan took a few more sips of water. His hand stopped shaking. The door shut.

His sister sat in the chair next to him. "What were you talking about?" she asked.

"Simple chat."

She tapped her foot on the floor. Her body kept fidgeting as she tried to maintain focus outside the window. "Should we move back to Earth?"

Xan lowered his glass. "No. Why would we move back there? Do you want to go back to Earth now? What's wrong with Mars?"

Ima shrugged and bit the corner of her lip.

"Mars is a great place to live," he said. "There's nothing wrong with it. We're just going through a little phase right now. That's all."

Ima kept looking out the window. She said nothing in response to his comments. After some time, she stood up quietly and left the living room. Xan watched out the window as he took another sip of water, lost in his thoughts.

Tiny chimes rang. Broken shards glittered in the sun. Rubble lined the streets like ornaments of dust.

The door slid open. Razan and Zola walked through the bright hall and into the blue-lit room. Razan turned on the lights, and Zola marched through the living room.

"Why are you sitting in the dark?" she asked. "Are you cold?"

He didn't answer. His eyes were out the window.

Razan focused on taking off her shoes. "Are you sick?"

"No."

She turned to him as she grabbed her shoe on her other foot. "Did something happen?"

"No," he said.

Razan was done taking off her shoes and walked towards Xan. She stood over the couch for a moment, looking at him. Then she sat down beside him, pulling some of the blanket towards herself. The stars were gleaming in the night sky. Each little bead of light looked different from the rest.

"Something needs to change," she said as she cozied up to him. "The future is bright. As long as this situation gets resolved soon."

Xan put his arm around her. He tried to put the visions away from his head, but they buried themselves deep inside his skull.

CHAPTER 36

In the furthest corner of the closet, he found his old long coat given to him by his father, the pair of boots from his mother, and the sand goggles from his old mentor at the station. Xan sat with them, feeling a vast distance between those times. Silence embraced him in the night.

Xan examined the small marks left on his jacket from wear, remembering how a few of them got there. As he set them back in their box, he heard his Vlex buzz on the floor.

Picking it up, he saw it was a private number and put it away. The call ended. He went back to his things when it rang again. Xan picked it back up and slowly put it to his ear.

"Evening sweetheart," said the voice.

"What do you want?"

"How's your wife and sister? I've seen you with them in the city. Good looking girls."

Xan felt breathless for a second.

"You had an old roommate in your first lodge, yeah?"

Xan recognised the investigator's voice.

"Come to the station tonight, real quiet, and maybe we'll both forget about that safe you have there in your closet."

"What are you after?"

"I have an old friend of yours. Maybe you can tell me if he looks familiar now that you're feeling better?"

Xan's heart ticked in his chest.

"Don't let anyone see you on the way."

The line cut and Xan sat silently on the floor.

* * *

Police officers patrolled the streets at night in tight-knit groups, wandering from lane to lane, each one armed with heavy rifles at their chests. When the group passed, Xan darted up the stairs to the station headed to the front door, which he found locked.

"Brave man."

Xan turned over his shoulder. He saw the investigator hiding in the dark, smoking his electric cigarette. The man put his smoke away and unlocked the doors. "After you," he said.

Xan stepped through. The investigator followed and then locked them in. The man jutted his chin to a set of stairs and pushed him on. They reached a small corridor lined with two-way glass cells.

They stopped outside one. The investigator rapped his knuckle on the glass. "Look familiar?"

Sven sat inside, his back propped in the corner. He tugged at his long matted hair.

"Is that a yes?"

Xan remained silent.

"Nasty scar you have there."

"Let me speak with him first," said Xan.

The investigator laughed. "No can do."

"I recognised his voice. If you give me ten minutes to speak with him -"

"I'll be listening."

Xan nodded.

The investigator unlocked the cell and held the door open for him. "Ten minutes."

As Xan stepped in, Sven bolted upright. His face soured for a second then a wicked grin spread across on his face.

"I swore you were dead," said Sven.

"Surprise."

"Surprise indeed."

Xan sighed. "What were you doing there?"

Sven studied Xan in his old jacket and boots. "Did you know that Meridien was once a cluster of small villages? No city or skyscrapers, just a few towns gathered around their main factories and plants."

"Why are you doing this?"

Contemplating to himself, he tied two long strands of hair together. "Everyone mined or worked the belts," he said. "Unless you owned a factory.

Then you made the rules. Could change the rules."

"I can help you."

Sven's face remained blank. "And one of them did," he said. "A plant owner who paid his workers a living wage. He made his employees citizens of their town. Owners of their own parliament. The workers. Not his friends or other village owners. His workers!"

Xan's eyes fixed on Sven.

"What do you think happened to that man?"

Xan squinted one eye at him, saying nothing.

"Everyone abandoned their own village when they heard of his kindness. Workers flocked in from every neighbouring town, hoping for a job there. But their owners tracked them down and carted them back. Breakouts were commonplace, and people died for the dream that they might be something more than a slave."

"Sven?"

"You've never heard this part of our history?"

Xan took in a deep breath.

"Raising wages would've been easy for those other plant owners. But instead of doing that, they killed the man responsible for their loss in labour and productivity." Sven clapped his hands together. "From then on, all the villages worked together to make sure that no town ever stepped out of line again."

Xan leaned forward. "It's in the past," he said. "Right now you're in big trouble if you don't let me help you."

Sven chuckled. He lay his head back and smiled up at the ceiling.

"Why did you go there that night?"

"I told everyone you'd died. And yet here you are. Working for the other side just like one of them."

"You think I own that farm?" said Xan. "Are you that deluded?"

Sven watched him.

"I'm not the one who sets your wages or is keeping you out of politics. I'm not rich. I'm comfortable."

"Comfortably paid off."

Xan scoffed.

"It's too late for you anyhow. For everyone on Mars."

Xan glanced at the walls. "This is being recorded."

"There isn't a damn thing any of you can do about it. Kill me. Tell them to sink a beam through my head. But it won't stop it. Nothing will."

* * *

Xan slipped into his room. Razan was fast asleep in the bed. She saw nothing but her dreams. He went to the window and gazed at the full moon above.

"What did they do to you in those moon circles?"

Shadows moved across the wall, touched at the walls, snuck around corners, and emerged from under ground.

"You'll be dead by tomorrow night if you don't let me help."

Razan shifted in the bed. Xan looked over his shoulder.

"What's the matter?" she said.

"Nothing."

"Is it your head?"

He took a while to reply. "No," he said. "It's something else."

CHAPTER 37

A faint beep echoed throughout the room. Xan slit his eyes open. The alarm sounded different than before. His sight was fuzzy until he rubbed them a few times. His Vlex continued beeping, and so did Razan's. She woke up and clicked on the alert.

Their wall turned into a giant news board. A file opened to a woman's voice speaking to them.

"All Martian citizens are to remain indoors today, as we are dealing with a protest. I repeat, all Martian citizens are to remain indoors as the authorities handle the situation. We will notify everyone when the situation has been cleared. Thank you."

Xan looked at Razan, and she returned his puzzled look.

"Turn on the local feed," she said.

Xan did as she said.

"...protests started in Mons early this morning. The protestors are refusing to leave the tunnel entrances until the government grants everyone access."

The screen flashed with images of workers gathered at the tunnel entrances. Angry murmurs sounded in the background as they shouted in unrest.

"Earth has been notified of the situation but has yet to comment on how they will respond," the speaker said.

Knocks hammered at his door. He opened it with his Vlex. Ima entered, looking frightened. Xan turned back to Razan.

"What's going to happen?" Ima said at the door.

"I'm sure this will blow over. The authorities won't allow anything to get out of hand. We'll sit tight for a little while."

The crowds buzzed like an angry swarm of bees. People were shouting at the top of their lungs, and angry veins bulged from their necks. The feed clicked between the entrances where the workers had gathered.

"We'll switch to the live feed until we receive further information," the newscaster said.

Ima swayed in the room. "Why don't they let them use the tunnels?"

"It's not that simple," said Xan. "The government doesn't own the tunnels."

A slow march sounded around the feeds. The groups stirred with rage. A band of riot police appeared at the corner of one of the surveillance cameras. They marched towards the groups, clad in dark armour and wore thick black face masks.

They halted in unison, facing the crowd. A loud voice echoed towards the protestors through an electronic amplifier.

"Return to your homes immediately," said the voice. "I repeat, return to your homes immediately."

The crowds grumbled and began their uproars again.

"WE ASK YOU AGAIN TO PLEASE RETURN TO YOUR HOMES. PLEASE DO NOT FORCE US INTO ACTION. PLEASE RETURN..."

Xan watched as a man broke from the crowds and ran towards an officer, swinging a blunt object in the air. An officer fired his weapon, knocking the protestor flat to the ground. An explosion of red burst from the side of man and splashed onto the ground as he hit the street.

Silence fell over the group. The other feeds showed looks of confusion as the other protestors searched for the source of commotion. The body twitched on the ground. His hands shook in a fit. No one moved to help him. He continued pulling his legs up and down into a foetal curl.

The officers kept their sights on the rest of the mob. Xan couldn't take his eyes from the feed. He heard his sister whimper, but he didn't look her way.

"AS WE'VE SAID, PLEASE RETURN - "

Niall stepped ahead, with a charged FOBEL launcher, firing an explosive beam into the crowd of officers. Shots broke out, volleying back and forth as the groups scattered in disarray. Explosions tossed up black clouds and bodies fell to the earth like lumps of clay.

Chunks of cement ruptured off the walls and fell upon the crowds. Xan watched as one man tried his best to free his trapped leg from a large piece of rubble. Blood seeped around him as he tugged at his deadened leg.

A police officer ran by the man and stopped for a moment to aim and shoot. The man dropped to the ground. The officer continued chasing the group inside the smoke. Xan could hear the echoes of chaos outside his window.

"Turn it off."

A few protestors pulled down an armoured officer with some wire string and hacked at him with their blunt tools. The officer put up his hands to protect his face, but his hands broke under the brunt of a few swings.

Another officer rushed to break up the group, but one man pulled out a laser and shot the officer through the opening near his neck. The officer tried to stop the blood as he fell to his knees.

"Turn it off."

Another group of protestors huddled behind a mound of fallen rubble shooting at the officers. An officer threw a ball towards the other side, engulfing them in flames.

"Turn it off!"

The protestors scattered, patting at the flames on their bodies. They rolled on the ground and grabbed their heads as the fire persisted. The officer stood over them, watching them burn.

"TURN IT OFF PLEASE!" Ima screamed.

Razan stood up, took the Vlex out Xan's hands and turned off the feed. They could still hear the muted battle sounds outside. The humming and thumps of explosive shots rang through the window.

Ima cried as she sat on the corner of the bed. Razan wrapped her arms around her.

"I want to go back to Earth," Ima cried. "I don't like this place anymore. I want to go home!"

"Wait," he said. "We don't know anything yet. We can't do anything until we figure this out. Let me think for a second. There's no need to make such rash decisions. We still don't know anything."

Xan left the room and went downstairs to the living area and turned the newsfeed back on.

Smoke filled the streets as men and women ran by the surveillance feeds in the city. Most of them seemed to be retreating. At the right corner of the screen, Xan saw one of the protestors limping away, trying to keep with the rest. Through the burning fog came a dark figure in his armoured suit and rifle in hand. The limping man picked up speed and dragged his broken hip. The officer raised his weapon and shot the man down.

The protestor fell. The officer strolled by him at a leisurely pace and paused for a moment above him. He shot the body two more times and then continued moving on his slow pace.

A clear wind cut through the heavy breaths of smoke, revealing a glimpse of the damage. A few more gusts opened the view of streets lined with bodies and the handful of remaining officers. Xan hadn't noticed that the reporter had started talking again.

A hand touched his shoulder and caused him to jump. "Sir?"

Xan turned to Zola, who was standing behind him.

"They're retreating," Zola said. "If we take the sandrover we might make it to the spaceport before they return."

Xan shook his head as he looked at Zola. His eyes were wide and full of fear.

Zola moved closer to him and grabbed him by the shoulders. "Sir?"

Xan couldn't say anything. His throat had closed off. His mouth produced syllables but nothing coherent.

"Did you hear me?"

Xan sat down on the couch for a moment and held his head. He buried his face within his palms. Faint cries echoed from upstairs.

"Yes," said Xan. "Yes."

Zola kneeled beside him. "We need to get out of here before they strike again."

Xan took his face out of his hands and looked up with red eyes. "The police will stop them."

Zola put his hand on his knee.

"This isn't happening," mumbled Xan.

"It is," said Zola. "Whether or not you want it."

"Sven was right."

* * *

Xan sat unmoved on the couch. Zola and Razan sped about, piling things at the door, prepping bags and shouting to one another in the house. Ima cradled herself on the floor.

"Xan?" said Razan. "We have to go!"

Xan's eyes were blankly fixed on the smoke outside the window. Razan grabbed his hands.

"I'll stay here," he said. "The rest of you go. I'll wait and see how it turns out."

The news feed continued on the wall with no newscaster speaking. Two police stations had black smoke billowing from their doors. A band of protestors pried apart a dead officer's armour, snatching up his rifle, helmet, and flame grenades.

"We're not going without you." Razan placed her hand on his face. "Xan, all the private ships have already left. If they're bailing out so fast..."

"It will blow over in time."

A pair of officers raced after the scavenging protestors. Red beams snapped from their rifles. The protestors cut the corner, one of them narrowing missing the fire.

"We need you. Don't flake out on us."

His eyes remained outside on the smoke.

"Now might be our only chance to make it to the spaceport."

Xan shook his head. "Just until it's safe."

"It might never be safe again."

CHAPTER 38

Xan lingered in between the doorway of his apartment and the hall. He looked at the little fish tank and the birds jumping about. Razan shut the door and pushed him towards the lift.

"Everyone says they're heading for the spaceport," said Razan.

The lift door opened. The lift was almost full to the brim with people, and they barely managed to squeeze inside.

Once they got to the lobby, everyone flooded out into a frantic mob. A receptionist stood on her desk, shouting into the crowd. "We will get to you one at a time! If you'd all please queue up!"

A sandrover appeared outside. The valet hopped out, and a family jumped in. Some of the crowd begged to hitch a ride and others grabbed at the sandrover. The owner sped up and dragged a man for a few meters until he fell off, rolling over in the streets.

The valet came back into the building and stood behind the receptionist who was standing on the desk. She tapped on her Vlex and then one of the crowd members moved towards the desk with her flashing Vlex.

A man raged inside the crowd as he knocked others out of his way. "Hey that's not fair I was here before her!"

"Please calm down. We will attend to you as soon as possible."

The crowd pushed back at him and then push back at each other. The few nudges turned into punches and slowly into a furious brawl. Xan edged away to the side near the doors.

"Let's get out of here," he said. "We'll ditch the sandrover."

"No," Ima said. "It's too dangerous. What if they shoot us on the way? I'm not leaving without the rover. I won't do it."

"There is no other way," Xan said. "If you want to go back to Earth, we have to leave now!"

Ima refused to budge, shaking her head dripping in tears.

Xan threw up his hands. "How the hell do we leave then?"

Xan felt a hand moving over his arm. Razan came to his side, pulling for his attention. "What about Mick? He has tons of sandrovers. Ask him. We're not going to be able to move her without one."

Xan looked back at his sister and pulled out his Vlex. He sent a message as quickly as he could. "We should leave," he mumbled as he typed the message. "Sitting here like sheep."

Ima covered her face and cried even more. Razan gave him a look.

"She's so intent on leaving yet she won't even listen to me," he said.

"She has a point," said Razan. "How are you going to save anyone's life if we're between the city and spaceport when they return?"

Xan turned his back to her and threw his Vlex to the ground. It bounced on its edges and shot off in a zagged line. "Answer me, god damn it!"

"Calm down," said Razan, holding his arm. "It won't do us any good to lose our heads."

Zola moved forward to retrieve Xan's Vlex. He handed it to him and went back to Ima's side.

"How am I supposed to stay calm? My life is collapsing right before me. How the hell am I to stay calm? Tell me, please!"

"There are more important matters right now." Razan stormed away from him.

Xan brushed his jacket a few times and held his Vlex with a pincer-grip. He looked down and saw a new message from Mick.

Ten minutes. Xan sighed relief and looked back at his family. "Ten minutes," he said.

They kept watch outside the doors. The crowd grew wild, taking the valet inside, ripping his clothes to shreds, and stomping a few people to death.

Almost there, get ready, the new message said.

"He's here. Hop in quick. We don't want to draw attention to ourselves."

Xan's group stepped outside. The streets were layered with dead bodies and smoke. Ima put her head down, refusing to look. Xan kept his eyes peeled for Mick's sandrover. He saw one in the distance approaching their building. It did its best to weave through the corpses along the way.

"That's him," Xan said.

The sandrover stopped beside them, and Mick jut his thumb towards the open seats. "Get in."

They jumped in the sandrover as quickly as they could. A few people came out of the building and waved towards them. Mick sped off, dodging the extended hands. They drove through the city streets, trying to avoid the rubble and bodies along the way.

The ride was silent. Everyone seemed to focus on the damage in the city. A few police officers shuffled through the streets, taking weapons from their fallen brethren.

They rode by a police station. Xan slapped on Mick's shoulder.

"Stop!" yelled Xan.

Mick slammed the breaks. Xan jumped out of the sandrover. A few pedestrians took notice and started running towards it.

"You have any kind of weapon on you?" said Xan.

"A tire iron bit in the back."

Xan went to the back and took it out and went to the side of the vehicle. "Circle the building. Give me five minutes."

"Are you crazy?" said Razan. "What are you thinking?"

"Five minutes. Hurry!"

The tires squealed, leaving the pedestrians behind. Xan ran up the stairs in the station and through the broken front door, pulling his jacket over his mouth in the wafting smoke. Fallen officers lay spread across the station.

Running down the stairs, he reached the cell floor and walked to Sven's holding. The tire iron relaxed in his hand. Xan hissed through his teeth at the empty cell then raced back outside. Mick charged down the street, stopping quickly to let Xan jump in.

As they drove on, they passed the last tunnel exit where people stampeded out in a dash to the spaceport.

"Everyone's got the same idea," said Xan.

"Course they do," said Mick.

The sandrover bumped as it rode over a body then onto the unpaved terrain. Dozens of sandrovers drove alongside them, heading for the same place. As they drew closer to the spaceport, they noticed mounds of vehicles piled at the entrance. Xan wiped the sweat from his forehead and chewed the sandy grit in his teeth.

Mick pulled the sandrover near the side, parking behind a mass of others. Everyone hopped out and looked around for safety's sake. Other sandrovers were pulling in and parking as quickly as they could. They moved along the side of the building where a small narrow path had been left open. Xan's group moved silently into the spaceport and through the crowds of people.

Ima looked around in a daze. "How are they going to fit us all on board?"

"I'm sure there are other ships on their way," he said. "If we miss this one, we'll just wait until the next one lands. They won't forget us."

Mick found the ticketing room and waved for Xan to follow. They entered the bustling room and waited for their turn to access the purchasing squares. The lines drifted. Some people threw fits when they could not purchase their tickets. Others bought them with ease and left.

A square block on the floor opened up for him to stand. His Vlex lit up and showed him the purchasing options available to him. Beside each option were the words "*Insufficient Funds.*"

Xan sent out an alert for help and waited for a flight assistant to arrive. A woman with a mean scowl approached him.

"What?"

"My Vlex is telling me that I have insufficient funds. I can afford all these options twice over!"

The woman scowled at him. "If all of your credits are in Martian dollars, then your Vlex is accurate."

Xan opened his mouth in disbelief.

"Sir?"

"That shouldn't matter. My credits are good. THEY ARE FINE! I'VE GAIN LOADS OF THEM!"

"That's too bad," she said. "Earth froze Martian credits this morning. Your money is no longer worth anything."

She held one hand open and pointed at the exit. "Now will you please move aside so that other passengers can purchase their tickets?"

He clenched his fists.

"Sir?" she said, gesturing towards the door again.

Xan stepped out of the square, his shoulders hung low. The woman turned away from him. He swung back and grabbed her by the arm.

"Wait a fucking minute!"

She flung her arm away from him.

"I've worked up here for years. I've earned my credits, and you're trying to tell me I can't buy a ticket out of here? I don't believe this shit! Get back here!" Xan grabbed her again.

She slapped him across the face. "Take your hands off me. I'll call security if you don't leave right now."

Xan felt a strong arm pulling him away as he struggled against it.

"Calm down," said Mick. "Relax. Don't get shot over this."

Xan stopped resisting and paused, looking at the woman.

"How does it feel like to join the rest of us?" she said. "Stupid people like you who can't share a damn tunnel."

Mick pulled him to his senses and walked him back out of the ticketing station.

"This is bullshit. How can they do this to us? We've worked our entire lives for what we have."

"I've been trying to contact Kane," said Mick "He might have enough Earth credits. I know his parents do. Maybe he could book a cabin or something?"

Xan approached his family with a pained expression. Razan pinched her eyes shut, and Ima's lips trembled.

"What happened?" said Razan.

Xan spit towards the ticketing room. "Tell me you have Earth credits?"

Her face turned white.

"They've frozen our Martian credits."

"We're stuck here?" his sister said. "We're stuck here. This is it?"

Xan breathed quickly. He said something then lost his breath. He dropped to the ground hyperventilating.

Razan kneeled to his side. "Xan? Xan!"

Mick had gone to the ticketing station again and rushed back. Xan remained on the floor, looking up at Mick.

"There's a lottery tomorrow," he said. "We have a chance. If the ship doesn't fill, then they'll throw the vacant rooms into the pot for the rest of us. We still have a chance."

CHAPTER 39

The spaceport grew congested as day turned into night. People slept in different areas, most of them on the floor. Xan snuck around all night, trying to figure out a way to get his sister onto the ship. Heavily armed guards stood at the entrances, never blinking an eye.

Xan then went back to the group that had huddled in a tight corner. Ima was asleep while everyone else lay awake on the floor.

Xan sat beside Razan. "Nothing," he said. "There's no way in."

He turned his head and saw Mick lying on the floor. "Any word from Kane?"

"Not yet."

***

The sun rose with the sound of explosions in the distance. A woman's voice reverberated through the spaceport.

"The lottery will take place in fifteen minutes in front of the security gate at Concourse B. I repeat, the lottery will take place in fifteen minutes in front of the security gate at Concourse B. Thank you."

The spaceport came alive.

Xan picked up his small bag and helped his sister and Razan to their feet. "This is it. We've a good chance. I know they aren't close to filling it all up. I bet there are over a hundred vacancies."

No one talked to him.

Bodies packed in front of the security gate. Families bound together amidst the crowds, and couples held their hands tightly together as everyone eyed the ship's entrance.

Xan kept his head up.

"Attention. The lottery is about to begin. I repeat, the lottery is about to begin. Please make your way to the security gate at Concourse B to take part. Thank you."

The crowd hushed. Tiny patters of sound lined the silent walls.

"Attention. The lottery is about to begin. Thank you."

The crowd erupted in a blue glow. Xan's Vlex flashed blue as did everyone else's around him.

The loudspeaker echoed against the walls.

"Attention. A blue screen indicates that the system has cast your ballot. If you have not received the blue screen, please ask for help now."

The room remained silent.

"Thank you. The drawing will now begin."

Xan kept his eyes on the entrance, knowing they would soon be walking through it.

"A green light indicates that you have selected to board the ship. If your Vlex shows green, please make your way through the security gate. Thank you. The drawing will now begin."

A shout erupted in the middle of the crowd. Xan saw the first person get chosen. Nervous energy shifted in the area. People mumbled to themselves.

A second burst of joy came from the back of the room where another person had been selected. The crowd shifted even more.

The next came quicker and then another. Pockets of excitement spread into hopeful prayers. More Vlexes lighted up green. The winners rushed to the front, breaking through the crowds.

Xan watched the room grow in flashes and waited for their turn.

"See how many spaces they have? I wouldn't be surprised if they took almost all of us."

No one answered him. Ima held her Vlex in front of her chest and watched the crowd spark in green. Her eyes looked desperate, fixed on the gates before them.

More green screens lit up. The hum of the crowd grew agitated. The shifting became bitter. The restless energy lingered over the walls like unpainted portraits.

"We can always wait for the next ship," he said. "Just think, if they do this lottery for each one, we'll be home in no time. This is very hopeful. Even if we don't get it this round."

He tried to smile at his sister. Ima lowered her head. He looked at Razan who gave a similar gaze of acceptance.

More Vlexes alerted their winning owners in the crowd. Xan looked at the family next to him. They gripped their children closer to themselves.

A flash of green lit up within his group. Xan turned with joy to see who would be going back. Zola stood, his Vlex flashing in his hands. He looked at the rest of the group in surprise.

"Hurry up and go," said Xan. "We'll get one of the next ones. Go. You don't want to miss it."

Zola nodded hesitantly, then weaved through the crowd towards the security gate. He made little parts in the mass of people as he walked through them.

"See? If Zola can get one, we can too. I told you it's just a matter of time before we all get on there."

Mick nodded his head.

More green flashed in the crowd.

The lights dwindled as the intervals between the next green lights grew longer. Then a darkened pause fell over the crowd. A final one shone.

A lone woman with her green Vlex made her way towards the security gates and talked to the ship officer.

"Attention," said the announcement. "The lottery is over. Thank you for your participation."

The crowd grumbled in a collective wind. Moans hardened into roars as everyone spilled their fists onto the gates. Feet stamped on the ground like a rushing herd.

The woman entered while the officer backed towards the ship. Five other ship officers rushed into the gate behind the woman and backed into the ship. The crowd rammed into the gates and banged on the walls. They threw themselves towards the security gates, shaking them in violent fury.

Shots ripped into the crowd. Everyone screamed as more shots were fired.

A large man knocked Xan to the floor, crawling amidst the mob, trying to regain his standing. A large woman's hip smacked across his face.

On the floor, Xan inhaled a gust of strength and threw himself up, then ran along with the crowd. He tried his best to keep his balance.

No one could stop the momentum of several hundred people. As he reached the exit, he nearly tripped over a few bodies that lay trampled beneath them. He saw a woman with long hair under his foot before he kept moving.

Xan felt his feet hit the sands. He moved to the side of the building to avoid the sandrovers ploughing through the crowd. He pushed himself up against the wall and walked in a narrow line with the pack.

People slipped past him. Some of them ran to the city and others bunched near the building. Dust permeated the air. Human figures blurred behind the veil of sand.

"Razan?" he shouted. "Ima? Mick?"

Xan felt a tug against his foot as he tripped over another person's leg. He pulled forward without apologising.

The noises died down, and the sands settled. Xan saw blotted figures running in every direction. As the particles lay back into the ground, he gained clarity.

Hundreds of bodies remained motionless on the ground, and a few sandrovers lay overturned or smashed. He saw two families amongst the fragments. Red streaks lined their faces as they lay in their conjoined wreckage.

Xan held his chest as he fell to the ground. He couldn't whisper his thoughts out of his constricted throat. His eyes spotted with liquid embers that burned within the dust. He drew his face in between his knees and let the tears flow out of him.

A firm hand patted him on the back. Xan felt too raw to lift his head. Then a gentle embrace wrapped around him. Then another pair of arms did the same.

"It's not your fault," he heard. "It's okay. We can wait for the next ship."

Xan pulled his head up and saw Razan to his left and his sister on his right. Razan held a firm grip around his shoulder. His sister patted sand off his back.

"They're still coming," Razan said. "They'll strike again. We need to find somewhere safe."

Xan fixed his gaze on the anxious city. It waited there for the next blow without flinching. The shadows crept, getting ready to strike once again.

CHAPTER 40

The city went off in fiery commotion with the last strand of officers holding out against the rioters. Thunderous volleys pattered off and on with longer spaces in between them. Xan watched it rage the whole night. Bright orange lit the city's core, flashing in ripples, then ended in a decrescendo.

The world hummed in deadened silence. Like sharp ticking hands on a clock, each silent note struck towards a swinging blade, reaching closer to their supple throats.

Razan shifted her back against the wall to lean against Xan. She opened her eyes for a moment to look at him whirling in a maze of mental torture. Then her eyes shut back into rest. Ima lay close to Razan as she slumped further into a nervous rest.

Metal clicks sounded within the warehouse, and large thuds shook the ground. Xan looked up for Mick but found it too dark to spot him. He moved out of Razan's touch and slipped up the wall with his hands behind his back. He saw a faint light coming from the opposite wall where the sounds were coming from. Xan drifted towards Mick.

Mick crouched over a metal grate that he had slid off the ground, with half his body inside the opening. Xan stood behind him. He saw a pile of metal objects thrown onto the floor next to them. Mick dragged his body out of the hole and slapped his hands together.

Xan touched the tools with his foot. "What's this?"

"Protection," said Mick.

Xan pulled up one of the large knives from the pile and examined its edge. "Why are these here?"

"Don't know. One of the other guys must've left them."

Xan picked up a sleek hatchet with a curved handle. He felt the power from it, throbbing through his hand, like an extension of his flesh.

"You never know what you'll find," said Mick. "I was searching for some food. I remember Pei talking about a hidden stock here somewhere."

Xan looked at the other open grates in floor. "Any luck?"

"Not one damn meal."

Xan exhaled.

Mick kicked the pile of tools lightly with his heel. "I haven't eaten much of anything in the past two days."

He thought about the city and the images he saw on the screen. The carnage unfolding on the streets. Bodies sleeping forever along the walks.

"Should we leave the girls behind?"

Mick nodded. "They'll be fine. It'd be easier for just the two of us to travel anyway. We could take one of the smaller vehicles."

Xan gripped the hatchet. "Okay."

Mick glanced at his hand. "I haven't searched the whole place yet. There might still be some food in here."

"Did they mention anything about water?"

Mick shrugged his shoulders. The two men stood over the pile of weapons in silence.

Mick moved away from the open grate and tapped on the others in the room. He bent down and tried to pry one of them open with no luck.

Xan moved towards the front entrance. He went to one of the smaller doors. It creaked as he slid it back. He peeked outside at the battered city in the distance. He saw the glimmer of light starting below the horizon. The sun would soon rise.

Xan flipped the hatchet from side to side, having a good look at it. He slipped it through his belt. He gazed back to the horizon as he rubbed the cold steel hatchet beside him. A tiny speck caught his eye. Someone was ploughing through the sands.

Xan's gaze widened as he watched the person struggling towards them. He pulled the hatchet from his side and ran to alert Mick. The two men went to the door and eyed the lone figure inching closer to their building. Xan gripped at his hatchet, causing his knuckles to turn white.

The figure was getting closer to them. Xan saw he had a few boxes in his hand and a cloth wrapped around his head. The man looked familiar. The lanky silhouette.

"Is that Kane?"

They stared at him from the door. Mick held the machete by his side and left his other hand on the door. He tapped on the metal door a few times with his thumb.

"Should we help him?" asked Xan.

Mick glared outside. Xan looked at the machete still in Mick's hand.

"What are you going to do?" A hot wind coursed through his chest. "Mick? What are you going to do?"

"Nothing. I'm waiting."

"Are you going to open the door for him?"

Mick didn't move.

Kane reached the door and set the box down in the sand. He knocked softly and whispered, "Mick? Mick?"

Xan wanted to slide the door fully open, but Mick refused to budge.

"What happened to you?" said Mick.

"Can you let me in?"

Mick slid the door open a bit more. "Where the hell were you? What are you getting at?"

"Mick," Xan said.

"I got knocked out cold," said Kane.

"Right. Sure you were."

Kane took a step backward. "Are you upset?"

Mick's knuckles bulged as he gripped the machete even tighter. His other hand held firmly on the door.

"What if I am," Mick said. "You tell me what's going on. You conveniently get knocked out and then walk around like it's nothing? What are you getting at Kane? I'm not messing about!"

Mick glimpsed at the machete through the door's crack.

Kane tripped over the box at his feet. "Mick. I've had nothing to do with this. I came here for some help. It was the only place I could think of. I work with fish. I work with god damn fish! How am I going to be a part of something?"

"Let the guy in," said Xan. "He's our friend. He stares at fish all day. Come on!"

Mick twitched back and forth. He finally slid the door open. Kane looked between the two men in the doorway. Mick averted his eyes from them both.

Xan stepped outside. Kane pulled himself off the ground, his eyes fixed on them. Mick pushed Xan back and went outside first. Kane backed away from him.

Mick put the machete to his side. He bent down to pick up the box and disappeared into the garage.

Kane stood and peered through the door. "What happened?"

Xan sighed.

Kane remained outside until Xan waved him in.

"What happened to you?" asked Xan.

Kane rubbed his hands together. "I blacked out," he said. "I don't know what happened. I woke up in my building's lobby, right before the shooting began again."

Xan saw Mick tearing into one of the food packets near one of the sandrovers.

"Did you see anything?"

Kane nodded.

"And?"

Kane bared his teeth.

Xan slid the hatchet into his belt. He turned and saw Razan walking around the sandrovers inside. His sister was still leaning against the wall, half asleep.

"You think we have enough food to last us until the next ship?" Xan asked.

Mick opened another packet of food and ate it over the box.

Kane looked down. His lips quivered. "It depends on when the next ship lands," he said. "If it does."

Xan nodded to Razan then looked back at Kane. "You think the police can hold out?"

Kane hesitated. Everyone's eyes lingered on him. He rubbed his hands together. "Not from what I saw."

CHAPTER 41

Gathered in Mick's garage, they stood near one of the smaller sandrovers inside. "Then we slide through the passageway," said Kane. "That'll lead us to the vault. There's plenty of water inside. If we do this quietly, no one will notice."

Mick tapped his machete on one of the sandrovers. "What if I drop the two of you off and keep riding? I'll pitch back around when you're done?"

Kane nodded while keeping his lips pursed. "That would work. I think we can carry the containers between the two of us." Kane looked to Xan for affirmation.

"Even if we can't carry them, we'll pick them up next time," said Xan. "Does anyone else know about your water supply? Are you sure there isn't anyone left on Mars who might have heard a rumour of it?"

Kane shook his head. "It's impossible. We hired an Earth contractor when we put it in. My father has dozens of these built back home. Old family investment according to him." Kane tried to laugh.

No one else laughed. Kane looked down.

"Is there any way someone could've found out about it?" said Xan. "Have you ever been down there before the riot? It could be easy for someone to have seen you."

"I've only checked there once," said Kane. "That was almost three years ago, and I'm certain no one saw me."

"Not like we have much choice," said Mick.

Four containers lay stacked side by side with only one of them holding water.

"Let's get to it then," said Mick. He stood and picked up two containers as he made his way to the sandrover. Kane grabbed the last two and placed them in the vehicle.

"You don't want to take one of the -" Xan stopped.

"What?" said Mick.

"Shhh!"

Xan held a finger over his lips and turned his ear towards the doors. A scraping carried through the air. Rusting murmurs sank into the winds.

Xan pulled the hatchet from his side and pushed his back against the wall. Mick crept into the sandrover while Kane waved frantically to the girls.

Whispers echoed outside. A loud metal twinge creaked the door open.

The sandrover growled as Mick started it up. "Get in!" he yelled.

Kane jumped into the passenger seat. Razan and his sister sprinted towards it. The main door slid open to shouts of fury. Xan ducked down as the group flooded inside. A shot blasted against the wall. Razan and Ima picked up their pace to get to the sandrover. The invaders, firing off more shots inside.

Xan edged himself along the wall, and he saw his sister trip as she was making her way to the sandrover. Razan leaped into the back, not realising what had happened.

Xan felt the shots run over his head, punching dark blots on the walls and raining shrapnel upon him. He looked under the sandrover and saw his sister still hiding on the floor. A burst of courage revived him from his paralysis, and he threw himself into a dash. He ran quickly and jumped closer to Ima. Xan swooped alongside her and tried to lift her up. Her weight brought him down and tripped him to the floor.

"Nice place you got here," one man shouted.

He tried again to pull her up, but his hands slipped out from under her. "Get up!" he yelled.

As he looked down, Xan saw scarlet red dripping from his fingers. A hot beam snapped above him. He ducked further down, grasping at his sister. He turned her over and saw an opening in her clothes draining blood. The room grew silent. The raining shots didn't matter. The commotion continued with a flattened pulse. He couldn't breathe. He couldn't move.

I'd like to live on Mars too, he heard. *It sounds fun. I'd like to live on Mars too. It sounds fun.*

Sandrovers crushed around him into different angles. Mick crashed into them, pulling up right next to Xan and hitting the rest out of the way. "Come on!"

Xan couldn't hear him. Bright beams coursed around him, and one of them nicked at his shoulder. Xan stroked her hair.

"If you wake up now, I'll take you back home. We - we can go to the spaceport together?"

Mick grabbed his jacket but lost hold. Xan wouldn't let go of his sister. Mick came back again, tugging once more, throwing them both in the back seats.

Razan screamed. "OH MY GOD! OH MY GOD!"

Mick ploughed through the garage, smashing into a man along the way. Xan felt something pulling at his head. He turned his to look behind him and saw Sven yelling and grinning as he shot at them. The eyes of an old friend caught his for a moment.

Razan screamed into her hands. "Oh my god. Oh my god!"

Xan looked back down at his sister and brushed her hair out of her face. "Do you want to go the spaceport now?" he asked her. "I'll take you home. I promise."

The sandrover shot out of the garage, leaving the hornet's nest behind. Shots followed closely behind them.

Kane hopped into the back seat and tried to revive her. He pulled open her clothes and worked around her wound. "Do we have any - "

Xan couldn't hear anymore.

I'd like to live on Mars too. It sounds fun.

CHAPTER 42

The broken shards of life carried their symbols into the physical world around him. People gathered, hoping their death might be painless. Chimes hung outside windows, like the industrial days of the past, to let everyone know when sandstorms started brewing. Xan looked about the room with a blank stare. His mind was always somewhere else.

A middle-aged man with a grizzly beard rested his hands on the table before him. His eyes were yellow and his face wrinkled.

"What are you carrying these days?" he asked.

Xan left his mouth open as he gazed into nowhere.

The middle-aged man picked up his hands off the table and scratched at his beard.

Xan looked up at him and opened his mouth further to say something but closed it back down.

The middle-aged man looked at Xan's hatchet. "That's the same one?" he said.

Xan reached down to the hatchet and touched it with his hand. "Same one."

The middle-aged man pulled at his neck folds, bringing them further off his skin. "You don't wanna take anything else with you?"

Xan shook his head.

The man picked at the front of his teeth with his thumbnail. His eyes looked at nowhere in particular, just as Xan's did. The man brought his hands down from his neck, letting it rest on top of his gun.

"How's that holding up?" said Xan.

The man pulled out the gun and turned over it a few times. "Not so good. Some days it works, others it won't."

Xan sighed as he touched the table with his fingers. The middle-aged man turned to the window in the narrow barrack. He let the gun rest limply in his hand.

"They found Eos street's hold," the man said. "Did you hear?"

"No."

"Found it a few days ago."

Xan looked over the man's shoulder through the window. He studied the large room filled with ragged souls waiting to die. Xan watched an older man walk around the room speaking to everyone but being listened to by none.

Xan bit at his lower lip. "There were a lot of older folks at Eos," he said.

The man took in a large breath. "That's right," he said. "They had the largest group."

Xan sighed through his nose.

The middle age man forced a laugh and tugged the folds on his neck. "I guess that leaves us and Central barrack," he said. "Which do you think'll go first?"

Xan looked at the faulty laser resting crookedly on the man's fingers.

"I'm only joking. Being stupid," he said, regripping his gun tightly.

Xan fixed the hatchet at his side. "I need to head out."

The middle-aged man stayed in his trance for a few moments. His yellow eyes focused back on Xan.

"You think they'll ever get their justice?" said the man. "I worked in the factories too."

Xan glanced down at his hands and rubbed his palms.

The middle-aged man tapped a brown package on the table. "Don't misplace this set," he said. "Yeah?"

Xan scooped up the package. "I didn't misplace the last one."

"Well, you'd better hang tight to those. She's done making them."

Xan looked at the wrapped package. "She's too tired?"

The man gave an empty laugh as he pulled at his neck folds. "That'd be nice," he said. "I'd like to think that maybe she just got tired and moved on, you know?"

Xan squinted his eyes. "I don't," he said.

The old man pulled at his neck with a red itch. A trembling smile ran over his face. "She stayed at Eos," he said. "You knew that?"

Xan held the package with reverence. He opened it a little, touching the chimes with his finger as he brought them closer to himself.

He saw the old woman making them. Taking care of every detail. He saw her hanging them in the air, listing to the wind pull through them, smiling to herself.

Xan opened his mouth. "When did she move from her dome? She was safe up there."

The middle-aged man shrugged. "Who remembers?"

Xan cradled the chimes in his arm.

The man looked through the window to the holding area. "Maybe she wanted to be with others?" he said. "No one stays in these barracks for the protection. None of us want to die alone."

Xan stared at the hopeless residences. The middle-aged man pulled at his beard again with a rough twist. His bared his teeth as he thought.

Xan looked at the chimes and returned to his thoughts.

The old lady sat in a small room making the chimes. Fire was erupting around her as she stayed focused on her artwork. A figure entered her room. The man's shadow stretched across her wall like a tall curtain. She turned her face to the intruder, gave him a pleasant smile, and then went back to her trinkets. A blast fired through her back. Her bloodied hands swept up and down the chimes as she smiled.

Xan pulled away from the window. "I need to head back," he said.

"Sure," said the man. "Do what you have to."

Xan moved a step and hesitated. "I'll stop by in a few weeks then."

The man went closer to him. "I'll walk you out."

The two men walked past the guards at the back entrance and bid their goodbyes. Xan went down a metal ramp towards the city streets. He walked past the corner and glanced at the vacant world around him. His shadow grew longer beneath his feet as the sun set. The winds tossed sand at his jacket. Xan pulled his leather goggles over his face and kept watch around the buildings.

He lingered at the outskirts behind a giant block of rubble. Then he pulled a telescopic lens from his bag and glanced up the hill. Nothing moved other than chimes hanging from their domes. They picked up their tune in the unsettled air.

He turned his attention to the streets one last time before he stepped out. He ran quickly up the hill. The maze of houses rang their welcome to him, each ringing their own tune.

Xan pushed himself faster to the top of the hill. He watched his back to make sure no one followed him. When he reached the dome, he knocked on the door in a pattern. A different pattern tapped from inside the dome.

He opened the door. Razan stood behind, it waiting for him.

"Did you get them?" she asked.

"Yeah," he said, handing her the package.

She unwrapped it.

"We have to keep a better eye on these," he said.

Razan picked up the chimes, rotating them in her hand.

"June died," he explained.

Razan sat at the little table and placed the chimes in front of her. Her eyes watered as she grasped them in her hands. Xan swallowed hard.

Razan let go of the chimes and placed them down on the table. She looked to the wall as a tear flowed down her cheek. "I didn't know she died," she said.

Xan nodded. "Me too."

He sat down beside her and thought about rubbing her back. She rubbed her eyes with the heel of her palm.

"There was a signal today," she said. "I saw it while you were out."

Xan glanced towards the window. "We'd better go then. It's nearly dark."

"I'm not going."

"What? Why not?"

"I'm just not going."

Xan pulled his seat back, rubbed his face, and let out a sigh. "It'd make me feel better if you came."

"No."

"Please?"

"Stop it," she said. "I said I'm not going."

Xan pursed his lips and looked away from her. With a sigh, he picked himself up and pulled the telescopic lens from his bag.

"I shouldn't have told you about June," he said, placing the lens up to his eye. Someone had marked a signal across the dome three houses below theirs.

Razan stood up from the table and stormed off into the bedroom. Xan heard the door slam behind her.

"For fuck's sake! What's your problem?" Xan marched towards the bedroom door. "I'll go by myself then. How's that for respect?"

Faint cries slipped under the door. Xan beat his fist on the door. "First you won't follow me to the barrack, and now you're backing out of the meeting?" His fist hurt from slamming it on the door. "Open the door," he said. "Razan! Open the door!"

She kept crying inside the room.

Xan moved back and watched the door, then he went to the table. He tossed a cup against the wall. It broke and fell to the floor in pieces. He glared at the door again and ran back to beat on it.

"It's not easy for any of us," he said. "We all die no matter where we are!"

Small cries filtered under the cracks.

He listened as he pulled a hiss through his mouth. "Fine. I'm going. You'll be all alone. While I'm off thinking the worst!"

There was no response.

He put his hands flat up against on the door. "I didn't mean to upset you," he said

Her sobs continued.

"I wish you'd come with me," he whispered. His fingers ran down the door. "I don't feel safe. Not even in my own head."

Xan pulled away from the door and pushed himself back. Nothing stirred from the room. He waited. Then after a long time, he picked up the broken cup pieces from the floor and laid it on the counter.

"I'm going now," he paused. "I didn't mean to upset you. I didn't know..." He opened the latch. The winds swept inside the dome and around his legs. "Bye..."

He stepped outside. Tiny grains of red sand crunched with each step he took. The winds flapped the tail of his coat behind him. Tiny dings piqued at his ears as the chimes sang louder.

Xan kept himself low as he weaved through the buildings. He peeked around each corner. He stopped to look up at his dome. No movement nor any lights on.

"God," he whispered. "Why won't you come with me?"

Xan leaned against the back of a dome and sat on the ground. The cool breeze licked at his face while sand shifted around his feet. "Sorry," he said, looking at his dome. "I'm sorry. For everything."

The chimes plucked their chords along the gust. Xan listened to them as he watched the stars unfold above. They had grown brighter since the city died.

"We'll take that ship back," he said. "You and I. We won't have to worry about a thing after that. They'll land right over there," he said, pointing towards the empty spaceport. "Even if I have to smuggle us on it. We'll do it. We'll get it right this time." He clenched his fists.

What would I tell them? he thought. *She was their favourite child.*

"What would I tell them?" he said.

He stared at the silent dome. He shook his head and pressed his eyes shut. He wanted to shake the nasty cobwebs out of his head. They clung to his skull like grime in the dark recesses of abandon.

"We wouldn't ever see them," he said. "We'd never go back there. We'll stay away from them, forever. We'd live somewhere else. We'd never let them know. It'd be for the best."

Xan felt the stars gazing down on him from the burning heavens. The small clock inside his head reminded him of the meeting. The hands pointed past the designated time. He pulled himself back up and snuck around the dome. Xan reached the door and tapped a pattern on it. A few knocks came back to him, and the door opened. Xan held his hatchet as he stepped in.

Mick sat at the table, giving him a half-hearted nod. Kane stood next to the open door. "Evening," he said.

"Yeah."

Xan entered and walked to the small table, pulling a chair from it. Kane shut the door and clicked the latch. Xan kept his eyes near the window. He saw Kane's chimes hanging outside. A small piece of crystal hung on the middle string, dangling in the wind.

"You heard about Eos?" Mick said.

Xan nodded. "Found out today."

The room went quiet.

"June lived there," said Xan. "She was making chimes when they broke in."

"Where'd you hear that?"

"Down at Centre Street. Got the last set of chimes she made."

Mick pulled a bottle out of his jacket and placed it on the table. He opened the top and took a swig. He then passed it to Kane who took a sip and then passed it to Xan.

"Did you hear the rumours about the frontier ship up north?" said Mick.

Xan passed the bottle back to Mick. "No."

Mick took another drink and passed the bottle. "It's a load of crap," he said.

Kane took a slow sip and then passed the bottle to Xan. "It's the reason I called the meeting," said Kane.

Mick looked down with dead eyes, too tired to care.

Xan held on to the bottle. He rubbed his thumb along it in thought. Mick kept his eyes down. Kane glanced at Xan and then Mick.

Xan took a swig and then passed the bottle along. "So what's the rumour?"

Kane scoffed. "What does it matter?"

Mick bobbed his head.

Xan rapped his thumb on the table. "At least tell me about it."

Kane brushed the top of his hand. "There's word about a frontier ship up north," he said. "Talk about some scientists fixing it up to fly."

"Right," spat Mick.

Kane ignored him. "It's plausible. Is it that big of a stretch to believe?"

"Where would they get the tools for a project like that?" asked Mick. "It's another rumour. Don't be stupid."

"What makes you so certain?" said Kane. "You don't know what these people are capable of. They've built and maintained atmospheric stations up there for years, and now you're convinced they're just sitting on their arses?"

"Wouldn't be surprised," said Mick.

"They have the resources to undertake such a project," said Kane. "Under normal circumstances, it might take less than a year to complete but it's been close to two years now, and you're telling me they couldn't do it?"

"How are they going to work on a giant ship without being noticed?" said Mick. "We can hardly walk out of our front doors without being killed, and I'm expected to believe these meek scientists up north are risking their lives every day to rebuild a ship?"

Xan took another swig and kept the bottle for himself.

Kane slapped his palm on the table. "You wouldn't do the same? You wouldn't risk your life every day if it gave you a chance at freedom?"

Mick snatched the bottle from Xan and lifted it even higher as he drank. "Word gets out." He wiped his mouth with his wrist. "Anything that happens around here catches someone's ear eventually. Doesn't matter what city you're living in. It's all the same."

Kane kept his eyes on the table, his nostrils flared. Xan raised the bottle higher as he drank, then passed the last sips back to Mick.

"Isn't it worth it?" said Kane. "The possibility that it's true. In the chance they've really done it. Isn't that worth it?"

Kane jerked his head up. "What is our plan for staying down here? Honestly, what do you expect will happen in the next few years? Do you genuinely think they'll come back for us? Is that what we're waiting for? Someone to come and get us?"

Mick finished the last of the bottle and put it to the side. He wiped his face with his open palm.

Kane continued. "Have you seen the ships up there? They left some of them almost fully intact. Not all of them are wrecks. I believe if anybody were to put one of those ships back together, it'd be Mons."

Mick crossed his arms.

Xan tapped his finger on the table. "Could it make the journey back to Earth?"

"They made it here once. Why can't they go back?"

"Would it be safe?"

"Compared to what?" Kane looked them in the eye. His hand still lay flat on the table. "Look at it this way, we either sit here and die or take the risk of exploding mid-air. Even then we wouldn't know. The explosion would make it painless. Nothing like having your throat sliced."

Xan put his hand up. "Kane," he said. "Get back to the ship."

Mick scratched his head roughly.

Xan sighed. "When does it leave?"

"Six months from now."

Mick laughed. "How are we going to get up there?"

"That's why I've called this meeting. If you'd let me talk."

Mick's mouth hung open a little.

Kane wiped his hands across the table. "If you're serious about going, then we need to discuss logistics." Kane pulled out a piece of film with a map of the two cities on it. "There are routes to Mons," he said. "People have done it before."

Kane pointed to a mountain ridge that snaked all the way from Meridien to Mons. "Look, if we keep to this ridge here, then we could find caves along the way to keep safe during the storms."

"And if we can't find a cave when a storm comes?" Mick said.

"We'll latch a portable dome above our rover," said Kane. "We'll go near one of the mountain bases and wait it out. It won't be as powerful near the base of a ridge."

"What if the sandrover only makes it halfway?"

"Then we'll walk. We could still make it in time. Especially if we give ourselves more than two weeks to get there."

Xan thought about the vacation he took up North. *His family was walking the city streets. The old atmospheric stations stood like giant pyramids.*

"You know," said Xan. "I vaguely remember seeing those ships. They weren't right beside the city, but they were in the background. It's possible they could've rebuilt one."

"That's what I'm saying," said Kane.

"You're sure we could make it up there?"

Kane looked around the table. "The old ground transports made the journey in a day. Even if we had to walk halfway, we could make it."

Xan paused for a second. "What about Sven?"

Kane scrunched his brow and pursed his lips. "We leave him. Let him rot to death like the rest."

Xan shifted. "What if he makes it out somehow?"

"He won't," said Kane. "Leave him to die. In twenty years, no one will be here. That'll give us both more peace than doing it ourselves."

The room went silent. The men kept to their thoughts. Mick brought out another bottle and opened the top. He passed it to Kane for the first swig.

"So," Mick said.

Xan took the bottle from Kane. "You loved her?"

Kane eyed him. "I cared for her," he said. "I want him dead too."

Xan took a swig. "Not like I do."

"Are you serious? You'd rather stay back and keep plotting his death when a golden opportunity sits right in front of us?"

"How are we to know a ship won't come in? What if they take him to Earth? Could you live in peace knowing that?"

Kane shook his head. "They're not coming back."

Mick laughed.

"How do you know?"

'They're not," said Mick.

Xan took another swig.

"You're not a killer," said Kane. "Face it, none of us are."

They sat in stillness for a while. Xan finally passed the bottle on. Kane nicked it from the table and took a drink.

"I have an old engine in one of my cellars," said Mick. "They've left some of the frames in the old garage. I saw them the other day." Mick reached for the bottle. "It'd take a while to fix it together. And I can't promise how far it'll get us."

Kane nodded. "I can help you with it. There's a small generator with a bit of juice left in my vault. We can use it for tools or to give it a charge."

"Save it for the charge," said Mick. "We'll rebuild it by hand. It'll be a bitch, but we'll manage."

"If we have the three of us?"

The two men looked at Xan. Xan's bitter eyes looked away. The bottle was passed around in silence. When it reached Xan, he looked up to see them waiting for his response. He said nothing more.

***

Xan knocked outside his dome for over ten minutes. Nothing echoed back to him. His heart thumped. He knocked faster. Then he threw his shoulder into the door. It flung open.

Pushing the door further, he crept in, pulling out his hatchet from his side. He twisted on a tubular light and illuminated the main room. The chimes tapped slowly outside his window.

"Razan?" he whispered.

He approached the bedroom, pressing his ear against the shut door. A quiet echo sounded from inside. He knocked a few times.

"Razan?"

The chimes dinged lightly outside. Xan beat on the door with his fist. "Come on Razan. I need to know you're okay. I need to talk with you!"

A few seconds passed. Xan grabbed his hatchet and readied his aim. The door creaked open. Xan lowered his hatchet.

"Didn't you hear me? I knocked outside for over fifteen minutes. What are you doing in there?"

She rubbed her red eyes and looked towards the wall behind him. "I don't know," she said. "I'm not feeling well."

She moved out of the doorframe and lay on the bed. Xan moved into the room, his heart thumping in his chest. He sat on the bed and placed his hand on her back. She refused to face him.

"How long have you been feeling unwell?" he asked.

She didn't respond.

Xan turned to the wall. "Can you please talk to me?"

Razan started to cry.

"Razan, I need to know!"

"Let me sleep," she said, moving away from him.

Xan reached for her back but ended up retracting his hand. Both of them did not say anything. He listened to her sniff between tears.

"Can you talk with me? Please?"

"What do you want me to say?"

"Anything," he said.

"There's nothing to say."

"Is it your lungs?"

"No."

Her eyes filled with tears as she rolled onto her back and placed her hands over her abdomen.

"Your head?"

"No."

Xan reached over, placing his hand on top of hers. "There might be a way back," he said. "If you open up to me, I can help you."

Tears ran past her cheeks. The winds picked up outside. The chimes clanged faster.

"You won't leave," she said. "You can't."

Xan licked his chapped lips. "I'm willing to," he said.

"I know you."

Xan took his hand from hers and placed the light further down the bed. He opened his mouth, but his words got stuck in his throat. Razan looked up at him.

"They've rebuilt a freight up north," he said. "One of the old frontier ships."

Her sniffs lessened.

"If we hold out for another few months," he said.

She dabbed her eyes on her sleeves.

"We can buy you new lungs on Earth," he said. "I'll get you on that ship. I'll get you back down there."

Her lips quivered. "It's not my lungs," she said.

Xan sighed. "Would you just tell me?"

She glanced down at her hands. Xan followed them to her abdomen. Tears built up in her eyes.

Xan shook his head. "What is it?"

He looked back at her stomach, and his eyes widened. "No. No."

"It's been a little over two months. And I can't get rid of it."

Xan touched her stomach. "What about Centre hold? They might have some tools."

"I'm not going to some butcher."

Xan moved to the side of the bed. "Okay," he said. "Okay."

She turned on to her side.

He looked into her eyes. "There's no other choice then," he said. "We have to go."

Another bead rolled down her face. "You'll never be ready for that. Not until he's dead."

Xan held her hand.

"I knew it."

He opened his mouth.

She glanced into his eyes and moved closer to him.

"Let him rot," he said.

She moved towards him and placed her head in his lap, wrapping her arms around his waist.

Xan stroked her back. "I'll get you there," he said. "I promise. Even if you're the last one aboard that ship."

"Don't leave me," she said. "I don't want to do this by myself."

Xan continued to stroke her back. "I won't."

CHAPTER 43

Xan kept gazing outside the window as he held a bag full of baby formula, water, and dry meals. The night whispered cool and steady.

"Anything?" she asked.

"Not yet."

Xan felt her pacing the dome behind him. A knock came at the door. Razan moved towards it, but Xan shot in front of her and motioned for her to be quiet and back away as he pulled out his hatchet.

He knocked three times in response. Two more knocks sounded.

"Something's wrong," he said. "Damn it."

Xan cracked the door, and Kane slipped inside. Xan closed it behind them. "It's not working is it?"

"The rover's fine," said Kane.

"Where's Mick?"

"There's a few groups patrolling the hills. Mick's lying low until they pass. I came by foot to let you know it might take some time."

Xan put his hatchet back. "This doesn't sound right."

Kane stood by the circular window, keeping watch. "They seem fixed on something over there," he said. "I thought Mick might arrive before me. I guess he's still waiting it out."

Kane turned back to watch Razan pace the floors. His eyes lingered on her rotund belly before he looked at Xan.

Xan eyed him back. "She'll be fine," he said.

"Is she ready for this kind of trip?"

"The same as us."

Kane peeked at her again. "If we have to go by foot. The strain..."

"We've discussed it. We understand the risks."

Razan rubbed her abdomen. "Losing the baby is the least of my concerns. I can handle that."

Kane set his gaze back out the window and suddenly ran to the door. "It's him. We're ready."

Xan glanced at Razan. "You ready?"

Razan nodded.

The group left the quiet dome and headed into the night. Their feet made faint crunches as they rushed through the sands. Xan helped Razan into the sandrover then jumped in himself. The vehicle took off with a silent breeze.

"Goodbye," Xan whispered to the domes.

No one spoke as they rode towards the northern hills. Their senses remained sharp and their mouths shut.

Mick pointed towards the mountain ridge. "This way, through here?" he asked.

"That's it," said Kane. "We'll follow them all the way up."

The sandrover drove along the outskirts of the darkened city. Whispers of old ghosts called to them. Xan could feel a heavy air upon his breath. He put his hand on his chest for a while.

"You okay?" said Razan.

"Yeah," he said. "I haven't been out for a ride in some time. I forgot how dry the wind can be."

She reached over and held his hand as she lay on his chest. "The stars are so bright tonight," she said. "It never felt like this in town."

Xan looked up at the sky and saw the glitter of blue and purple specks. "It reminds me of my time on the ship," he said. "It looked like this on the flight deck. It was the one thing I looked forward to."

Razan smiled at him. "I wish we'd known each other back then."

"Me too," he said. "That would've been one more thing to look forward to."

The stars clustered in the dark sky. The sandrover pulled away from the city and worked towards the horizon. A giant bump threw them around their seats and Mick struggled to regain control.

"Damn," Mick said.

"Turn on the lights," Kane suggested.

"Not until we're far enough out."

"It's no good if we end up wrecking before we get there."

Mick pursed his lips and continued driving under the starlight.

Xan lay his head back to look at the flickers above. He searched for a blue star amongst them. The thought of his sister roused inside him. The sandrover jerked to a sudden halt. Xan crashed into the seats in front. Razan's belt kept her in hers. Xan rubbed his head.

"Are we being followed?" said Mick.

Xan turned his head and saw movement in the darkness. Suddenly, headlights snapped on, blinding him. The sandrover shot out of its stall. Two vehicles roared behind them, steadily gaining more speed.

"Get down," Xan told Razan.

Red beams sailed above their heads. Fire erupted alongside their rover, knocking their wheels off course. Voices chanted behind them, laughing and shouting with glee.

Another blast exploded in front, causing the sandrover to swerve into an uncontrolled twist. The machine snagged, launching Xan from his seat and flat onto the sand.

The sandrover sped off again. Two vicious machines raced behind them. Xan pulled himself up, watching the chase. A dull laser shot him square in the back, burning through his clothes and knocking him to the ground. Touching the leathery mark on his back, he grimaced, then rolled away quickly, narrowly missing a set of wheels.

Xan pushed to his feet and ran. Mick swerved, dodging the explosions and savage machines behind him. Xan watched, his eyes reflecting the lights when the sandrover crashed, and Kane dove out from it.

Zipping past them, the two sandrovers sped on, then circled back. Xan reached the side, and he saw Mick unable to restart the engines. Razan was lying still in her seat.

Another beam pierced straight through Mick's hand, splashing blood and shrieks into the air. The red warmth splattered onto Xan's face. Mick rolled out of the vehicle, holding his hand, screaming with rage.

Xan tugged at Razan. "GET OUT," he yelled.

Her eyes opened. Another explosion rippled beside him, throwing him from his feet. Kane was lying nearby, holding his bloody shoulder and trying to get to his knees. A silent pause hung in the air for only a second before a loud crack set the sandrover ablaze.

Xan stood in the outline of the giant fire. He leaped to the side of the vehicle and got hold of Razan. She moved her hands frantically, grabbing onto him with her weak hands.

"Hold on," he said.

A final gust erupted within the machine. Xan was thrust backward, and he watched the sandrover get engulfed in flames. Xan clawed towards the machine. He gripped the scalding bars and ripped Razan from the inferno. Her eyes lay open, but they gazed at nowhere.

"No," he said. "Wait. Razan! Wait!"

He struggled to pull her dead weight from the heat. The flames pushed him out. He waved his hand in front of his face to diffuse the heat, then rushed back in and threw her body away from the machine. Red blisters covered her skin. Xan smacked the flames off her clothes quickly and then felt her abdomen.

Another explosion made him duck. The machine ignited the sky. Xan rolled over and screamed. Razan's body lay a few meters away. Dark figures gathered at the fire, chanting their praise. Xan crawled towards her and pulled her body closer. Then he dragged her behind a large rock. Grabbing her face, he pulled it up and tried to look into her eyes.

A crack sounded on the other side of the rock. Xan cowered in time. His eyes widened. Fury burned in his chest. He gently rested Razan up against the rock and stood, hatchet in his hand.

Another blast erupted close to him. He threw his body over Razan as a shield. He hugged her neck with fear in his eyes. He rubbed the back of her head, thinking of when they first met, how she put the gun down from his chest.

A man stepped around the side of the rock, his weapon charging in his hands. He grinned as he aimed it at Xan. Xan looked into his eyes then turned back to Razan. He pulled her closer into his chest and put his head around her neck.

The man spat on the ground. "Get up and take it like a man," he said.

Xan clenched tighter. "You'll have to shoot me like this, Sven," he said.

Sven backed a few steps, his FOBEL launcher still aimed at Xan. "You had your chance," he said. "I handed everything to you on a silver platter."

Xan held on tightly to Razan, waiting for their journey to end. Sven clicked the trigger, but it hissed a dud. Xan looked up at him.

Sven growled, charging it to a quarter full, and re-aimed his FOBEL at Xan.

"It won't make you feel any better," said Xan.

Sven clicked the trigger, throwing them from their position. Xan felt the warmth of death upon his face. His breath laboured, and his chest grew too cold and heavy to continue.

CHAPTER 44

Xan woke up in a strange bed. His head was spinning. His face burned with unbearable pain. He sat up and scratched his head, and he screamed. Kane ran into the room.

"You're all right," he said. "You're all right! We're safe. We're safe." He grabbed Xan's hands.

Xan flung away, hitting the bed with his fists. He tried to pull the hatchet from his side but found it missing. Kane approached him. Xan shoved him away then stopped to look at his shaking hands.

They looked like scarred leather, covered in red blisters and scabs. He felt a deep pain wrenching throughout his entire body. Xan fell to the floor, trying to stop his arms from shaking. He then curled into his chest.

Kane stood over him with a small liquid cup. "Take this," he said. "Trust me, it will help with the pain."

Xan couldn't hold his hands steadily enough to take the liquid.

"Here," said Kane, placing it under his mouth for him.

Xan drank the top, feeling a cooling sensation rush over his body. He could catch his breath again.

Xan leaned his back against the giant window and focused on Kane. "You're shot?"

Kane touched his shoulder. His eyes remained fixed on Xan with a strange grimace on his face.

"What?'

"I thought you would die," said Kane. "You've been out for three days. Do you remember waking up to scream?"

"No. Why are you looking at me that way? Huh?"

Kane averted his eyes.

"Answer me damn it!"

Kane turned his back to him.

Xan stared at his hands again, shaking like chimes in the wind. "Why are you looking at me like that?"

Swallowing his breath, Kane glanced over his shoulder. "Your skin..."

"What do you mean?"

Beside a large cabinet, Xan spotted a mirror shard on the floor. Grovelling towards it, he caught sight of the red face looking back at him, smooth as leather, yet covered in scars.

A blast sounded, throwing him into the sand.

Xan lifted the mirror.

He reached into the vehicle, trying to pull Razan from it. "GET OUT!" Another blast threw him back to the ground.

Xan chucked the mirror onto the wall. He felt hot again. The flames charred his innermost senses.

"Give me more of that stuff," said Xan.

"You shouldn't take any more."

"GIVE IT BEFORE I BREAK YOUR GOD DAMN HEAD!"

Kane stared at him and then slowly poured another dose. Xan snatched it out of his hand and downed it in a single gulp. Cooling waves pulsed within him. The thick liquid numbed his veins. The chill drew deep into his chest.

Red flames ignited across the sands.

Xan gagged.

Razan was limp sitting in the sandrover.

Xan coughed.

She opened her eyes.

Xan spewed out dry heaves.

He held her close to his chest.

Xan vomited a glob of purple mucous lined with blood.

Razan looked up at him.

More bloody mucous shot out of his mouth and onto the floor.

Xan's eyes filled with warm tears. His tears fell, mixing with the hacked up mess. Kane kneeled down and patted him on the back with his good arm. Xan couldn't say anything. His system wouldn't stop its heaves.

He placed her up against the rock.

Xan's head fell to the ground as he passed out.

CHAPTER 45

Flames ripped through the sandrover.

"Kane?"

Ima slipping through his bloody hands.

"Yes?"

"The stars are so bright tonight," she said. "It never felt like this in town."

"Where's Mick?"

"It was the one thing I had to look forward to."

Kane mumbled in the silence.

"I wish we'd known each other back then."

"Kane?"

"Me too. That would've been one more thing to look forward to."

"Yeah?"

"What happened to Mick?"

Xan could hear Kane scratching at the floor as he mumbled.

Silence hung inside the walls. The night was dark while the broken city snagged the winds with a somber lull.

"I don't know," said Kane. "There was too much commotion."

Mick's hand burst into a bloody mess.

"He got out of the sandrover," said Xan. "It was his hand."

"I saw him on the ground right before the others came," said Kane.

"More of them?"

"No. Another group heading up north."

"Oh."

"Sven lost his focus on you and started to go after them…"

Xan put his face down.

"You were still breathing," said Kane. "So I dragged you back."

Xan opened his mouth to ask but he couldn't. It had been a long time since he'd stayed in the city at night. Bittersweet memories pricked faint reminders in his head.

Xan moved out of the bed and walked to the door. "Where's my hatchet?"

"In the main room."

Xan walked out to the main room. Kane followed him. He saw his hatchet sitting on the torn couch. He picked it up and put it back at his side.

"I'll be fine now," said Xan. "You can go back to your dome."

Kane said nothing as he stood in the silent room. Xan entered the abandoned hallway, each step echoing softly. Gone was the old city he had lived in. Reconstructed materials were left to rot. Rooms were left like dead empty spaces.

Xan headed into the breezy night. He turned his head in every direction, looking for something he could recognise. He drifted, talking to himself. His feet clambered in front of him, not taking instructions from his mind. It didn't matter to him where they took him. Nothing did.

"Me too. That would've been one more thing to look forward to."

Xan opened his eyes. It was all so familiar to him.

"Me too. That would've been one more thing to look forward to."

Xan opened his eyes again.

"Me too. That would've been one more thing to look forward to."

Xan opened his red eyes.

"One more thing..."

Xan clenched his fist.

"Look forward to."

The familiarity rang inside him like a barren tree with black roots.

"One more thing..."

Xan fell to the ground, his blistered hands catching the tears from his eyes.

"Look forward to."

Xan dropped his face to the floor. He beat his swollen fists on the floor.

A taste of cheese.

He stayed in his position of tearful prayer.

Their lips met.

Xan dragged his body into a standing position. He knew this place. He looked at the aquarium that once housed a little crayfish. The deactivated birds now lay lifeless on the floor. Xan touched the couch he had sat in every night, stroking it back and forth. Back and forth.

"Zola?" he called.

"Zola?"

Yes sir?

"Is Razan running late again? Was there another strike?"

I believe so sir. She asked me to pick her up later than usual. Shall I prepare your dinner now?

"She's been working herself pretty hard," he said. "Those damn workers. They're all bastards don't you think?"

Yes sir. Bastards indeed.

"Has my sister come back yet?"

No sir. She's gone on a date with your friend Kane.

Xan laughed. His laughs gradually turned into painful whinges. He fell to the floor again, placing his back against the couch.

"They're an item aren't they?" he said. "I knew it. What can I say though? He's a good man."

Indeed, sir.

"He saved my life you know?"

Is that so?

"Oh yes. Just a few nights ago in fact. Although if I'm honest, I don't know if he did me a favour."

Oh dear, and why is that?

"Because everyone else is dead."

Oh.

"Except for you Zola," he said. "You made it back. They gave you a ticket. Lucky man. I guess if any of us deserved it, it was you."

Thank you sir.

Xan stood up to talk with Zola in his moment of excitement. Then he saw the vacant, hollow doorframe that led to the kitchen. Only the moon's light shone through the windows.

Xan stroked the top of the couch again. He felt the cold steel hatchet at his side. He pulled it out from his strap and lifted it over his head and then swung it into the couch. He pulled it back out with a tug and threw it back in. Over and over, he smashed the hatchet into the couch. Pieces ripped into the air. Back and forth, he severed into the torn couch.

Xan yelled as he flipped it over. He walked away towards the stairs and went up into his old room. He went to the window and looked down at the pavement below. "Ahhh," he said.

Xan drew his hatchet back and slung it into the window. Shards of glass chipped away. He slung it again and again until it burst open. A large gash split along the back of his hand. He didn't notice as he gazed down at the pavement.

This is it, she said to him.

"It is," he said. "Down we go."

Xan brought his foot towards the edge. He felt the winds pouring through the glass, thrusting him back into the room. He inched closer but kept getting pushed inside by the flowing winds.

Xan snapped around quickly and threw his hatchet into the room. It smashed into the mirror, raining shards onto the floor. He meandered towards it. He kneeled down in search of his hatchet. His hands and knees bled, leaving him with a cold warmth. The pain felt beautiful to him. He felt he deserved it.

His body shook as it lost more fluid. He slowly lowered himself down on the shards, refusing to fight it anymore. Xan thought about getting up to escape the slices in his flesh. But his body already understood. The winds blew in through the broken window, chilling his bones and cooling his blood.

And soon the night took him in.

* * *

His hands stuck to the floor from his own dried blood. His face was cold and smeared with crust. His eyes were the only thing he could move. They looked straight into the old closet at the hanging clothes of people he once knew.

It haunted him, knowing those fabrics touched their skin at one point. Dead cells and loose hairs lingered in their fibres. His eyes scanned the closet and paused upon an item inside. He recognised that old lump against the wall.

Xan whispered to himself. "It's still there," he said. "Waiting for me to open it."

A low pulse rose from inside the safe.

Sven was crawling on the ground. Xan was shooting at his body, again and again, filling him with reddened bullets for all he'd done to him. Each fire brought him less pain.

Razan was smiling. His sister was happy again. Mick and Kane reverted to their old selves with big grins on their faces.

Xan tried to pull himself up but found his body too weak. He lay staring at the safe, praying to it like an alter god.

His fingers twitched, and his hand became unstuck. He climbed to his knees with a blistering pain as his healing wounds stretched open again. He pulled himself up and slumped into the closet. His fingerprints smeared blood upon the safe.

Xan tried to drag it out further but found it too heavy. He sat down beside it in the silent closet for a while.

"I'll come back for you," he said to the safe. "Trust me."

He pulled himself up and crunched pieces of glass under his feet. Xan stopped by his old bed and touched her pillow. "I'll be right back," he said. "You take care while I'm gone."

She didn't answer.

He went down the stairs, then up into his sister's old room. Her bed lay undone like she had just woke up. He stepped over to the wall above her bed and opened the scabs on his hand. Tracing with his finger, he left a bloody message on the wall.

Sorry, it read.

* * *

Xan walked along the city's outskirts, looking at the charred wreckage from the fight. The sands absorbed the red blood. Black twisted remnants of sandrover frames aimed their sharp edges into the air.

Xan saw a few people scattered on the land. Their faces were silent as he approached them. Every one of them had their own story to tell. A man had his arm outstretched as if reaching for something above his head. Another was missing his leg.

Xan walked by a mangled sandrover, moving his hand over it and touching its burnt remains. The wheels had melted into dripping clocks that bled their tar onto the ground below.

Xan turned over his shoulder. He saw the large rock a little way off and took a deep breath before he marched towards it.

The winds blew a soft caress upon his face as he walked towards her. He saw that time had already eroded her life away. Xan turned his head back to the city as he kneeled down next to her. He put his head down and took hold of her hand. Yellowed bone peeked out from her leathery skin. He couldn't face her yet.

Xan stayed for what felt like forever, with his eyes shut and hands upon her hand.

He opened his eyes. She gazed off into the distance, her face covered in red blisters and open flesh.

Xan moved closer to her and touched her face. He pulled at the side of her head, running her remaining hair in between his fingers. He pushed her into his chest and closed his eyes, imagining she was alive.

"I'll make it right," he said.

He placed his hand on her abdomen, feeling its flatness. The sun hit brightly upon his face. The world seemed calm for a moment. The wreckage no longer cried out to him.

* * *

He pulled her head up over the pillow and then brought it down softly. Xan went to the end of the bed and dragged the covers over her, up to her neck. He stepped back to look at her.

Her eyes were closed as best as he could manage. Xan took another step back and went towards his closet, picking up the safe, and stopping near the bed.

"I'll be back soon," he said. "There's someone I need to kill."

CHAPTER 46

Xan stalked him to no end. The thought of red strung him along.

Hack after hack, chopping right through Sven's flesh, cracking his bones with a vicious grin. Sven bleeding dry before him, raising his hand in the air.

Without realising it, Xan's finger slid across the blade of his hatchet. It started to bleed. A dull throb grabbed his attention. He shoved his finger into his mouth and left it there.

Speaking loudly with a small tight clan, Sven ambled along, acting like the proud owner of the broken town. A tall man with long peppered hair walked at Sven's right. A bald lady and man followed closely behind, scanning the buildings.

Xan eyed them from the shadows. One by one, they entered an old barrack, the bald man first, then followed by the lady. The long-haired man kept watch behind them, and Sven slipped inside.

Retracting his head around the corner, Xan hid from sight, and the door locked shut across the street. He lingered throughout the day, studying the stolen barrack and the members going in and out.

At sunset, Sven left the barracks, followed tightly by his clan. Xan stalked them all the way to the furthest skyscraper on the eastern side of the city. They entered the building every night at sundown, never returning until the next morning.

"Where do you go?" he whispered. "Roaming the tunnels? They're yours now."

Xan waited for the sun to move lower behind the ridges before he went home. He dragged his bones up the hill and went inside his dome. He passed by a reflective shard of glass and looked into it. A bitter man stared back at him with scars dragging every inch of his face down into bitter resentment.

He stepped away from the mirror and thought about the young man he once was. His smooth face and bright eyes were now gone.

Xan sat for a moment, feeling mad, before he pulled out a small hidden jug of water near his makeshift bed and drained it. He let out a large sigh of relief and hid the jug back in its spot.

* * *

Knocking his code on the door brought a reply, then his friend appeared in the threshold. Kane stood there with a blank gaze. His face was drawn down in sullen ridges with dark moons under his eyes.

"Anything?" said Xan.

Kane shuffled in his cluttered dome and fiddled with some items on the counter. Xan shook his head, stepping into Kane's house.

Staring out the window, Kane remained in a trance, looking at his wobbly chimes and the sad crystal dangling from its string.

You're losing it, Xan thought. *Calling me down here all the time for a stupid chat. You're lonely. You can't stand dying off in this hollow dome.*

Still lost in thought, Kane started tinkering with an item on his counter, ignoring the chimes. Xan closed the door and sat down. He looked past Kane at the sad chimes struggling to ding. He couldn't take his eyes off the piece of crystal Kane had added to them.

You're the one that wanted to go up north.

Kane turned from his piddling. "Did you hear about the chimes?"

Xan shifted in his chair. "What about them?"

Kane paced the room, picking up an item along the way. He squeezed the trinket in his hands as his eyes glassed over. Kane eventually sat in a chair with his back to Xan.

Xan glanced at the chimes. "What about them?" he mumbled to himself.

Kane continued to fiddle with the trinket. "They had them in the industrial days," he said. "Before everything was well connected."

Xan sighed.

Kane looked at him for a moment with a tired glance. "I can't do it anymore," he said. "I don't have the strength."

Standing to his feet, Xan went to the window, tapping it with his knuckle. "You're tired? You signalled to tell me this?"

"If we could open your safe."

"It won't open."

"They've already won. Two men against how many?"

Xan shut his eyes tight. "You're losing sight of our mission."

"I've found someone who might help us," Kane said. "A younger guy."

Xan stepped back from the window, glaring at him. "You what?"

Kane gazed between the window and door. "He knows Sven's clan. He says he's willing to help."

Xan gripped at his hatchet.

"How long can we keep this up?" said Kane.

A knock sounded at the door. Kane drifted over.

Xan tightened his grip on his hatchet. Kane opened the door, letting a younger man with a round face and cold grey eyes inside.

"This is Geil," said Kane. "If the three of us sneak attack them."

Xan stood to the side, watching them both. Kane walked between the two. Xan quickly rushed out the door. He dug his boots into the sand and pushed himself up the hill.

Kane ran behind him. "Don't you want to hear what he has to say?"

Xan stopped. He thought about continuing on without saying a thing.

"This is it," said Kane. "We can finish it. And finally, be done."

"Have you looked this kid in the eye? He's dead inside."

"And our eyes are still alive?"

Xan closed his mouth and turned his face away. "What are you offering him?"

"Offering?"

"He's not here to be our new pal. What does he get out of this?"

Kane hesitated. "Some water," he said. "Not the location but enough to keep him happy."

Xan looked back at Kane. "Has your brain rotted away?" he said.

"There's more than enough."

"He's not after a case of water, he's sniffing out our location!"

"You can't do it."

"He'll kill us both, given the chance."

Kane spat a bitter laugh. "You don't want this to end, do you?"

Xan leered at him.

"You know nothing else," Kane said. "It's not about revenge anymore. We're busy bodies! Neither of us will ever take a stab. We're two pathetic survivors filled with delusions of heroism and vengeance!"

The corner of Xan's lip flickered.

"We're inches from finishing it. But you can't do that. Once he's dead, you'll have nothing else left."

Xan bared his teeth. "Go on then. Walk off to your death. I'll finish him off myself!"

Kane's face tightened.

"Let him bleed you dry for all I care!"

"You know I'm right," said Kane.

"Where were you when my sister died? Where Kane? Just tell me where?"

Kane's eyes narrowed, and his nostrils flared. He stepped forward to face Xan.

"Exactly," said Xan. "Running to save your own ass."

Kane punched Xan in the mouth, then grabbed him by the neck. Xan knocked Kane in the ribs and pushed him off. Grabbing his arm, Kane held to Xan, and pulled them both to the ground. They struggled to throw more punches at each other as they toppled over into the sands. Kane thrust his heels up into Xan's side, launching him to the ground.

Xan jumped to his feet, coughing, as Kane did the same. Kane held his knife out by his side. Xan grasped at his hatchet.

"Don't you blame me for what happened," said Kane. "Where were you? Hiding under a sandrover? Having a breakdown!"

Xan balled his fist around his hatchet, losing all circulation. Geil stood in the doorframe observing the little brawl. Xan looked over Kane's shoulder at the listless man. He put his hatchet back to his side and turned away.

Kane held his knife and watched Xan leave. He yelled at Xan. He screamed something about death. But Xan ploughed ahead in silence, no longer listening to his friend.

***

Xan waited inside the building, crouched near the door, waiting for the group to pass by.

"You don't need him. You don't need any of them." His finger stroked his hatchet.

Voices rippled in the air. Xan fixed his back tighter against the wall, his heart throbbing.

"Perhaps we'll leave her tied up outside when the next storm blows in?" said Sven. "Don't you all think it's petty the way she acted?"

Xan closed his eyes and listened to their voices. Both hands were wrapped around his hatchet.

"Don't you feel so?"

Xan's heartbeat pounded inside his ears. Xan tightened his grip.

A slap. "I asked you a question!" Sven slapped the lady again. "Do you think it's petty the way you acted?"

Looking around the side, Xan saw Sven and his clan gathered around a woman who had been tied up on the streets. The long-haired man pushed his ponytail to his other shoulder, then lifted his makeshift spear and poked its flat end into her ribs. The group laughed.

Sven raised his hand in the air to stop them. "Let me ask you something else," he said, kneeling down. "Do you think you own this city?"

Dirty rags remained stuffed in her mouth, leaving her unable to talk. She tried to shake her head. The bald lady smiled a toothy grin. The bald man with a tattooed face handed a small hammer to Sven.

"Do you know who does?"

Tears ran down the woman's dusty cheeks. Sven brushed the cold hammer along her face.

Xan swallowed hard, his hatchet shaking in his hands. "You don't need anyone," he whispered. "Do it. Do it now."

"We do," said Sven. "This is our land. God has returned it to us, his faithful servants."

Xan crouched into a squat.

Rubbing the hammer along her back, he stopped near her crotch and held it in place. "Does it feel good?" he said. "Women can be so sensitive."

Pushing himself along the wall, Xan began to stand. Sven curled his finger at his group. The bald lady kneeled down with a knife, cutting off the woman's gag. She ripped it out of the lady's mouth and tossed it behind herself.

"Are you ready to talk like an adult?" said Sven.

The woman spat into Sven's eye. "You schiz!"

Wiping the spit off, Sven shook his head and sighed. "No, I'm God's child. Owner of these lands." He lifted the hammer high over his head.

Xan turned his eyes as Sven dropped it. A loud crack sounded. Then a blood-curdling scream. Another crack of the hammer smashing bones. More screams.

The hatchet trembling in his hands, Xan closed his eyes and tried to shut his ears to the commotion outside.

CHAPTER 47

Xan sat alone in his empty dome, watching the chimes outside his window. Memories trickled into his head. He grimaced with a tremor.

"Play it right," he growled.

The chimes reflected off his withered eyes, taunting him, whispering through his mind.

His upper lip curled. "Play it right."

They sang their lament without care. His voice dulled to a twinge of helplessness.

"Play it right," he said. "Just play it right!"

Xan whacked his face then tugged at his grey hair. He felt a burn in his chest. A pain in his mind. A reality he refused to acknowledge. He shook his face, spittle-flinging out the sides of his lips as he rose from his seat, holding on to his aching joints.

The chimes behind him whispered in his mind. *Where are you going? You can't outrun us. We know it isn't done yet.*

"Shut up," he said. "Shut up!" He pushed away, closing his eyes for a moment. A bitter growl escaped his lips. The chimes continued to sing through the window.

Xan paced the large room. His chairs were old with rust. The table slanted with uneven mats placed beneath their legs. Backing away from the window, he glared at the chimes.

"I don't want this anymore," he said. "Why do you nag at me?"

Xan glanced at his door then back to the chimes.

"Incessant," he whispered. "As if I don't know?"

The chimes swayed as soft dings sliced through his window.

"And what if I finished it? How would you sing then?"

The room gave a silent response. Xan reached for the door latch. He pushed it open to soft winds and harsh sunlight. He stepped out, crunching bits of sand beneath his feet. His eyes blinked in the brightness.

The hill covered in matching domes soon came into focus. Xan ambled down slowly, bracing himself against the empty homes until he reached the base of the hill where a natural dune had grown.

Xan climbed to the top of it and looked over into the city. Large chunks of cement lay scattered along the streets. Fragments of old sandrovers bent into their own shapes of deformed art.

He walked along the abandoned roads, mumbling to himself all the way. The winds howled alongside him as they struck jagged chords from broken glass and worn towers. He felt an unsettled nerve twinge through his skin. He closed his eyes to listen to the crying city. A beautiful song sang inside his mind. The faint sound of the old melody echoed through his head.

He pushed himself off the wall and continued on, grains of sand gritting beneath his feet. Xan slowly stepped inside a building that had no doors and was filled with crushed glass upon the floor. He turned over his shoulder a moment to listen outside. The winds coursed steadily.

Xan licked his lips, then moved towards the staircase in the room. He walked up to the seventh floor, stopping at the top, keeping his ears pricked for any odd sounds.

"Keep going," he said. "No one's there."

He approached a door that was jammed in the centre, leaving a narrow crack just wide enough for him to slip through. Xan pushed through the sliver and entered the old supermarket. He walked under a leaning shelf and kicked litter on the floor.

He reached the back of the room where a fallen shelf lay and picked up a green can to place in his satchel. His mind ticked like the hands of an old clock.

Xan kneeled down behind the shelf and listened. A light rhythmic click hovered along the floors. The sound increased with each passing moment. It grew louder and louder as he crouched behind the shelf.

They didn't see me, he thought. *They don't come here at this time. Can't be them. Has to be the winds.*

The clicking sound entered the room.

"Someone's here," he whispered to himself. "Get up."

The steps clicked faintly as if the owner was creeping gingerly. Xan grabbed his hatchet from his side. The room went silent. Nothing for a few seconds.

Click, click, click.

He pulled himself up. He kept his head low and pulled the hatchet over his head.

The footsteps sounded near the corner of the fallen shelf.

Xan held his breath, waiting to swing.

The footsteps stopped at the edge.

He could feel them. He could feel their blood pumping the same as his.

A rustling noise sounded at the corner.

Xan swung quickly, and the blade grazed the intruder's jacket. Jumping back and pulling out a gun, the young girl cowered, aiming her barrel at him. Xan lifted his arm up and stared at her.

"Wrong move," he said. "Who do you think you are, sneaking up on me like that?"

The young girl fumbled backward, her gun still aimed at Xan.

Xan raised his hatchet again. "You little shit. You little piece of shit!"

"I'll shoot you," she said. "I'll shoot you dead right now."

Xan gazed into the girl's eyes and stopped. His hatchet lowered as he studied her.

Her gun shook, and her voice trembled. "Right," she said. "Stay there."

He took a step closer as his eyes grew wider.

The girl backed up. "I'm serious!"

Xan stepped nearer. "Why are you so young?" he said.

The girl creased her eyebrows. "What?"

"Why are you so goddamn young?"

The girl paused, her hands shaking even more. "I - I don't know," she said.

Xan smiled for a moment. "You're from Earth?" he said. "To take us back?"

"No. No, I was born here."

"DON'T LIE," he shouted. "DON'T YOU FUCKING LIE!"

The girl moved back, her eyes filled with confusion as she watched Xan. "I'm not," she said.

"THEN WHY ARE YOU SO DAMN YOUNG?"

The girl continued trembling. "I don't know? I don't know what your point is!"

Xan stepped towards her.

She jabbed the gun in the air. "I SAID DON'T MOVE!"

Xan looked down at her weapon. Then he looked back into the girl's eyes.

"It's okay," he said. "Tell me. You can say it. You're from Earth? I'm no barbarian. I'm on your side."

The girl shook her head with vigour. "What are you talking about? I'm not. I'm not from Earth!"

Xan glanced down at his hatchet. His eyes lost hope.

The girl thrust her gun at him again. "You have water?" she asked. "Go on. Hand it here."

Xan ignored her. His head hung low as he walked in her direction.

"HEY," she shouted. "STAY THERE!"

His eyes were blank as he walked past her.

The girl turned and clicked the gun, ready to charge. "You think I'm kidding?"

"Should've known," Xan said, walking on.

"What?"

Xan stopped and turned to her. The girl pushed her shaking gun at him. He breathed a heartless laugh and walked to the door.

"Wait," she said. "I'm not going to shoot you."

Xan paused with his back to the girl. "I know," he said. "I can tell you're not from here."

The girl knit her lips. Xan lingered with his hand on a shelf.

"How would you know?" she said.

Xan glanced back. "Where are you from?"

The girl lowered her gun. "Here."

Xan sighed. "Where are you from?"

She brought the gun to her side. Her mouth opened, but she hesitated. Xan looked her in the eye.

She relaxed her shoulders. "Mons."

Xan laughed.

"It's not that much better up there," she said.

Xan hummed.

She looked down at her gun. "Is there anyone else with you?"

Xan watched her, perplexed for a second.

She moved to the nearest shelf. "Are you alone?"

His eyes wandered. A painful furl creased across his brow. Then he hissed as if struck by a knife. She looked him up and down.

Xan ground his teeth back and forth. "You're not from Earth?"

"I was born here..."

"Mons." He shivered. "Mons?"

The girl squinted her eyes. "Yeah..."

"Damn." He hissed again. "Damn."

She flinched. Xan yelled as he shoved a shelf over, knocking the entire row down to the floor. Following a loud crash, the room filled with dust and pushed them both outside. Xan stormed to the staircase.

The girl rushed behind him. "Maybe you could help me out?"

He continued down the steps. "Get away from me."

"We can trade?"

"You've got nothing I want."

She pressed her laser against his back. "Nothing?"

Xan whipped around, snatching the gun out of her hands and set it upon her neck. Her eyes widened in fear.

"The hell do you want?"

She swallowed hard. "A safe place."

"There are plenty," he said. "You don't need my help for that."

"The city's dangerous," she said. "I've already spent a few nights here.'

"Go back to Mons."

The girl's lips trembled. "Please, help me out?"

"Help yourself."

"I wasn't going to shoot you! I swear!"

Xan laughed. "You think you scared me?"

Her mouth hung open a few seconds. Xan clicked the trigger. A dull tick sounded from the end of the barrel. "You look like a fool carrying this. We all know they don't work no more."

The girl looked at the dead gun touching her throat.

Xan threw it to the ground. "No one will fall for that here."

She looked at the laser for a moment and rubbed her shoulder. His eyes narrowed on her as she did. He touched his heart, feeling strange. She chewed on her lower lip with her head hung low, and continued to rub her upper arm. Xan studied her longer.

"Sorry," she whispered.

His eyes widened then squinted at the sound of her voice.

"They said there was water still down here." The girl pulled a small dagger from her side. "This is all I have left for protection."

"Good god."

The girl put the dagger back.

Xan let out a snide laugh, then slipped out the staircase. The girl followed him. They made their way through the city, avoiding the debris, and pushed through the little pelts of sand tossed at them by the dry wind. They climbed over the sand dune lining the city's outskirts. Xan continued walking up the maze of domes on the hill without paying her any attention. When they covered a fair distance, he stopped and slapped his hand on a dome as he looked at it in confusion. The girl grimaced. Xan talked to himself as the girl watched him.

"This should do," he said with hesitation. "No one will bother you in here."

"You're sure?"

Xan glanced at the dome, chewing on the corner of his lip.

"Maybe I could stay with – "

"Yeah," he said. "You'll be fine."

She nodded.

Xan held his hand on the dome for a moment. He looked back down at the city.

"You should think about returning to Mons," he said. "No other soul will treat you this nice down here."

The girl said nothing for some time. The winds pushed faster along the grounds. The city hummed louder.

"I can't," she said.

"You'd better."

She shook her head. "None of us can," she said.

Xan stepped back an inch and raised one of his eyebrows.

She looked up at him with soft eyes. "There are no more supplies up there. We're finished."

Xan toed the sand with his boot. "What makes you think we have enough down here?"

The girl kept her lips tightly shut. Xan patted the dome a few times and then shuffled back up the hill in silence. The girl watched him leave without following this time.

CHAPTER 48

The memory consumed him.

He placed his brittle finger on a dome as he watched the winds, circling small twisters. His hand scratched at his beard with nervous fury. A clattering sequence shuffled uncomfortably in his heart.

His fist banged on the oval door. "Open up you big sissy. Let's talk man to man."

His hand returned to his beard and then slowly down to his hatchet. He shouldered the door open and took a step inside. Stale air wafted the scent of decay.

"You don't mark lines after you take water anymore? Huh?"

He stood, looking out the window for his friend's chimes. Xan went closer to the window to search for the missing item. He turned to a door at the back of the room and gently tapped on it. Silence returned.

"Kane? Let's discuss this new guy," he said. "Kane?"

No answer.

Xan pushed the door. It slid open with a creak. He took one step inside the darkened room.

"Kane?" he called.

Xan lifted his foot to take another step. They were stuck to the floor from a dark adhesive grime. "The devil is this?"

He kept moving, pulling his feet up with more strength, un-sticking himself from the ground below. Echos ripped throughout the hall. As he rounded the corner, he saw Kane lying on the floor. He grabbed the side of the wall to brace himself.

"Oh god," he whispered, turning his head.

He held his arm over his face to shield himself from the sight. Kane lay with a wide slit in his neck. Xan glanced down at his feet. The dark blood had burnt to a cinder beneath him. Xan pulled his foot up with horror as he listened to it un-stick.

He stepped back down the hall, echoes following him. Xan panicked, tripping over his feet, as he went back into the living room. He heard them on the floor.

The sound of chimes rang inside the house. Xan raised his eyes. There were no chimes outside Kane's window. They were gone. The chimes grew louder. They rang faster.

Xan opened his eyes, waking from his trance. He scanned his dark home and saw his own chimes swaying outside the window. A string kept pulling the memory back through his consciousness.

Kane's eyes were wide open with is mouth agape, gasping for air.

Xan clenched his fist. The memory wouldn't fade. It sat in the corner, watching him with sharp eyes.

"It's almost done," he whispered. "I'm so close."

"Will that help?" said Kane. "Will it end?"

He could see the memory of his friend waiting at the table to remind him. *"If we went along the mountain ridge," said Kane. "We could reach it without a sandrover."*

Xan looked at his friend, sitting at his table. His neck was slit, but he was speaking as if he were alive again.

"Did you hear about the chimes?" said Kane.

"I didn't hear that part," said Xan. "I never heard the rest."

"Did you hear about the chimes?" said Kane.

Xan slammed his fist into the table. "No, I didn't hear the rest!"

"If we went along the mountain ridge," said Kane. "We could reach it without a sandrover."

Xan closed his eyes. *Kane's chimes rang in the wind. A small piece of crystal dangled at the bottom of its string, causing them to wobble unsteadily.*

"What about the chimes?" said Xan, slowly opening his eyes. "I'll listen this time."

His friend was gone. The room was empty. Xan's chimes dinged outside his window. He sat down on the floor and swished away the clouds of dust. The dust settled back into the ground.

"Will you all forgive me?"

* * *

Xan brought his face down near the floor. He blew away a stream of dust, revealing a slight crease in the ground. He slid his finger along the groove until he reached a wider gap, then pried it up with his hands.

Slowly, the floorboard rose into the air. Billows of dust exploded then vanished as they glided over the dark cavern. Xan placed his foot into the hole, catching it on the first rung of a metal ladder.

The metal bars echoed throughout the cellar. Xan entered further into darkness. When he reached the base, he twisted on a torchlight, illuminating the small cave before him.

The light shone on various cabinets etched into the walls. He picked up an old useless Vlex and brought it closer to his eyes. He gave it a few taps with his thumb before throwing it back into the pile of other defunct Vlexes.

In the middle cabinet, he picked up a paperback book: *2001 More Jokes for the Office Party*. He flipped through the pages, indulging in the old paper smell. Xan placed the book back on the shelf and gave it a kind pat.

He squatted lower to see into the bottom cabinets. Xan wiped sweat from his forehead as he stared at the safe resting on the ground. He let out a forced sniff and continued to repeat the action. He closed his eyelids, mumbling to himself an incoherent mantra.

A small tear crept out and landed on top of the safe. Brilliant lines ignited with a red glow, fading in and out. Xan watched as the lines waned.

He paused for a moment, watching it as if something else might happen. Xan lifted his head up to the opening above.

"YOU SEE?" he yelled.

He threw his light onto the floor. It smacked against the safe and then rolled down below his feet. Xan let out a harsh growl, then put the light in his satchel and pulled himself up. He looked back down at the safe.

"What good have you done?"

Xan shook his head and then leaned down to pick up a worn container with a small amount of water in it. His eyes went back down to the safe.

"I'm not ready," he said. "Not yet."

The safe said nothing.

* * *

He pulled out a telescopic lens from his satchel and threw it over his eye. The old Martian hill burned calmly in the morning light. Xan focused his lens towards the outskirts of the city. His sights narrowed upon a specified point.

After some time, a man walked into his line of sight. He dragged himself along the dune at the outskirts.

"One," said Xan to himself.

The man stood near a circular skyscraper with an aimless gaze. His clothes flapped in the winds as he waited. Soon, another figure appeared beside the man.

"And two," said Xan, as he watched the figures confer at the bottom of the hill. With their heads nodding and a few hand gestures, their conversation ended almost as fast as it had begun. The two men slowly left together, heading further into the city.

Xan collapsed his telescopic lens, put it in his satchel, and slung the water container over his shoulder. He opened the oval door and trekked down the dusty hill. The sun welcomed his red skin into the Martian lands.

Xan ducked below the domes and stretched out his hands to balance himself on the old houses. He slowed his pace, almost stopping. His eyes scrutinised the domes across the hill. Xan felt drawn to one in particular. He reached out his hand to graze it, hoping the touch might ignite the remembrance he asked for.

His palms slid back and forth along the dome's rough form. Little pieces of dead skin caught themselves in the jagged cracks. He took his hand off the dome and moved back, shaking his head. He kept going down the hill, pausing to touch each dome along the way. He passed by one that caught him, only after he'd walked by it.

Shouldn't it be dinging?

He turned back and saw Kane's old home. The chimes were gone, but the body remained.

***

He crept into the tall building unseen. Inside, he found himself surrounded by old aquariums, full of decay. At the back, he pushed one in, opening a slight passageway for him to slip into.

Xan turned on his portable light, dispersing the darkness. He slid down the tight passage, reaching an alcove with a large vaulted door. The door rested open enough for him to push his fingers between. He pulled the door back with all his might.

Xan squeezed through. His water jug caught as he tried to push into the opening. He jiggled it a few times until it fit. The placid room met him with a cool humidity. Xan held the light over his head. Its rays caught the sparkling reflection of a crystal vat before him. The sight of pure water filled his soul with comfort. He would survive another day.

Xan placed his body on the ground, lay next to the pool, and let his hand dip in. He pulled his fingers up with tiny beads of vapour accumulated at his tips. They fell into the peaceful vat, rippling to each end.

"I didn't know it'd end like this," he said. "Nothing like this."

Another bead fell from his forefinger, making a soft patter as it landed. He sat up and submerged his container into the pool. It sank inside with a fair bit of resistance and then filled all the way to its brim. Xan lifted it back out of the water and sat it beside himself. He thought about the young girl for a moment.

Xan stood up and squeezed through the exit. He pushed the vault to a sliver, without shutting it fully back. He slid through the passage and stopped at the end.

Rustling grains of sand swept across the floors. Xan peeked from a small crack between the display and wall but saw nothing threatening. He pushed out and closed the aquariums behind him.

As he left the room, he heard a faint hum of human voices. Xan rushed to a round pillar in the centre of the room, placed his back to it, and held the water against his chest. He could hear the hum growing as it echoed into the building's lobby.

"Might have a bigger water supply than all of ours combined," the voice said.

Xan peeked around the pillar to see them.

"I don't believe it," he heard.

"I know I saw him carrying a huge jug. He's hiding out. Somewhere in plain sight."

Two men appeared at the edge of the furthest window. They paused to look inside the building. Xan peered around the pillar to study them. He saw the tall man with a long ponytail talking to a hairless man covered in tattoos.

"Did you hear this from Geil?" said Tattoo. "You know he makes up all kinds of stories."

"Shhh," said Ponytail, as he scanned the building intently. Xan watched the two figures march towards the steps. He threw his back against the pillar.

"This is where he told you to go?" said Tattoo. "There's nothing in there. I've checked."

Xan strained his eyes far enough to see them walk by the next window. Tattoo-face pat his machete at the side of his leg. Mr. Ponytail used the shaft of his makeshift spear like a walking cane.

I can't kill those two.

Xan could hear the spear tapping on the streets, growing louder. He could not break away from the pillar. He stood frozen between two dangerous options and refused to choose either.

"According to Geil he already killed the guy," said Tattoo. "Or his friend, I can't keep up with his nonsense."

"Maybe we should look for his dome," said Ponytail. "I bet there's still chimes up there. If he's careless enough, we'll find him."

Xan rushed out of his position and ran to the staircase inside the building. He saw the two men jump back as they caught sight of him. Xan continued running down the stairs. Footsteps rang loudly behind him.

"TOLD YOU HE WAS HERE! HEY PRETTY BOY! COME HAVE A CHAT WITH US!"

Xan reached the basement and found an old emergency passage to the tunnels. He fumbled as he tried to open it. His fingers weren't strong enough to pull it out and keep it up. Their voices echoed louder as they hammered down the stairs. He struggled to keep the hatch open. Their feet hit the basement floor.

"Open the god-damned hatch," Xan said to himself.

In one smooth grip, he lifted it and slipped his legs inside, catching the indented ladder with his foot. He went down the ladder quickly as the hatch fell shut above his head.

The dark tunnel greeted him with an eerie tone of silence. Whispers echoed from darkened pits. Xan froze as an animal does when cornered. His eyes tried to probe the dark and his ears shot around the passage for lurking horrors.

The men spoke loudly above the ceiling of the tunnel. Xan moved away from the hatch and touched the wall, guiding himself to the nearest exit. He left his light off to keep from drawing any attention to himself.

A sliver of light entered the tunnel as the hatch behind him opened. He heard them barking to one another. Xan increased his pace and arrived at an intersection. He turned left, keeping his hand to the wall. He saw lights flickering from the intersection behind him and heard their voice floating nearer.

Each indent in the wall gave his heart a leap of hope only to let him know he had mistaken cracks for a ladder. The voices lurched over his back, building up behind him.

"Where's the exit?" he whispered. "Please."

"He can't be far," echoed one voice. "There's nowhere to hide."

Xan burned his fingers in search of the exit. The two men laughed like children playing a cruel game.

"Tell us where you've been drinking from pretty boy," they called. "We promise to share it with you!"

Another dip in the wall caused his finger to jam. Xan wasted no time re-examining it. It was the ladder he had been looking for. He quickly climbed up each rung and pushed the hatchet open. He saw a light coming from the intersecting passage below him as he threw himself onto the floor of the exit above. He shut the hatch down and turned on his portable torch.

Tensing up in fear, he saw three figures sitting in chairs before him. He peeked at them with his hand upon his hatchet. The men taunted underneath him. The three figures sat still. They never moved and never would.

Xan stood up and walked around them. Their faces had blackened with gristle upon their yellow bones. They all wore suits as if it was just another normal day at work.

Xan wasted no time in grabbing the first body to pile it on top of the hatch's door. He went back for the second, threw it over the first body, and then rushed to grab the last one. When he threw the final body on top of the hatch, he brushed the sticky residue from his coat and backed up to the nearest stairwell. The hatch rang with pounding fists as the men beat against it, trying to get in.

Xan leaped up the stairs, creating as much distance between his followers as he could. The beats abruptly ended. Xan drifted up the stairs like a mouse, reaching halfway and listening. Footsteps and whispers were talking below him.

"Check the floors," a man said. "I'll wait here."

Xan kept climbing with quiet grace. He reached the top level and pulled out his hatchet.

"This is it," he said. "They've got you." He glanced down the stairs. "Try to swing your blade before they can."

Xan backed into the top-most floor and out of the stairwell. Two hands came around his throat, throwing him to the floor. He hit the ground and lost his grip on his hatchet. It slid away from him. Xan held up his hand, struggling under the weight of his water jug. He saw the girl rushing to pick up his hatchet.

She came back with a scowl on her face. "You're trying to kill me?" she said. "Did you know there was a dead body in there?"

Xan squirmed to pull himself up, but the strap pinned him down. "No," he coughed. "I didn't know. I didn't remember. I promise kid. I forgot. I promise you!"

The girl stood before him, holding Xan's hatchet. Her eyes were red as she bared her teeth at him.

"Why would you do that?" she said. "You know that's a death threat up north?"

Xan eyed the girl, pulling himself to his elbows. "Let me explain," he said. "Please."

The girl lifted the hatchet up with tears in her eyes. "Do you know how that felt?"

"Girl, you need to listen! We're not the only ones in here. I can explain!"

She stared at Xan with anger in her brow.

"Please," whispered Xan. "Go to the stairwell. You'll hear. We have to do this together now. Trust me!"

She kept her eye on Xan and backed towards the stairs. She glanced down for a moment and then came back.

"You knew there was a dead body in there?"

"Not at the time. I promise."

The girl looked at the stairwell and then back at Xan. She handed him the hatchet then offered her hand.

"You're making the right choice," he said, getting to his feet. He quickly went around the room, picking up fallen debris in search of protection. "Damn," he said. "All right kid. This is the real thing."

The girl stood next to the lifts and slid one of the doors open. "Hide in here," she said. "Quickly!"

Xan went over to the lift. It remained stuck halfway between the floors. He shoved her inside, letting her topple over, and jumped in behind. He slid the door back, leaving just enough space to look inside the room.

"Ow," she said. "What'd you push me for?"

"Shh."

The girl stood up behind Xan. "You'd better explain why you put me in that dome. Doing something like that is a death threat you know?"

"Quiet," said Xan, keeping watch through the crack. "Don't talk."

Tattoo walked into the room, tapping his machete on his leg. He flipped over a few pieces of debris in the room, mumbling to himself as he tipped them. He then walked along the walls, slowly scrapping his machete on it. He paused for a moment and glanced at the lifts. He grit his teeth and walked towards them. His blade scrapped all the way. Tapping on each lift, he mumbled to himself, eyes wide and ready to kill.

The girl moved behind Xan and grabbed the hem of his jacket. With a nasty grunt, Tattoo stepped away, scrapping his machete along the wall. He went back towards the stairwell, pausing to eye the room once more. His gaze seemed to stare in through the crack in the lift doors.

Tattoo exhaled a dry laugh. "Nothing," he shouted out of the room. "Let's check the other buildings."

Xan could hear Ponytail yelling up the stairwell, but could not make out what he said. Tattoo reached into his pants, pulled out his penis and urinated in the room. When he finished wagging his penis, he sniffed and went down the stairwell.

Xan hit the wall and slid down to the floor of the lift. He let out a large sigh and lay his head back. The elevator shook around them as they hung stuck in the air.

"They're gone?" she whispered.

"They're gone," he said.

The girl grabbed the sliver and opened the lift door. She pulled herself out, walked with her back against the wall, and peered down the stairs. She waved behind herself to signal that they had gone. Xan fell further into the lift and closed his eyes.

CHAPTER 49

The girl stood above the windows, staring wide-eyed outside. Xan swayed in the hanging lift, his heart thrashing in his chest.

"They're leaving," she said, over her shoulder. "They're going into another building now."

Caught in his thoughts, Xan could not respond. The girl watched out of the window for a long time.

"Are you all right?" she called.

Xan didn't answer.

"They're searching the building across the street too," she said. "There's another person with them now."

Xan talked to himself in a dull murmur. The girl turned and strolled to the lifts. She looked in and saw Xan sitting against the wall, and leaned in to give him a hand. Xan pushed her hand away.

"I don't want to get up," he said. "I can do it when I'm ready."

The girl brought her hand back. Xan drew in a deep breath.

"Why are they chasing you?"

Xan glanced at her. "They're after my water supply," he said.

The girl kneeled outside the lift. "Oh."

He hugged his jug closer to himself and watched the girl's eyes darting back and forth, stopping a moment on his water. Some moments passed in silence before either spoke.

"You left me with a dead man," she said.

"I'd forgotten about that place," he said. "I forgot when I left you there. You can understand that?"

She shook her head. "No, I would remember that."

"Don't go shaking your head at me," said Xan. "As if you would know. As if you've gone through it like I have."

Xan rose from his seat, threw his water outside the lift and pulled his body up. He glared at the girl for some time and then shuffled towards the window. The lights were dim, and the sun fell lower in the sky.

Xan held his hatchet as he muttered to himself. The girl stayed back near the water for a second then joined him at the window. Xan pushed her back with his hand.

"Don't stand so close," he said. "They'll see you."

The girl stepped back and sat down. Xan kept his eyes outside, not concerned if they might see the girl up in the window, but more so what she might see if they found someone else in the buildings. Xan watched the group leave the building across the street. Geil was with them now. Xan's heart beat with anger at the sight of him.

"Did you kill him?" the girl asked.

Xan raised an eyebrow. "What?"

"In the dome, you killed whoever it was."

Xan snorted then pointed out at the group. "You see the younger guy there? With dark rings around his eyes?"

The girl peered out. "Yeah?"

Xan watched him. "That's who killed him."

The girl eyed the group as they entered the next building. "Him?"

Xan nodded. The girl checked his face. Xan turned away and continued watching them carry out their search.

"Did you know him?"

Xan clicked his tongue in his mouth. "For about a second," he said. "I never trusted him."

The girl moved closer to the window. "Why not?"

"You can see it in his eyes." He pointed out the window. "They're dead inside. Look."

The girl put her head high enough to see. "Can you see it in young men?"

Xan backed away. "Doesn't matter the age," he said. "Some people are born that way."

The girl nodded, a shade of fear descending over her face. "Oh," she whispered.

Xan sighed as he backed away from the window and sat on the floor. He pulled his water jug close and took a swig from it. The girl eyed the liquid. He set it down and pushed it towards her. The girl picked up the jug and gulped as much as she could, spilling drops from the side of her lips onto her clothes.

When she put it back down, Xan pulled it nearer to himself.

She reached into her bag, grabbed a half-inflated black pouch, and lifted it in the air.

Xan looked at it. "That's all you have?" he said.

The girl squeezed it at both ends. Its contents moved to form a bulge of water in the centre.

"I had two others," she said. "I lost one on the way down here."

Xan looked at his water and then at the pouch. "Let me see it," he said.

She handed it to him. Xan opened the water jug and dipped the pouch inside. It filled up like a sponge, expanding far beyond his expectations. He handed it back to the girl.

"I'm not your fill up station," he said. "You'll have to find your own source in time."

"I will."

Xan looked back out the window. The group moved to another building. Night grew darker and stars poked through the violet skies.

"There's four now," said the girl. "Only this new one doesn't seem to be with them."

Xan studied the new figure. The newcomer kept his distance, dodging in shadows, stalking them with precision. Xan scratched his beard.

"What's he doing?" said the girl.

"Tailing them."

"Is he going to kill them?"

Xan narrowed his eyes on the dark figure. "I've never seen anyone else follow them before."

The group left the building and crossed over to the next. The lone figure continued to trail them, walking in the shadows and keeping low. Xan pulled his lens from his bag to have a closer look. The lone figure carried a long knife in his hand that peeked out from the edge of his overdrawn sleeves. The tip winked in the fading light, reflecting off its sharp end, like a beacon blipping in and out. The figure moved around one of the buildings, disappearing as the group exited. Xan put his lens back.

"We'd better get moving," he said.

"Shouldn't we stay?"

"Never stay in the city at night."

"But they're still looking for you."

Xan stood up, ignoring her comment.

She quickly followed. "Are you sure?"

He took his water and went out towards the exit. The girl followed behind him.

A steady whistle sounded inside the staircase. Dust particles levitated above the steps as the winds rose. Xan pulled out a pair of leather sand goggles from his satchel. He wrapped them around his head. The young girl pulled out a black rectangular box and strapped a pair of sand goggles around her face.

"We might be able to make it out of the city tonight," said Xan. "We'll have to leave before the storm picks up though."

He exited to the ground floor. The winds poured sand through broken windows as small tornadoes whipped in the streets. Xan inched his way to the exit. He peered outside, holding on to the wall as he did. The lone figure was gone, and the group had begun their journey back eastwards.

Xan fixed his goggles. "That's it, let's go."

He pushed out into the winds. The air steadily increased with sudden gusts, knocking them about. The sand dune sprayed dust in a constant blast as they reached the outskirts. All the little white domes sat covered by a veil of diaphanous sand. Xan held his arm over his face as pelts of sand pierced into his skin.

"Are we going to make it?" said the girl.

"We're almost there."

Xan ploughed up the sinking sands, doing his best to keep his balance in the wind. A strong gust punched him to the ground. His face sank into the sand, and he quickly turned over and sat upright. The girl rushed over to help him.

"I can do it myself," he said.

She retracted her hand. "Hurry up," she said. "It's getting worse."

Xan lifted himself up with effort and continued walking up the hill. Each step he took required more strength than he had. One foot over the next. Another nudge from the wind. The dome was now a few yards away as he heard a loud roar behind them.

"One step at a time," he said. "This isn't how you die."

A small white dome stood before them. He reached for the oval door and tried his best to click it open, but nothing happened.

"Shit."

Xan wrestled at the door, failing to push it open. The girl came between him and the door and gave it a few thrusts, cracking it out of its frame, and disappeared inside. Xan jumped in and kicked the door shut with his legs.

The house was dark. The girl lit a torch and placed the light in the middle of the floor. She then retrieved another torch from her bag and searched the house. Xan lay down and held his chest. His heart fluttered with an uneven tick every fourth or fifth beat. The girl stopped to look at him.

"You don't look well."

Xan held his hand in the air, waving her away, breathing heavily.

The room was filled with restless dust floating through the air like a fine mist. He sat up, pulled himself into a chair, took hold of his water jug, and downed a few gulps.

Still one more mission, he thought. *Keep ticking. Keep on ticking. No stopping until you finish.*

He listened to the howls outside the dome, feeling something amiss. The absence of dings outside the house.

The girl returned from the back room. "It's clear," she said. "No one's here."

Xan stood up from his seat and placed his water down. He took the extra light on the floor, kneeled down, and traced his finger along the ground. He placed his fingers inside the small groove and slowly lifted the middle of the floor open. A hidden cave appeared before them. Xan shone his light down within. Nothing moved.

The girl leaned over the hidden cellar. "Do all the domes have these?"

Xan pushed the hatch back, closing it into the floor. "No," he said. "But most of them do."

Xan went to his chair and tossed the extra light to the ground beside him. The girl picked up a fallen chair and sat down too. She held up her light, examining the room with it. Then something caught her attention, and she jumped from her seat, running to a fallen shelf. She picked up a metal-cased book and flipped through it.

Xan dropped his head against the back of his chair. He watched the dust stir in the air. He listened to the winds scream outside as his mouth hung open and his cheeks weighted heavy off his face.

"Is it really like this?" she said.

"What?"

The girl walked to him with the book. "Earth? The pictures must be fake."

Xan leaned over to see the book. He glanced at the images of his old blue planet. Just as he had remembered. Full of clutter, blinded in light, and wrapped in a grey haze.

The girl flipped to another page. A brilliant orange moon peeked through the clouds as a tiny opening shown it clear as day.

Xan scoffed. "I've never seen it like that," he said. "It's probably fake."

The girl continued flipping through the book, stopping at certain pictures to admire them. Xan spied the book. A beautiful mountain scene full of luscious trees.

"Don't look at that stuff," he said.

The girl paused with her hand on the page. "Why not?"

"It's fantasy. There's no point."

The girl shrugged and continued flipping through the book. Xan watched over her shoulder. He snarled to himself and turned away if she glanced at him. Then he abruptly threw his hand upon the book.

"Wait," he said. "Hold on."

She furled her brow. Xan saw a familiar city on the page. The girl handed the book to him. He took it and leaned as far as he could into the picture, staying silent as he stroked the city towers with his thumb. He closed his eyes for a moment.

"You miss it?"

Xan opened his eyes a little and silently returned the book to the girl.

She turned the picture right-side up. "Do you know this place?" she asked. "Is it a tunnel?"

"No."

"Have you been there?"

He closed his mouth.

The girl looked at the picture again. "I think I'd miss it if I'd lived there," she said.

Xan ignored her as he closed his eyes. He saw his younger self, standing among the sea of bright advertisements.

Come to Mars! Every day is an Adventure! There were pictures of happy people riding sandrovers atop the Martian hills.

The girl closed the book and picked up a new one: *The Tragedy of the First Martian Colony.*

Xan pushed further into his seat and allowed his eyes to shut.

A young man stood in a large crowded street. He looked up at the flashing ads above him. A red glint shined in his youthful eye. Come to Mars! Every day is an Adventure!

Xan stood beside his younger self and watched from behind his memory. The ad decayed. People lost their smiles. Their skin cracked. A red tint weaved through their faces.

The young man saw none of this. He smiled with them. He didn't see the lies yet.

Come to Mars! Every day is an adventure!

* * *

Books cluttered the living room floor. Xan opened his eyes. The girl had left for one of the back rooms. He sat up, listening to the slow beat of his heart.

His joints clicked as he stood. No sounds whispered around the dwelling. A silent latch opened. He walked into the night. A darkened sky with speckled lights guided him back.

Xan kneeled alongside one of the domes, spying down the hill. He saw a lone figure standing at the base of the dune. Xan pulled out his telescopic lens, seeing the dim figure with a knife sticking out of his long sleeve.

"Following me too?" he said.

The figure stood motionless. Xan watched.

After some time, the figure moved again, hovering around the outskirts before passing within the city. Xan stood and continued up the hill. He hurried into his dome and shut the door behind him and pulled the latch back. He moved away, keeping his eyes on the door.

Soft dings filled the house. Xan eyed them. "Still off," he said. "Still off."

He then went inside his hidden cellar. His feet touched the ground as he lowered his body to the floor.

Beautiful eyes winked at him. She lay her hand upon his.

He shook away their gaze.

A playful kiss graced his lips.

He shook his head.

Xan sat beside the safe. He slapped his face until a small tear formed and fell unto it. A red circuit circled the case and then pulsed its final light.

Xan took his light and smacked it against the safe. The light flickered. He whacked the safe again, killing the light. Darkness filled the cellar. He sat at the bottom of the cave, this time refusing to stand.

CHAPTER 50

Broken glass whistled an eerie tune in passing currents. Sand piled through the building's floor unswept by man. Ponytail spoke to Sven, both carrying jugs of water to their base. Xan watched behind the broken glass.

Where do you go next? he thought. *Tell me where it ends.*

Xan put his lens away and slipped down the stairs to follow them. He scanned the exit quickly, then tailed behind them, keeping a safe distance from them. They spoke of water supplies and a scarred man with a hidden vat somewhere.

Xan hid behind a large piece of cement in the streets as he listened to them. Both men vanished into a building and out of sight. Xan tapped his cold hatchet at his side.

"Where do you go from here?" he whispered. "Where do you bastards stay?"

Xan went into the opposite building and perched on the second floor. He sat waiting. For any sign. The sun sank lower in the sky.

Xan pulled himself up when he caught sight of another figure walking about. The figure crawled along the buildings, keeping himself out of sight. Xan saw a glimpse of his knife hanging out from his sleeve.

"You again," he said.

The figure lingered outside the building where Ponytail and Geil had gone. He circled it for some time then eventually entered. Xan left the building and crossed the street. The burning sun drew long shadows onto the pavement. He peered inside the building then took a step in.

He edged over to the stairwell and listened. No sounds or human voices. Xan backed out and went towards the door.

"Trailing us..." he heard. "Can't be too sure..."

He kept quiet.

"Gut him the way we did those goats," said the woman.

Knots writhed in his gut. Xan ran and jumped behind a broken art piece in the lobby. He ripped a small hole, large enough for him to see through. Tattoo and Ms. Baldy stepped inside.

"Twisting the blade is more painful than the actual stab," she said with a small laugh.

"Yeah? You've felt it?"

Ms. Baldy grinned. "No."

"Then how do you know?"

"The screams, listen to the difference when you wrench a firm twist."

Xan's eyelid flickered.

"You're a real cunt," said Tattoo.

"Ever tasted one?"

"Fuck off."

"We all know you prefer your boys young."

Both snapped around fast, drawing their weapons, as Geil fumbled into the building. He raised his hands high in the air. Xan pressed his eye further into the hole.

"Speaking of bum boys," she said. "Here for a quick one? Should I turn my head for you two?"

Shoving her hand down, Tattoo grunted at her. "Shut it," he said. "The fuck are you doing here?"

"There's some girl running about trying to nick our water supplies," said Geil.

Tattoo licked his teeth and grinned. "Then why didn't you handle her? I know I would've."

The woman sniggered.

Tattoo shook his machete back and forth. "You need me to handle her for you?" He raised his eyebrows up and down.

"This kid is actually a kid," said Geil. "Not a woman. I mean she's a goddamn kid. Not a single wrinkle on her face!"

Ms. Baldy laughed. "That's bullshit! You make up half the mess you tell us."

"Oh," said Tattoo, grinning even more. "Don't forget the ugly man stalking him too. Poor little boy here has a teenage girl he can't nab, and some creep trying to squeeze him."

Geil's eyes remained flat. "And your little scare the other day?" he said.

"Who did you chase through those tunnels? What happened to your ghosts roaming the city?"

Setting his machete on Geil's throat, Tattoo stepped closer, bringing his mouth inches from his face. "Shut your mouth. Shut your dirty mouth... Don't you ever talk to your elders like that."

Ms. Badly drew closer, brushing his hair. "Poor baby."

Geil jerked his head away.

Tattoo laughed as he lowered his machete. "Who said it was a man? Maybe we saw a woman?"

Tattoo grabbed Geil by the back of his neck and led him towards the entrance. "How about you show us where you found this kid. Yeah?"

Ms. Baldy continued to snigger behind them. "Afraid she'll bite you?" She rubbed his hair again as they left.

Xan lingered a while longer. When the echoes petered off, he ran out of the building straight to the hill, checking a few domes along the way up to his.

Let her go, he thought. *She's not worth it. Don't get attached. You'll just lose her in the end.*

Xan kept walking past the dome and drew his hatchet when he noticed someone leaning behind one of them. He paused, glaring at her as he drew in a deep breath.

The girl rubbed her arms. "Can I stay with you tonight?" she said.

Xan snarled at her. "You almost got killed today," he said. "I'm not here to watch over you like some nanny. That's not my job you know. That's what your parents - " he stopped.

The girl buried her face in her arms. A welt of shame burnt across his face. She lifted her head and wiped her eyes on her sleeve.

"I get it," she said. "You don't have to help me then. Go be lonely. See if I care." A tear ran down her cheek.

Xan let out a deep breath. "You have to learn how to survive like the rest of us," he said.

"I needed water. I had no clue it was their supply!"

Xan hissed through his teeth. "You should've asked me then."

The girl glanced at him. "But you're not my parent," she said. "You've made it clear from the start that I'm a burden to you. Same as everyone else in my life before they died."

Xan opened his mouth to say more. She stood up, picked up her bag, and walked away.

Xan reached his hand out towards her. "You can stay with me tonight," he called.

She stopped with her back to him.

"If you're thirsty, then take from my supply from now on."

The girl slowly turned to look at him. "You don't have to," she said. "I can manage myself."

"It's fine. Everyone's left me too."

The girl kept her arms crossed.

"I've failed a lot people in the past." His throat numbed.

She lowered her head and walked toward him. "Did your parents die here too?"

"No."

She swallowed a dry breath and looked up at him. He gazed down the hill and then cocked his head to the side.

"Let's get out of here before anyone sees us."

She nodded and followed him. Xan watched her, looking at her hair, and was reminded of his sister for a moment. They both had the same colour and texture. He almost touched her head, but he caught himself.

They went back up to the dome, listening to the chimes dinging lightly outside. The girl went up to the oval door and reached out for it when Xan grabbed her by the arm and threw her behind himself, accidentally knocking her over. He slung his hatchet out before him.

"Don't move," he said. "Something's off."

The door wasn't fully closed. A small line ran down it, and Xan saw a person inside. He took a step back, motioning to the girl behind him.

"Keep quiet and go back down the hill."

The door opened, and a knife shone in the faint light. Xan gripped at his hatchet, keeping the girl behind him. "GET OUT HERE AND FACE ME LIKE A MAN!"

The knife pulled away in the darkness. Then the door pulled all the way open.

"I thought you might be dead," said the figure.

Xan said nothing.

"Put it away Xan. I'm here to help."

Xan whispered under his breath. "Mick?"

"Yeah."

Xan stepped towards the door. Mick turned on a light near the back, showing his face inside the room. Xan went into the house, the girl following behind him.

"I don't understand..."

Xan looked at Mick's weathered face and then down to his hand. A knife peaked out of from his sleeve, flashing with a soft glint. Xan lowered his hatchet and placed it to his side. He pointed at Mick's knife.

"You can put that away," Xan said.

Mick let out a rusted laugh.

Xan slipped his hatchet back out. "You're mad at me?"

Mick gave a weary sigh and lifted his arm, pulling his sleeve back and revealing the knife attached to a stump on his wrist.

Xan stared at it for a rude amount of time. "Oh..."

Mick nodded, his eyes fixed on the floor. Xan examined the stump where Mick's hand used to be. The knife was fixed to his wrist with a brown metal brace that rose up to his elbow.

Mick pulled his sleeve back down and lowered his arm. "Where's another fight going to get us?"

"Tell that to Sven."

"I'm surprised you're still here," said Mick. "I swore that night..."

Xan touched his face, running his finger along the withered lines. "What happened to you?"

Mick mumbled. Xan studied him.

"I went to Kane's dome," he said. "That's him?"

Xan looked at the young girl. "Go into the back room," he said. "We need to talk."

"I know him," she whispered. "He came round the orphanage."

"I said let us talk," said Xan. "Now!"

The girl nodded and walked past Mick, who eyed every step she made. Xan watched him uncomfortably. Mick turned back to Xan and nodded his head.

"What happened to you?" he said.

Mick nodded with vacant eyes.

Xan turned on his light. "It wasn't my fault if that's what you're here to say. I warned Kane against it."

Mick shuffled slowly to a chair and sat down. "I've nothing more to say. We've seen enough to know how this place works."

Xan relaxed.

Mick looked at the walls as he spoke. "I saw Sven. I thought if he was still alive that maybe you'd..."

Xan felt anger throttle his veins. "You know how many of his group I've slashed over the months?"

"Sure."

"What is your damn problem?"

Mick's eyes remained impassive.

"Where have you been? Why are you coming up here to push me around when you're the one who left us?"

Mick sighed. "I'm not guilting you. I may have the answers you want."

Xan walked around the table and pulled a seat back.

"They don't stay in the old barrack at night, do they?" said Mick.

"I already know that."

"But you know where they rest at night?"

"The tunnels," said Xan. "But I'm not stupid enough to follow them."

"Then I guess I am?"

Xan tapped his finger on the table.

"They built their own tunnels. All the way out to your old factory. That's the one you first met him at, right?"

Xan sat down in the chair. The room went quiet. The two men sat in their broken silence.

Xan looked up at Mick. "Where did you go?"

Mick rubbed his face a few times. "Mons," he said. "Ever since that night..." His mouth hung open for a moment, a flash of life shone in his eyes. "I heard everything."

Xan tapped on the table faster.

The sandrover was consumed in fire.

Mick looked into Xan's eyes with an apprehensive gaze. He leaned across the table, leaning on his arms, whispering to him.

"At some point, they left, and it wasn't long after that I heard it."

"Talk about something else."

"I heard a cry."

Xan shook his head. "I don't want to know."

Mick raised his eyebrow. "You know she was almost due."

Xan jabbed his finger at him. "Mick I'm warning you."

"It was screaming when they left. It must've come out of her, so I ran to see." His breath increased as he spoke. "I thought the bodies were yours. If you'd seen how black..."

Xan rubbed his face.

"When I picked her up," he said. "I knew I had to make it up there." He shook his head with his mouth hanging open. "It doesn't make sense but when I held her in my arms. I knew I had to."

Xan threw his hands down.

"If I knew you'd survived, I would've come back."

Xan gradually slumped in his seat. *It's a lie. No one survived. Don't listen to this asshole.*

"I gave her to a family of scientists," said Mick. "But I never saw her after that. They housed a few other orphans, you see?"

"Enough!"

Mick quit talking.

"It's time to finish this," Xan said. "To make it right. Tomorrow morning, both you and I."

Mick tried to smile. "Is that how we erase the past?"

Xan looked down at the table. A vein pulsed at the side of his neck.

"I miss the old days," said Mick. "What a life we had."

Xan's eyelid flickered.

"Nothing can bring that back now."

"Sven thinks he's a god."

"So did we."

'No. No, we did not."

Mick reached inside his jacket, pulled out a bottle, and placed it on the table.

"Just like old times," he said, tipping the bottle towards Xan.

Xan glared at the bottle. "Not until it's done," he said.

Mick pulled the drink towards himself, leaving it upright on the table.

"Your choice," he said. "This is one of the good ones."

The two men sat in the night's aura. Their lights kept total darkness at bay. The chimes spoke outside. The winds were picking up.

Mick stood from the table and picked up the bottle. "I'll call it an early night then," he said. "You sure you don't want any of this?"

"When we're done," said Xan.

"And when is that?"

No response.

"You mind if I stay here tonight?" said Mick. "I've been sleeping poorly for too long. Never know who's outside."

Xan pointed to the second room. "She didn't really survive, did she?"

Mick walked towards the room and stopped in the doorway. He opened his mouth to say something, then stopped.

"You know, there weren't any ships up there," he said. "They're all shot to hell. Not a single one of them could break the atmosphere in this lifetime."

Xan clenched his jaw harder. Mick held the bottle in his hand and wiggled it a few times as he laughed.

"Hindsight's a bitch," Mick said. "A real bitch to live with."

Chuckling loudly, Mick lumbered into the second bedroom, singing a song to himself. His voice grew louder and quivered at certain notes. Xan stayed at the table, listening to his friend sing.

No ships, he thought. *There never were.*

ChAPtER 51

Xan snapped upright in his chair, drenched in sweat. Chimes dinged outside in the dark. Picking himself up, Xan went to Mick's door and placed his ear against it.

"Mick? Let's go. The sun'll rise anytime now."

No response.

Xan jiggled the door then rapped his knuckle louder. "Get your drunk ass up!"

Pulling away, Xan wiped spit from his mouth, still glaring at the door. "Come on Mick, let's go. We're not doing this again. It's time to finish it."

Mick's room remained silent.

"We're done after this! Don't you get it?"

Inching towards the door, Xan put his hand upon it, then curled his fist. "Mick! Stop being a damn fool!"

Silence.

Stepping back, Xan cocked his arm, then punched into the door.

"Open this door!"

He thrust his heel into the door, cracking a fine line down it.

"Mick? Mick?"

Xan shouldered the door out of the frame. He clawed his way into the room and slapped the sleeping man. "Wake up!"

Mick remained still.

Xan shook him with both hands. "Get your drunk ass up," he said. "For god's sake! What the heck did you come down here for?"

Mick fell limp on the bed. Xan eyed the half-empty bottle next to the bed. He picked it up and brought it under his nose. It smelled of corrosive acid.

Placing the bottle down, Xan's hands trembled as he stared at Mick. His face twitched. "You came here to die?"

His eyelid flickered. "You coward," he said. "YOU BIG COWARD!"

Xan threw his fists into Mick's chest. Up and down he hammered until he heard a rib snap. Standing up straight, he spat on Mick's body, then fled the room. He flipped the table outside, crushed all the loose trinkets under his boot, then smashed his cabinet doors. The girl stood in the doorframe watching him.

Xan yanked up the hidden cellar and slid down the ladder. Items scattered to the floor as he grabbed one of his spare lights from the cubby hole. It shone upon the safe.

"YOU PIECE OF SHIT! YOU WORTHLESS PIECE OF SHIT!"

Xan slapped the light into the safe, breaking its glow. He smashed it into broken fragments, then threw his body over the safe. He convulsed as his eyes weakened.

A vision popped into his head. *The investigator rang his doorbell. Everything and everyone was being snatched from his hands.*

Razan, Ima, Kane, and Mick. No one left but himself. Him and his haunting memories playing on a permanent loop inside his head.

The gun slipped into the safe. He didn't want to lose them. He didn't want to lose any of them.

Xan sniffed. "I thought he spared my life. I never thought any of this would happen!"

He hugged the safe. "How could I give up what we had?"

He saw everyone he loved huddled beside him.

His eyes salted and his nose dripped. A tiny bead squeezed from his closed lids and fell onto the safe.

"Forgive me," he said. "Please forgive me."

Xan opened his eyes to the blazing lights. The safe reflected a brilliant green on his swollen eyes. It pulsed in the dark cellar like fire in the sky.

Then a faint click sounded. The door opened a sliver.

The room faded to dark once more. Nothing stirred. He reached slowly into the safe and wrapped his fingers around the handle. Xan stood in the cellar, stroking the old revolver for some time before he tucked it into his belt.

"You'll forgive me," he said, "when I make this right."

He slowly crawled out of the cellar, sitting with his feet dangling inside it. Xan took the gun from his belt and spied the six worn bullets loaded inside. He snapped it back together with a sigh. The girl watched him from the corner of the room.

* * *

Xan flew out the door. He felt the sun brush against his skin and listened to the chimes singing a sad lament.

"Where are you going?" the girl asked.

Xan kept his gaze on the city. She ran out to follow him.

"What happened?" she said. "Where are you going?"

Xan legged it down the hill, keeping his hand near the gun.

"What's going on?"

Xan halted.

"Tell me!"

"I'm going to die," he said. "If that's something you'd like to do, then, by all means, join me."

The girl held her arms. "Why?"

"Because I made this city what it is. And now I have to fix it."

"You can't."

Xan stared at the rising sun.

"Nothing you do will mend the past."

Xan pulled his satchel to his side and searched for an old cleaver inside it. He turned it over, thumbed its edge, and marched down the hill. She stood in place, the distance expanding between them.

The city cried old worn memories. Rubble scattered along the streets told stories of where they used to lay. *The windows were whole. The streets brushed clean.* The old city reached for Xan. It asked for its glory back.

He continued walking through the road. Shards of glass mixed with the sands, crushing beneath his feet. He marched onwards to the eastern end where the factory sat.

The winds moved around him. The city howled, and the sun rose high above him. Xan kept his gaze on the old factory. He took his first step and then his next. He marched on without looking back. Nothing could pull his attention away from the large factory before him.

Xan dropped his bag to the ground. He touched the hatchet at the side of his leg, gently dragging it out. A man emerged from the shaded entrance. It was Tattoo, licking his tongue along his blade. Laughing to himself, he set his machete on his shoulder and walked to meet Xan. Another man trailed behind him by a few steps. Xan turned his cleaver in his hands, readying his attack.

Tattoo laughed as he picked up his pace. "Hey buddy?" he said. "You feeling okay? Let me give you a drink of water?"

Xan moved closer.

Tattoo lowered his machete and put it at his side.

"I've heard about you." He readied his swing. "Maybe we could talk over some - "

Tattoo swung his machete at Xan.

Xan backed a step, then lunged at him, slamming the clever into his skull. A splatter of blood hit Xan's face. Tattoo fell to the ground like a fallen rock. Xan quickly pulled the hatchet from his side as the second man raced towards him, yelling.

"Son of a bitch!"

Xan watched the other man barreling towards him. He tossed his hatchet, slicing the large vein at the side of the man's neck.

Grappling at his neck, the man dropped his blade, attempting to close the wound. Blood drenched his clothes as he fell to his knees. He yelled curses, then begged for help before he plunged to the ground, draining blood into the red sands.

Xan wiped his face then walked back to retrieve his cleaver. He tugged hard, placing his foot on Tattoo' head, then gave up.

Xan collected his hatchet, kicking the man's body once before he kneeled down to pick it up. The shaded entrance called for him. Gusts of nostalgia ran through him as he entered the old factory he first worked in.

Xan stopped as he listened to cries of help. He heard them screaming, pleading for someone to save them. Voices rang through the air, telling their killers not to swing. Telling their killers not to shoot. Telling them to leave their families be. Xan closed his eyes as he listened to phantoms within the passage.

The old lady was making chimes, smiling to herself, while her killer closed in behind. Crafting those chimes with old shaken hands.

He opened his eyes and gazed over his head. The passage shrieked echoes of stolen chimes dangling above. Strewn throughout the long hall, chimes tapped painfully against themselves in the coursing breeze.

Xan listened to their cries for help. He walked slowly through until a glimmer or light blinked for his attention. Xan squinted at a pair of chimes with a crystal suspended from its centre string.

"Kane..."

Xan knew why they screamed to him. *These aren't chimes*, he thought. *They're trophies.*

Xan touched his chest. He fastened his hatchet back to his side and rubbed his waist. Xan drew the gun as he eyed Kane's chimes.

"I'll make everything right," he whispered.

Xan walked towards the main lobby, basking in the play of chimes above him. He heard voices echoing at the end of the hall. His finger crooked at the trigger.

The voices cheered.

Xan edged towards them.

The voices roared in banter.

Xan came to the opening and saw them.

Geil with his lifeless eyes. Ms. Baldy laughing beside Ponytail and Sven sitting on top of the old statue in the centre of the lobby. Their attention slowly turned to him standing before them, gun in hand.

Ponytail sneered at him. "I think you've got the wrong house, pretty boy."

"That's the guy," said Geil, pointing at him. "He's the one with the water!"

Sven's face flushed as his eyes widened.

"He's crazy," said Ms. Baldy. "Look at him with his little gun. Aww, darling, don't you know, those things don't work anymore."

Everyone barked with laughter. Xan stood steadily, examining every single one of them with a slow, steady gaze.

"Come to tell us where you've hidden it?" said Geil.

Xan pointed his revolver at Geil. "You killed him," he said. "You killed my friend."

The room burst into laughter again.

"He's getting sentimental now!"

An explosion broke through the room. Geil's chest erupted with a bloody hole. His eyes glazed over, helpless in shock as he dabbed his chest and dropped to the floor. The room rang quietly only for a moment.

Xan aimed the gun at the bald lady and fired off another round. *Crack*. It hit her in the shoulder, and she shrieked in pain. He fired again, *crack*, opening her chest and her crimson body fell to the floor.

Ponytail bolted for the other exit. Xan shot him in the back of the head. *Crack*. His body flung to the floor in the weight of his momentum.

Xan raised his gun to Sven who was climbing over the statue. *Crack*. He shot him in the back of the leg. A scream echoed through the dome. *Crack*. He fired again, hitting him in the side. *Thud*. He heard Sven hit the floor on the other side of the statue.

Xan walked around the statue, following the faint whimpers echoing off the walls. Sven scrambled his wounded paws across the floor, dragging his body to the nearest exit.

Xan dropped his gun, then slipped his hatchet out. Sven whined as he pulled his bloody legs along the ground.

Xan moved behind him. Sven turned over onto his back and threw a dagger at Xan, nicking his shoulder. Xan continued walking towards him, paying no attention to his wound.

Sven spat out a mixture of spittle and blood. "Fuck off!"

"You want to talk about fairness?" said Xan. "Tell that to Razan."

Sven lifted his chest from the floor. "IT WON'T MAKE YOU HAPPY. IT WON'T MAKE YOU FEEL ANY BETTER!"

Xan walked over Sven's foot. "Tell that to Ima."

"YOU DID THIS. YOU HAD ALL THE CHANCES IN THE WORLD TO BE A PART OF IT, LIKE BROTHERS!"

Xan walked over his chest. "Tell that to Kane and Mick."

"IT WON'T MAKE YOU FEEL BETTER."

Xan put his foot on Sven's chest. He raised his hatchet and said. "It's not for me."

He swung the hatchet across Sven's neck. Sven gripped his throat as he convulsed. He gurgled in his own blood, rolling and twitching, until his hands moved in a slower panic, and then fell to the ground at last.

Xan dropped his hatchet and turned his back to Sven. His eyes watered. The chimes no longer pleaded. They played as they once had. No more cries. No more pleas.

* * *

His hands shook as he wiped the last remnants of blood from them. Xan wandered the lobby, circling the statue twice, then found a handcart near Geil's body.

Xan dragged the cart to the hall and reached above his head, taking down every chime with care. He placed them in the cart and moved further towards the exit.

When he took Kane's, he held onto them until he had brought the rest down, then he laid Kane's on top of the pile. The sun poured its bright rays onto the sand as Xan stepped out of the factory. He breathed in the fresh air that surrounded him.

Xan bounded through the city, touching the buildings along his way. He closed his eyes to recall their former state. How tall they stood with pristine glass welded together in a circular mass.

When he opened his eyes, he saw them strong again. The winds whipped through the city, catching the shards of glass. It didn't sing the bitter song it used to.

Xan paused in the middle of the city, looking up at the tallest tower. He closed his eyes and then glanced up at his old flat. He climbed into his old bedroom and wrapped Razan's bones in the blankets and fastened them with some rope.

"I did it," he whispered to her. "You can rest now dear."

Xan put her on top of the cart. He pushed her to the outskirts. The girl sat near one of the domes waiting for him. Xan waved for her to join him. She rushed down the hill and slowed when she saw him. She glanced at the traces of blood on his clothes.

"I thought you were going to die?" she said.

Xan reached out his hand and placed it on the girl's shoulder. "You have beautiful eyes," he said. "Still full of youth."

He nodded at her a few times and then dropped his hand back to his side. She lowered her head.

"Will you help me hang these back on their domes?" he said.

Glancing at the cart, she contemplated the task, then slowly nodded her head. "Okay…"

Xan reached into the cart and picked up the blanket resting on top of it.

"What's that smell?"

"Don't mind it."

She pinched her nose and picked up the first chime she saw.

Xan grabbed Kane's chimes from her. "Wait," he said. "I'll take care of this one."

The girl looked at Xan's hands and then glanced back at the chimes. "What are they for?" she said.

"How else will we know there's a storm coming? There's no electricity. Our Vlexes don't work anymore."

She squinted. "You can feel it, no?"

Xan walked up the hill. The girl then hung chimes on every dome she could. Xan reached Kane's old dome and pat it a few times. He set the blanket down and hung the chimes back up at their rightful place, on the little latch outside his window.

"I got them back for you."

They dinged with a wobble, because of the crystal hanging on the centre string.

Xan sighed and picked the blanket up from the ground.

The girl continued re-stocking the domes as Xan walked up to his home. He watched the young girl replace them for quite some time. She hung the final one and ran up to meet with him.

"That's it," she said. "There's no more."

Xan patted the blankets and then gave it to her. "Take this up the hill, right at the peak," he said. "I'll meet you there."

She took the blanket in confusion, then scrunched her nose and coughed. "What is this?"

He pointed up the hill. "Just take it up there. I'll join you in a minute."

She squinted her eyes, held her breath, and went up the hill. Xan sighed as he opened his door. He went to the second bedroom and took Mick's bottle. He put it in his jacket and headed back out. He stopped in the doorframe, listening to the chorus of chimes outside.

"That's it," he said. "That's right. You're playing it right."

He walked up to the hill and met with the girl sitting at the peak. Each chime played its own tune as the sun dipped.

Xan watched the sun falling behind the horizon with the bottle in his hands. He smiled at the city's amber hue. It was a sunset he wasn't sure he had ever seen before.

The girl looked at the dying light shone upon the city. A symphony of dings sang out to the world.

The girl glanced at the bottle in his hands and then up at him. "What'll we do now?" she said.

He rubbed the stopper with his thumb as he watched the sun dip beyond the horizon. "There's someone I might need to find."

the end

NOTE FROM THE AUTHOR

Word-of-mouth is crucial for any author to succeed. If you enjoyed the book, please leave a review online—anywhere you are able. Even if it's just a sentence or two. It would make all the difference and would be very much appreciated.

Thanks!
Jon

About the Author

Jon Vassa is a Creative Writer and Editor at Asian Cinema Entertainment, helping talent to draft, edit, and refine scripts for the screen. When writing fiction he enjoys Crime, Sci-fi, and blends of Horror. His fiction works have appeared in *Aphelion* and *Crimson Streets Magazines*, and forthcoming on more.

Thank you so much for reading one of our **Sci-Fi** novels.

If you enjoyed our book, please check out our recommended title for your next great read!

Culture-Z by Karl Andrew Marszalowicz

In the year 2190, mankind has made great strides forward in the worlds of technology, science, and greed. However, when all three get together one last time, this oblivious generation may not exist much longer.

View other Black Rose Writing titles at www.blackrosewriting.com/books and use promo code **PRINT** to receive a **20% discount** when purchasing.